THE WORLD OF THE GATEWAY

The Gateway Trilogy (Series 1)
Spirit Legacy: Book 1 of The Gateway Trilogy
Spirit Prophecy: Book 2 of The Gateway Trilogy
Spirit Ascendancy: Book 3 of The Gateway Trilogy

The Gateway Trackers (Series 2)
Whispers of the Walker: The Gateway Trackers Book 1
Plague of the Shattered: The Gateway Trackers Book 2

SPIRIT PROPHECY

SPIRIT PROPHECY

Book 2 of The Gateway Trilogy

E.E. HOLMES

Lily Faire Publishing

Lily Faire Publishing
Townsend, MA

www.lilyfairepublishing.com

ISBN 978-0-9895080-3-2 (Paperback edition)
ISBN 978-0-9895080-4-9 (Digital edition)

Publisher's note: This is a work of fiction. Names, characters, places and incidents are either the product of the author's imagination or are used fictitiously.

Cover design by James T. Egan of Bookfly Design LLC
Editing services by Erika DeSimone of Erika's Editing
Author photography by Cydney Scott Photography

To my mother, my biggest fan always; and to my father, who taught me many things, including how to devour a good book.

EPIGRAPH

After great pain, a formal feeling comes –

The Nerves sit ceremonious, like Tombs –

The stiff Heart questions 'was it He, that bore,'

And 'Yesterday, or Centuries before'?

The Feet, mechanical, go round –

A Wooden way

Of Ground, or Air, or Ought –

Regardless grown,

A Quartz contentment, like a stone –

This is the Hour of Lead –

Remembered, if outlived,

As Freezing persons, recollect the snow –

First – Chill – then Stupor – then the letting go –

—Emily Dickinson

CONTENTS

UP IN THE AIR

BREATHE IN. BREATHE OUT. BREATHE IN. BREATHE OUT. Now repeat to yourself: We are not going to die. We are *not* going to die. People do this every day. So what if this seemed to defy all logic as well as the natural order of where and how human beings are supposed to exist? So what if the only things keeping us dangling thousands of feet above the open ocean were the sketchy—and, in my opinion, totally unreliable—laws of physics? Know what I remembered from physics? Gravity. That inescapable force that could send us plummeting to a watery grave at any moment.

"Barf bag?"

I unclenched my face enough to open one eye. Milo was grinning at me from the aisle. "No, thank you."

"Are you sure? It looks like your airline food may have purchased a round-trip ticket."

I considered hitting him, but that would have required releasing my white-knuckled grip from my armrest. It also would've been completely pointless, all things considered.

"I'm fine. Besides, if I throw up, I fully intend to aim for you."

"Empty threats, darling."

Damn it, he was right. Someone as annoying as Milo had no right to be dead. It seriously depleted my options for revenge—physical violence being my first choice.

My twin sister Hannah leaned across me, placing a gentle hand on my arm. "Milo, be nice, please."

"Come on, Hannah, let's not set him up to fail. Give him an easier one."

Hannah tried to scowl at me, but she smiled instead. "Milo, can't you find something else to do other than bother Jess? I think I saw a woman up in first class reading the new *Vogue*."

"Ooh, *Vogue*? See you later, sweetness." Milo winked and shimmered out of view.

"Yeah, go haunt someone else for a while," I mumbled, fighting a wave of nausea.

"Just take some deep breaths, Jess. We'll be there soon, don't worry," Hannah soothed.

Her words did little to ease my tension. What I was heading toward was just as stressful as how I was getting there. I felt like someone had hijacked my life.

I was supposed to be a regular college student, testing my maturity level with some hard-earned freedom and spending school vacations with my loving, if somewhat disastrous, mother. Instead, my mother was dead, and I was now flying across the ocean with a twin sister I never knew I had, in order to develop a newly discovered talent for seeing ghosts everywhere I went. I knew the first year of college was supposed to be full of change and new experiences, but come on, how much change could one person take?

I closed my eyes and tried to imagine myself somewhere, anywhere, else. My thoughts wandered back to my good-byes at St. Matt's the day before.

§

Pierce's office door was open, revealing a familiar jumbled disaster of papers, files, and used coffee mugs. He was encased in an enormous pair of headphones and crouched over a legal pad, writing feverishly. His face was a masterclass in concentration. If this hadn't been my only chance to say good-bye, I wouldn't have disturbed him. But it was now or never, so I knocked on the doorframe.

He looked up, startled, and then his face broke into a grin. He yanked off his headphones. "You're alive!"

"No thanks to you."

"Hey, don't look at me. Crazy shit like that didn't happen on my investigations until you showed up."

I shrugged. "Yeah, well, I had to uphold my reputation as 'ghost girl.'"

Pierce's smile shriveled a bit. He gestured to his decrepit sofa. "So, you really are okay?"

I sat. "Yeah, I'm okay."

Pierce looked me in the eyes, as though searching for a hint of the "otherness" he'd seen there the night he found me in the library's bathroom. Then he sighed and flopped back in his chair. "I'm so sorry, Ballard. I had no idea anything like that was going to go down. I never would've suggested it if I thought—"

I held up a hand to silence him. "Don't. Please don't blame yourself. No one could have predicted what happened in there. I don't even think the spirit knew what was happening. I'm okay now, really."

Pierce still looked slightly miserable. I tried to distract him.

"What are you listening to?"

"Your parapsychology homework," he said, plucking a little silver voice recorder off of his desk. I recognized it at once as the one he'd given me to record EVPs while I slept. I'd forgotten all about it.

"So, did it catch anything spooky?" I asked, trying to keep my tone light.

"Spooky, Ballard, is the freaking understatement of the century," Pierce replied. He pressed the "play" button.

At first I heard nothing but the innocent noises of sleep—a little tossing and turning, a bit of deep breathing. Then a whispering began, soft enough that it could have been dismissed as the breeze or the rustling of a sheet. A second whispered joined in, and then a third; the vague swishing began to resolve itself into sounds and words.

"Take her! What are you waiting for?"

"Something's wrong."

"I can feel it, she's the one."

More voices joined in and echoed the first.

"She pulls me. She draws me."

"She is incomplete. There is no light here."

"Wake her! Enter her! We must get through."

Pierce stopped the tape. Our eyes met across his desk. "That goes on for about six hours," he said.

It took me a few moments to make sure I could suppress the tremor in my voice. "Right. So, as far as homework goes..."

"I'd say you passed." He looked down at the recorder like it was his firstborn child and then slid it across the desk to me. "Here."

"I don't want it!" I cried, before collecting myself. "I mean, I'm not going to listen to any more of that, so you can just keep it."

"No, actually, I don't think I can," Pierce said grimly.

"What do you mean?"

"I mean, someone has made it abundantly clear that I'm not supposed to keep any evidence related to you." He waved a hand toward a large box perched on the radiator. It was full of cassette tapes, CDs, video tapes, and memory cards. "That's every piece of A/V captured from our investigation. And every single one of them is blank."

"Blank?"

"Wiped clean. Someone broke into my office while we were at the hospital. The only reason they missed this recorder is because I still had it in my pocket. They did a very neat job of it, too. Dan's spent hours trying to retrieve the files, but it's no use. Iggy's in a state of depression, and I think Oscar may never recover." The corner of his mouth twitched into a sad little smile; Pierce looked like he was the one who might not recover.

I shouldn't have been surprised, but I was. Karen had told me the Durupinen had been protecting their secrets for centuries, and that they had complex systems and methods for doing so. If we'd been willing to wait, Finvarra could have arranged Hannah's release from New Beginnings psychiatric facility using her own mysterious connections, instead of Karen and I breaking her out. Pierce's video and audio recordings were exactly the kind of evidence that the Durupinen would go out of their way to destroy. I imagined Lucida scaling the side of Wiltshire Hall and slipping into Pierce's office, like some kind of Bond-girl super-spy. I almost laughed until I realized how plausible that scenario actually was.

I took the voice recorder from Pierce's desk. I'd have to choose my words carefully to protect him.

"I'm really sorry that I can't tell you what's going on. If anyone deserves to know the truth, it's you. You believed me when almost no one else did. You did so much to help me, and I'll never, ever forget that."

He nodded. "I had a feeling we'd be having a conversation like this. Are you leaving?"

"Yeah, for a while. 'Study abroad program,'" I said, with air quotes.

"Do you know how long?"

"Two years. Karen promised I could come back and finish my senior year here at St. Matt's."

"And I'm guessing that joining our ghost hunts won't be on your list of approved activities when you get back?"

I shook my head sadly.

"Well, I would've kicked myself if I didn't at least ask." Pierce stood up and shuffled through the mess to his ancient coffee maker. "Want a hit?"

"You know me. Can't resist caffeine," I smiled.

Pierce turned his back on me to doctor up my coffee, but he kept talking. "I guess I've always been a bit of a glutton for punishment. Stubborn as hell, y'know? Whenever someone told me I couldn't do something, I'd turn right around and do it, just as a 'fuck you.' That attitude followed me right into academia. The world said parapsychology wasn't legitimate science, so of course I studied it. But it wasn't just that. I really believed in it. That's why I knew I had to help you; I recognized another kid scared shitless by stuff she couldn't explain."

I took the chipped mug from him and cradled it in my hands. "So... you had your own experience when you were younger?"

"Sure did. When I was just a kid, my older brother Teddy came home from Vietnam the night of my eighth birthday. He woke me up just after midnight to wish me a happy birthday, still in his uniform. I was so happy to see him I didn't even stop to wonder why he still had his helmet on and an M-16 assault rifle slung across him. We talked for hours... talked until I couldn't keep my eyes open anymore and fell asleep. When I got up in the morning, I ran downstairs to have breakfast with him, and my mother told me I must've been dreaming; Teddy hadn't come home. I didn't believe her—I searched the whole house, wouldn't let it go for days. Then, about a week later, two uniformed officers showed up and destroyed my mother with three sharp knocks on our battered screen door."

I was speechless. I'd felt like I knew Pierce pretty well in a way, but for all I'd confided in him, I knew almost nothing about his personal life. Finally, I choked out, "I'm so sorry."

Pierce drained his own mug. "No one was going to tell me ghosts weren't real after that. But naturally, being me, I made it my mission to study the most mysterious, most elusive subject in all of ghostlore: the Durupinen." He winked at me and grinned. "You realize that sharing a cup of coffee with you is like going for a swim with the Loch Ness Monster."

I snorted. "You sure know how to flatter a girl."

"Well, there's something I've heard exactly three times in my life, and only two of them were sarcastic," he replied.

We sat in silence for a few moments.

"If I could tell you everything, I would," I offered.

"Can you at least tell me if you'll be okay now? What happened to you in the library, that's not going to happen to you anymore, is it?" There was a fatherly concern etched into his face.

"No, I'll be okay now. They'll help me."

"Good. That's good."

We chatted a bit longer while I sipped my coffee. Pierce showed me the syllabus he was working on for the fall semester. Due to the popularity of the parapsychology course, the college had added another section. Pierce lit up like a campfire as he described the course content. He gesticulated wildly, arms knocking files to the floor in coffee-ringed avalanches. As I watched him, some terrible knot inside me loosened.

Half an hour later, I stood to leave.

"You sure you can't initiate me and tell me all your mystical secrets?" asked Pierce. "I promise I won't tell anyone—except the entire scientific community, and maybe a few geeks who read academic journals."

I just smiled. "I'll see you, Pierce."

"Don't be a stranger, eh? Keep in touch."

"You got it. I'll send you lots of letters with blacked-out names and details," I said. I couldn't find anywhere to put my mug down that looked safe, so I handed it to him instead. "Say thank you to the guys for me, okay? And to Annabelle, too."

"Are you going somewhere, Jessica?"

I spun around and saw Neil Caddigan hovering in the doorway. As was his general style, I had neither seen nor heard him approach, and therefore jumped in surprise.

"Neil, hey. Sorry, I didn't know you were there."

"It is I who ought to apologize. Am I intruding? I can come back, Pierce. I just wanted a quick word," Neil said with a polite little bow. His gaze never left my face; I'd never seen eyes so blanched of color.

"No, I was just leaving," I said, suddenly glad Neil had appeared to shape this odd moment of good-bye for us. "Good-bye, Pierce. Thanks for everything."

"See you around, Ballard. Take care of yourself."

He thrust out a hand and I shook it. Then I turned and brushed past Neil. I could feel his eyes burrowing into me all the way down the hallway. For one strange moment, I wanted to turn around and run back to Pierce's office. There was something incredibly important I hadn't said to him. But since I couldn't put into words what that something was, I just kept walking.

§

"Jess? How are you feeling?"

My Aunt Karen's gentle voice burst my thoughts as if they were soap bubbles. I opened my eyes to find her back in her seat with her belt buckled and magazine in her lap. I hadn't even heard her sit down.

"I'm fine," I lied. "How much longer until we land?"

"About another four hours."

I whimpered pitifully. Four hours.

"Here, they have this map on the TV, you can track where the plane is and—"

"Nope, no maps, no pictures of planes above water, please," I muttered. "I really don't need any more reminders about what we're doing. I just need to be distracted. Or unconscious. Is there a blunt object nearby that you could just hit me over the head with?"

Karen smiled sympathetically. "How about a sleeping pill?"

I actually picked my head up off of the headrest. "Do you have one?"

"Yes, I thought I might need them for the time change, but I think you need one now." She pulled her purse out from under the seat and extracted a pillbox and a bottle of water.

"Take one of those, you'll be out cold in fifteen minutes," she advised.

"Oh my God, I love you," I sighed, as I popped open the pillbox. As I realized what I'd said, I felt Karen stiffen a little beside me.

Things had been strained between Karen and me ever since I'd discovered the truth about my abilities. I'd been torturing myself for months, first by trying to understand the circumstances of my mother's death, and then with questioning my own sanity. Karen had known all that time what had happened to my mother and, to a certain extent, what was happening to me. But she hadn't told me the truth until she was forced to: When two of the Durupinen arrived in my room in the middle of the night, Karen could no longer keep her secrets. Her excuse was that she was trying to protect both me and our family's ancient secret. A part of me knew that she had done what she thought was right, but a much bigger and angrier part of me kept telling that first part to shut the hell up.

The Durupinen had torn apart my family and destroyed my mother. Now they were commandeering my entire life, and everyone expected me to be happy about it—like this was all some big honor, like I'd won the freak lottery. Well, I wasn't about to start waving any Durupinen flags just yet, they still owed me too much. In fact, the only reason I was on this plane was for Hannah. She'd dealt with the Visitations all alone for far too long. I wasn't about to deny her the chance to learn how to control our abilities, and becoming a Durupinen Apprentice at Fairhaven Hall was the only way to do that.

As I started trying to imagine what Fairhaven might look like, the sedative hit my bloodstream with a dizzying rush, and my thoughts slid out of my control and into a highly colored dream. I was flapping around the campus of St. Matt's with a giant pair of feathery wings I had just sprouted. I landed in a tree to watch the haute couture fashion show Milo was coordinating on the quad. Every model that strutted down the runway was a ghost with gruesome injuries. When I pointed this out to Milo, he just rolled his eyes and said, "Get with it, Jess, it's dead chic. You are *so* bourgeois."

I resurfaced groggily to the sounds of seatbelts unsnapping and overhead compartments popping open. The plane itself was wonderfully, blessedly, stationary.

"Jess? We're here. How are you feeling?" Karen nudged me.

I shook my head. I felt a bit woozy, but was too relieved to care. "I'm good. Remind me the next time I have to do this that I only fly unconscious."

Karen laughed. "Will do."

A businessman who'd been flirting shamelessly with Karen in Logan airport retrieved our bags for us, and we shuffled off the plane and into Heathrow. As we made our way through customs, I realized I hadn't been able to move past my crippling aviophobia and appreciate being here. I glanced over at Hannah, who was wheeling her carry-on bag and looking anxious.

"Nervous?" I asked her.

"Yeah," she said. Her voice was a hoarse whisper.

"Afraid they'll make you declare Milo?"

She laughed, a fluttery sound. "No, I think he'll sneak into the country okay. There was no reason for him to wait with us in this line. He's checking out the airport shops until we get through."

We inched closer to the crumpled-faced man at the customs check-in booth. "I guess I'm just... nervous about what will happen when we get there," Hannah said.

I snorted. "Which part?"

"Well, all of it, really."

"I think they're the ones who should be nervous, after letting us go for so long without the truth. I, for one, expect full apologies, with groveling," I said with more bravado than I felt. Hannah's smile was a little too understanding, but at least she was smiling again. I considered it a little victory as I finally reached the front of the line.

The gray-haired man signaled to me with a little wave of his hand. I shuffled forward and handed him my packet of paperwork. "Good morning, Miss, and welcome to the United Kingdom. I trust you had a pleasant flight?"

The polite "Yes, thank you," that came from my lips did not match the sardonic "Hah!" in my mind.

He flipped through my documents carefully. "Well, that all seems to be in order." He stamped a few things and handed the papers back to me. "And what is your reason for visiting the United Kingdom?"

For one insane moment, I wanted to grab this mild-mannered man by the lapels of his jacket and scream, "You've got to help me! I've been kidnapped by an ancient ghost cult and I want my life back!" Instead, I smiled blandly and parroted the party line, "I'm attending University here at Fairhaven Hall."

"Very good, very good," the man replied with a smile. "You may proceed through. A pleasant day to you, Miss."

"You too," I said, and stepped aside to wait for Hannah and Karen.

We stopped at an airport café for coffee, which I started to gulp down immediately despite the fact that it was scalding my throat. Between the nerves, the time change, and the horse-tranquilizer-strength sleeping pill, I had never needed caffeine more.

Just as we finished our coffee, an airport security guard offered, quite cheerfully, to find us a luggage cart. He then proceeded to load all of our baggage from the carousel and wheel it out to the cabstand, whistling as he did so. Milo lounged atop the pile of suitcases like Cleopatra. The only thing lacking was an entourage of half-naked men feeding him grapes and fanning him with giant palm fronds.

I couldn't help but be struck by how friendly and polite everyone was. I don't think a single airport employee had so much as cracked a smile at us during our two hours at Logan airport, unless you counted the snide smirk from the woman at the security checkpoint when I'd lost my balance trying to remove my shoes.

The cabstand was crowded with vehicles. The hackneys looked nothing like the taxis back home—their slightly bulbous shape reminded me of antique cars. I started toward the first available hackney, but Karen held up a hand. "We don't need one of those," she told me. "Our cars are here."

"Our cars?" I repeated in surprise.

Karen nodded and pointed to two sleek black Bentleys pulling up to the curb. With almost military precision, two drivers in dark suits and chauffeur caps emerged, walked quickly around their vehicles, and popped open the trunks. Then they stood straight-backed and wordless beside their cars.

Karen, who was obviously expecting this Secret Service-style treatment, slid into the backseat of the first car. She poked her head back out when we hesitated. "Come on, girls. You can ride with me. The second car is for the bags."

Hannah and I exchanged a nervous look, then followed Karen. The chauffeur didn't so much as glance at us, and I was reminded of the unflappable Queen's Guard at Buckingham Palace, who were famous for their ability to hold stock-still, even as tourists like myself tried to goad them into reacting. It took great effort not to wave my hand tauntingly in front of the chauffeur's face as I passed him and ducked into the car. The Bentley, with its posh leather interior, was by far the nicest car I'd ever been in. It was cool and dark behind the heavily tinted windows.

"So, did you order these cars, or does Fairhaven Hall have its own army of chauffeurs?" I asked Karen. I watched as the chauffeurs slid into what looked to my American eyes like the front passenger seat, but which was, of course, the driver's seat.

Karen laughed. "Don't let them hear you call them chauffeurs. They're Caomhnóir."

"Come again?" I said.

"Caomhnóir. They're the guardians and protectors of the Durupinen," answered Karen.

"Who are they though?" Hannah asked. "How do they know about us? I thought only women were a part of the Durupinen."

"It's true that only women are part of the actual Gateways, but over the centuries we've learned that we need protection if we're going to keep our world a secret. The Caomhnóir are men descended from the same Clan Families; they have latent abilities to sense spirits as well. They are trained to watch over us, just as we are trained to watch over our Gateways."

"And are they all this strong and silent?" Milo asked, while trying to sneak a peek at the driver through the divider.

Hannah repeated his question for Karen, who laughed appreciatively.

"For the most part, yes, actually. Interaction between the Durupinen and the Caomhnóir is very... limited."

"Why?" Hannah asked, frowning.

"Oh, that's a long political discussion," Karen said with an airy wave of her hand. "I'll let your teachers bore you with that in class. For now, let's just say that you shouldn't feel offended if they aren't very friendly to you; they're like that with all of us."

"At least they make nice eye candy," said Milo.

Hannah laughed and once again repeated the joke to Karen.

"Milo is quite the comedian. I look forward to meeting him for myself shortly," she said.

"What do you mean?" I asked.

Karen smiled broadly. "I was talking with a few of my Council friends yesterday. It seems that, although the Binding was broken when your mother died, it still needs to be formally removed. Once that happens, it's almost definite that I'll be able to see the spirits again." It could not have been more obvious that Karen was thrilled about this.

"That's great!" I said, since that was the expected response. Privately, I thought her enthusiasm for seeing ghosts was insane. I would've traded with her in a heartbeat and skipped on my merry way back home.

"Couldn't you just have removed it yourself?" Hannah asked.

"Not by myself," Karen said. "You need four Durupinen to complete the ceremony. It's very complicated. I'll go see the

Council when we get there to take care of some loose ends, and they'll do it then."

"That's wonderful, Karen," Hannah said, before turning and pressing her nose to the glass. Milo rested his chin on her shoulder, sharing the view. I tried enjoy the scenery too, but had to lean back and close my eyes after only a few minutes; it was too disorienting to be barreling down the left side of road instead of the right. Our driver seemed to have little regard for silly restrictions like traffic lights and crosswalks, and I spent much more time fearing for our lives than sightseeing. Shit, and I thought New York cab drivers had a collective death wish.

After what felt like one long near-death experience, the twisting and turning gave way to a smooth, straight ride, and I risked opening my eyes. The last of the suburban houses were fading into the distance behind us as we continued on into the open country.

I'd seen some beautiful places on my drives in the Green Monster across America with my mother—the red geometric rock formations of Arizona, the golden wheat fields of the Midwest. But the English countryside had a beauty unlike anything I'd ever witnessed before. The fields rolled gently past us, undulating waves of the truest greens; the fields were speckled with sheep and crisscrossed with fences and tumbledown stone walls. Here and there, a quaint farmhouse or cottage perched like a sparrow upon a hilltop. It was as though I had stepped back into a simpler time, and suddenly even the car I was driving in felt like an anachronism—like an intrusion of sorts. Even though I had never been here before, I was struck by a sense of familiarity, and not by a sense of "otherness," as I had expected. There was a tiny but insistent part of myself that was singing with joy because it knew that I belonged here. The song scared me a little; I tried to hush it, to ignore it, but it continued to sing, a whisper of a tune, in the recesses of my mind. Hannah turned from the window and her eyes, saucer-wide, were aglow with that same understanding; I knew she felt it, too.

The ride could have been a few minutes or a few days—I was too entranced by the scenery to know for sure, or indeed to care. But long before I expected to hear it, Karen's voice broke my thoughts.

"Fairhaven Hall is just over the crest of that hill. You should be able to see it coming up on the left-hand side in a moment." I craned my neck and gasped. My gasp was echoed by both Hannah and Milo. Karen heaved a sigh of contentment.

Fairhaven Hall, a stately and ancient castle, was nestled between two embracing curves of a valley. Four tall, turreted towers—each a weathered collection of windows and balconies, bastions and crenellated ramparts—seemed to anchor the castle to the ground. Fairhaven Hall was bordered on the east by a vast forest, on the west by a rushing, diamond-bright river, and to the north by the most expansive set of gardens and orchards I had ever seen.

"Holy shit," I whispered. "We go to Hogwarts."

2

WELCOME AND UNWELCOME

K AREN WAS PRACTICALLY BOUNCING IN HER SEAT, as though she were five years old and we'd just arrived at Disney World. But the castle before us was decidedly different than the one in the Magic Kingdom.

"Isn't it wonderful?"

Nobody answered her. I was so awestruck that I had no room left for any of the other emotions that had been wreaking havoc on my psyche for the past few weeks—they simply shriveled up and vanished. My one and only coherent thought was a silent curse: My sketchbook was packed away in my suitcase. My fingers twitched with longing; no place I'd ever been had ever begged more desperately to be drawn.

We gawked, open-mouthed, as Fairhaven Hall loomed nearer. Massive wrought iron front gates, their bars twisted and curled into delicate, vine-like tendrils, opened smoothly as the car approached. At first, I thought the gates had parted of their own volition and had opened my mouth to ask about it; then I spotted the heavy chains, concealed in stone niches, that were pulling the gates apart and were vanishing, link by link, into small openings in the thatched gatehouses on either side of the cobblestoned drive.

The moment we reached the gates, a strange feeling swept over me, as though I had stepped through a heat haze or an atmospheric disturbance. Hannah closed her eyes and swallowed hard, as though the sensation had made her feel nauseous. Milo flickered momentarily out of view and then back again, with a wary expression on his face.

"Um... what was that we just passed through?" I asked. My head was swimming slightly.

"Sorry, I should have warned you about that," said Karen. "We just crossed the Wards. There are protective charms all around the grounds, sort of like barriers. Wards are designed to protect the Durupinen as well as the spirits that harbor here. Is Milo still here?"

"Yes," Hannah answered.

"Well, I mean obviously I assumed he would be. The Wards are only meant to keep out hostile spirits, and we know he's not hostile—"

"Speak for yourself," I said.

Milo responded by batting his eyelashes and blowing me a kiss.

"Oh, you know what I mean," Karen said. "It's good to know that the Wards won't affect him negatively or keep him out. If so, he would've been stopped right at the boundary to the grounds."

"Are hordes of hostile spirits something we're going to need to worry about?" I asked.

"No, not exactly," Karen replied. "Spirits are drawn to this place in huge numbers, just as they are drawn to you both. They can feel the pull you exert on them, the connection you have to the Gateway. Obviously, that pull is exponentially stronger with so many Gateways gathered together in a single place. The Wards keep us safe from any spirits with less-than-good intentions."

"I could've used one of these Ward-thingies back at St. Matt's," I said.

Hannah nodded fervently. "Will we be taught how to do that? Create Wards?"

Karen smiled a little sadly at her, and I knew what Hannah was thinking at once. My sister's life had been defined by unexplained Visitations that left her terrified, marginalized, and eventually institutionalized. She probably would've done just about anything to be left alone. As happened so often when I looked at my twin, a terrible anger rose in me from the thought of what her life had been. I wished I had been there to protect her, or—at the very least—stand by her through that nightmare of a childhood.

Karen answered, "Yes, Hannah, although it's bit difficult, and it will probably take a few months before you can Cast one powerful enough to be effective. The Wards around Fairhaven Hall have been in place for centuries and are nearly impenetrable. Ah, here we go," she added, as the gates finally opened wide enough for our car to pass through.

The car bumped along the cobblestoned drive, wound through impeccably manicured lawns and flowerbeds, and finally came to rest at the front doors. The doors were constructed of ancient wooden planks studded with nails and held together with well-aged metal crossbars. In the middle of the left door, which remained closed, an intricately carved door knocker depicting a woman's face, with her mouth open in a silent terrified scream, stared out at us. The right door stood open, as though the castle had been expecting us.

If this had been an old horror movie, a hunchbacked butler with a disfigured face would have hobbled out to greet us; the entire theater would have shouted at the heroine, "Don't go in! Don't do it!"

But this wasn't a horror movie. This was my life, and yet, like every epically stupid heroine in every scary movie I'd ever seen, I didn't turn around and leave, but squared my shoulders and walked right in the front door... and toward certain doom. Or, at least, that's how it felt as I crossed the threshold with my heart curled and cowering in my throat.

Hannah, Milo, and I stopped short just inside the vast, echoing entrance hall. A great marble staircase stood before us, flanked with curving stone banisters. Tapestries and paintings that looked like they should have been hanging, under heavy guard, in the National Gallery adorned the wood-paneled walls. The second floor comprised a balcony that ran the perimeter of the chamber. Behind its heavy wooden railings, I could see a number of arched doorways interspersed by stained glass windows. The stone ceiling was latticed with cathedral-like wooden beams, and right above our heads hung a magnificent chandelier worthy of The Phantom of the Opera.

Any single feature of this room could have captivated us, but it was not the architecture that stopped the breath in my lungs. The entire place pulsed and buzzed with a palpable energy, as though the very stones themselves were alive; the irony was not lost on me, considering that this feeling was caused by the constant and powerful presence of the dead. Even as my eyes made the initial scan of the room, I spotted several spirits: One walking up the staircase; another peering curiously over the gallery railings; and a third crouching defensively in the shadows of a sculpture. I was definitely getting better at distinguishing between the living and the dead—although whether that was a good thing or not, I still hadn't decided.

"Wow," Milo murmured. "There are a lot of us here." He turned to

Hannah, looking excited. "Mind if I leave you ladies to it and have a strut around the place—y'know, to meet the rest of the floaters?"

"No, of course not," Hannah said, barely able to tear her eyes from her new surroundings. "Have fun."

Milo winked and dissolved on the spot.

"Ah, Clan Sassanaigh has arrived at last!" a voice echoed down at us. I almost looked behind us to see who this woman was talking about, when I realized that she was referring to our ancient family name. *That* was going to take some getting used to.

The voice belonged to a slender woman with long hair and prominent cheekbones who was descending the stairs toward us; her arms were open in a gesture of welcome. Karen's face broke into a smile of true pleasure when she saw her.

"Celeste!" She walked forward to meet the woman at the base of the stairs, and the two embraced with mutual cries of delight.

"Karen!" the woman named Celeste said. "Welcome home!"

"Thank you, Celeste! I can't tell you how wonderful it is to be back," replied Karen, squeezing Celeste's hand affectionately. Then she turned to us. "Girls, come over here! I want to introduce you!"

As I crossed the entrance hall, my footsteps echoing resoundingly. Hannah followed half a pace behind me, like a shadow; her were feet somehow much quieter than mine. Okay, so combat boots were clearly a poor footwear choice for a place like this. I grumbled inwardly, thinking how gleeful Milo would be if I stopped wearing them.

"Celeste Morgan, these are Elizabeth's girls, Jess and Hannah," said Karen, pointing each of us out in turn.

"A pleasure to meet you both," Celeste said, shaking my hand. She then held her hand out to Hannah, but seemed to sense Hannah's hesitancy almost at once, and turned the motion into a wave instead.

"Nice to meet you, too," I answered for the two of us. Hannah nodded diffidently.

Up close, Celeste seemed to be about Karen's age, and had a few gentle lines around her full-lipped mouth and wide, blue eyes. Here and there, a strand of silver glimmered in her auburn hair, which fell past her shoulder blades in shining tendrils.

"Celeste and I were Apprentices together. She serves on the Durupinen High Council and teaches here as well. Do you still teach History and Lore?" Karen asked her.

"Yes," Celeste said with an apologetic expression. "I'm afraid I will be boring you both to tears three days a week."

"I like history," Hannah said quietly, speaking for the first time.

"I'm glad to hear it!" said Celeste. "At least I'll have one pupil listening, and that's something, isn't it?" She paused and gestured grandly around. Well, what do you think of the place?"

"It's... unbelievable," I managed.

Celeste gave a knowing smile. "It is overwhelming at first, but you'll get used to it. We all do. Pretty soon you'll be knocking around the old place just like you would at home." She turned back to Karen. "And how was your journey? Uneventful, I hope?"

"It was fine, thanks," Karen said. "And... how's everything here?"

There was something loaded about the question, about the hesitant way that Karen had asked it. Celeste understood whatever it was, and her smile faltered a bit as she answered.

"Pretty calm. The Council met last night. I'll tell you all about it once we get these ladies settled into their room. Also, I told Finvarra that I'd take you to see her when you arrived."

"I figured as much," said Karen, with an expression like a kid who'd been caught sneaking in after curfew. "Where are they going to be staying?" she added, gesturing to us.

"The East Wing, first door after the tower, of course. Your old stomping grounds! Where did you suspect?"

Karen grimaced. "I thought perhaps, given recent events, we might have been... reassigned."

Celeste took Karen's hand again and gave it a friendly squeeze. "Not while I'm on the Council." She handed Karen a large and ornate brass key, like the kind of thing that might open a pirate's treasure chest or the wardrobe to Narnia.

"Thank you," Karen said, then dropped her hand and pointed up the stairs. "Come on, girls, I'll show you where your room is. You'll be staying in the same room your mother and I had when we were here. Our family has been housed there for centuries. Pretty cool, huh?"

We mounted the huge staircase, then walked along the balcony and into a second floor corridor that seemed to go on forever. How could there possibly be this many doors in a single building? Each door had a gold plate engraved with the room number, but no indication as to what was behind it. On a few doors, a symbol had been burned into the wood, a sort of pictographic shape not unlike a closed eye.

"What's with the creepy hieroglyphics?" I asked.

"Remember I told you about the Wards around the buildings? Some of the individual rooms have Wards as well. Spirits aren't allowed into certain areas of the castle, including bedrooms and some ceremonial areas and offices. The Wards keep them out as effectively as walls would keep you or me out."

We twisted and turned down a half-dozen more hallways—a left, a right, another right, a short staircase, another left... this place was a labyrinth. I gave up all hope of remembering the way back to the entrance hall and started to wonder if the ghosts we'd seen so far were people who'd died trying to find their way out.

Finally, Karen rounded one last corner and came to a halt. "Here we go!" She fumbled in her pocket for the key Celeste had given her, and inserted it into the old-fashioned lock. It twisted with a whining screech, clicked loudly, and then door swung heavily forward.

The room was large and high-ceilinged, with richly paneled walls and a stone fireplace. Two four-poster beds stood against the far wall with a large, mullioned window between them. The beds were dressed with pale gold silk drapes, and were made up with matching gold bedspreads. In front of the fireplace, the wide-planked floors were spread with an ornate but threadbare Persian rug. Two wide and cozy-looking purple armchairs faced the fireplace. Two antique mahogany desks with matching chairs stood against the wall opposite the beds, and a tall bookcase took up most of the remaining space on the wall beside the door. A tapestry hung above the fireplace. It depicted a huntress, with her bow drawn, astride a rearing white unicorn; both were in pursuit of a creature that seemed to be half jungle cat, half bird of prey.

Hannah hovered in the doorway taking it all in, but I followed Karen into the room, and crossed to the window. I peered out at the grounds below. We had a view of the same gardens that we'd spotted on our approach to Fairhaven. As I looked out, a spirit flitted from pathway to pathway, fluid as a shadow, but bright as a star.

I turned to Karen and pointed back over my shoulder at the window. "So is this where we let our excessively long hair down to receive visitors?"

She laughed out loud as she tossed me the key. "I know, the whole thing is pretty surreal. I remember feeling the same way when we first came here. I know it doesn't look like it, but you've got all the modern amenities here."

I looked around a little more carefully and saw that she was right. There were outlets along the baseboards, and even, absurdly, an Ethernet port. The fireplace was spotlessly clean, with logs piled decoratively in a brass stand, but no sign that the fireplace was ever actually used. Despite how much more appropriately candles and torches would have fit the decor, there were several polished silver reading lamps, and the chandelier above our heads was fitted with light bulbs, not wax tapers. I turned to Hannah, who was still framed in the doorway.

"What do you think, roomie?" I asked.

Hannah stepped over the threshold with a most peculiar expression on her face, as if she were a child being submerged in a swimming pool for the first time. She stood there with her eyes closed for a moment, and took a deep, cleansing breath. Then she opened her eyes and her face broke into the biggest, most radiant smile I'd ever seen on it. It was absolutely transformative, as though the years of hardship had, just for a moment, been lifted off of her.

"I can't feel them. Any of them!" she said, her voice a gush of wonder. "It's wonderful!" Her whole body seemed to relax, and she fairly skipped over to the beds; with a little hop, she flung herself onto the right one and started moving her arms up and down in great arcs, as if she were making snow angels in the down of the comforter. "Can I have this bed?"

Karen and I looked at each other, stunned but delighted to see Hannah so happy. "Of course you can," I answered. I bounded across the room, landed with a plop on the other bed, and then—just because we'd never had the chance as kids—flung one of my many pillows playfully at her head. She caught it, still grinning that wonderful, light-hearted grin so foreign to her features.

Just behind Karen, two of the Caomhnóir appeared silently in the doorway, wheeling two brass luggage carts, like the kind found in Ritz-Carlton lobbies. Karen thanked them, but the Caomhnóir didn't acknowledge her. Instead, they deftly unloaded our bags before they slid out of sight.

"Why don't you girls get unpacked and take a rest? I'm going to go see Finvarra," Karen said.

"Sounds good," I replied.

"Before you go, Aunt Karen," Hannah asked, almost apologetically, "I've been wondering... Why does school start now? Why not in the fall? It's... weird."

Here we are in a strange country in a centuries-old castle filled with spirits and Wards and Bindings and who knows what else, and my twin thought the *schedule* was weird? I couldn't quite suppress a smile of both amusement and pride; my sister was deeply thoughtful in her own quiet way.

"It's tradition," Karen said. "The school year for Apprentices at Fairhaven Hall always begins on the third new moon after the spring equinox. You'll find a number of things here are governed by the lunar calendar. The new moon is always a time for beginning things, and the third new moon is symbolic of the Triskele, the symbol of the Durupinen. The Triskele is a powerful symbol which I'm sure Celeste will teach you about in History and Lore."

Hannah smiled and her shoulders relaxed. Clearly this explanation resonated with her, as if something in her mind had been fully quelled.

"When I get back," Karen said, "I'll show you around a little bit, and then we can head down to the dining room. They'll be serving lunch in a couple of hours, and you'll be able to meet some of the other Apprentices."

Karen closed the door behind her, and I rolled onto my elbow to face Hannah. She was gazing wistfully into the folds of her canopy.

"Are you happy we came?" I asked her.

"Yes," she breathed, still looking up, as though she were stargazing. "I mean, I'm still nervous about what it's going to be like, but not like I was. Before you found me, every time I went somewhere new, I was always so scared. It wasn't just starting over with new doctors or a new foster family. It was never knowing who else would be there, and what they would want from me, you know?"

I decided to prod Hannah just a little. As gently as I could, I asked, "But why did starting the school year now seem to worry you? I mean, this isn't exactly a regular school."

"Well... I guess, I..." began Hannah, timidly. I was almost sure she'd crawl back into herself, but after a moment of hesitation her answer emerged, with an almost-hopeful tinge in her voice.

"I guess it's because when I was moved somewhere new, whether I wanted to go or not, it always seemed to happen in the spring or summer. I almost grew to expect it. But maybe this time Fairhaven Hall will really be a fresh start. Maybe this is where I was supposed to be all along."

As I always did when Hannah talked about her childhood, I had to choke back my anger and sadness for the nightmare her life had been. I resisted the urge to leap onto her bed and fling my arms around her, and instead contented myself with a nod and a "Yes."

Somewhat to my surprise, Hannah went on. "There were some places where the spirits were quiet and calm. It was like they noticed me, but they didn't need me, so they mostly left me alone. But even then, they were always there. I could hear them all the time—like someone had left the TV on in the next room of my brain." She tore her gaze from above her and turned to look ruefully at me. "When I was little, I tried everything to block it out; I blasted music, I stuffed cotton balls in my ears, sometimes I would just scream for them to stop. But that was before I understood my hearing had nothing to do with it."

"Jesus, Hannah," I murmured. "How did you cope with it?"

"Not that well, obviously," she said, with an oddly cheerful little laugh. "If I'd dealt with it well, they wouldn't have stuck me in the psycho ward with the rest of the nutjobs."

I swallowed a golf ball-sized lump in my throat. Hannah glanced over at me and that rare smile faltered. "Do I make you sad when I talk about this stuff? I can stop."

I shook my head. "No... I mean, yes, it makes me sad that you had to go through all of that, and that I wasn't there to help you. But I'm really, really glad that you talk to me about it. I would rather hear about it, honestly—as long as talking about it makes you feel better and not worse."

Hannah's smile twitched back into place. "This is the first place I've ever been where it's really and truly quiet *in here*," she whispered, tapping a long slender finger against her temple. "And it's wonderful. It makes me feel like I can deal with whatever else happens, as long as I can have this quiet sometimes."

I relieved my own emotions with a joke. "Is this your subtle way of telling me to shut up and leave you alone?"

Hannah giggled. "No, you know that's not what I mean."

I peeled my reluctant limbs from the bed and jumped off of it. "Good, because I want to get unpacked before I completely pass out on this bed."

It took us far less time than I expected to put everything away, especially given the excruciating amount of time it took to pack. At first, we were puzzled as to where we would put our clothes; there were no dressers or drawers to be seen, but a little exploration on Hannah's part revealed a large closet hidden behind one of the wall's panels. Many of our belongings looked absurd in our grand new surroundings, especially our laptops, which—miracle of miracles—connected without a problem to the Internet, although of course there was no Wi-Fi. I was really convinced, when I'd first seen the room, that we'd be communicating with the outside world via smoke signals and the occasional homing pigeon, but instead it looked like we'd be Skyping and tweeting like the rest of civilization. These days I clung like a drowning woman to any shred of normalcy that might keep me afloat.

Finally, we heaved our empty bags into the corner. Hannah collapsed, exhausted, into one of our armchairs, but I stayed on my feet.

"Do you want to go look around or something?" I asked.

"Aren't you tired?" Hannah asked incredulously. "I thought I might try to take a nap before lunch."

"I'm exhausted," I admitted. "But I'm afraid if I lay back down on that bed, I'll sleep until next week, and I don't want to miss anything. Let's at least try to find the bathroom."

"Okay," Hannah agreed. "I was hoping to track down Milo anyway, and if he isn't allowed to come in here, I'll just have to—"

I never heard the end of her sentence. I had just opened the door and stepped into the hallway when the figure—small, pearly, and utterly desperate—attacked me like a bat out of hell.

3

AMBUSHED

I WAS TOO SHOCKED TO CRY OUT. With the force of a hurricane's gale, the spirit knocked me clear off my feet and sent me tumbling painfully across the stone floor. Then she was on me—a blur of skeletally thin arms and legs, scrabbling little fingers, and a tangle of long hair. Instinctively, I threw my arms up in front of my face to protect myself. But I realized almost at once that although the sheer force of her presence had been enough to hurl me through the air, she could no more make direct contact with me than a captive animal on the other side of observation glass. With my heart hammering, I lowered my arms and focused on the apparition's face.

She was a young girl, maybe eight or nine years old, with hollow cheeks, wide sunken eyes, and an expression of all-consuming terror. A white nightgown hung in tatters from her bony shoulders. Her mouth was opening and closing frantically, forming words or cries which, for some reason, I couldn't hear properly. Her voice was distant and warped, muffled into unintelligibility.

My fear drained away as quickly as it had flooded me. "What? What is it?" I asked as she continued to struggle wildly at the invisible barrier between us. "Do you need help?"

The girl shook her head, then started tearing at her hair like a wild, feral thing.

"Hey! Get away from her!" Hannah cried, bursting out into the hallway and running toward us.

The girl's face snapped up and locked onto Hannah with an animal-like intensity. Then, with one last disappointed frown at me, the spirit skittered across the floor like a crab and disappeared through the wall.

Hannah knelt beside me, panting. "What was that about? Are you okay?"

"I… yeah, I'm fine," I replied, staring at the spot on the wall where the girl had vanished.

"I don't understand, I thought that kind of thing wasn't supposed to happen here. I thought the Wards were supposed to protect us from hostile spirits!" she said, helping me to my feet.

"She wasn't hostile," I declared, without consciously deciding to form the words. They escaped my lips as though someone else had thought them, and yet I knew absolutely that they were true.

Hannah raised her eyebrows. "What are you talking about? She just attacked you!"

"Yeah, I know, but it wasn't like that. She was…" I groped through the tangle of emotions I'd just encountered and pushed aside the ones that didn't belong to me. "She was scared, not angry."

"Yeah, but still, she could have really hurt you," Hannah continued. "We should tell Karen or Celeste or someone."

"I… yeah, okay," I said absently. I was running my fingers along the stones of the wall where the girl had vanished, as though a door might open there so I could follow her. A nagging worry about the girl took deep root in my mind.

"I'm sorry I didn't warn you. I didn't hear her coming. It must be all these Wards. I can't hear anyone in our room, but even when I came into the hall, I couldn't really hear her," Hannah said.

"I couldn't hear her either. She was trying really hard to communicate, but I couldn't understand a word. I wonder why?"

"I'm getting really hungry," Hannah said, in an obvious attempt to change the subject. "Do you want to wait here for Karen to come back, or should we try to find the dining room?"

I tore my eyes from the wall and tried to focus on her. "Sure, let's go find some food."

"Did you still want to find the bathroom?"

"Yeah, bathroom first." I felt dazed. I shook my head a little to clear it, and started down the hallway.

The bathroom turned out to be just a couple of doors down from our room, but it took us nearly a half an hour to find the entrance hall again. When we finally did, it was much more crowded than when we'd arrived. Trunks, suitcases, and bags were stacked neatly along the walls, and knots of women and girls were embracing, shaking hands, and conversing together. I spotted Celeste with her clipboard near the base of the stairs, handing out keys and pointing out rooms to the newcomers.

"Well hello, again," she said as we approached her. "All settled in?"

"Yeah, thanks," I said. "Have you seen Karen?"

"I think she's still up with Finvarra and some of the other Council members," she said, gesturing vaguely over her shoulder.

"Okay. She said she would meet us back at the room, but we're starving. Is there anywhere we can eat?"

"Of course!" answered Celeste. "I'm sorry, I should have pointed it out to you as soon as you arrived. They've laid a luncheon for you all in the dining room, just over there. It's buffet style. You can go in and help yourselves to whatever you'd like."

She pointed to one of the large arched doorways. It had been closed when we'd arrived, but it now stood open. I could see a few people already milling around by the entry passage, carrying plates and teacups.

"When Karen comes down, I'll let her know where you've gotten to," Celeste promised.

"Great, thanks," I said, and turned to Hannah. "Shall we?"

"Okay." She'd gotten quieter and quieter all the way down to the entrance hall, and now she had resumed her habitual imitation of a living shadow, half-hidden from the world behind my shoulder. I gave her what I hoped was a reassuring smile, then walked down the passage and into the dining hall.

The dining room had the same cathedral-like ceilings and dark wood paneling as the entrance hall. A stone fireplace, big enough for both Hannah and me to stand in, dominated the far wall. On either side of the fireplace, a series of doors stood open, through which we could see a bustling kitchen staff clattering away at their work through clouds of steam. Women and men in crisp white uniforms darted in and out of these doors, carrying beautiful antique silver trays laden with sandwiches, pies, pastries, and salads; they placed each of these trays upon one of four long buffet tables. The rest of the room was set with about twenty-five smaller round tables, each set for eight diners. Groups of women were milling around them, flitting from table to table. From what I could tell, there was no rhyme or reason to who sat where; the room had been arranged, it seemed, to encourage socializing and mingling. Since Hannah and I both decidedly sucked at socializing and mingling, we made a beeline for the buffet and loaded up our plates. I didn't know a lot about English food, but everything looked pretty familiar. I snagged a ham and cheese sandwich, a small garden salad, and a pastry-type thing that looked like it was probably filled with meat and vegetables. I reached for an apple just as a girl beside me did the same.

"Please pardon..." she began, but her voice trailed away as our eyes met. She was tall and willowy, with sleek black hair and a swanlike neck. She would've been stunning if a sour look hadn't twisted her mouth into a severe little knot.

"Oh, sorry," I said, as she released the apple. I offered it back out to her. "Here, you can have it."

"No, please. You have it. I really don't want it. It looks like it might be... *rotten*," she said with a haughty toss of her head. Then she turned on her heel and walked away without putting a single item of food on her plate. I watched her flounce purposefully over to one of the other tables, where she settled like a frost over the other girls congregated there. Within moments, all of their eyes were flickering in our direction like little forked tongues.

Hannah, who had been ladling soup from a large tureen, hadn't noticed the exchange. Conscious now of the hostile looks on the back of my neck, I picked my way over to a deserted table tucked in the corner by the windows. The place settings looked so delicate that I was almost afraid to touch anything on the table. By the time I'd convinced myself that I couldn't eat without touching my silverware, Hannah had already begun tearing her roll into tiny pieces and floating them, like little starchy icebergs, in her soup.

I kept my eyes on my food, but the atmosphere in the room was perceptibly changing. I could feel it circulating like a cruel breeze from one end of the hall to the other. Although I had been keeping my eyes down and my mouth busy chewing, I chanced a glance up through the curtain of my hair. Every table greeted my glance with whispering voices, pointing fingers, and staring faces.

My memory spiraled back to a dozen different school cafeterias in which I had sat, a lone figure at a corner table trying to be invisible yet failing miserably; I stuck out as if I had been placed center stage in an auditorium under a blinding spotlight. And it was dispiriting to see how little people changed between six years old and sixty... a span of time that could have revealed the mysteries of the universe, but still hadn't taught these people that openly pointing and staring at the "new kid" was rude and sophomoric.

Just as I was deciding whether to point this out at the top of my voice or just flip everyone a general but sincere middle finger, Karen walked in. She scanned the room for us and, as I could tell at once from the stony look on her face, immediately processed the atmosphere. She barely lost a step though, and, with a magnificently feigned indifference, she strolled casually over to our table and slid into the chair beside Hannah.

"Here you are," she said, stealing a cherry tomato off of my plate and popping it into her mouth. "All unpacked, and finding your way around by yourselves—I'm starting to think you girls don't even need me here! Maybe I should just head back to Boston and stop cramping your style."

I tried to smile, but couldn't quite manage it. "Sorry we didn't wait for you. We were really hungry."

"Don't be silly, I'm only kidding. I'm glad you're starting to feel at home."

"I wouldn't go that far," I muttered.

Karen shot me a quizzical look and I gestured to the room at large. "Have you noticed they've set up a perimeter? We appear to be quarantined."

Karen closed her eyes for a brief moment and took a deep breath. Then she opened them again and gave us a rueful smile. "I was afraid that it might be like this, but I was hoping..."

"Karen?"

We all turned. It was as though the girl I'd met at the buffet table had instantly aged thirty years; even her expression of thinly veiled disdain was identical to her daughter's.

Karen greeted the woman in a diplomatic voice. "Hello Marion. It's been so long. How are you?"

"Oh, I'm well, thank you—although I must admit I'm a bit surprised to see you here," Marion said in honeyed tones. "We weren't sure if after... recent events... you'd be coming. She inclined her head toward Hannah and me, looking us over for the first time. This must be the new generation, then?" It couldn't have been more obvious that she was unimpressed with us.

"Yes, these are Elizabeth's girls, Hannah and Jessica," Karen said, pointing us out. I nodded curtly to Marion. Hannah didn't even look up from her soup, and instead kept her eyes firmly on the bits of roll swimming in her broth.

"Welcome to you both. I hope you enjoy your time here," said Marion, without a trace of sincerity. "My daughter Peyton is right over there," she added, waving toward the girl from the buffet table, who merely glared back. "Her cousin Olivia is here too, my sister Claudia's daughter."

"Peyton's... very like you," Karen said carefully. "So how have you been?"

"Busy as usual," replied Marion, running a manicured finger lovingly over a large golden locket resting in the hollow of her throat. The charm was engraved with the Durupinen's Triskele. "I've been working almost nonstop in preparation for tonight's welcoming festivities; there's just so much to organize, so many little details to oversee. The Council keeps my nose to the grindstone, dealing with all manner of things. Of course, now that one of our most pressing matters is resolved, perhaps things will lighten up."

She looked pointedly at Hannah and me again. With a derisive laugh, Karen dropped her tactful air and crossed her arms.

"You know what, Marion? I'm actually not in the mood to play this particular game of social graces," she said. "You and the other Council members can blame me all you want for the last eighteen years. I've explained everything to Finvarra, and I've been as helpful and cooperative as I could in every way since the moment that Elizabeth disappeared. Finvarra is satisfied that I've done my best to preserve our family's legacy, and if my actions are good enough for her, they should certainly be good enough for you."

A hush fell over the room as the surrounding women dropped their pretense of not paying attention to Karen and Marion's conversation. Even Hannah looked up warily, with her hands tensed against the tabletop as though readying herself to flee.

"Finvarra isn't the only one who has opinions about your family," Marion hissed. "You've disgraced your clan and neglected your sacred duties!"

"I've neglected nothing," Karen said firmly. "I care as much about our family's duties as you do about yours."

Marion let loose a laugh that was nearly a cackle. "Don't you dare compare *my* family to *yours*! No member of my clan would dream of abandoning the Durupinen! We have upheld our laws for centuries!"

"Despite what you may think," Karen interrupted, thrusting her chair away from the table and rising to her feet, "being a member of the Council does not give you the right to pass judgment on all those you deem beneath you. Nor does one scared girl's mistake wipe out centuries of a clan's devoted history."

"Maybe it should!" Marion spat.

"Then why don't you and your precious Council cronies have a vote on it!" Karen laughed derisively.

Marion bristled as though Karen had just cursed at her. "I would think you'd show a little more respect for the Council given the amount of hardship your family has put us through."

"Oh yes," Karen scoffed. "Yes, all those extra meetings and votes, I'm sure it was just torture for you, Marion—I don't know how you survived. I'd love to hear all about it, truly. But in the meantime, know this: These two girls," and she pointed at us, "have been through hell and back because of Elizabeth's decision. If anyone has a reason to be angry, it's them. But here they are, ready and willing to take up a burden they understand very little about. And I will *not* stand by and watch you, or anyone else here, punish them for their mother's mistake. Do I make myself perfectly clear?"

Marion swallowed whatever diatribe she was longing to hurl at Karen and instead nodded imperiously. "Oh, yes. I think we know where you stand, Karen."

"Lovely," Karen replied, settling back into her chair with every appearance of being completely at her ease. "Please feel free to report all the details of this little chat to the appropriate committees."

Marion turned and marched away without another word.

To break the loaded silence that followed, I asked, "Friend of yours?"

Karen ground her teeth. "That woman," she said, "has driven me to the brink of violence since I was eighteen years old. Honestly, I don't think I've ever come closer to hitting someone in my life."

"Not even Lucida?" I asked.

Karen poured herself some tea. She looked down into the cup as though wishing it contained something a bit stronger, and then drained it. She looked around to make sure no one was within earshot before continuing. "It seems you're going to learn this the hard way, so I might as well explain it so you know what you're up against. I'm sorry I didn't warn you earlier, but I had hoped, foolishly I suppose, that the Council would be a little more forgiving."

"I think we got the gist of it," I said, as I pushed my plate away; I was no longer even remotely hungry. "Mom screwed up and everyone is pissed about it. They can't take it out on her because she's gone, so they're taking it out on us instead."

Hannah nodded in agreement, shredding another roll into a little heap of bread dust. She hadn't touched her food either, except to destroy it.

"Yes, that is, as they say, the gist of it," Karen said, "But it's more complicated than that. There's a hierarchy here, just like in any society. Council members are elected to run things, and despite how I may have sounded to Marion just now, I don't deny that their jobs are very important. There are twelve representatives, one from each of twelve different clans. Of course, there are more than twelve clans—there are dozens at Fairhaven Hall—but only twelve are honored with Council seats. Council members wear gold lockets to identify themselves; you probably saw the one that Marion was wearing. Celeste has one too, although she doesn't feel the need to have it on constant display, like some members do."

I looked around the room and spotted Marion at a table with six other women. All of them were wearing lockets; they looked thick as thieves.

"Technically," Karen continued, "any clan can be elected to the Council. Elections are held every five years, but it's really all for show. The same twelve clans have held Council seats for the last four hundred years, simply passing the lockets from mother to daughter, from aunt to niece. The only change in all that time came eighteen years ago, when our family was thrown off the Council and a new clan took our place."

"Our family was one of the twelve?" I asked, surprised.

"Oh yes. Your grandmother was very proud of our position. She, like many still on the Council, felt that to be a member family made you practically royal. I'm sorry to say that she and many of the other families have abused their status over the years, seeking special consideration and offering political clout in return for favors and payment."

Hannah frowned. "She took bribes from people?"

Karen nodded with a grimace. "It's standard practice, I'm afraid. Politics are politics, no matter where you go, and there's always corruption to be found. But all the status and favors in the world couldn't save our family from disgrace when Lizzie left. There were many who took great pleasure in seeing your grandmother dethroned... and I can tell you, she did *not* go quietly. She'd already been devastated by the loss of her husband, and then by her daughter's betrayal; losing the Council seat was the final blow. Her heart gave out only a few weeks later. And of course no one was happier to see her go than Marion's clan, as they were the ones who finally clawed their way to the top to take our place."

I couldn't even begin to formulate a response; it was all too much unpleasant information to process. I tried to swallow it down, chasing it with the ham and cheese sandwich—which I only ate because I knew that I'd be ravenous later if I skipped lunch. No one else came over to talk to us, although Karen did exchange waves with a few people and excused herself a short time later to talk with Celeste and another older woman with short, spiky, gray hair.

"You really should eat something," I said to Hannah, who was now drawing shapes in the pulverized remains of her bread.

"My soup is cold," she replied sadly, as though this ended all possibility of consuming food ever again.

"I can get you some more."

She shook her head. "I don't want any." Her eyes looked glassy and her bottom lip trembled.

"Look Hannah, it's going to be okay," I said, reaching out to touch her arm, but she jerked it violently out of my reach. "They'll get over it."

"I never even knew her," Hannah whispered fiercely. "I never even knew her and she's still ruining everything." She stood up abruptly. "I'm going to find Milo. I'll see you back in the room."

I watched her scurry away, my mouth hanging open. I wanted to call after her with the words that could make her stay, but they wouldn't come; I had none.

I'd always known my mom was haunted by something. No matter how angry I was with her, no matter how tired I was of packing up the car or cleaning her up after she'd passed out, I always knew that there was something there, something I didn't understand, something that drove her to do the things she did. It wasn't just the drinking. I watched her every day, battling against her demon, fending it off for all she was worth. And so, even on the days when she lost, I still gave her credit for fighting. Because on the days that she won, she was my whole world. She braided my hair and drew murals on the bedroom walls with me. When our car radio finally stopped working, she sang made-up songs to me—sometimes even going so far as to change songs, mid-tune, when I pushed the channel button on the Green Monster's defunct stereo. She poured salt into the sugar shakers at greasy all-night diners, and we'd shake with silent giggles when the man behind us coughed and sputtered over his salty coffee. And late at night, in the middle of nowhere, she'd pull the Green Monster to the side of the road and shake me awake, just so that we could lie on the car's roof together and look at the stars. I had all of these wonderful memories to soften the bad ones; I heaped them like precious jewels onto a scale to balance out her mistakes, weaknesses, and lies.

The good memories were my shield. All Hannah had was a stranger's name typed onto her birth certificate, leaving a gaping hole in her life where her mother ought to have been; Hannah's life was a legacy of terror, confusion, and abandonment, and there wasn't a damn thing I could say or do to change that.

Karen arrived beside me, interrupting my thoughts. "Where did Hannah go?"

"Back to the room."

"How is she?"

"I don't really know. She didn't really want to talk about it. But I think we can both guess."

Karen sighed. "I wish I could head back up with you. We had a lot of paperwork and details to get through this morning... it took much longer than I expected. And now I have to go back for the removal of the Binding. I'll see you shortly."

"Good luck."

I watched her go and then, tired of being stared at like a sideshow oddity, I abandoned my half-eaten lunch and went after Hannah. By the time I'd caught up with her, she had found Milo and was sitting with him on a stone landing, telling him all about Karen's confrontation with Marion in the dining room.

"Glad to hear Karen has some claws tucked away for special occasions," Milo said with approval. "Do you want me to go down and give 'em hell for you, sweetness?"

Hannah shook her head.

"Pretty please? It'll brighten my day to darken theirs, I promise you."

"Probably not the best idea," I said.

"I wasn't asking you!" Milo shot at me.

"Yeah, but you heard Karen when we pulled up. They use Wards to keep out hostile spirits. The last thing Hannah needs is you getting yourself labeled hostile and kicked out because you started harassing people."

Milo considered this. "I hate to admit it, but you have a point."

"It happens occasionally," I replied.

We made the long trek back to our room in silence. As we turned the last corner to our hallway, I spotted the ghost of the little girl who had attacked me earlier peeking around a pillar. I opened my mouth to call to her, but she shook her head and pointed to our door. Celeste was standing in front of it. Then the little girl vanished around the corner.

"Hi, Celeste," I called as we approached.

Celeste spun around, startled; she pressed her back to our door, and quickly concealed her hands behind her. "Hello, girls. That was a quick lunch!"

"Yeah, well, the company left something to be desired," I said darkly. "What are you doing up here? Were you looking for us?"

"I... uh, yes," said Celeste. "I thought you might like a tour of the grounds. Are you up for a little field trip?"

I'd just noticed a bucket of soapy water on the floor by her feet. "What are you doing?" I asked, pointing to the bucket.

"Nothing, just a bit of last minute cleaning," she insisted. "What do you say, shall we explore the gardens? There's a really lovely—"

"Celeste, is there something on the door? Can we see it?" asked Hannah.

Celeste's too-bright smile faded. "I'd rather you didn't."

"Why, what's going on?" I asked.

Celeste looked back and forth between us, then sighed resignedly and stepped away from our door. As she did so, her hands dropped to her sides, revealing a sodden cloth, stained pink. "I was hoping I could clean it off before you saw it."

Smeared in red paint across our door was a "welcome" message that Celeste hadn't yet been able to fully scrub into obscurity.

Go home, traitors!

4

PASSING OF THE TORCH

"**O**H, NO THEY DID *NOT*," Milo said angrily, then faded away without so much as another word.

"Milo, come back! It's not worth it!" Hannah called after him, but he didn't reappear.

"I'm so sorry," Celeste said, dropping the rag into the bucket and raising her hands in a helpless gesture. "I don't know what to say. Your family's return has been a rather—"

I cut her off. "It's not your fault. Karen explained the whole thing to us downstairs. Thanks for trying to clean it off, but I think it's probably better that we saw it—so we know what we're actually up against here."

"I think I need to find some paint remover. The soap doesn't seem to be working," she said, wiping her hands on a towel and picking up the bucket. "I'll get the maintenance staff on it straight away. I've alerted the Council, and we will be sure to investigate—"

"I don't think the Council will care very much," Hannah said. "They're the ones who hate us, aren't they?"

"The Council doesn't hate you," Celeste said reassuringly, as she placed a hand on Hannah's shoulder and gave it a gentle squeeze. Hannah didn't pull away this time. "I'm on the Council, and I can say that with certainty. There are a few members who have a hard time forgiving and forgetting, and I'm afraid they've passed their prejudices on to their daughters. But on the whole, the Durupinen honor and respect each other, regardless of any bumps in the road. We will make a full investigation into this incident. The Council will take it very seriously, I promise you."

"If you say so," I muttered, as I watched the hate-speak drip in pink, soapy rivulets down the grain of the wooden planks.

"Whatever their personal opinions may be, the Council knows how detrimental this sort of behavior can be amongst Apprentices, and they won't risk the trouble it could cause in the long run. Why don't you go rest for a bit before tonight's Welcoming Ceremony? I'll take care of this," she said, with a wave at the door. "And your aunt will be up in a few minutes. She's just getting your clan garb for the ceremony tonight."

"Clan garb?" Hannah asked.

Celeste nodded. "Yes, you'll see what I mean when she gets back. The whole evening is really quite beautiful; I'm sure you'll enjoy it." With one last disgusted look at our defaced door, she turned and left.

We walked back into our room and Hannah shut the door behind us to keep the unpleasantness firmly on the other side. She took one of the dusty old books off of the shelf by her bed, seemingly at random, and curled up with it.

"Are you okay?" I asked.

She didn't answer, but opened the book and hid herself behind it. I didn't blame her. It was a stupid question—we were both a long, miserable journey from okay. My gaze fell on our pile of empty suitcases, and I wondered how long it would take to just pack them all up again and get the hell out of here.

A quick knock resounded on our door and it opened before we could respond. Karen poked her head in; an ugly look was on her face.

"Hi."

"Hey," I said, gesturing for her to come in.

She slipped through the door and shut it behind her. She had shopping bag in one hand and, tucked under her arm, an antique wooden box, which she placed on my desk. "Celeste told me—"

"How did the removal of the Binding go?" I asked pointedly.

Karen glanced at Hannah, then took my cue and changed the subject. "Very well. I can see spirits again. I saw several just on my way up here."

"Congratulations," I said, without enthusiasm.

"I realize you can't really understand this, Jess, but it's a big relief for me. This is how it's supposed to be for me. Being cut off from it was unnatural. It felt wrong."

"You're right, I can't understand it," I said. "What's in the box?"

"Your clan garb for tonight."

"I don't suppose they include two plane tickets back to the States?" I asked.

Karen ignored the question and opened the box instead. "It's a really beautiful ceremony. I'm sure you'll both really enjoy it."

"That's what Celeste said. What do we have to do?" came Hannah's muffled voice from behind her copy of *Geatgrima: A Historie of the Durupinen in the British Isles.*

"Do?"

"What's our role in the ceremony?"

"Oh, it's really just a bit of pageantry to welcome all of the Apprentices. All you need to do is show up in the appropriate attire and hold a candle."

"What attire?" I asked, eyeing the box warily. It didn't look big enough to hold entire outfits, but I still cringed to think what bizarre possibilities lay within it.

Karen laughed. "You need to wear white, but it can be your own clothing. The box only has a few accessories in it, see?" She pulled out two purple silk sashes and two gold necklaces.

Hannah peeked over the top of her book as Karen handed me a sash; the fabric was soft and cool to the touch, almost as though it were woven of water. A Triskele, large and golden, was stitched onto it.

"This goes over your left shoulder," she explained, pulling it over my head and adjusting it carefully. "We'll pin it here so that it doesn't slip off. And then the necklace..." She handed one to me. It depicted the Triskele as well, intricately shaped from intertwining bands of gold. Tiny amethysts, winking like fireflies in the lamplight, were set all along the edges.

"It's beautiful," I said, caressing it with a tentative finger. "You realize, of course, that there is not a single white item in my wardrobe."

Karen winked at me. "I knew that, which is why I took the liberty of buying you some." She reached into a large paper shopping bag and pulled out a pile of white fabric, which she thrust into my arms.

"You can be pissed at me later, but for now just try the damn things on, okay?" she said as I opened my mouth to argue. "We don't have a lot of time to find you something else if they don't fit." She held another white garment out to Hannah. "Hannah? Would you try this on, please? You already had that white button-down blouse, so I just got you a skirt."

Hannah slid off the bed and pulled the skirt up over her hips. It was a long and ruffled, Bohemian-style, and it suited her. She even cracked a smile and twirled around once, so that the fabric billowed out around her.

"It's really pretty, Karen, thanks."

"You're welcome. There will be several more occasions coming up when white dress will be required, so you should get some good use out of it."

My own white ensemble turned out to be a long-sleeved fitted T-shirt and a pair of bleached-white skinny jeans. They were even strategically shredded and torn a bit, I noted with satisfaction. Karen had obviously chosen them carefully.

"You know, Karen?" I said, revolving once in front of the mirror to admire the outfit from all angles. "I might actually consider wearing this in public."

Karen smiled. "Hallelujah! You can change out of them for now, if you want, but just make sure you're both dressed and in the entrance hall by 8:30 PM. I've got some more business with the Council to deal with," she said, with a poisonous look at our door. "I'll be back before dinner. And speaking of the Council," she added, perching now on the arm of a chair and now looking quite serious, "there's something I need to discuss with the two of you. Hannah, it's about you, really."

"Me?" Hannah asked, looking up. Her hands still held her skirt out, which made her look like a small child who'd gotten in trouble for splashing in puddles.

"Yes. It's about what happened on the night that Jess and I came to get you from New Beginnings, and what you did to escape from the nurses."

"What about it?" Hannah asked.

"What you did was unusual, Hannah. Really, really unusual, maybe even unheard of. I can't even explain it, to be honest, and I've been trying to figure it out ever since. That's why I asked you so many questions before we came here."

Hannah continued to stare at her, motionless, with her hands still clutching handfuls of skirt.

"Our connection to spirits exists so that they can find us, not the other way around. I've never known any Durupinen to Summon spirits to them, let alone so many at once."

I thought back to the moment when, crouched in Hannah's closet, I watched in frozen terror as she Called the spirits to her.

She had sucked them from the surrounding air and wielded them like weapons to enable our escape.

"I think it's best," Karen continued, "if we don't tell anyone here about it until I can find out more. As we've all learned the hard way, there are too many Durupinen here who resent our family, and we don't need another reason to draw unwanted attention."

"But shouldn't we tell someone?" Hannah asked. "Someone here must know why I can do that, and if it really is that unusual, shouldn't they know?"

"I think they ought to know eventually, yes," replied Karen. "And I'm not even sure how long we will be able to keep it from them once you start interacting with spirits in front of your teachers. I don't want you to lie to them, exactly, but I don't think there's any reason to clue them in if it doesn't come up."

"Is something wrong with me?" Hannah said, almost as a statement instead of a question.

"No. Many people here have unique spirit abilities. I'd just like to find out what I can about yours before Marion and her entourage have a chance to pounce on it and draw their own conclusions. Agreed?"

"Agreed," we both said, Hannah a little late.

"Good. Thank you." Karen's expression cleared. "I'll be up to get you for dinner."

"Can we eat up here?" Hannah asked.

"Yeah, I wouldn't mind avoiding the snake pit for tonight," I agreed.

Karen hesitated. "I appreciate that it's tough, but you girls are going to need to adjust to being here and—"

"Karen, we're stuck here for the foreseeable future with these people. We're going to have plenty of time to adjust. Can't we just... start adjusting tomorrow? I think we've had about all the adjustment we can handle for one day," I said. By "we" I meant Hannah, but I had to admit that hiding out in our room sounded like a pretty nice alternative to further humiliation.

"It won't stay like this, you know," Karen said in a gentle voice. "Things will get better."

"Yeah maybe, but probably not by dinner time."

Karen picked up the antique box and tucked it back under her arm. "You're right. I'll bring up some plates for you, okay?" Without waiting for an answer, she slipped out the door and closed it behind her.

I plopped down in one of the chairs in front of the fireplace. I could tell that if I ever came to feel at home here, this would quickly become one of my favorite spots. I tried to close my eyes and rediscover the exhaustion that had been ready to overwhelm me that morning, but I couldn't find it. It had been replaced with a manic kind of energy that was buzzing under my skin. I wanted to run through the halls and rip the stupid old tapestries off the walls. I wanted to find the girls who had painted the message on my door and scream in their faces. I wanted to kick and claw at the stones of this horror-story castle until it was a pile of rubble.

I needed and get some fresh air before I gave in to one or all of those urges. I stood up and announced to Hannah, "I'm going for a walk."

Hannah, curled again behind her book, and with her new skirt fanned out around her like a cloud, didn't even look up. "I'll see you later."

"Right." I grabbed my sketchpad and some pencils, shoved them into the depths of my bag, then slung it over my shoulder. I flung the door open only to leap backwards as Milo streaked in.

"Knock much?"

He turned to me with a withering look and gestured to himself. "Knock? Really? I sort of lack the necessary tools for that sort of thing—you know, like a corporeal existence."

"You know what I mean. Can't you at least—Hey, wait a minute. How the hell did you get in here?"

Milo raised a perfectly arched eyebrow. "Through the door, oh brainy one, you just watched me do it. By the way, what happened to your dismal wardrobe? Did you trip and fall into a tub of bleach?"

I chose to ignore this last comment. "No, I mean, how did you get past the Wards?"

"The what now?"

"The Wards!" I pointed to the symbol carved into our bedroom door, which was now partially obscured with dripping graffiti. "This symbol is supposed to keep all spirits out of our room."

"Oh. Well, maybe it's broken," said Milo with an unconcerned shrug. "Anyway, don't you want to know what I found out?"

I rolled my eyes. "I don't know much about all this ancient Durupinen stuff, but I'm pretty sure these things don't just break."

Milo snuggled up onto the bed next to Hannah, who, rather than shying away from what ought to have been his intensely cold and uncomfortable energy, leaned into him as if he were a throw pillow. I shivered involuntarily.

"Huh. Well, now that you mention it, that sort of explains a few things." Milo quipped.

"Such as?"

"While I was exploring the place, there were a bunch of rooms I couldn't get into. It was like the doorways and walls had turned solid, which was really weird for me—since solid isn't really something I deal with anymore. Then I came back here and tried to get in, to see if you were back yet, and I couldn't do it. Maybe I can only enter when you're in the room?"

"I don't know," I said, tracing a finger around the grooved shape of the Ward. "I don't think it's supposed to work like that."

"I want him to be here. Maybe a ghost can come in if you invite him. You know, like vampires," Hannah offered.

"Vampires? Okay seriously, can we just stick to ghosts? I think that's about as much paranormal interference as my life can handle right now," I said, raising my hands in front of me.

"I was just kidding," Hannah giggled.

"Hello? Doesn't anyone want to know what I found out?" Milo said with a pout.

"Okay, okay. What did you find out?" Hannah asked.

"I know who left the love note on your door," sang Milo in triumph.

I dropped my bag, bounded across the room, and clambered onto the bed. "Really? Who?"

"There's at least three of them. One of them is named Peyton; she lives across the hall, three doors down from here."

"Yeah, I had the displeasure of meeting her already," I said.

"Her roommate is involved too, Olivia. They were talking with a third girl, but I didn't catch her name. I heard them plotting in the alcove by the staircase. They were talking about how to get rid of the paint without anyone finding it."

"You didn't let them see you, did you?" Hannah asked.

"No," Milo said with a sigh. "I took Jess' advice for once and didn't materialize. It would've been much more fun to tell them off, but I think it's better that they didn't know I was there. I tried to follow them back into their room, but I couldn't get in—probably because of those Ward thingies. That's where the evidence is, though."

Hannah bit her lip. "Who should we tell? Celeste? Karen?"

"Nobody," I said firmly, getting back up.

Milo's mouth dropped open. "You aren't going to bust them?"

"No." I picked my bag up off the floor.

"But how else are we going to get those bitches kicked out?" Milo asked.

"I don't want to give them the satisfaction of knowing that they got to us," I said. "Besides, even if we did tell someone, do you really think the Council is going to do anything about it? Peyton's mother pretty much runs that show, from what I can tell."

"You're probably right," said Hannah.

"Can I at least go wreak some havoc?" Milo pleaded, as he clasped his hands in supplication. "You know, go all poltergeist on their asses? Pretty please?"

The corner of my mouth twitched in spite of how hard I was trying to stop it. "We'll see. For now, I think we've got all the trouble we can handle, don't you?" I turned to Hannah. "I'm going outside to sketch. Can you bring my clan stuff down to the entrance hall? I'll meet you there."

I spent the intervening hours out on the grounds, lost in the pages of my sketchbook. If Fairhaven Hall's castle was something out of a gothic horror story, then its grounds were something out of a fairytale. The gardens were full of forgotten corners and statues worn down to vague suggestions of their former detail; the stone walls were so old it seemed as if the ivy and brambles tangled across them were trying to hold them together. Every so often, I would catch a glimpse of a figure here or there that faded away before I could study it. Once I heard a snatch of a woman humming; it sounded almost like a lullaby, and made me at once both sad and comforted. I sketched until my fears and anger dulled to the same vague, featureless masses as the statues standing watch over the flowerbeds. As it always did, drawing calmed me down, gave me a sense of control, and allowed me to think more clearly.

We were here. We were here and we were going to stick it out, but not because we didn't have a choice: It was simply that our choice had already been made. We would have to deal with a lot of unpleasantness and uncertainty as we found our footing. But giving in wasn't an option. Both Hannah and I had dealt with a lot of shit in our lives and, quite frankly, I couldn't really think of anything they could dish out here that could top what we'd already faced in the past. It was a weirdly comforting thought, and I lit it like a talisman in my chest. We would do our best to learn what we could here, and then our lives would—once and for all—be our own.

As I trudged back up to the castle, I felt renewed from my artistic release and my mental regrouping. I tried to hold on to that feeling as I entered the crowded entrance hall at 8:25 PM to prepare for the Welcoming Ceremony. I pointedly ignored the crowd's parting for me as if I were carrying a particularly contagious form of leprosy, and found Hannah and Karen by the fireplace.

"I was starting to wonder if I'd have to come looking for you," Karen said, draping my sash over my shoulder.

"Just needed some air," I replied as she handed me a safety pin. I secured the sash in place and pulled the Triskele necklace over my head. "Have I missed anything interesting yet?"

"No, we're just about to line up in formation." Karen smoothed out my sash, which was now secured to my shoulder, and looked with satisfaction at us. "Perfect. Now when the music starts, I'll show you where to line up. Just follow the procession outside. You'll be on the western side of the courtyard."

"Aren't you coming with us?' asked Hannah in a slightly panicked voice.

"I'll be out there, but I have to take my place among the other Senior Durupinen. When the moment comes, I'll come to light your candles and stand with you." At this, Karen handed us each a white taper in a brass candlestick.

A sharp echoing gong resounded throughout the hall, and, like a flock of doves taking flight, the Apprentices fluttered around, arranging themselves into two long rows. Peyton, I noticed, was at the very front of the line, bearing her own candle and an expression so smug that I could have cheerfully slapped it off her face. "Maybe I *should* let Milo loose on her," I thought. I glanced around for him, but he was nowhere in sight. In fact, for the first time since I'd arrived here, I didn't see a single spirit anywhere.

"Where's Milo?"

"Upstairs. He's not allowed at the ceremony, none of the spirits are," Hannah said.

"Why not?"

Hannah just shrugged.

Karen guided us quickly into position about a third of the way from the front, where we hurried to imitate the other girls around us—chins up, shoulders back, and candles raised. As nervous as I was, the fact that I felt like a complete tool still managed to register; I barely succeeded in covering a nervous laugh with a snorting sort of cough. Hannah looked paler than I'd ever seen her.

"Relax, or you're going to snap that candle in half," I muttered.

She threw me half a smile, then drew a long, slow breath and relaxed her grip on her taper.

Just behind me, a tall gangling girl with freckles and a long blonde braid was chewing nervously on her lip and standing on her tiptoes, searching the hall. She was so preoccupied that her candle was dangling loosely in her hand, tipping out of its holder. Just as I opened my mouth to point this out, Celeste came sweeping by, righting the candle and adjusting the girl's sash.

"Phoebe, mind your taper, please," said Celeste, and then her eyes fell on the empty space beside her. "Where is Savannah?"

"I don't know," Phoebe said nervously. "Haven't seen her since lunch." Celeste raised her eyes to the ceiling as though praying for patience, and then hurried away though the crowd.

A haunting, wailing melody began to reverberate through the hall. Every head turned to the rafters where a woman in a long white dress was playing a rustic set of panpipes from the balcony. Then a second melody rose to meet and intertwine with the first, this time played on violin by a blonde woman. By squinting into the shadows, I realized that the blonde woman was Catriona. The last time I'd seen her, she'd been casually lounging on my window seat in my bedroom in the dead of night as though she and Lucida hadn't just broken in. Seeing Catriona now, like a wraith in the rafters, was nearly as dreamlike and surreal as that first time we met.

The music signaled the start of the procession. As we shuffled forward, torches and lanterns all along the stone edifices flared to life. With a deafening groan, the great front doors creaked open to reveal a sky on the rosy brink of twilight. We crunched along a gravel path between the trees, and entered the central courtyard for the first time.

The courtyard was circular, flanked by the curved inner walls of the castle itself. The four turreted towers loomed over the space, which contained a wide, perfectly round pathway of stone and—at its very center—a crumbling arch raised on an ancient stone dais. It looked as though someone had transported one of the famous mystical structures of Stonehenge right into our midst. I could barely take my eyes from the thing, so strong was its allure.

"What is it?" Hannah whispered.

I managed to tear my eyes away from the arch for just long enough to see her enraptured expression. "I don't know."

I looked around us. Every face was staring at the arch with unmitigated reverence. A thrill of terror jolted through me like electricity. I was awed to be so close to something that had so much power, something that could, I knew, hold us here or cast us off—or even simply swallow us all. All it would take was one tiny, tempting pulse of energy and I knew I would have no choice but to sprint right through the arch to whatever lay beyond. It was, I realized, the physical manifestation of the Gateway which lived in each of us.

The Apprentices formed a circle on the inner walkway and turned to face the center. Then bagpipes joined the other instruments, and the music swelled as the Senior Durupinen processed in. Each was dressed in a long white gown with a clan sash, and each carried a lit white taper in a gold candleholder. The expression on each face was eerily similar... reverent and peaceful. I felt a sudden flutter of panic as I wondered if they'd all been hypnotized or brainwashed or something. They walked in two-by-two, although here and there one of them walked alone. Karen was one of solitary ones, and I knew that the empty space beside her was meant to be my mother's place. The absence of my mother suddenly expanded inside me like a silent explosion; I forced myself to look away before it consumed me.

I concentrated instead on the other faces parading past. Though some of the women were quite average looking, a disproportionate number of them were strangely beautiful—that same flawless, airbrushed sort of beauty that I had noticed immediately upon meeting Catriona and Lucida. It was thoroughly disconcerting, and somehow I had a feeling their beauty had little to do with moisturizers and expensive hair care products. I mean, Karen was attractive, but not in that almost eerie, otherworldly sort of way. It was like the freaking *Stepford Wives* out here. I scanned the Apprentices around me, but none of them shared this preternatural glamour as far as I could tell.

The music changed again. Its melody shifted from something

that floated and buffeted on the wind to a regal march. The Senior Durupinen formed a larger circle around our smaller one, and then turned expectantly toward the North Tower. The Apprentices all followed suit. Two columns of Caomhnóir marched in strict formation from the tower doors and spread out across the ramparts; there they turned, as one, to face the courtyard at attention. Several of them, I noted in surprise, looked barely older than me. A moment later, a woman, flanked by Catriona and the panpipe player, appeared upon a small balcony above the Caomhnóir and raised her arms: Silence fell.

I knew before she spoke that this must be Finvarra, the woman who, from the shadows, had been pulling the strings on the twisted puppet show that was now my life. She was the High Priestess of the Durupinen, the woman who had sent Lucida and Catriona to find us, the woman who had made sure that every trace of my ability to communicate with spirits was wiped clean from Pierce's investigative equipment. She was the singular most powerful force within the Durupinen, yet I had imagined many times walking right up to her and giving her a piece of my mind. But now, as every one of us held our breath in anticipation of her words, I knew that I never would have dared to do such a thing. Finvarra fairly glowed with an aura of power. Her face looked like it had been carved from marble, from her high cheekbones to her full lips. Her hair was pure, shining white, and I realized that if the wind hadn't been lifting it into billowing waves all around her, her locks would easily have reached her waist. Even from below, I recognized the Triskele locket around her throat; a much larger amulet—clearly a symbol of her status as High Priestess—hung from a ribbon around her neck. Her expression, as she gazed out at us all, contained the kind of peace and surety only seen in paintings of saints and martyrs.

A last quavering note from Catriona's violin shivered on the air, and then Finvarra's voice rang out into the attentive silence. Catriona and the other woman left the balcony quietly, presumably to join us in the courtyard.

"On behalf of the generations of Durupinen who have graced this place before you, I welcome you all with an open heart to Fairhaven Hall," began Finvarra. "Apprentices, you step today onto a path that has been forged ahead of you, over many centuries, as the Durupinen have played our crucial role. We are the Gatekeepers, protectors of the portals between the spirit world and the living world. We have maintained, through our commitment to our gift and traditions, a delicate balance between light and dark, between life and death. We are eternal and enduring..."

A tiny orange light bobbed around in the corner of my eye. I turned to see Lucida creeping out from between two bushes with a lit cigarette dangling from her mouth. She was slinking her way toward the empty space beside Catriona, whose formerly solemn face was now twitching with repressed laughter. Lucida, in her wildly inappropriate stilettos, stumbled slightly on the uneven cobblestones and had to grab onto Catriona's arm to steady herself. I don't know why Lucida bothered trying to sneak in; her little black dress and leopard-print coat, over which she'd hastily thrown her blue clan sash, contrasted so strongly against the white costumes of the other women that she might as well have been wearing a blinking neon sign. She fell into ranks, ignoring the sideways glances from the women around her. As she turned to flick her cigarette away, she caught my eye and winked.

I snapped my head back around. My dislike for Lucida welled up inside me even more strongly that it did upon our first meeting, when she'd shown a total lack of regard for both my feelings and the gravity of the emotional baggage she unloaded on me; she'd treated the whole encounter like a performance put on for her amusement. Apparently her lack of respect extended into all areas of her life, including sacred Durupinen ceremonies. I mean, okay, I wasn't exactly sold on all of this Durupinen stuff yet, but I was here wasn't I? I was standing here, holding my stupid candle, feeling like a tool but still behaving myself, making an effort.

I tried to pick up the thread of Finvarra's speech. If she had noticed Lucida's unceremonious interruption, she wasn't letting on. Her voice cut through the twilit silence. "For some of you, the knowledge of the Durupinen has been a part of your lives from your earliest memories. Your childhood was steeped in our lore and traditions, and therefore your arrival here seems natural—a long anticipated step on the path you've always known you would travel. For others," and here I felt sure her gaze flickered down to and Hannah and me, "the discovery that you are one of us has opened heretofore unimagined vistas of possibility before you."

I leaned slightly toward Hannah. "No shit," I murmured under my breath. She giggled softly and gave me an admonishing nudge with her elbow.

"Whatever paths you took as individuals to arrive here tonight, your journey forward will be the same, and all of you will be united in the exploration of your gift. I hope that you will help each other, support each other, and look to the guidance of your teachers and mentors to shepherd your way. With our gift comes enormous responsibility—a responsibility that you may now fear, but that, in time, you will come to cherish as a sacred duty for the good of all humankind as your destiny and your calling. As a symbol of this, your clan elders will now light your candles."

At this, Karen and many of the other Durupinen stepped out of their circle towards us, the tiny flames of their candles bobbing forward like synchronized fireflies. Karen tipped her flame first to Hannah's wick, then to mine; both candles flickered to life. All around us voices were murmuring, but it wasn't until Karen's voice joined them that I could make out what they were saying.

"This light I bestow upon you as the next Gateway. And thus, my door closes... and yours shall open."

Karen's eyes were full of tears as she said it, but she managed a small smile. I felt a lump rising in my throat and swallowed it back—along with the impulse to thrust the flame, and everything it stood for, right back at her. A strange battle was raging in my chest between a previously dormant yet surprisingly innate desire to do all that Finvarra asked of us, and a louder and much more logical instinct for familiarity and self-preservation.

"And now, Apprentices, please bring your flames to the *Geatgrima* in the center of the courtyard. The *Geatgrima* is the physical manifestation of the Gateway within each of you. By placing your flame in this Circle, you are pledging your life to the protection of your Gateway, and promising to serve the spirits who shall Cross through it."

As though the *Geatgrima* itself was waiting for this instruction, I suddenly found its pull irresistible, and before I could consciously decide to do it, I was walking with sure and steady stride toward the dais. It was just as I had realized in the garden: It wasn't that we didn't have a choice, but that the choice had already been made.

We all knelt around the dais, and placed our candles carefully upon the roughly hewn stone. No sooner had we done this than the individual candle flames were whipped into a frenzy, as though by a wind that none of us could feel. They danced higher and higher, their flames spreading until a ring of fire encircled the *Geatgrima*, which continued to pulsate with its own formidable energy. And as the ring rose higher and higher, the smoke began to swirl and undulate, twisting itself into strange shapes as it climbed to the sky and obscuring the first of the evening stars above us. At last, as the flames climbed to the very top of the *Geatgrima*, they exploded into a final halo of sparks.

We stood transfixed until the smoke cleared away. Through the last trailing tendrils of smoke, my eyes met Finvarra's. Her visage, so calm a moment before, looked troubled as her gaze lingered on my face. I nodded once to her, but she did not return the acknowledgment. Instead, she said something to the spirit of a tall man who had materialized just behind her. Then she turned her back to me and disappeared back into the yawning black mouth of the North Tower.

5

GENDER POLITICS

D AMN YOU, JET LAG. Damn you straight to the ninth circle of hell where you were undoubtedly concocted by the devil himself. I wasn't a morning person by any stretch of the imagination, but getting out of bed usually didn't resemble scraping roadkill off the freeway to quite this extent. I groped around for the alarm clock on my bedside table and bashed it into silent submission. It was seven o'clock in the morning on my first day of classes.

"Kill me."

"I don't think that would make a difference around here," came Hannah's voice. "They'd probably just make you go to class anyway."

"Ha ha," I said, blinking the sleep out of my eyes and trying to bring the room into focus. Hannah was loitering by the door, fully dressed and with a backpack at her feet, as though our room were a stop on the midtown bus line. She was also chewing her fingernails obsessively.

"Hannah, you might as well sit down and relax for a few minutes. I still have to shower and everything," I said, sliding out of bed. The drop was higher than I expected and I had to grab onto the bedpost to keep from falling. I'd forgotten how high off the ground these old-fashioned beds were; Hannah could barely get into hers without using the little footstool we found tucked under it.

"I can't sit, I'm too nervous," she said.

"What time did you wake up?"

"Five-thirty. I couldn't fall back asleep so I just got ready instead."

"Ew. Okay, well, I'll try to be quick. You don't have to wait for me if you want to go eat."

She looked at me like I'd just suggested she jump off of the roof of the school.

"Or not. Be right back." I grabbed my shower caddy and slipped past her out the door.

Everybody thinks they want to live in a castle until they actually try it. It's beautiful to look at, but a castle in the English countryside the first thing in the morning is flipping freezing. I cursed under my breath in the deserted bathroom while hopping back and forth from one bare foot to the other as I fumbled with the shower taps and waited for the water to warm up. The goose bumps were just relaxing back into my skin when the bathroom door banged open. Without warning, my shower curtain was ripped back and a girl jumped right into the stall with me.

What the hell?—"

"Shh!" She clamped a hand over my mouth.

I froze with my arms folded protectively over my bare chest, and stared into the panting face of this complete stranger. I knew she wasn't a spirit; the hand still covering my mouth was far too solid and warm, and it smelled like nail polish.

Before I could even think past my own shock or consider what to do next, I heard the bathroom door swing open again.

"Savannah? Are you in here?" It was Celeste.

I looked into the girl's face. She shook her head with a pleading expression. I wrenched my face away from her hand and called, "It's just me in here, Celeste. It's Jess. Who are you looking for?"

"Oh, hello Jess. Sorry, I didn't mean to intrude. I was just looking for one of the other Apprentices."

"In the bathroom?"

"Yes," she said with a wry laugh. "Sorry about that. I need to talk to her, but she's being... anyway, didn't mean to disturb you. Have a good first day of classes. I'll see you after lunch in History and Lore."

The door closed with a gentle bump. We stood motionless another moment, listening to footsteps fade away down the hallway. The girl heaved a sigh of relief and collapsed back onto the shower bench.

"Cheers, mate," she said with a laugh. "That was a close shave, wasn't it?"

"Yeah, I'm not your mate, so will you please get the hell out of my shower now?" I replied.

She grinned at me. "I suppose so." She hopped up, pulled the curtain, stepped out, and shook the water out of long red hair as she left the stall. Her clothes were soaked.

I pulled the curtain, finished my shower, and shrugged into my bathrobe. When I emerged a few minutes later, the girl was sitting cross-legged on the radiator and sucking on a lit cigarette. She watched me as I towel-dried my hair and began tugging a brush through my tangles.

"Fag?" she asked, extending the crumpled pack toward me.

"I'm good, thanks."

She continued to stare at me, smoking her cigarette with relish.

"So, are you Savannah?" I finally asked.

"Guilty as charged," she said.

"Why was Celeste looking for you? What did you do?"

She shrugged as she expelled a plume of smoke over her head. "It wasn't so much what I did as what I didn't do."

"Which was?"

She didn't answer at first. She seemed to be sizing me up, trying to decide if I were trustworthy.

"Look, if you're worried I'm going to tell someone, I think you've got the upper hand on personal information here. I mean, you did just see me completely naked."

Savannah gave a grunting snort of a laugh and flicked the spent cigarette into the sink. It was actually a pretty impressive shot; she sunk it from about fifteen feet away. "No need to be embarrassed, love. Nothing I ain't seen before, and you've got a nice set there."

Her accent was so strong that it took me a moment to register what she'd said, and then my face went crimson with mortification. "Uh, thanks, I guess."

"No problem. And to answer your question, I skived off the ceremony last night in favor of another social engagement."

"Social engagement?"

"One of my friends from home was throwing a party and I wasn't about to miss it," she said, hopping off of the radiator. At the mirror over the next sink, she rubbed vigorously under her eyes, trying to remove some of the previous evening's makeup.

"You skipped the Welcoming Ceremony for a party?" I asked.

"I know, I know... and it wasn't even worth it. That cab cost a bloody fortune and the coppers broke it up before things really got going. Still, I bet it was a damn sight better than all that candle nonsense."

I smiled in spite of myself. "You're probably right."

"What's your name, then?" she asked me.

"I'm Jess Ballard," I said, bracing myself for the same negative reaction we'd gotten from most of the other people we'd met, but Savannah just wrung my hand with a vice-like handshake.

"Alright, Jess? I'm Savannah Todd. Folks call me Savvy, and I suppose you can too, if you fancy. Thanks again for covering for me. I'll have to face them eventually, I know, but I was hoping I could have a bit of breakfast first." She crossed over to the door and peeked into the hallway. "Coast is clear. See you down there?"

"Yeah, sure."

She flashed a toothpaste-commercial smile and left.

§

When Hannah and I entered the dining room about half an hour later, the ranks had already closed. Like a high school cafeteria in a made-for-TV movie, dirty looks followed us as we made our way through the buffet line and over to the same corner table we'd eaten at the day before with Karen. I could actually feel the absence of an angsty acoustic soundtrack. I was prepared for another meal in isolation, but a few moments later Savannah came strutting over to us, tray in hand, and dropped into the chair across from me.

"Alright?" she said genially. "Almost didn't recognize you with all your clothes on."

"Hello again," I said through a mouthful of scrambled egg. "Hannah, this is Savannah Todd, my, uh... shower buddy." Hannah, blushing in apparent empathy, barely looked up from her oatmeal as she flicked her hand feebly in greeting.

"So did Celeste track you down yet?" I asked.

"Oh yeah, she gave me a right good talking to," Savannah said, waggling her finger sternly at me. "Sadly, she didn't chuck me out, but there's always next time."

"Do you want to get kicked out?" I asked, a little surprised. "Is that really even an option?"

"Don't think so, but I thought it was worth a try anyhow." She reached across the table, stole my knife without asking, and started using it to butter her toast. "I've been pretty successful at it before, but this ain't exactly your typical school, is it?"

"No, not exactly," I said. "Why do you—"

"Hello there!"

A tall, lanky girl with a heavily freckled face and a pixie cut had walked up to our table. She was strawberry-blonde, and wearing a name tag that said, "Mackenzie." She was carrying several purple folders under one arm, which had a blue silk armband tied around it.

"Hi," I said; my greeting came out a moment later than was probably polite, but I was too surprised by another friendly greeting to answer right away.

"As my totally unnecessary name tag says, I'm Mackenzie Miller, but please don't ever call me that, because I'll completely ignore you. Just call me Mackie, alright?" She thrust out a hand to each of us in turn and we all shook it.

"Nice to meet you all," Mackie said.

"Uh, you too," I said.

"My aunt is Celeste Morgan, so she's got me on welcoming duty," Mackie said, rolling her eyes. "Not that I wouldn't have welcomed you anyway, seeing as I'm the First-Year Head, but now I get to look like a prat while doing it."

I smiled tentatively at her. "Sorry about that."

She sighed. "No worries. Anyway, let me get through this official stuff, so you can get back to your breakfast. These are for you." She handed each of us one of the purple folders. "Your class schedules are in there, and also a map of the school, so you don't get lost—although you probably will anyway. There's also a list of what to bring for classes and a letter about meeting with your mentors. Just have a look through it, and if you have any questions give me a shout."

"Cheers," said Savannah, as she chucked the folder aside without opening it and returned to her toast.

"Also, if you have any questions during the day, just find somebody with one of these blue armbands on. They're the ones that already know their way around the castle, and can help you if you need it."

I leaned past her and looked around the room. I could see several girls with blue armbands scattered among the tables.

Peyton appeared just over Mackie's shoulder. "Ah, you've already done the reject table, I see," she said in a positively saccharine simper. "How chivalrous of you to take on the less pleasant tasks... but then, that sort of thing always falls to the First-Year Head, I suppose."

Mackie forced a smile and imitated Peyton's sugary tone. "Yes, you know me, I'm a giver. Now why don't you make yourself useful and take these," she shoved a few more purple folders into Peyton's hands, "and sort out the last table by the windows. And try not to scare them away, would you?"

Peyton glared at Mackie, but held back whatever snarky comment she was formulating. She stalked off with her nose in the air.

Mackie slid into the chair beside Savannah and cocked her head in Peyton's direction. "I should warn you now that not everyone with a blue armband will be equally helpful. In fact, don't ask Peyton or any of her minions for directions unless you want to wind up in the dungeons."

I laughed, but Hannah squeaked, "We have dungeons?"

Mackie smiled at her. "Well, yeah, but nothing that's been used in about four hundred years, so I wouldn't be bothered about it."

"Alright," Hannah said, and relaxed enough to attempt another bite of oatmeal.

"Look," Mackie said, dropping her camp counselor demeanor. "Don't let Peyton or the others get to you. They're just terrified of anything outside of tradition. The truth is that every clan is just as important as the next, and the instructors will teach you everything you need to know to fit right in."

"And if we don't want to fit in?" asked Savannah, taking an interest in the conversation for the first time.

"Then you just learn what you need to know, and get out of here as quick as you can," Mackie said with a shrug.

We all must have looked surprised, because Mackie laughed before continuing. "Probably not what you expected to hear from your First-Year Head, right? Look, some of us make this our lives. We live here, we teach here, we get elected to committees and plan Durupinen cocktail parties. We define ourselves by it. But many others—most of us, in fact—finish our training here, turn our backs, and never see the bloody place again if we can help it. We do what we are required to do, but no more. We choose to define ourselves by other things. And that's okay, too. I know it doesn't feel like it now, but a time will come when you can take control of your life again. But you need to put in the time here first, get the skills and training you need. I know you've all had a taste of what it's like if you try to deal with your gifts on your own... and some of you have had more than a taste."

Here she stopped and smiled a little sadly at Hannah. Hannah caught her eye and, although she didn't return the smile, she didn't look away either.

Mackie went on, "Fairhaven will help you make the best of it, I can promise you that. So," she jumped up from the chair so quickly that I slopped half a cup of tea into my saucer in surprise, "good luck today, and chin up!" And with a sort of salute to the three of us, she turned jauntily and headed off to greet another table.

"She was friendly," Hannah murmured.

"Yeah, she was," I said. "It's nice to know we won't be total outcasts."

"What's with you two, then?" Savannah asked. "I thought my cousin and I were the only outsiders here."

Despite the fact that this girl had, quite literally, seen all of me there was to see, I wasn't about to go into the whole sad and sordid story with her—there were two different kinds of naked, after all. "We didn't know we were Durupinen until a few weeks ago. Our family had sort of... stopped the whole thing and never told us about it, so now we have to start over."

"Well, you're still a step ahead of me," Savannah said, picking her teeth with the tines of her fork. "I'm the first one in my family to do this at all."

"What? How is that possible? Aren't the clans all supposed to be ancient? How can you be the first one?"

"Yeah, well one of your ancient clans died out recently, and you lot needed a new one to 'maintain the balance' or some rubbish like that. Are you going to finish that?" She pointed to Hannah's untouched blueberry muffin. Hannah shook her head and Savannah slid the plate across the table and began wolfing the muffin down with gusto.

"So what, they... recruited you?" I asked.

"Suppose you could say that," Savannah said after a huge swallow. "They turned up and told me that I needed to join up, said they found me because of my abilities."

"What abilities do you have?"

"Same sort of thing as you, I'd think. When I went places, I'd sense stuff, like feelings and thoughts that weren't my own. I've been like that my whole life. When I was very small, I used to tell my mum all about my grandparents, even though I'd never met them. In year four of primary school, I knew all the answers to the tests like someone was whispering them in my ear, even though I hadn't studied a thing. It was brilliant. I got the best marks of my life."

"That happened to me once," Hannah said, with just a hint of a mischievous smile playing around her mouth. "My seventh grade history classroom was haunted by a former teacher. My living teacher thought I was a genius."

"It had its benefits sometimes," Savannah said. "In the end I learned to tune it all out, or at least ignore it in public. But then about six months ago, that Celeste woman turned up on my doorstep and told me I had to come here. She said my abilities meant that I was supposed to be one of you. Well, I very nearly slammed the door right in her face. I thought she was a complete nutter. But she kept coming back, and finally one day she started talking about my grandparents, told me all sorts of things she never could have known. In the end I believed her, and so here I am. They needed two of us though, so they brought my cousin Phoebe as well."

Savannah jerked her head over her shoulder toward the table behind us. The blonde girl who'd stood behind us during the Welcoming Ceremony was sitting there by herself, chewing with her mouth slightly open as she picked the raisins out of her toast.

"I only met her a few times as a kid. My mum and hers don't get on very well, and they live three hours from London in the tiniest, most boring village—nothing in it but a few rundown cottages and about a million sheep. She's probably the dullest person I've ever met, and now we're stuck together for life. And I tell you this—if she thinks I'm moving to the sheep capital of the UK she can think again."

I laughed. "I guess we've all got some adjusting to do."

"You said it," Savannah agreed.

Somewhere in the castle, a deep bell began to clang, and all around us people rose from the tables like a flock of startled birds. I dropped my spoon and checked my newly adjusted watch. It was 8:20 AM. I fumbled to open the purple folder Mackie had given me and extracted my class schedule.

"Okay, we're going to Ceremonial Basics in room 481, which according to this," I quickly scanned the map, "is only a few corridors over from our bedroom. It shouldn't be too hard to find. Let's go."

§

Famous last words. Ten minutes and three wrong turns later, we had found seats in the back left corner of the classroom, which looked more like a wealthy gentleman's private study than any real classroom I'd ever been in. The walls were covered in beautiful, tall mahogany bookcases, and a fire crackled gently in the fireplace behind the teacher's elaborately carved, claw-footed desk; an imposing, high-backed chair sat positioned behind it. Instead of traditional desks, we were seated at small, highly-polished tables, all of which were carved in the same style as the desk at the front. I wasn't really surprised by the decor, since most of the castle had the same opulent, almost ostentatious kind of feel, but I couldn't shake the feeling that I ought to be wearing a stiffly starched dress and reciting my multiplication tables under the threat of a teacher's ruler. Hannah was shooting covetous looks at the vast array of books, which were all richly bound in leather with gold titles stamped onto their spines.

Phoebe walked in a minute or two after we did, but chose a seat three rows away from her cousin; she seemed too intimidated by Savvy to try to strike up a conversation. The other Apprentices looked totally at home, lounging in their seats; most of them were chatting comfortably with each other. The floor was inlaid with a line of black stone, which ran from the fireplace at the front all the way to the back wall, dividing the room in half and making a clear aisle down the center of the desks. Every desk on the right hand side of the aisle was empty.

Mackie walked in, followed by a girl who looked so much like her that they were obviously sisters. They came down the aisle and headed for the tables right in front of ours, which had remained conspicuously empty.

"Jess, Hannah, meet the bane of my existence, my little sister Brenna," Mackie said, clapping her sister on the back. Brenna smiled and gave us a little wave.

"Thanks for the introduction, Mack," Brenna grumbled, then turned to us with a friendly smile. "Hiya."

"Hi," we both replied.

"You've noticed the great divide, I see," said Mackie, dropping into the seat in front of me. Brenna slid into the seat in front of Hannah.

"Yeah. What's that about?"

"It's to keep us all pure," Mackie said, her expression very grave.

"Sorry?"

She snorted and her face broke into an easy grin. "It's the Sanctity Line. Many of the classrooms have one. It's to keep the Caomhnóir and the Durupinen separate when they have to take class together."

My mouth dropped open. "You can't be serious?"

"Deadly serious," Mackie said with a chortle, and nodded toward the door.

As though on cue, a Caomhnóir entered the room, followed by a line of silent and unsmiling Caomhnóir Novitiates, who filed into the empty section of seats. A few of them snuck sideways looks over to where we sat, but most averted their eyes, ignoring us completely.

Savvy, who'd been slouched in her seat, perked up at once. "Hang on, now," she said, running a hand through her long auburn curls. "You mean we actually take classes with blokes here? I thought it was just women!"

"Whoa, girl. Don't go turning on the charm just yet," Mackie said. "Interaction between Caomhnóir and Durupinen is strictly monitored. The only times we'll be together will be chaperoned, during classes and ceremonies. Socializing is expressly forbidden."

"What century are they living in around here? And why are we—" I began.

"Shh!" Mackie hissed. "Here comes Siobhán. I expect she'll lay it all out for us."

Our teacher lingered on the threshold, engaged in a brief exchange with the Caomhnóir standing just inside the doorway. I couldn't be sure, but I thought this Caomhnóir might have been the same one who drove us from the airport; all the Caomhnóir I'd seen so far had the same emotionless faces, so it was difficult to distinguish one from the other. After a few whispered sentences, he nodded curtly and took a seat that had been placed by the open door for him.

As Siobhán swept further into the room, the Caomhnóir all leapt to their feet respectfully. Startled, I half-rose from my chair as well, but Mackie caught my sleeve and shook her head; all of the other Apprentices had remained in their seats.

"Good morning," Siobhán said, as she raised her hands in a gesture of welcome.

"Good morning," we all responded automatically.

"Welcome to your first day of classes here at Fairhaven Hall, and to your very first lesson, which is Ceremonial Basics. In this class, you will learn the routines and rituals that will guide your interactions with the Gateway and the spirits you will encounter. Let me begin by clarifying a misconception." She swept a long strand of dark hair from her cheek and leaned back on her desk. "This is not a class in magic. Magic, as the world would envision it, does not exist. We do not cast spells, and we do not brew potions. We do not wave wands or deal in witchcraft. The world sees these things as strange and unnatural. We do, however, seek to effect change and harness some measure of control over our interactions with the ebb and flow of the cycle of life and death in this world, and nothing could be more natural than this."

Here she stopped, and surveyed us all with a piercing gaze from her pale blue eyes to ensure our complete concentration before continuing. Even Savvy had stopped winding her chewing gum around her pinkie finger and was staring at Siobhán.

"We deal with the natural order of things, and to do this, we need to harness the power that exists in the natural cycle of life. The Durupinen have had this duty entrusted to us. It is not magic, and it is not witchcraft. It is merely knowledge that others do not possess."

She walked over to the nearest bookcase and ran a hand delicately across a row of spines. "Words have immense power. No learned person would ever dare deny this. Words can evoke the most powerful emotional reactions or calm them into submission. They can incite the world to action or bind it together in common empathy. All of this can be accomplished by the right combination of words. The words of our rituals and ceremonies are no different, but we are the precious few who know how to wield them.

"And who would be foolish enough to deny the power of actions?

Any human that walks the earth could, through the right combination of actions, ignite a war, build a cathedral, or end a life. The rituals of the Durupinen are just such actions, but they are ours alone to learn and pass along, and their immense power is ours to protect. I know that you will therefore treat the content of this class with the reverence it deserves, and give it your fullest and most attentive efforts."

Siobhán turned smartly and sat herself behind her desk. I looked around. Hannah's hands were splayed across the tabletop, with her fingers tensed as though she were holding them over the keys of a piano. Savvy appeared very uncomfortable, and she caught my eye with a look that clearly said, "What the hell have we gotten ourselves into?"

I couldn't help but share in a bit of her alarm. Based on that speech, missing a homework assignment in this class would be akin to disrupting the natural order of the universe. I suddenly thought of Tia; she would have an aneurysm from this kind of academic pressure.

I turned to see Mackie smirking at me. She'd obviously heard all of this before, living with a Council member, and was merely enjoying the reactions of the newcomers.

"This is one of three classes this term," Siobhán continued, "in which the Apprentices and Caomhnóir Novitiates will share a classroom, so it falls to me to lay the ground rules for your interactions with each other."

Several people shifted uncomfortably. A few surreptitious glances floated across the aisle; the line separating us suddenly became a gaping chasm.

"Caomhnóir and Durupinen have long had a very important and sacred relationship. The Durupinen are the Keepers of the doors between our world and the world beyond. It is the job of the Caomhnóir to protect us as we carry out our duty to the Gateways. Throughout our history, the Durupinen have been discovered and persecuted. There are those who would expose our secrets to the world, would seek to destroy the balance of the system. The Caomhnóir are sworn to stand between us and these dangers, and to lay down their lives, if necessary, in the defense of the Gateways. Many have done just that, and we honor them."

Heads bowed as though in prayer all around me, but I felt like I was in the middle of some bizarre dream I couldn't wake up from. A fear flooded through me: Was it really likely that one of these boys sitting across the aisle would have to sacrifice himself to protect me? From what? From whom?

"It is crucial," Siobhán went on, oblivious to my silently mounting anxiety, "that this relationship is never tainted or abused in any way. The abilities of the Durupinen and the Caomhnóir must remain in harmonious, but separate, balance. This means that romantic relationships are expressly forbidden. I cannot impress upon you enough how important it is to preserve the inviolability of this system. The Sanctity Line, which divides you in this classroom, is symbolic. You will of course need to speak with one another, and to work together in close proximity. But the Sanctity Line is there to remind you of the limits set upon your interactions, limits that I expect you all to heed with the greatest of reverence."

Her words fell like a frost over the room. No one spoke, though Savvy looked like she had a few choice words she'd like to let loose—if she'd had the nerve.

Siobhán accepted our silence as assent and continued. "Very soon, each Gateway will be assigned a Caomhnóir, who will be pledged to its protection. These assignments will be permanent, until such time as the next generation of the Gateway is initiated. You will continue to work throughout the school year to develop a cordial and functional working relationship built on mutual trust. All of that begins with study, and so, trusting that you will all heed my words and abide by them, I will now hand out your textbooks."

I shook my head to clear it. The idea that a speech like that could conclude with something as mundane as the handing out of textbooks seemed inherently wrong. I looked over at Hannah, who seemed to be taking it all in stride; I was struck by how much better she accepted the magnitude of all of this than I. Then again, she'd been submerged in a sort of alternate reality for her entire life, whereas I had only forced myself to accept this existence a few months ago.

I took a deep, steadying breath, blew it out slowly, and then reached my hand out for the textbook that Mackie was passing to me. It was bound in leather and looked as though it should have been kept in a glass case in a university archive, and handled only while wearing gloves. As I turned the book over in my hands, I caught Mackie's eye. She was smiling as though she knew exactly what I was thinking and was thoroughly entertained by it.

"Am I amusing you?" I asked.

"Immensely."

"Glad to hear it," I said, carefully placing a book onto Savvy's table. She looked at the textbook as though she had never seen such a thing before, and proceeded to ignore it wholeheartedly.

"Talk about culture shock, right?" Mackie said. "On a scale of one to ten, how ready are you to hop across the pond back to the States?"

"Seventeen."

"Look, it sounds crazy. But you'd be surprised how quickly it all starts to feel normal. First day speeches are always meant to sound impressive. They figure the more important they can make it all sound, the better students we'll be."

"Obviously haven't met me before then, have they?" Savvy said, fluttering her lashes in mock innocence.

"My point is, the biggest hurdle has already passed for you, hasn't it?" continued Mackie.

Hannah looked up from her book in mild surprise. "How do you mean?"

"You've already done a Crossing, haven't you?" asked Mackie. She raised her voice a bit as she said this, and I saw several heads turn to listen.

"Yeah," I said, feeling the spotlight of unwanted attention glaring in my face. "How did you know that?"

"Celeste told us. She said the spirit activity was so intense that you had to get special permission to perform a Crossing before you came here, just to protect yourselves."

Brenna was leaning on her hand, looking eagerly at us. More heads turned. Was staring openly at people only considered rude in America?

"That's right," I said.

"Well, there you go!" Mackie said, clapping her hands. "None of us has ever performed a Crossing before. You're several steps ahead of everyone else in this room."

A few of the surrounding faces looked impressed in spite of themselves, which I'm sure was Mackie's intention. But it didn't last, of course.

"Oh Mackie, that's really not fair," Peyton chimed in from a few rows ahead. She had painted a politely incredulous expression on her face.

Mackie turned to face her. "What's not fair?"

"Several steps ahead of everyone else? Really? Are we meant to be awed by this vast wealth of experience?" Peyton laughed delicately, then turned to me. "Look, I know Mackie's trying to make you both feel better, sweet thing that she is, but I think it's really much kinder to let you know exactly where you stand."

Awesome. Here we go. Junior high cattiness rears its ugly head.

"And where's that?" I asked, feigning interest.

"As far outside of this inner circle as you can possibly be," said Peyton, gesturing around her. Here and there, a smug face nodded in agreement. "We've all been groomed for this training since birth. We've grown up learning about our history and respecting our traditions. I wouldn't want you to get a false sense of security about fitting in here just because you stumbled your way through one barely sanctioned ceremony."

Mackie glanced over to find Siobhán, but Siobhán was occupied with handing out books to the Novitiates on the other side of the room. "Peyton, give it a rest, okay?"

But I held up a hand to silence her. I'd had enough of the *Mean Girls* routine. "No, no, please go on," I said. "You've obviously got quite a bit you'd like to say to us, and to be honest, I'd rather you got it over with. I'm not really one for bullshit pretense and snide comments, so by all means, say your piece."

Savvy snorted appreciatively.

Peyton's smirk vanished. "Blunt, aren't you? How very American. Very well, if you insist. Your family might've been important here once, but those days are long gone. And whatever a few riffraff might've told you to spare your nerves and help you feel at home, you should know that they're just pitying you. The truth is that we don't forgive or forget very easily around here. Some stains don't wash away. We all know of the absolute disgrace your family wallows in, and we don't intend to let you forget it."

I smiled brightly. "Excellent," I said. "Glad we had this little chat. I don't know how we'd ever remember all those pesky details about how we got here if you didn't feel the need to constantly remind us. We're just so forgetful, aren't we Hannah?"

"Very forgetful," said Hannah. Her voice quavered a bit, but her expression was determined.

"Oh, we'll be pleased to remind you as often as necessary," Peyton said. Behind her, three or four girls laughed.

"Shut up, Peyton."

We all turned in surprise. Across the aisle, slumped low in his seat, one of the Novitiates was scowling at Peyton. He had long, dark hair that hid most of his face, but from what I could see his features were hard and angular.

"Excuse me?"

"I said shut up. Let them alone."

"And why should I do that?"

The boy clenched his jaw and hesitated. Judging by his expression, he regretted entering into the conversation in the first place, as if he'd done it without thinking. "Because you don't own this place, and they're here to learn just like the rest of us. So just... let them get on with it, then."

Peyton raised an eyebrow. "Getting carried away a bit, aren't you, Finn? I mean, I know you're meant to swear an oath of protection to the Durupinen, but you needn't take it so literally, especially with clan traitors like them. Where's your family pride?"

"I guess I left it at home, much like your sense of common courtesy," Finn replied, no longer looking at us.

"What's happening over here? Not arguing, I hope?" Siobhán interjected, finally noticing the exchange and pouncing upon it. No one answered her.

We spent the remaining hour slogging through a very long syllabus detailing exactly what we would be covering during the semester. I might not have been at St. Matt's anymore, but my workload was still going to be impressive.

"At the end of the class, you are all to report to your mentor meetings," Siobhán said. "Details about who your mentors will be and where you are to meet with them are in the folders you received this morning. I will be happy to answer any questions I can before you go. Hannah?"

Hannah, who had been rummaging in her tattered old backpack for her folder, looked up in alarm.

"You have been assigned to me for mentorship," Siobhán said, smiling encouragingly. "Our meeting will take place here, so you needn't pack up your things."

Hannah nodded without saying anything and placed her bag back down on the floor.

I pulled out my own folder and found the mentor information.

"Where are you headed?" Brenna asked me.

"The the East Tower, to meet with Fiona Cassidy. I have no idea how to get there. Savvy, where are you going?"

Savvy started out of a daydream. "Sorry?"

"Where are you going next?"

"Dunno," she said, and went back to staring out the window.

A cacophonous bell marked the end of the period while simultaneously scaring the living daylights out of me. I stood up and slung my messenger bag over my shoulder. With the addition of the new textbook, my bag was much heavier than I had realized; I overbalanced. I stumbled and fell right into the same Novitiate who'd spoken to Peyton as he rose from his own seat.

"Ouch... Sorry about that."

He helped me to right myself again, but pulled his hands away at once and shoved them into his pockets, as if I had somehow contaminated them.

"Watch where you're going," he spat, and started elbowing past several of his fellow Novitiates as he stalked down the aisle and out the door.

6

ARTISTIC TEMPERAMENTS

I STARED AT FINN AS HE STOMPED AWAY. "What the hell is his problem?" I said, more to myself than to anyone else.

Mackie followed my gaze and said, "That's Finn Carey," as though that explained everything.

"Wasn't he just telling Peyton to leave us alone?"

"Yeah, but that was probably just because he can't stand her. They're cousins; his sister Olivia is the other half of Peyton's Gateway. That's her, walking out with Peyton," Mackie said, and she pointed out a sharp-faced brunette who was clutching her books to the front of a conservative pink cardigan.

"You mean he and Peyton are actually related to each other?" I asked.

"Yeah, most of the Caomhnóir are related to one branch of the Durupinen or another somehow. I'll explain it on the way to the East Tower. I'm heading that way anyway, and it will probably take you until next Tuesday to find it by yourself."

"Okay, thanks," I said. I turned back to Hannah. "So, I guess I'll see you in a little while?"

"Yeah." She looked so tiny and lost in the now-empty section of seats. The room seemed to swallow her up.

"Are you going to be okay?"

"Yes," she said without conviction.

"She'll be fine," Siobhán said, as she sat herself at the table in front of Hannah's. "We'll have a nice chat together."

"Right," I said, grateful that Siobhán, at least, seemed unfazed by our status as resident pariahs. "Thanks. I'll meet you at lunch?"

Hannah nodded again, and I followed Mackie out of the room. As we turned into the hallway, I caught Savvy's voice saying, "Folder? What are you on about? I never got a folder!"

"She's pretty shy, huh? Your sister?" Mackie asked, cocking her head back over her shoulder at Hannah.

"Yeah," I said. "She's hasn't had a very easy time of it, so she doesn't trust a lot of people."

"She'll be alright with Siobhán. I think your aunt requested her specifically, because she's not... y'know..."

"A total bitch?" I supplied.

Mackie grinned. "Something like that, yeah."

"What are these mentor meetings for anyway? Is it just to have someone to talk to, like an advisor?" I asked.

"For the most part, yes," Mackie said. "The mentors are usually randomly assigned, just so that we'll have someone we can go to if we need advice or help, that sort of thing. But in certain cases, the assignment isn't random at all. Some of the Apprentices have demonstrated special abilities that need to be explored, so they get paired up with a mentor that has a similar gift."

"What kind of special abilities?" I asked. "Shit, we see spirits! Isn't that special enough?"

Mackie let out a bark of laughter. "It usually has to do with the way we sense the spirits. Like me, for instance—I'm an Empath. When a spirit is near me, I start to experience their emotions really intensely. We all do it, to some degree, but for me it's really pronounced. My own mood and emotions will start to change at the first sign of a spirit who's trying to make contact. I used to burst out screaming or crying for no apparent reason when I was a kid. That was how my mum first knew I'd inherited the gift."

"Doesn't that sort of... mess you up? It can't be easy, getting flooded with negative emotions that aren't even yours."

"Yeah, it was pretty scary at first. I'd be playing in the garden, having a grand old time, and suddenly I'd be running and screaming, hiding behind the shed. But I've learned to mostly sort it out—you know, recognize when the emotion isn't mine. I'm still working on it, though, so I've been paired up with the language teacher, Agnes, because she's a pretty powerful Empath herself. I'm hoping she can help me minimize the effect of spirit emotions."

"Huh. What about your sister? Does she have any extra abilities?"

"Nope. At least nothing that stands out right now. It's possible something will still manifest. She's a year younger than me, and she's only just been getting Visitations within the last year."

"How do I know if my assignment is random? I don't think I've got any sort of extra special abilities going on."

"I'd expect yours isn't random at all. You draw, don't you?"

I stopped walking. "Yes. How did you know that? Why does everyone here already know everything about me?"

"Calm down, now," said Mackie. "I was giving a tour yesterday, and I noticed you out on the grounds with a sketchpad."

"Oh. Right, sorry," I said. "I'm still just... adjusting to the way things are done around here."

"I know," Mackie replied, clapping me on the shoulder so that I stumbled a little. "It's like being tossed into a den of the vipers around here. They make it their business to know your business. But don't be bothered, you'll get used to it."

I said nothing. I had a feeling I was rapidly reaching the limit of stuff one person could possibly get used to.

"I mentioned the drawing because Fiona is our artist in residence. She cares for all of the artwork here, and produces her own as well. They probably matched you two up because of your art background."

I perked up at this. An artist? Maybe I would actually get a transferable life skill out of all of this. "Does this mean I might get to talk about art with her?"

"I don't know her well, but I think you'll find it hard to talk about anything but art, actually," answered Mackie, with a hitch in her voice like a laugh.

We set off along a corridor I hadn't entered before. It was hung with a series of tapestries, each depicting a different woman; each was wearing a long, robe-like gown and was surrounded by celestial bodies and various creatures, some of which were mythical.

"Gallery of High Priestesses," Mackie explained with a flick of her hand. "The royals do paintings, we do tapestries. Creepy, aren't they? Celeste will bore you to tears with all their names and accomplishments in class, so I won't bother now, but this one might interest you."

She stopped in front of a tapestry depicting a dark-haired priestess who stared haughtily down her long, straight nose at us. Something about her features gave me a touch of déjà vu. At her feet, I could just make out a name stitched in gold thread: Agnes Isherwood of the Clan Sassanaigh, 1016–1073.

It took a moment for my clan name to register. "She's from my family," I said in mild surprise. "She was a High Priestess?"

"That's right. Your history's always been here, even if you never knew it. And I'll tell you something else: You'll not find any of Peyton's great-great-great-grandmothers knocking about on one of these walls. Tell her to put *that* in her pipe and smoke it."

Mackie punched me genially on the arm and continued down the hallway at a brisk pace. I stared for another moment, transfixed by the face on the tapestry; it was at once foreign and yet uncannily familiar.

I caught up to Mackie. "So can you explain what you started to say before, about the Caomhnóir?" I asked. I nearly had to jog to keep up with her—her legs were about a foot longer than mine.

"They're chosen because of their abilities, just like we are, and their lines go back as far as ours do. Most of the Caomhnóir are related to the Durupinen clans in some distant way, but it used to be a real mark of status to have both male and female offspring in one direct line with the gift."

"What abilities do they have?" I asked.

"They can sense spirits, just as we can, but they have the ability to repel them, rather than attract them. They can keep them away, which is a very useful skill to have when ghosts are constantly trying to make contact with you."

"No kidding. I wish I had it," I said.

"Me too," Mackie agreed. "It would've helped me to avoid some awkward situations as a kid, I can tell you. Anyway, the Caomhnóir use their abilities to protect the Durupinen from spirit hostility. Some Caomhnóir are really powerful at repelling"

"But if they're supposed to be working with us so much, why are they so..."

"Rude?"

"Yeah."

"It goes back to what Siobhán was saying about forbidden relationships. Our abilities aren't supposed to be combined. It would be really dangerous—or so they tell us—so we're not supposed to fraternize much. But Caomhnóir culture takes it a step further. They're taught from childhood that the Durupinen are these manipulative temptresses who will try to lure them into relationships."

"Excuse me?" I laughed.

"Yeah, I know," Mackie said, shaking her head. "It's supposed to be a mark of their strength and manhood if they can resist us, so most of them will barely speak to us or look us in the eye."

"I... I don't even... wow."

"So I think your question was, 'Why was Finn Carey so rude?' And the answer is, 'Because he's the quintessential Caomhnóir.' He wants as little to do with the Apprentices as possible, and when he's forced to interact with us, he does it with an attitude."

"Otherwise I might seduce him with my evil feminine wiles?" I asked, still laughing.

"Not if I get him with mine first!" Mackie giggled.

We were still laughing as we turned a final corner. The hallway ended abruptly in front of us in a gently rounded wall of stone.

"Okay, here it is, the East Tower." She pointed at an arched entryway in the wall, which opened to a tightly spiraled set of stairs. "Up those steps, as far as you can go, and make sure you knock at the top. Fiona's a bit protective of her space."

"Thanks," I said. "Well, I guess I'll see you later."

"I'll see you at lunch, if Celeste hasn't found another silly job for me to do," Mackie said, straightening her armband and pasting on a forced smile. "Bye, then. Good luck."

§

By the time I reached the landing at the top of the tower, I was gasping for air and the muscles in my legs were seizing up. I hadn't realized that getting to my classes would require quite so much cardio; I'd never played an organized sport in my life, but I thought I'd better take up some form of exercise or I'd have to start every mentoring session as a sweaty disaster. I took a minute to catch my breath, and then knocked on the door.

No one answered.

I tried again, a bit more forcefully.

I heard something metal crash to the floor and a voice cry, "What? What, what, what, damn it! I'm trying to get some bloody work done in here!"

The door flew open and a woman stood before me, with her livid expression barely six inches from my own face. I took an involuntary step back.

"What do you want?"

"I... I'm here for my mentor meeting. I'm Jess Ballard."

"Mentor meeting?" Her eyebrows drew together into a single severe line over her narrowed, deep-brown eyes—eyes so dark that they were nearly black.

"Yes. Aren't you Fiona?"

I held out the paper with all of the mentor information on it, and she snatched it out of my hand, glaring at it through the bifocals she had perched on the end of her nose. Her hands, face, and clothes were smeared in a chalky white substance that might have been plaster.

"Dogs!" she said, and stalked back into the room. I hovered in the doorway, unsure if "dogs" meant I was supposed to follow her. She turned and sighed dramatically. "Well, come in if you must. Don't touch anything."

I followed her into the room, which wasn't really an office at all, but a cavernous artist's loft. The rafters that crisscrossed over our heads were hung with canvases and empty old frames stripped of their innards. The floor was obscured by a jumbled carpet of tarps. A steady drip, drip, drip sound pattered; a row of paintbrushes were drooping and weeping as they dried. All around the space, paintings and sculptures were piled atop mismatched furniture. A potter's wheel sat in one corner. Next to the wheel was what had once been a suit of armor, but had now been dissected, welded, and reassembled into something that would have looked at home in a Picasso painting. A massive metal scaffolding encased the entire left wall, caging in the largest and most faded tapestry I'd ever seen. The tapestry's very topmost section was being restored; the image of a sun, in shining new thread, was slowly emerging from the tapestry's dull antiquity.

It was like stumbling into the forgotten lair of da Vinci. It was fantastic.

"Sit down," Fiona said, gesturing vaguely toward the windows; a desk and several chairs lay half-buried under the artistic carnage.

I shifted a canvas and a dried palette of oils off of a rickety wooden chair and sat down gingerly, testing to make sure the chair would hold my weight before settling onto the threadbare seat.

Fiona took her time scrubbing her hands in a large metal sink in the corner, then finally seated herself cross-legged on her desk, facing me. "So," she said, still picking plaster out from under her fingernails. "What am I supposed to do with you?"

"I have no idea," I said, feeling slightly annoyed. "You're the mentor."

"I told them not to send me any more randomly assigned Apprentices. I don't have the time for it. But they never listen to me. What did you say your name was again?"

"Jess Ballard."

"Hmm. One of Lizzy's girls?"

"Yeah," I said, surprised. "You knew my mom?"

Fiona ignored my question completely, but instead grabbed a small wire wastebasket off of the floor and dumped its contents all over her desk. She picked through the refuse until she found a somewhat crumpled piece of paper, which she smoothed out on her knee and started reading. Her eyebrows disappeared up into those tendrils of hair that had escaped her bandana. When she looked at me again, it was with a first glimmer of interest.

"I should properly read the stuff they send me more often," she said. She waved the paper at me. "You weren't randomly assigned at all. This letter says you're a Muse. Is that true?"

"I'm a what?"

"A Muse," said Fiona impatiently. "Christ on a bike, don't they tell you girls anything before they drag you in here? It means that you channel the spirits through some form of art. The spirits use you as a tool to tell their stories in an artistic medium. We haven't had a legitimate one for years, other than me."

I opened my mouth to say no, but stopped myself. My memory raced back to the day last winter, when I was sitting in a crowded lecture hall at St. Matt's and trying to sense what was hidden underneath a chair draped in black fabric.

"Well, there was this one time I was communicating with a spirit and I drew her without having ever seen her before," I said. "Is that what you're talking about?"

"Just the once?"

"Yes."

Fiona's face fell. "That's not much to go on, just one poxy sketch. I don't suppose you still have it, do you?"

"Yeah, I do. I've got it with me, actually," I realized, and extricated my sketchbook from my bag. I'd taken the book with me that morning, hoping to find a few minutes between classes to sketch in the gardens. I wasn't overly eager to show this woman anything I'd drawn, given her attitude, but I flipped back until I found my drawing of Lydia Tenningsbrook and handed it to Fiona.

Her face, so skeptical at first, fell into a deep concentration as she gazed at the little girl's smiling face. Her head began to nod slowly. "How did you produce this? Were you trying to picture her when you drew this? Did you have a vision, or see her in your mind's eye?"

"No, I wasn't even looking at the paper. I was focusing on listening to her, and when I looked down, I had drawn this without even realizing it. It would have taken me half an hour to do a sketch like that normally, but I looked down after maybe a minute of communication, and there it was. My hand was all cramped up. It was like... it was like someone else borrowed my hand."

She started leafing through the other pages without asking, continuing to nod. As she pulled back the final page, she revealed the first likeness of Evan I had ever drawn. I snatched the sketchbook out of her hands, flipped it closed, and shoved it back into the depths of my bag.

"That one is... private," I said firmly.

Fiona seemed not at all offended by this. She then began firing questions at me like projectiles. "Was that last one a spirit as well?"

"Yes." But I wasn't going to talk about Evan now, not to someone I barely knew.

"How long have you been drawing?"

"As long as I can remember. We lost the security deposit on one of our apartments when I was five because I drew a mural on my bedroom wall in Sharpie."

Fiona might have smirked, but it was hard to tell in the half-light coming in from the windows. "What mediums do you prefer?"

"Usually just pencil. Sometimes charcoal."

"Do you have experience with anything else? Oils? Acrylics? Watercolors?"

"Not really. A little bit with pastels."

"What about sculpture?"

"Not even a little."

Fiona frowned and scratched her chin. "Any formal training? Art classes or lessons?"

"Just a couple of art classes in junior high," I said. "I moved schools so often that I didn't usually have time for electives. It's always been more of a hobby for me."

She made a sound halfway between a groan and a hiss, then jumped down from the desk and started pacing like a caged animal. "You know what they do. They dig around and send me the most pathetic excuses for Muses they can unearth. You wouldn't believe what passes for a Psychic Drawing around here. One spirit-induced doodle, a bloody stick figure, and they just can't wait to ship 'em up to me. And I tear my hair out trying to coax repeat performances out of them, these Apprentices who've never picked up a brush or a sketchpad in their lives, and what's the result? Hours of wasted time, that's what. And look at this! Look at all of this!" She gestured wildly around the space. "Do I look like I've got time to waste? All these bloody paintings and tapestries to restore... I'm left with barely a moment to work on my own pieces."

She glared at me expectantly, waiting for an answer. I opened my mouth, but could not formulate a single coherent thing to say. I snapped it shut again and shook my head.

"And forget about real art. Forget about actually sending me someone who can make *art,* for the love of all that's holy! I don't know what they think I do up here all day but they sure as hell don't think it's art."

She kicked a defenseless paint can across the room; its amber-colored contents soared through the air in a graceful arc and then splattered gruesomely across a nearby tarp.

"That," she shouted, jabbing a finger toward my bag, "was possibly the first real Psychic Drawing I've seen from an Apprentice in years, and certainly the first I've seen from anyone who can actually draw worth a damn."

I blinked. I was getting ready to be dismissed at best, or to have a paint can hurled at my head at worst. Did this mean she thought I had potential?

"What's your name again?" she shot at me.

"Jess."

"Well Jess," Fiona flung herself into the chair next to me and folded her arms. "Congratulations on being the first Apprentice I haven't chucked out on the first day."

"Uh, thanks," I said.

"Do you want to do something real with that?" She cocked her head toward my sketchbook. "I mean, do you want to develop your skills? Create something?"

I hesitated. Yes, I wanted to improve as an artist, but I wasn't sure if I wanted to do it with this woman. I was about seventy percent sure that she was nuts. I looked around the room, playing for time, and my eyes fell on a partially completed painting on an easel behind her. One of the towers of Fairhaven Hall leapt from the canvas. On its balcony, a woman gazed out over the twilit grounds. A breeze had caught her hair and pulled it over her shoulder; it twisted out into the night, as though hoping to catch itself on an early-evening star. It was breathtaking. If, in the midst of all this uncertainty and hostility, there was a chance I could learn to create something that beautiful...

"Yes." The answer escaped me without my consciously deciding to give it, but I felt no urge to take it back.

Fiona gave a grim nod, as though we'd both just agreed to something mutually unpleasant. "If we're going to do this—I mean, properly do this—I need to lay a few things out for you. First, you need to understand that I'm not promising I can actually do anything with you. You're raw. And I have no idea if you'll improve with training—it may all come to naught. I can already see there's a good deal I'll have to unteach you, but you've got a good eye, I'll give you that. And if I see you aren't improving, I'm not going to keep wasting my time."

"Okay..."

"Now as far as the Psychic Drawing, I can't say for sure if you're a Muse or not. One isolated incident doesn't mean you've been gifted like that, so we'll have to experiment and go from there. It's not unusual for an Apprentice to have very varied forms of spirit communication before a gift settles into its regular patterns, and we may find that a spirit never uses you in such a capacity again. You have to be prepared for that. If that's the case, I'll be shipping you off to another mentor. I don't have time to hold your hand and bond with you and talk about your feelings, or whatever other rubbish a mentor is supposed to do."

"Okay," I said again. What else could I say? She wasn't really giving me a choice.

"Alright then," Fiona said. "Dogs, I've got my work cut out for me. We begin then."

I spent the next hour in an interrogation scene from a film noir, minus the cigarette smoke and saxophone-heavy soundtrack. Fiona wanted to know every detail about every bit of art I'd ever done, but grew increasingly snappish with each question she asked. She grew impatient if I had to consider my answer, and bored if I gave what she considered to be an irrelevant piece of information. She yelled at me no less than ten times about things I had no control over, like which great paintings I'd seen or when I'd first started sketching. She actually threw a chair when I said I didn't know how to mix paints, then rounded off the whole bizarre encounter by slumping into her chair, banging her forehead repeatedly on the desktop, and pointing wordlessly at the exit. As I hightailed it for the door, she shouted after me, "Next Monday, same time. Bring your sketchbook."

As I closed the door behind me, I didn't know whether to laugh, cry, or sigh with relief. Clearly, my mentor was a complete lunatic. On the other hand, she was also a brilliant artist. If I could avoid being concussed by her throwing furniture, I might just learn something remarkable.

And then there was this Muse thing. Could this actually be true? Did I have some sort of additional ability? I didn't like the idea of spirits being able to use me like that; it seemed invasive, like being possessed. My drawing had always been my own private escape, something I had done purely for the joy of it. Was it possible that spirits were going to invade that last, secret corner of my life? Couldn't I have this one tiny portion of normalcy?

§

A cold, creeping sensation crawled its way up my spine and broke into my inner monologue, and I realized I had been pacing, lost in my own thoughts, in the hall outside of Fiona's studio for a good five minutes. I stopped in my tracks and scanned the corridor around me. It seemed to be completely deserted.

"Hello?"

No one answered. The chill deepened, and I shivered violently.

"I know you're there," I said, turning on the spot and squinting into the shadows.

A dark place under a nearby tapestry suddenly rippled, as though the shadow itself was breathing.

I took a tentative step toward it. "Hello?"

A tiny, grubby hand materialized from the darkness. It was pointing at me.

I took a deep steadying breath and crouched down, trying to get to eye level with whatever it was that was looking at me. "Do you want to talk to me?"

The hand vanished, and for a moment I thought I'd scared it away. Then, with no warning, the very same spirit who had attacked me the day before shot out of the gloom and was hovering barely an inch from my face.

I would have leapt back in fear if that same fear had not immobilized me where I stood. I swallowed hard and tried to keep the quaver out of my voice. "What do you want?"

The spirit started yelling—her face screwed up with the effort of it, and her thin shoulders heaved—but not a syllable of her cries reached my ears.

"I'm sorry," I told her. "I can't hear you."

Her mouth opened wide in a silent scream, and then, in frustration, she began to beat her fists upon the air, which remained solid and impenetrable between us.

I stood there, helpless, watching her efforts to communicate drain her energy, so that her form started flickering. Finally, with one last furious swipe, she gave up, exhausted.

"I'm sorry," I whispered again.

The little girl stared up into my face. As I watched her eyes fill up with ghostly tears, I found that my own vision became clouded—that I was, in fact, sobbing. I closed my eyes, but before I could even process the emotion, or do anything to control myself, she faded into nothing but a strange, negative imprint behind my closed eyes. As she disappeared, so did the alien emotion that had seeped into me, and after a moment the tears on my cheeks felt as though someone else had cried them. I brushed the moisture away quickly with the back of my hand and calmed my breathing.

"Hey!"

I looked up to find Finn hurrying toward me. I swiped again at the tear streaks on my face. He came to a sudden halt a few feet from me, as though he'd met the boundary of another Sanctity Line hidden beneath the carpet.

"Are you okay?" he asked.

"Yes. Yes, I'm fine." I tried to get up, but my knees couldn't quite remember how to straighten.

"What's wrong with you?"

"Nothing's wrong with me!" I snapped, struggling to find my bearings.

Finn hovered indecisively on the spot, staring at me as I tried awkwardly to get to my feet. He made a sound that might have been a sigh of frustration, and when he spoke his voice came out in a growl. "Do you need me to fetch someone?"

I glared at him. "No. There was just this ghost and she..."

"A ghost? What ghost?" he asked. He shook his hair back from his face and peered around, his expression skeptical.

"Forget it. I said I'm fine."

He didn't move. He just kept staring at me. I finally straightened up, although my knees were shaking.

"What is this, a spectator sport? The show's over! Nothing to see here," I announced, swinging my bag over my shoulder.

Finn scowled at me. Then he turned on his heel and stalked down the stairs, with his hands shoved deeply into his pockets.

Awesome. I'd met this guy twice. The first time, I had stumbled right into him; the second time, I'd been on my knees and sobbing in the middle of the hallway. Nothing pissed me off more than coming across as the damsel in distress, especially to someone who clearly had not the slightest inclination of helping me. Not to mention the fact that I'd barely been here two days yet already seemed to have a spectral stalker. I started for the stairs, glancing this way and that for any sign of the ghost child. There were dozens of us in this castle, why was this little girl harassing me? And, more importantly, what did she want?

"Well, look who it is," said a sultry, smoky voice that I recognized instantly, despite having heard it on only one other occasion.

I spun around and looked down the staircase; Lucida and Catriona were on the landing below me. They were both as uncannily flawless and beautiful as I'd remembered them from the night they'd invaded my bedroom. I'd thought perhaps I'd exaggerated their beauty in my mind, or that the moonlight combined with the strangeness of that encounter may have created a false impression, but no. Here, with the afternoon sun streaming in through the stained glass window, their glamour was even more apparent.

"Well, you made it then, I see," Catriona said. "I thought I saw you at the Welcoming Ceremony."

"Yeah, we made it," I said, stiffly. "I saw you there, too. Nice playing."

Catriona rolled her eyes. "Thanks. They always make me do that."

"Oh, come off it, Cat, you know you love to show off with that bloody fiddle," said Lucida.

"How would you know?" Catriona shot back. "You barely made it to the ceremony."

Lucida grinned. "You got me there." She turned back to me. "I'd have thought Marion and her mates would've driven you out by now. Going to make a go of it?"

"I don't see that we have much of choice," I said.

"Suppose not. And what about your sister? What state did you find her in?" Lucida asked.

"What do you mean?" I asked, frowning.

"I mean after all the docs and shrinks had finished with her. Has she completely lost her marbles?"

Lucida's avid, gleeful expression sent fury pulsing through my body. "I don't see how that's any of your business."

"Lay off, Lucida," said Catriona, but she was pulling a hair absentmindedly from her sleeve as she said it, and it was obvious she didn't really care.

"No need to get sore with me, Jessica. I'm the one that found her in the first place," Lucida said. "Haven't I earned a few details? Come on now, just spill a bit. Was she drugged up? Restrained? Electroshock?"

"Do me a favor," I spat at her, "and don't talk to me again. Ever."

I stalked past them down the stairs.

"Aw come on, don't be like that, love!" Lucida called after me, and I could hear the barely repressed laugh in her voice. "Can't we be mates?"

"No," I muttered under my breath. As wended my way down the staircase, I caught a snatch of Catriona's voice from behind me, saying something that sounded like "...such a bloody troublemaker."

I seethed about it all the way down to the dining room, where I found Hannah already seated at our table, with her knees curled up under her chin, buried in our Ceremonial Basics textbook. I took a moment to compose myself, then grabbed a plate, loaded it up, and joined her. I'd been too nervous to eat much at breakfast; it was only as I bit into my sandwich that I realized how hungry I was.

"How'd it go?" I asked.

She looked up and smiled. "It was fine. Siobhán is very nice."

"Great! What did you talk about?"

Hannah placed a scrap of paper into the book to mark her place and carefully closed it. "She asked me a lot about how I was feeling, and I told her. That part was a bit like seeing one of my therapists, but better, because I didn't feel like she was trying to find something wrong with me."

I nodded in sympathy. After my one and only foray into therapy, I would have gladly watched all psychiatrists jump off a cliff—while holding hands and talking all about their feelings, obviously.

"She asked me questions about when I first started seeing spirits, and what that has all been like for me. She's not at all like that other woman, Marion. She knew Elizabeth when she was here."

I was pulled up short. "Elizabeth?"

"Yeah. You know... our mother," Hannah said, squirming uncomfortably at the label.

"I know who you meant. It was just weird hearing you call her that."

"I don't usually call her anything," said Hannah, in barely more than a whisper. Then she shrugged and went on. "Anyway, Siobhán wants to help me adjust to being here, and wants me to talk to her if I need help or advice."

"I'm really glad, Hannah," I said, just as Mackie slid into the seat beside me.

"How's it going, alright?" she asked us.

"Hannah's meeting was fine. Mine was bizarre."

"Why? What happened?" Hannah asked.

I snapped at Mackie. "I think you left out a minor detail about Fiona."

Mackie tried to look innocent, but couldn't quite manage it. "What do you mean?"

"Oh, I don't know, how about the fact that she's completely—"

"Off her nut? Mad as a hatter?" Mackie suggested.

"Yeah, something like that."

"I was a bit surprised they assigned you to her. They don't send many Apprentices her way."

"I can see why," I said, then told them both all about the meeting.

"So that's the end of that then, eh? She chucked you out?" asked Mackie.

"Actually, I go back again on Monday."

"You're actually going to go back?" Hannah asked. "But she… she threw a chair at you!"

"Well, not exactly *at* me," I hedged. "It was more in my general direction."

Mackie looked impressed. "Wow, I've never heard of anyone who's been back for seconds with Fiona. Good show there."

"Thanks," I said, starting to rethink my whole decision-making process and wondering if I'd do better to ask for a new mentor.

We finished our lunch and walked over to History and Lore of the Durupinen, which was held in Celeste's bright and airy first-floor classroom. It was one of the classes we shared with the Caomhnóir, who were already seated silently on their side of the Sanctity Line.

Celeste was a passionate lecturer, and although all we received on the first day was an introductory speech, I had to grudgingly admit that her class would be fascinating. As reluctantly as I'd come here, I couldn't deny that I was interested in learning about my family's culture—even if that culture was creepier and more clandestine than most.

By this point in the day, Peyton and her crew had apparently decided to pretend we didn't exist, which suited me just fine. The same was true for Finn Carey and the rest of the Caomhnóir, who tended to ignore us in general anyway. The session was uneventful; the most exciting thing that happened was Savvy's strolling in ten minutes late, reeking of cigarettes and claiming that she'd gotten lost, though the classroom was only a few yards from the entrance hall. Celeste, with extreme difficulty, restrained herself from shouting at Savvy.

§

When we finally arrived back in our room that night after dinner, I was exhausted. Hannah dragged her bag over to one of the armchairs by the fireplace, pulled out our Ceremonial Basics textbook, and started reading the chapters Siobhán had assigned for homework. The thought of trying to absorb anything else about Durupinen culture made my head throb, but I was still too wired to go to sleep. I decided what I needed was a friendly face and a nice dose of normality; I needed Tia. So I took my laptop out of its case and began unraveling the various cords. As I worked, Milo drifted in.

"What up, biatches?" he trilled. "How was the first day of classes? Do tell all!"

Hannah smiled, closed her book, and launched into a full description of the day's events. Hearing her talk to Milo was a little strange—she never spoke that much to anyone living. I felt a petulant little stab of jealousy that took me by surprise, but I tried to ignore it; I was too desperate to connect with the outside world.

"Do you two mind if I Skype with Tia? If she doesn't hear from me by tonight she'll probably have a panic attack."

"Be our guest," Milo said, not even looking away from Hannah.

"Thanks." I signed into my Skype account. It seemed to take forever to connect to Tia, so while I waited, I tried to decide what exactly I was going to tell her. I couldn't just unload all my woes on her in miserable detail, as I would have liked. I resented that.

My instructions from Karen and the rest of the Durupinen had been very clear. I had to stick to the official cover story for my time here: I had been accepted into a prestigious study abroad program in England at Fairhaven University. When I finished my Apprentice training, I would be provided with a transcript, and all of my credits would be fully transferable back to St. Matt's so that I could still graduate on time.

Tia was a little bit of a special case, since she knew about the ghost stuff, and so, although I couldn't tell her any of the specifics, she knew that part of my "educational experience" would be getting the spirit activity under control. Even this tiny concession came at the expense of a lot of begging and pleading on my part; I had to convince Karen—and then Karen had to convince Finvarra and the Council—that Tia was simply too smart to accept the bullshit explanation of my suddenly deciding to study abroad on a whim. It was a hard sell, but finally I convinced Karen that if I didn't give Tia some idea of what was happening, Tia would investigate on her own. And, as Karen knew, Tia was exceptionally good at getting the answers she wanted—it was better to put Tia off the attack. As far as I was concerned, this arrangement was far from ideal, but this way I could at least control what Tia knew, and the Council could avoid having to do the kind of damage control that had left poor Pierce with a huge box full of blank tapes and empty memory cards. Fortunately, Tia—as I had promised she would—accepted that I couldn't tell her everything, and settled for the knowledge that I was getting help.

"Hello? Jess? Is that you?" Tia's voice, stilted and tinny, rang from my speakers. I could barely make out the shape of her head in the pixelated image.

"Yeah, Tia, it's me. Hang on, I can't see you. Come on, come *on*," I grumbled, fiddling with the power cord, the screen angle, and the resolution in turn before resorting to whacking the computer with my fist out of sheer technological incompetence. Oddly enough, this last method worked suspiciously well, and Tia's heart-shaped face, framed by her sleek curtains of glossy black hair, emerged from the pixels and broke into a smile.

"Jess!"

Just the sight of her had me swallowing back a threatening onslaught of tears. "Hey, Ti! How are you?"

"I'm fine, I'm fine, don't worry about me, for goodness sake!" she said with a wave of her hand. "How are you?"

"I'm okay," I said, hardly daring to hint at my misery in case I dissolved into a useless puddle.

"Well, you obviously got there okay. What's it like? Oh, sorry. Can I ask that? I probably shouldn't have asked that."

I laughed. "That's okay. It's beautiful here, you would love it. It's like going to school in a Jane Austen novel, without the dress code. See?" I picked my laptop up and panned the room with it so that she could see my digs.

"Oh, wow!" Tia sighed. "Is that a fireplace in your room?"

"Yup! Kind of drafty, but it beats the hell out of our old room in Donnelly, I can tell you that."

"No kidding! What about your classes? I probably shouldn't ask you about that either."

"I think the classes will be challenging, but in a good way."

"And I suppose you can't tell me what any of those subjects are, huh?"

"Well... I'm taking a study in old Celtic languages. And a private tutorial in art and art history," I said.

"Yeah, and I'm sure those are the most interesting and unusual things you're learning," said Tia with a laugh.

"Oh, yeah, everything else is really boring and predictable." I chuckled.

"Alright, I'll be good. Enough about all the stuff you can't tell me. How's Hannah?"

I glanced over my shoulder. Hannah was deep in conversation with Milo. "She's... adjusting."

Tia smiled a little too knowingly. "It'll get better. For both of you. It may just take some time."

"Normally I'd say you're right as usual, but this time I really don't think so," I said. My vision began to cloud as the tears started to win their fight for domination.

"Oh, I knew it, I knew you were upset! Your voice sounded all quivery. I wish I could help," Tia said, picking at her fingers fretfully. "Can't you tell me about any of it?"

"No, not really. It's just that... well, we don't feel very welcome here. And I never thought I'd say this ever in my life, because I never really stayed anywhere long enough to think of it as home, but I think I'm homesick." I brushed the tears away with the back of my hand and took a deep breath. "I miss St. Matt's, and you, and Sam, and..."

"And Gabby?" Tia suggested.

I burst out laughing. "Especially Gabby."

Tia bent over to pick up her mug of tea and I focused on her surroundings for the first time. I'd recognize that institutional cinder block wall anywhere. "Wait, are you at St. Matt's right now?"

Tia nodded, her mouth full of tea. She swallowed and said, "Yeah. I'm in MacCleary Hall."

"What are you doing back there in the middle of the summer?"

"Didn't you read the email I sent you? Never mind, stupid question, you never check your email. I'm here for summer sessions!" Her face lit up with the kind of glee only rigorous academics could ignite in her. "They were offering some science intensives for the pre-med track, so I signed up!"

"You signed up to do extra bio labs in the middle of your summer vacation," I said. It wasn't a question. It was a statement of the absurd, yet obvious.

"Of course! It seemed like a great opportunity to get ahead with my requirements, especially if I'm going to pick up that economics minor I was thinking about."

"Tia, don't you want a break? You know, to relax a little bit before the fall semester?"

Tia's forehead wrinkled as she considered this apparently foreign concept. "Oh. Well, there's a week off between the end of this session and the start of regular classes in the fall. So that will be a break."

"Right. Because one week off is enough of a break for anyone."

"Are you making fun of me?"

"Nope. Wouldn't dream of it."

"Yes, you are. Well, you might be interested to know that the classes aren't the only reason I decided to stay," said Tia, dropping her eyes to her mug and grinning shiftily.

I perked up. "Okay, I'll bite. What other reason could you possibly need to do more schoolwork? You know, other than the fact that you're an academic masochist?"

I watched as a pink flush crept up her neck and stained her cheeks. "Sam. He's here, too, for orientation leader and RA training."

I tutted, shaking my head. "Tia Vezga, you sly, sly dog—using school work as an excuse to get some nookie."

Tia's head shot up and her mouth dropped open in horror. "I am not getting—"

"I know, I know," I laughed. "Here in jolly old England we call that a joke. So, you and Sam Lang, huh? And how are things going?"

"Really, really well," Tia said, growing pinker with every syllable. "He's taking me to Bellini's for dinner tonight, actually. He'll be here soon."

"That's great!" I had suggested that restaurant to him ages ago, knowing that Tia admired it. There was hope for that boy after all. "And what are we wearing? Come on, give us a little spin."

Tia rolled her eyes, but stood up, backed away from her screen, and executed a slow twirl. She was wearing a very simple blue sweater with a black pencil skirt.

"Are you sure that's decent? I can see your ankles."

"Oh, shut up," she said, and sat back down.

"Just kidding, just kidding. You look adorable," I said, which was true—even if her outfit was better suited to a job interview than a romantic candlelit dinner for two.

"I just hope everything works out. I mean, I know I said I wasn't at St. Matt's to date, but that doesn't mean I can't find some time to have a social life, right?"

"Yes! You aren't going to get any argument from me, Tia. I think you need to find a healthy balance of work and play." I infused the last word with just enough innuendo to make her blush again. If we'd been in our old dorm room, she definitely would have thrown something at me.

"He's got a lot going on too, and he knows how important my classes are to me. That's why I feel like this can work."

"He's no slacker himself," I pointed out. "What does he have, a 3.7 GPA?"

"3.8," Tia said, with a faint note of pride in her voice, as though she had somehow been partially responsible for Sam's enviable score.

"Exactly. Plus he's got a million other things to keep him from distracting you too much. He's got all of his RA stuff to keep him busy, not to mention the fact that Pierce will probably work him to death, and—"

"Not this semester," Tia interjected.

"What do you mean, 'Not this semester?'"

"I mean Sam isn't working for Pierce this semester, not while he's on sabbatical."

"Not while who's on sabbatical?"

Tia looked at me like I was crazy. "Pierce. He's on sabbatical in the fall. Didn't he tell you that when you went to see him? I just assumed he would've."

It was as if she'd suddenly started speaking ancient Greek. "What are you talking about?"

She frowned at me as if I were the one no longer making sense. "What are *you* talking about?"

"I'm talking about how there's no way Pierce is on sabbatical," I said. "When I went to say good-bye to him, we talked all about the new class section he was supposed to be teaching in the fall. He was really excited about it; he showed me his syllabus and everything." A strange panicked flutter was starting in my stomach.

"Maybe the class is starting in the spring?"

"No, it was definitely a fall class. He was talking about a curriculum tie-in with Halloween."

"Oh," Tia said, frowning. "Hmm. Maybe something came up? Like a ghost hunting opportunity or something?"

"Yeah, I guess..." I began, but the fluttering grew stronger; I couldn't convince myself to finish the sentence. "No, I really don't think so, Tia. Sabbaticals take a long time to plan. I can't believe Pierce would take one just when St. Matt's is offering him more classes. He was always complaining how they don't take him seriously. Why would he take off right when was about to get some validation?"

"I guess that is pretty weird," Tia said, tapping her thumb thoughtfully against the rim of her mug.

"Did Sam talk to Pierce in person?"

"No. Sam was really confused about it, actually; he was just telling me about it a few days ago. He said that he went up to Pierce's office to talk about a work schedule, and there was a sign on the door saying that Professor Pierce would be unavailable for the fall semester, and to direct all inquiries to Professor Borkowicz. He's the head of Pierce's department. Sam went to see Borkowicz, and he told Sam that Pierce was on sabbatical."

"Did he give Sam any details? Did he tell him where Pierce went or what he was working on?"

"No, nothing like that at all. He just apologized for the scheduling confusion and asked Sam if he'd like to be reassigned until Pierce got back. Then he shunted Sam over to one of the psychology professors. Sam was kind of upset about it; he really liked working for Pierce. He said it was much more interesting than any other lab work he'd ever done." Tia paused, scrutinizing me as if I were a particularly tricky homework question. "What's going on, Jess? Do you think something's wrong?"

"Not... wrong exactly," I said, although I wasn't sure that was strictly true. "Just... off. I can't understand why Pierce would suddenly take off like that. He must've had some kind of emergency or..."

My mind began to spin with half-formed fears. Did Pierce know too much? Had he revealed information to the wrong person, or said the wrong thing? Would he actually have been stupid enough to try to find out more about where I was or what I was doing, even after all of my warnings about secrecy? Part of me said no, but then again, nothing had ever sparked as fanatical a gleam in his eye as that mystical, shrouded word *Durupinen*.

I made up my mind at once. "Tia, I need you to do me a favor."

"Anything Jess, you know that," Tia said.

"I need you to help me find out where Pierce is. I know that you don't really know him, but I just... I have a bad feeling about this. I need to know why he's suddenly dropped off the grid. It might be nothing, but I'm going to worry about it until I know. I'd do it myself, but I'm stuck here, so my options are limited."

Tia bit her lip, but nodded. "Okay... I'll look into it. I'm sure Sam will help me, if I ask him."

I grinned. "Aw, sleuthing dates. How romantic!"

Tia rolled her eyes. "Yes, nothing says romance like a missing person." She caught the look on my face and backtracked at once. "I didn't mean that. I'm sure he's not missing, Jess. There's bound to be a perfectly logical explanation for his being gone. We'll figure it out."

"Thanks, Tia, you're the best," I said, as that nervous flutter in my stomach calmed slightly. "I'm lucky to have my own personal Sherlock Holmes for a best friend."

"Elementary, my dear Ballard," replied Tia; her feigned British accent was pathetic.

We chatted a little while longer, mostly about what was going on with Tia, since my life was now classified information. Tia promised to get in touch again as soon as she had some information on Pierce. I knew she'd find out what was going on, and in some ways that made me feel better; in other ways, it made me terrified about what she might uncover. In the meantime, determined to do what I could, I drafted a casual email to Pierce, asking him how he was and what he was up to. I kept the tone light and joking, just in case I was overreacting. Then I hit "send" and tried not to spend every waking minute of the rest of the night checking to see if he'd responded.

7

THE CALLER

N O RESPONSE FROM PIERCE WAS WAITING FOR ME the next morning when I rushed to my computer. My heart leaped when I saw the "fifteen new messages" icon, but it sunk when I discovered they were all junk. I tried to tell myself that I was being paranoid—if Pierce really were on sabbatical, he could be anywhere in the world. Knowing Pierce, he was probably holed up in some ancient haunted ruins in the middle of the Peruvian jungle somewhere. Twelve hours without a reply was hardly a reason to call out the National Guard—or, in this case, Scotland Yard. I resisted the urge to pack up my laptop and lug it around with me all day, and instead forced my brain to concentrate on whatever Fairhaven Hall had to throw at me today.

It was pretty easy to get distracted. Our first class Tuesday morning was Introduction to Ancient Celtic Languages, which Mackie explained was necessary for understanding and pronouncing all of the different instructions and "Castings" we would have to perform as a part of our duties. Indeed, the *Book of Téigh Anonn* was crammed with words I could neither comprehend nor pronounce.

"You are here at Fairhaven Hall because each of your clans hails from somewhere in the British Isles," our instructor Agnes explained. "The Castings and Incantations you must learn have been passed down to you in the ancient languages of your ancestors. We will be dealing primarily in Gaelic for the purposes of pronunciation, but you will find that a mixture of old Celtic languages has survived in the words you must learn in order to perform your duties. This includes elements of Irish and Scottish Gaelic, as well as traces from the various branches of Common Brittonic.

"You know, they're real fond of saying that none of this is magic,"

Savvy muttered to me from across the aisle, "but they use a fair few magic words, don't they? Castings? Incantations? Sounds like some bloody hocus-pocus to me."

"You've got a valid point," I whispered.

I didn't understand another word Agnes said for the rest of the class. In the interest of total immersion, she began speaking in an ancient form of Gaelic; she spent much of the class pointing to items in the room and encouraging us to repeat after her. Although I tried, I couldn't force my mouth to make the right sounds. I'd never heard a language like it; it was spoken with strange cadences and filled with odd consonant clusters—the language felt as foreign as if it were from a different planet rather than a different country. We all struggled through, with the exception of Peyton and one or two others who, during their Durupinen upbringing, had obviously been exposed to the language. It was only with extreme difficulty that I restrained myself from rolling my eyes every time Peyton made a point of raising her hand so she could show off her pronunciation with relatively long and complicated sentences. By the time the bell began clanging, my head felt like it was clanging also.

"Our next class isn't until after lunch," I said with a sigh of relief as Hannah and I left Agnes' classroom. "Do you want to go take a walk or something?"

"Sure," she said. "The sun is out for a change."

Our first few days at Fairhaven had been cloudier than we were used to, although the heat had hung low and heavy like a wet, smothering blanket—much like the humidity could do back home. But today was blessedly bright, and as we ambled along the cloisters on the north side of the castle, I thought how glad I would've been if this weather lasted forever. The breeze that snatched at our hair and lifted it playfully around our faces was cool and fragrant. We dropped into the shade of a small but gnarled old tree that was covered in dangling, knobbly, green fruit.

"Where's Milo?" I asked.

"Oh, still exploring. He's determined to make some dead friends to keep him entertained while we're in classes," Hannah said. "He hasn't had much luck so far."

"What, no wisecracking, *Vogue*-reading ghosts wandering the halls of Fairhaven?"

"He'll be lucky if he can track down a ghost that's even heard of

Vogue, let alone read it. Most of the spirits here have been dead for hundreds of years."

We sat quietly for a few minutes, enjoying the sunshine. I pulled out my sketchbook, flipped it open, and started adding some detail to a recent drawing of the castle. The sun created a whole new world of shadows to play with.

I glanced up at Hannah. She was tracing a finger absentmindedly over the scars on her wrist. Each scar was a little dermal reminder of the way she used to cope with the overwhelming reality of being herself.

"So, three classes and our mentoring sessions down, with one class left to go. What do you think so far?" I asked her, lowering my eyes so she wouldn't know I'd seen her tracing her scars.

"I think we have a lot to learn," she said slowly, "but I'm really interested in learning it. All of this ghost stuff never felt like it had any rhyme or reason to it. It just sort of happened, and I had to deal with it as best I could. It's nice to know there are actually guidelines."

"Yeah," I said. "It creates the illusion of control, doesn't it?"

She smiled gently. "Exactly. But honestly, it does seem fascinating—all that clan history over hundreds of years, all recorded and documented. It's like the most interesting genealogy ever."

"Definitely more interesting than finding out your ancestors were sheepshearers or something." I said. I was somewhat surprised when I realized that I actually meant it.

"I used to imagine all kinds of crazy family histories," said Hannah as she pulled up little blades of grass and shredded them, "to explain away what was happening to me. I didn't know anything about my biological family, so it was easy to convince myself that there was a genetic explanation for things. For about two years, starting when I was eight, I told everyone that I came from a long line of serial killers, and the ghosts of all our past victims were haunting me, looking for revenge." Hannah giggled at the horrified look on my face. "I know, right? What a morbid little kid."

"Well, you *were* surrounded by dead people," I replied, trying to keep my tone light to mask the sad little hollow her words had dug into the pit of my stomach, as they so often did. "Being morbid was probably a foregone conclusion."

"I remember I used to watch their faces when I told them, waiting for their fear to show. I always felt so satisfied when I saw it. I would think, 'There. See? Now I'm not the only one who's scared.' It was just a macabre little thing that I invented to make myself feel better. Misery loves company, right? No wonder they institutionalized me."

I couldn't think of a single thing to say.

Hannah's smile faded. "That wasn't me trying to spread the misery again. Sorry. You must think I'm so fucked up."

It was such a shock to hear her swear that I couldn't keep my own mouth shut. Maybe I just couldn't stand to see her sitting there all alone under a thundercloud so terribly dark, but the words started flowing from me before I could stop them.

"When I was twelve, we were driving from Houston to Albuquerque," I began. "Mom pulled off the interstate and left me in the car while she ran in to a bar for a 'quick drink.' Three hours later, I woke up and had to drag her out of the place. I managed to get her into the passenger seat, and then I drove. I drove the car the whole rest of the way to Albuquerque. I don't even know how I knew how to drive—I must have just absorbed it because we spent so much damn time driving to the next place we were going to live. Around two in the morning, I hit an animal—I think it was a coyote or some kind of dog. I saw it dart out into the road, then it turned and looked at me with glowing eyes just before I felt that awful 'thump.' I was too scared to stop and see if it was still alive, so I just kept going, sobbing my eyes out over the death of some random desert animal. I pulled over to the side of the road just as the sun came up. When Mom woke up, I told her she'd driven the whole way herself. She was too terrified to admit that she didn't remember any of it, and even more terrified when she saw the blood on the front of the car. I watched her staring at it; I could've told her what had happened—or even just assured her that she hadn't hit a hitchhiker—but I didn't. I guess I just wanted her to be scared for a while, too."

I chanced a glance up from my own hands. Hannah was staring at me, with her face hovering somewhere on the border of an incredulous smile.

"Just thought you'd like to know that you haven't cornered the market on fucked up," I said. Although, with the two of us together, we might have."

She started to laugh. Before I realized what I was doing, I had joined in. Before long, we were both in hysterics, clutching our stomachs and begging each other to stop as tears of laughter rolled down our cheeks. It was equal parts cathartic and euphoric.

We lapsed into silence for a moment, recovering from the spasms. "If you ever do want to know more about our mother," I said, "just let me know. I can tell you a lot about her—what she was like, and all of that. Just so you could start to get to know her a little bit."

Hannah didn't answer at first. I felt the last warmth left behind by the laughter ebb away. "I don't think I want to get to know her. Not right now, anyway. I'm still just so... I just don't think I want to."

"That's fine. It's up to you—I just thought I'd offer."

"Thanks Jess," said Hannah, "but you can't answer the questions I really want the answers to, so the rest of it just seems... unimportant."

"Okay. Well, the offer stands." I tried to shrug her reply off, but a little voice inside me wanted to tell Hannah that nothing about our mother was unimportant. She was a person worth knowing, as screwed-up and troubled as she was. Between the binges and the evictions and the frantic cross-country moves, there was laughter and spontaneity and music. But then I wondered if knowing those details might only make things more difficult for Hannah.

I looked back at my sketch, then at the castle. A cloud had swept in swiftly while we talked, and the shadows I'd been hoping to incorporate had faded to nothing. With a sigh, I thumbed through the pages, looking for another sketch to work on.

"Who's that over there?" Hannah asked suddenly, her voice still not quite steady.

I followed her gaze. At first I couldn't understand what she was talking about, but then a tiny movement, lower to the ground than I'd expected, caught my eye. At the edge of a nearby copse of trees, a small figure peered out from behind a trunk. I recognized her at once.

"Hey, that's her! It's that little girl again!" I said.

"What little girl?"

"The one who sort of attacked me on the first day."

"That's her?" Hannah asked, squinting into the trees. The sun had come out again; the sunlight, while brightening everything else, seemed to make the girl dimmer, more difficult to see.

"Yeah. I saw her yesterday, too, in the hallway after I met with Fiona."

"You saw her again? You never told me that."

"I forgot. Fiona made the rest of my day dull by comparison."

Hannah rose up onto her haunches to get a better look. "She didn't attack you again, did she?"

"No, no... not like the first time. But she did really want to talk to me," I said. I waved tentatively at the girl. She didn't wave back.

"I wonder why she's so shy all of a sudden," Hannah mused. "She had no problem asserting herself before."

"I don't know." I gestured for the girl to come nearer. She shook her head, and continued to stare at me.

Hannah shivered and took out our new textbook. "She gives me the creeps."

I looked at her in surprise. "Really? I'd have thought you'd seen plenty of creepier things than her."

"I'd have thought so too," Hannah said. "It's not how she looks, it's just... something about her."

I found a fresh page in my sketchpad and began to draw the girl. If she knew what I was doing, she raised no objections. In fact, she stood so motionless that she might have been posing for me.

"There's definitely something wrong with her," I said.

"How do you mean?"

"I mean she really can't communicate with me no matter how hard she tries. It's bizarre. I can tell that she's shouting as loudly as she can, but I can't hear her. Have you ever met a spirit like that?"

"No," Hannah answered, "but there are an awful lot of things about spirits we haven't learned yet. Maybe you could ask Fiona about it."

"And get a can of paint chucked at my head? I think I'll ask Celeste instead. Or, you know, basically anybody else in the entire world other than Fiona."

The girl continued to watch me as I drew her. She never ventured a single step closer, and kept darting back behind her tree whenever someone else walked by. Her eyes were so sad, even from this far away. I was entranced; I wished I could dive into those eyes, read whatever story of sorrow was within them, and understand what it was she so desperately needed to say.

"Why are you drawing her like that?"

"Huh?" I looked up at Hannah, who was frowning at my sketchpad.

"Like what?"

"Like that!" she said, pointing.

I looked down into the little penciled face. She stared back at me, looking pretty much exactly as she did over in the trees.

"I don't know what you're talking about," I said. "That's just what she looks like. Well, I mean, it's not perfect, but I can't see her that well from here, so—"

"No, look! Look at the rest of the drawing!" Hannah cried, her voice unnaturally high. She snatched the pad out of my hands and held the drawing up. This time I focused not on the girl's face, but on the entire image.

"What the hell?"

The girl stood surrounded not by a forest trees, but by a forest of flames; they were leaping, licking, and smoking around her like a hellish inferno, ready to swallow her whole.

"I... I didn't mean to draw that!" I gasped.

"What does that mean?" Hannah asked. "How do you draw something without meaning to? Couldn't you see what you were doing?"

I took the pad from her with a trembling hand, taking in each flame and plume of billowing smoke. "I was concentrating on her face, trying to understand what she couldn't tell me, and..."

"And this is what you drew? Without thinking about it?"

I nodded.

"Have you ever done anything like this before?"

"No... Well, actually yes... but not really like this. It was just a spirit's face, one I'd never actually seen before," I said. "It's why they assigned me to Fiona. It's called Psychic Drawing."

Hannah stared transfixed at the drawing. "What does it mean?"

"I have no idea," I said. I looked back into the grove. The girl in the trees, the girl in the flames, was gone.

§

That afternoon we all met in one of the side courtyards for our first Meditation and Bonding class. Our instructor Keira gestured toward a number of small circles that had been chalked onto the cobblestones. She gave us no further instruction, though, so we all just meandered pointlessly for a few minutes before each pair of us settled uncertainly inside a circle. At the very moment the bell clanged two o'clock, the Caomhnóir filed in with their usual military precision. They stood in two rows, like dominos that no amount of poking and prodding could topple.

"Aren't there going to be... you know... chairs?" Hannah asked. She shifted her weight, wincing on the uneven stones.

"Nah, not in Keira's class," Mackie said. "We'll spend most of the time on the grounds, I expect, until the weather gets too poor." Tucking her bag under herself as she talked, she added, "And even then, we'll hardly ever see a regular classroom."

"Does your ass need to be numb to bond and meditate?" I asked, but Keira was clearing her throat, and all chatter was dissolving into an expectant silence. Keira had one of those faces that could render a class mute with a single unpleasant twist of the lips.

"Good afternoon to you all, and welcome to Bonding and Meditation," Keira said, although her tone didn't make me feel particularly welcome. The courtyard, or at least the part of it in which she stood, at once amplified and scattered her voice; the words were alternatingly loud and difficult to hear. "Each teacher you have this year will tell you that her subject is the most important in your journey toward mastering your gifts. I'm here to tell you the same thing—the difference being that, in this case, what I tell you is true."

She paused and gazed combatively around, as though daring each of us, individually, to contradict her. No one did, of course.

"Your Castings, your knowledge of our history, your pronunciation of our Incantations, none of it will matter at all if you cannot connect and communicate effectively with the spirit world. This is the class in which you will hone these most important skills."

I shifted on the cobblestones, which already felt unbearably jagged beneath me.

"These skills shall require you to all open yourselves up to a variety of unknown entities. Theory will be of little help in this class; only real connection and interaction with spirits will teach you what you need to know... and that means that protection may, at times, be needed. That is why the Caomhnóir will share this class with you. Although you will be working on different skill sets—the

Durupinen to engage, the Caomhnóir to interpret and repel—the melding of these skill will be crucial to your future success. Thus, your cooperation during our sessions will be expected, and I do not foresee the need to remind you of this in the future."

Not one of the Caomhnóir betrayed even a hint of reaction to the pronouncement of his role in the class. Keira took their complete lack of emotion as assent, however, because she nodded with satisfaction and went on.

"Very well. Novitiates, when I call your name, please join your assigned Gateway. There will be no need to talk until I deem it proper."

As Keira extracted a sheet of paper from a folder, a murmur rolled through the Apprentices like a ripple in the water after a pebble had broken the surface. Did this mean that the Novitiates had already been assigned? I vaguely remembered Siobhán mentioning something about this is Ceremonial Basics, but couldn't quite recall it. Were we about to discover which of the stony-faced young men would scowl at us, aloof and stoic, for the rest of our lives? One whispered question to Mackie confirmed this.

"They could still swap people if an issue arises, but yes, most likely these will be the permanent assignments. I didn't realize we'd be getting them so soon," Mackie mumbled. Even she had lost her confident air and looked, for once, just as nervous as the rest of us.

Somehow, I had avoided thinking very much about this aspect of my future, probably because I found the idea so repugnant that I simply repressed it. I mean, seriously, a man assigned for my protection? Some gorilla with a culturally-ingrained superhero complex, intent on protecting me? Even in a theoretical sense it was archaic and infuriating.

My internal feminist rant was interrupted by Keira's roll call. "Isaac Brown, please join Mackenzie and Brenna Miller."

A cube of a guy with a face like a bulldog swaggered self-importantly out of the line of Novitiates and planted himself beside Mackie. Other than a swift glance exchanged with her sister, Mackie did not betray any reaction to their Caomhnóir assignment.

One by one, the Novitiates wordlessly joined their assigned Gateways, and the Apprentices watched them just as wordlessly. If anyone had an opinion about who they were paired with, they didn't let on. Until Keira got to us, that is.

"Finn Carey, please join Hannah and Jessica Ballard over there."

My mouth dropped open. Peyton gasped; she looked back and forth between her cousin and us, and then at Keira. I half expected her to insist that Keira had made a mistake. Finn closed his eyes and took a deep breath, as if he were fighting to hold something terrible at bay; he then quickly recomposed himself and stalked over to us. He stood there with his back turned to us, leaving us devoid of even basic acknowledgment.

Come on. Come *on*. I'd only had direct interaction with exactly one of these guys. Why did it have to be him? Why? And, even worse, why did he have to appear as horrified about it as I was?

The last Novitiate, a stringy, pallid boy named Bertie, took his position beside Savvy and Phoebe. Savvy gave him one disgusted look and then gazed longingly around at some of the handsomer, more muscular Novitiates standing guard over the other circles; it was obvious that she'd been hoping her placement would yield a dating opportunity. Bertie, who was now absently picking at a scab on his chin, was clearly not her type. To be honest, I don't think he was anyone's type, the poor kid.

"We are going to begin with basic relaxation exercises today," Keira said, as she began handing each of us a leather-bound book and a tall white candle in a protective glass container. "Many spirits will force their company upon you. They will seek your council and find many different ways to make themselves known to you. But many spirits will lurk in the shadows, afraid or unwilling to show themselves. They are unsure of what they want, or else they fear the pull of the Gateway. These are the spirits you must seek out and coax into communication. You must draw these spirits to you, so you can discover what they need and how to help them. This type of communication can only be achieved through complete mental focus along with true relaxation of the body. You sit now in what we refer to as a communication Circle."

Everyone looked around. For the first time I noticed a small black-velvet drawstring bag inside our Circle. I opened it and saw that it was full of pieces of white chalk, along with a strange collection of polished stones.

"Today, I have drawn the Circles for you. From now on, you will be expected to do so yourselves. Instructions on creating the Circle can be found in the first chapter of your books. I have provided you with the necessary materials for future use. Circles afford you with a basic level of protection from unwanted spirit contact. Each communication Circle establishes a boundary, but does not prevent the spirit from crossing it. Think of it as a warning—like the proverbial line drawn in the sand; unless you establish further rules of engagement, a spirit is free to decide whether to cross it or not."

I looked again at the dusty, jagged circle. I couldn't imagine such a feeble thing stopping even the least insistent of spirits, despite what Keira said.

"Most of your Castings will require that you first draw, or in some other way create, a Circle. Once you have done so, the Circle is given its more specific purpose through the use of runes and other materials. How many of you are familiar with runes?"

Every hand went up, except for mine, Hannah's, Savvy's, and Phoebe's.

Several Apprentices were smirking at us, but Keira just nodded firmly, as though she had anticipated this but did not resent it. She went on in her same businesslike tone. "Runes are characters that exist in many ancient alphabets, including our own. They will look like symbols to you, and indeed many of you have encountered them already without even knowing what they are. The Wards on your own bedroom doors, for instance, have been created with runes."

I pictured the strange symbol on our door that looked like an eye; then remembered the half-washed red paint over it, dripping like tears. I shivered for some reason.

"Learning and creating accurate runes will allow you not only to designate a purpose for your Circles, but also help to protect yourself and create a set of rules by which the spirits can interact with you. If you want a spirit to be seen and not heard, you can do it with a rune. If you want to hear them without ever seeing who you're talking to, you can do that as well. A few strokes of chalk, and a spirit can approach no closer than I am to you now. Another stroke, and a spirit can inhabit your body and walk you through his own memories."

The class was utterly still. The little velvet bag I was clutching in my hand suddenly seemed to weigh a ton. I put it down and wiped my hand on my jeans.

Keira's expression was all grim approval. She had us captivated and she knew it. "Apprentices, today we require no runes to invite a spirit in, because we are not attempting contact. However, this does not mean that contact cannot be initiated on the part of a spirit who is drawn to one or more of you. Apprentices, should this happen, you must alert your Caomhnóir at once. Caomhnóir, should this happen, it will present you with your first opportunity to practice your expulsion skills in a real setting. However, you should alert Braxton so that he can oversee your attempt."

The Caomhnóir who had led the Novitiates into the courtyard detached himself from the shadows of the cloisters for the first time and nodded his head sharply in acknowledgment. He then resumed his half-hidden position.

"Now Novitiates, I understand that you have all had the opportunity to work on creating Guardian Circles. Each of you will now please create one at your assigned place."

All around us, the Novitiates pulled their own small black bags out of their pockets and set to work. I watched Finn, who still had not so much as looked at us, as he unraveled a long leather cord attached to a piece of white chalk and then dropped to one knee. Using the cord as a kind of compass, he drew a large circle around himself; it overlapped with ours, creating a rough sort of Venn diagram. All the while he muttered a steady stream of words in an ancient Celtic tongue. When Finn's Guardian Circle was complete, he drew a rune in the space where the two circles overlapped; the rune looked like an arrow with three wavy lines below it. Then he stood up, stuffed his chalk into his pocket, and took his place standing at attention again.

"Very well, then," Keira began. "Apprentices, please notice the runes that your Caomhnóir have drawn in the Guardian Circle. This rune will stop a spirit from entering beyond the Guardian Circle, so that you will have the opportunity to concentrate and relax without unwanted spirit contact. Any questions?" She glanced cursorily around the courtyard. "Good. We begin. Apprentices, close your eyes and focus your attention, as fully as you are able, on the beating of your own heart."

I was completely caught off guard by the sudden commencement of the exercise, and found myself watching everyone else closing their eyes before I remembered to do so myself.

"Listen to your own heartbeat; it will tell you everything you need to know about your state of relaxation. Breathe slowly and deeply—see what this does to your heart rate."

The afternoon sun was low now, and stubbornly attempting to

penetrate my eyelids. I turned my head slightly to avoid the worst of it. All around me, I could hear the Apprentices as they sucked in the air. I hastened to do the same, and then told myself to calm down before I got dizzy, passed out, and caused a scene.

"Now I want each of you to begin with your toes and relax each individual part of your body all the way up to the top of your head," Keira continued. "I do not expect that it will take all of you the same amount of time to do this, so continue at your own pace until you feel that your entire body is relaxed. Continue to breathe. Also be sure to keep your senses alert to the possibility of spirit contact."

What followed for the next twenty minutes was a long, drawn-out, fairly painful silence, interspersed with Keira's soothing instructions. I did my best to relax my body, but all I could think about was how horribly uncomfortable I was. My buttocks were alternatingly tingling, numb, and throbbing with pain. Sweat trickled down my back as though the individual droplets were racing each other to the ground. My hair stuck to my neck and made my skin itch. How the hell was anyone supposed to relax like this?

I opened one eye and looked at Hannah. She was the picture of Zen tranquility; she was so relaxed that she could have been asleep. I chanced a glance over at Savvy; she was *actually* asleep, with her head lolling to one side. I could hear her snoring from across the courtyard; Keira was already wending her way through the group to rouse her.

I closed my eyes again, but they flew open again immediately as Hannah started talking.

"Finn," she said, her voice monotone. "I've got a visitor. She's quite calm, so I don't think you need to expel her."

Finn was staring down at her, frowning. He caught my eye and I shrugged. He snapped back to attention, but his eyes kept flitting to Hannah. He looked troubled.

I looked around. I didn't see any spirits, but that didn't bother me. I knew that spirits could manifest in a variety of ways, and that I didn't need to see a spirit for it to be there. Hannah began a murmured conversation, talking so quietly that I only caught a word or two here or there. She had a gentle, easy smile on her face. I scanned the courtyard. No one else seemed to be communicating with a spirit.

"Here's another one, Finn" Hannah said softly. "Oh no, two actually. Yes, two."

"Where?" Finn muttered.

"In here with me," Hannah said.

"But, how did they... I didn't feel them enter. They didn't even stop," said Finn.

"I sensed them out there, so I invited them," Hannah replied, almost dismissively.

"Yes, but I still should've been able to sense their entry," he said. He opened his eyes and crouched down, studying the boundary of his Guardian Circle. He hovered his fingers over the chalk, probing the air for something invisible.

I tried to ignore him and went back to the impossible task of relaxing my body. I had left off with my midsection, but everything below my waist was tense again, so I gave up and started over with my toes. The sun continued to beat down. My throat felt parched.

Finn cleared his throat and I opened my eyes again. He had raised his hand to alert Braxton, and Braxton was marching his way across the courtyard toward our Circle. I watched as they put their heads together and carried on a whispered conversation. After a few moments, Braxton waved Keira over to join them.

A number of people were watching us now; apparently I wasn't the only one who was having trouble relaxing.

"I do not remember giving the order to cease your relaxation exercises," Keira said sharply over her shoulder. Several heads whipped away; others seemed too interested to care about the reprimand, and continued to gawk as Keira joined Finn and Braxton's conversation. Keeping my eyes carefully closed and my expression neutral, I listened with all my might.

"Tell her what you told me," Braxton said.

"They aren't stopping." Finn said. "I'm trying to sense them on approach, but all of a sudden they're in there... I never felt them coming. The Circle and even the rune seemed to have no effect. I can't understand it. I'm sure I did it properly."

Keira looked at Braxton and asked, "How is his precognition generally?"

"Excellent," Braxton answered. "He is one of our most sensitive Novitiates. Very strong connective ability and above-average aura reading skills. The rune and Circle both seem in good order, and I can sense the Casting in its borders."

"I see," Keira replied, and I could almost hear the frown in her voice. I opened my eyes enough to make out her shape as she walked around our Circle, examining it closely for gaps or flaws. She found none. She let her hand hover in the air over the arrow-like rune, and also over the entire shared space between our Circles. She shook her head bemusedly and returned to Braxton.

"Braxton, why don't you take Finn's place in the Guardian Circle and see what you can do? It may simply be nerves or a lack of experience."

Finn slouched out of his Circle, looking bad-tempered, and watched as Braxton took his place. I no longer bothered pretending I wasn't paying attention, and neither did anyone else. Some Apprentices were actually kneeling to get a better view. Hannah, with her eyes still closed, was still murmuring to companions unseen, and had yet to notice that anything unusual was going on around her.

Braxton closed his eyes and stayed very still for several minutes. As I watched him, a shadow passed slowly over his face; when he opened his eyes again, his expression was very troubled.

He leaned over to Keira and spoke directly into her ear so that there was no chance of being overheard. When he pulled away, Keira's expression was utterly unreadable. She bent down and touched Hannah lightly on the shoulder.

"Hannah, may I have a word with you?"

Hannah started and her eyes, round as coins, flew open. As she did so, I felt a rush of energy blast out of the Circle. It left a ringing in my ears.

"Sorry?"

"I said, may I have a word with you?"

"Yes, of course. Sorry, I know we were supposed to be relaxing but I was just..." Her voice was snuffed out, smothered by the eager stares directed at her. She seemed to shrink, retracting into herself like a turtle into its shell. "Is something wrong?"

"No, no," said Keira lightly. "I just wanted to speak with you for a moment. Privately."

Hannah looked at me for help. I spoke up at once. "What's going on?"

"Nothing that anyone here should be so very interested in," Keira said loudly, returning to her usual brisk manner. "What are you all gawking at? You're supposed to be relaxing your bodies and minds! Snap to it, chop, chop!" She clapped sharply. "Braxton, please oversee the class for a few minutes until I get back."

Everyone except for me returned to their tasks, or at least pretended to, but none of our postures seemed very relaxed anymore. Bewildered, Hannah stood up and followed Keira out of the courtyard. Hannah looked back at me with barely contained panic in her eyes.

"I'll wait here for you," I called after her.

The minutes stretched by, but they did not return. I sat in my Circle, staring at the archway through which Hannah and Keira had exited, and feeling the sun beating down on my hair.

After a lengthy silence, Finn spoke, startling me. "Are we going to carry on without her?"

"What?"

He kept his eyes on his hands, which were turning his little velvet Casting bag over and over. "Shall we carry on? We ought to keep practicing."

"You go ahead. I can't concentrate right now," I said.

"There's no point if you aren't going to participate."

"Well then, I guess we're done," I said curtly.

"We oughtn't waste this time," he pressed on, still not meeting my eye. Was Finn one of those people who never looked anyone in the eye when they spoke, or was it just with me? I didn't know him well enough to tell. "This time is important for—"

"Well, I'm sorry, but relaxation is out of the question right now," I said. "If you were so worried about staying on task, you should've left Hannah to her own devices. What was that all about anyway?"

"I don't know," he replied. "She was doing something strange. It was like she was snatching spirits out of the air and pulling them in. The Circle wasn't stopping them."

"Keira said they could still decide to enter," I pointed out.

"Yes, but there was no decision. There was no approach. One moment they weren't anywhere nearby, and the next they were inside the Circle with her," Finn said. "That isn't how it's supposed to work. I had to alert someone."

I pursed my lips but didn't reply... I knew I wouldn't say anything fair. He was a student, just like we were; it was his right to ask questions. I was sure that I'd have about a million questions I'd need my teachers to answer before I walked out of this place, and Finn, in that respect, was no different. But did he have to do it like that, in front of the entire class? Did we have to be constantly reminded of our outsider status in every single setting? I mean, for heaven's sake, why couldn't we at least fit in here, in this strangest little corner of the world, in this place for people who didn't fit in anywhere else?

The bell reverberated through the courtyard, signaling the end of class. Everyone rose sluggishly to their feet, yawning and stretching. Braxton shouted instructions on how to negate the Circles, and passed out little silver jugs filled with water. For a few minutes, the courtyard was filled with splashing sounds as the Apprentices poured water over the chalk lines. The Circles dissolved into cloudy rivulets, which trickled first between the cobblestones and then into the grass. Savvy had nodded off again, although how she remained asleep through the clanging of the class bell I had no idea. Phoebe was trying to prod her awake.

Peyton lingered, waiting, it seemed, to see what Finn would do. When he didn't get up and follow the other Caomhnóir out, and after her many attempts to catch his eye went unnoticed, she flounced away with Olivia, looking sulky. Guess she'd have to wait for the latest chapter of Ballard sister gossip, just like the rest of them. The courtyard cleared in twos and threes, until only Mackie, Savvy, Finn, and I remained. I glanced at Finn, who had pulled out a book that looked like a journal and was scribbling away in it, oblivious to my gaze.

"You don't have to stay, you know," I said.

"I know," he said without looking up. He had gnawed on the end of his cheap ballpoint pen so much that it was pinched shut and covered in teeth marks.

"So why are you?"

He crossed out something on his page. "This is my Caomhnóir assignment. Whatever just happened affects my ability to do my job. I want to know what it is." He scratched something else out.

"What are you writing?" I asked.

He completely ignored me. I snorted with disgust and turned to Mackie, who was walking toward me and swinging her Casting bag in circles; behind her Savvy remained, yawning.

"How'd it go?" I asked. "Feeling relaxed?"

"Oh yes, ready for a kip," Mackie answered. "And more relaxed than you are, I'll bet. What was that all about?" She cocked her head in the direction of the archway into which Hannah and Keira had disappeared.

"I don't really know. Something about spirits showing up

unexpectedly in our Circle. You'd be better off asking him," I said, and hitched a thumb at Finn.

Before Mackie could ask, Hannah appeared in the archway and started walking calmly across the lawn. When she reached us, she was smiling gently.

"Everything okay?" I asked, although I was relieved to see her smiling.

"Oh, yes," replied Hannah, and she knelt to pick up her books. "I have to go and see Finvarra."

"Huh? Why do you need to do that?" I asked.

"Keira says that I may have a special ability after all. She wants to confirm it with Finvarra first, though."

She sounded very happy. I, on the other hand, was becoming increasingly nervous as I remembered Karen's warning. "What ability is she talking about?"

Hannah shrugged. "She didn't explain it, really. She just asked me a few questions about how I got those spirits into the Circle, and then told me that we should tell Finvarra about it. That's where I'm going now. I'll meet you at dinner." She turned to Finn, who had finally looked up from his writing. "Keira is speaking with Braxton now, but she'd like you to come with us up to Finvarra's office."

Finn nodded, snapped his book shut, and jumped to his feet. Without a word to anyone, he marched off.

Hannah turned to go. I blurted out, "Do you want me to come with you?"

She turned back. "No, I'll be fine. I might see if I can find Milo."

This caused the familiar little stab of jealousy, but I was prepared for it. Stronger, though, was my resentment at knowing that Finn would be there to hear whatever Finvarra had to say to my sister. I tried not to glare at Finn as he retreated, and focused instead on what seemed like an important reminder.

"Don't forget what Karen said when she was giving us our clan garb." I said firmly.

"I won't," Hannah said, her eyes shining with genuine excitement. "See you later. Wish me luck!"

I watched Hannah turn towards Keira, who was now beckoning to Hannah from the cloisters. I felt a little pang of loss as she walked away with her tiny shoulders squared and her long hair swinging behind her. Someone that small ought to have someone holding her hand.

"Wow, a summons to the North Tower," Mackie said with a low whistle. "That must be some special ability she's got. Finvarra doesn't often deal with new Apprentices directly."

"Straight to the headmistress is never good, in my experience," Savvy added, lighting a cigarette then immediately dropping it in the grass as she failed to stifle a huge yawn.

"Don't be daft, she's not being punished," Mackie said. "Come on then, let's go eat."

§

I had waited in the dining room for Hannah until my soup went cold before finally giving up and going back to our room. To take my mind off of her, I sat down at my computer and checked my email. There was still nothing from Pierce, but there was a message from Tia.

Seeing Tia's unopened message made my nerves jangle even more; the subject line was "Pierce." I clicked it and read Tia's cryptically short message: "Skype me as soon as you get this."

With my heart hammering, I signed into Skype and requested a chat with Tia. My leg bounced up and down, waiting for the connection.

"So?" I said as soon as her face appeared.

"So, you're not going to like it."

I waited, but Tia just sat there, avoiding my gaze.

"Just tell me already!" I cried.

"I started with the yellow pages. I thought that his home address was the most logical place to find him. He lives right in Worcester, not even fifteen minutes from campus.

"And?"

"He hasn't been there for a couple of weeks."

My heart sank. "How do you know?"

"His grass hasn't been mowed and his front porch is covered in newspapers and mail. Wherever he is, he forgot to forward his mail or have it held at the post office."

"And if he knew he was going away for the whole semester, he would have taken care of that," I said. "I know he's a little eccentric, but he's not irresponsible."

"Right. I tried to call his home number too, but no luck. He isn't having his calls forwarded, and his voicemail message doesn't give any information about where to reach him. Also, his voice mailbox is full. I couldn't leave a message even if I wanted to."

"Well, I guess that's it then," I said with a sigh. "Thanks for trying, Tia."

"What do you mean, you guess that's it? I wasn't going to give up that easily! Who do you think you're talking to?" Tia said with mild indignation.

"Oh! Right, sorry," I said with smile. "I'm not trying to underestimate you, but it's only been a day since you started looking! I can't believe you've found out that much already. Continue, super sleuth!"

"I thought our next best bet was to find out what we could about this alleged sabbatical, so I had Sam snoop around the science department a bit to see what he could dig up. None of the professors had any conversations with Pierce about his leaving, and several of them were very surprised."

"I knew it! I knew this had to be a sudden thing! He would've mentioned it to me!"

"So then Sam sort of... broke into Pierce's file in the department head's office."

"He did what?" I asked.

Tia grimaced. "I told him not to, but he's just as mystified about this as you are. He really loved working for Pierce, and he agrees that the whole thing seems kind of fishy. He thought maybe Pierce was fired or put on leave, and that the administration was trying to cover it up."

"But he was getting those new classes..."

"But you've said it yourself, he's had a hard time proving himself as a real scientist here. And he does have a temper. Sam thought Pierce might have flown off the handle and said something that got him suspended or something, and that the school could just be trying to save face."

I couldn't deny this was a definite possibility, and one I hadn't considered.

"So, Sam offered to file some papers in the department office, and then he just slipped into the faculty records. He found Pierce's folder and there was some very hastily filed sabbatical paperwork in there."

"How hasty? From when?"

"Filed and approved the day after you left."

"Did it give any details about where he was going?"

Tia ducked out of the camera's range for a moment, and when she reappeared she had a yellow legal pad in her hand. "He's supposed to be in upstate New York, at a two hundred-year-old hotel called the Deer Creek Inn and Tavern. It has a long history of intense paranormal activity and was being renovated under new ownership, but the renovations have stopped."

"Why?"

"The ghost activity had grown so violent and constant that all of the workers walked off the job and refused to return to the site. There have been lots of injuries and even one death."

"Is that all it said? He's just going to check out a haunted building? Pierce could do that on the weekends or over the summer, couldn't he? Why would he need to miss an entire semester?"

"You're asking me? I don't have a clue. You or Sam would have a much better idea about how long something like that would take. But the paperwork said no one has ever been allowed to investigate the place; the last owners refused to let ghost hunters in. But the new owners are eager for the activity to stop so they can continue with their renovations."

I said nothing, taking in the new information.

"This sounds pretty serious," Tia said, looking down at the writing on her legal pad. "In the world of paranormal investigation, this sounds like an emergency case. Injuries? Deaths? It might be the kind of thing he'd drop everything else to go and help with. There was even a preliminary book proposal included in the paperwork."

"I guess so," I said, still not convinced. "Pierce *was* always really eager to get into places that other teams hadn't explored. He practically did a tap dance when he got the permission to investigate the library... mostly because St. Matt's had never allowed paranormal teams into any of its buildings before." I paused for a moment, considering my own words. "Well, if he was going to New York, did he leave any contact information for where he'd be staying?"

"Yes—for motel near the inn. We've already tried the phone number. It rang a few times and went to voicemail, but it was one of those automated voices. Sam left a message, but we haven't heard back."

"Okay," I said, and slid out of my chair and began pacing. "No emails being answered, no phone messages being returned. Something is definitely still off. There has to be someone else we can... Wait! Pierce couldn't do this alone. I've seen what one of those investigations entails, and there is no way it's a one-person job. The whole team must be with him, right? We just need to get in touch with one of the other team members. I'm sure they could tell us what was going on!"

"That's a brilliant idea!" Tia exclaimed. "But, Jess, um... could you come sit back down? You're making me dizzy and I can only hear like half of what you're saying."

"Right. Sorry," I said, and hopped back into my chair. "Does Sam have any way of getting in touch with any of the other team members?"

Tia bit her lip. "I don't know. I'll ask him. Do you?"

"No, I only met them that one time. Well, except for Annabelle, and she—wait, I think Pierce said she's got a shop in the city."

"Oh, really? Do you know what it's called?"

"No, but she does palm and tarot readings, and she sells all that mystical garbage... you know, like candles and crystals and books about auras."

Tia raised an eyebrow. "Mystical garbage? Really, Jess? Haven't we had enough experience with all of this to at least acknowledge that it isn't garbage?"

I pressed my hands over my eyes and took a deep breath. "I know, I know. My entire existence right now is a sea of this 'garbage.' I'm trying to kill my inner skeptic, but she's not going down easily. She's a plucky little bastard."

"One of the many reasons I love her," Tia said. "But seriously, how hard can it be to find? How many shops like that can there be in town? I'll hop on the Internet and get searching. In the meantime, tell me what you know about the other team members and I'll put Sam to work tracking them down."

I racked my brain for any details I could come up with about the rest of the group. "I don't even know most of their last names. Dan was a recent MIT grad. Oscar was a local historian—I think Pierce said he'd written some books on haunted locations in the area. Iggy was... huge and tattooed, that's pretty much all I know about him. And come on, Iggy can't be his legal name anyway, can it? I mean, who names their poor kid Iggy?"

Tia's lips twitched as she continued scribbling.

"Annabelle's last name is Rabinski. And Neil's last name is Caddigan, but I'm not sure if he'd be much help, he wasn't a regular team member... But actually," I said, with a sudden spark of realization, "Neil was there the day I said good-bye to Pierce. He came by Pierce's office as I was leaving."

Tia stopped writing and looked up at me. "Really? Do you think it's possible he knows something? Could he maybe have told Pierce about the Deer Creek Inn?"

"Yeah, maybe," I said. "Pierce said Neil is a demonologist. Maybe Neil even thought the activity at the Deer Creek Inn was demonic, because of how violent it was?"

Tia shivered. "Wow, I really hope not. Ghosts are bad enough, aren't they?"

"Yeah, they are," I said. "But even if he isn't involved in the Deer Creek thing, he could still have some information. Pierce could've mentioned something to him. Plus!" I suddenly remembered, "Neil's from England. Maybe I could track him down over here."

"Good idea," Tia said. She looked down at her notepad and sighed. "Well, I've got a few good leads here, so Sam and I will get started."

Sam's name made me remember something else—something equally important, if totally unrelated.

"Hey, I never asked you! How was dinner at Bellini's?"

Tia flushed and a broad grin slowly crept across her face. "It was really, really nice. We had a great time. He brought me flowers and everything."

It was my turn to grin. "And?"

"And what?"

"Oh, come on, Ti, don't make me beg! Did he kiss you or not?"

Tia flung her hands up over her face, and I watched her ears turn from pink to scarlet. Then she nodded, emitting a little high-pitched giggle that was muffled by her hands.

"Woo-hoo!" I proceeded with an elaborate celebratory dance that turned Tia's giggles to gales of laughter, and by the time I had completed the finale—a truly epic kick-turn complete with jazz hands—we were both wiping away tears of mirth.

Finally, we laughed ourselves into silence. I caught my breath and said, "Thanks for helping me with this, Tia. And I'm really happy for you and Sam."

"Thanks Jess. We'll figure this out, I promise."

"I know. And in the meantime, just tell me one other thing."

"What?"

"Is Sam a good kisser? Too much tongue, or...?"

Tia hung up on me. As I expected.

I was still cackling to myself when the door opened and Hannah came in.

"Who were you just talking to?" she asked me. She glanced around as if expecting to find someone, living or dead, sitting in the room with us.

"Tia. She was filling me in on what she found out about Pierce."

"Oh, what is it? Did they find him? Is he okay?" she asked, crossing to her desk and depositing her bag onto it.

"No, we still don't know where he is. But never mind that for a minute," I said, with an impatient wave of my hand. "I can fill you in on that stuff later. What's going on? Tell me what happened... I mean, if you want to... obviously you don't *have* to," I finished lamely.

"Of course I want to," said Hannah, and she smiled at me; her smile lit an answering smile on my face.

This was still such a shaky, fragile thing that had grown up between us. I felt like one mild disagreement or even one stiff breeze could topple it right to the ground. I sat and waited patiently for her to talk.

"Well, once Keira had me away from the rest of the group, she explained that Finn's rune should've stopped any spirits from getting across, even if I wanted them to be there," Hannah said. "And so she asked me about how they got there in the first place, and I told her as best I could."

"How *did* they get there?" I asked. "Because I wasn't really paying attention and they weren't interacting with me at all, so I didn't know they were there until you told Finn."

"I could feel them out there, wondering about me," Hannah explained. "I knew they wanted to come closer, and I could tell they wanted to talk, so I just thought about inviting them in. I didn't even really mean to do it. I was bored with all that relaxation nonsense, and I started thinking how nice it would be to have someone to talk to. I guess that's all it took. And then they were there inside the Circle. That was it."

"But the rune should have stopped them," I said.

"Yes. They should've been stopped at the border of the Guardian

Circle; Finn should have had to open it to let them through. But I guess I sort of skipped that part without really meaning to."

"Wow. And that was a big deal?"

"Yes. So Keira told me that, because I was able to Summon the spirits to me, I must be a Caller."

The word sent a little shiver through my body before I could even form a single thought or feeling about it, which was disconcerting.

"What's a Caller?" I asked cautiously.

"They're very rare," Hannah said, and I could detect a note of pride in her voice that I had never heard before. "A Caller is someone who has the ability not only to communicate with spirits, but to exercise some control over them without the use of Castings." She almost sounded like she was reciting the definition out of a textbook, and I knew that she was just repeating back what she'd been told. "There have only been three in the last century, other than me!"

"This must be what Karen was trying to find out about. Did you tell Keira about the escape from New Beginnings and—"

"No, I didn't forget what Karen said," said Hannah, a little impatiently. "I didn't mention that part of things, even though I probably should've. But it doesn't matter, because I didn't need to. Keira seemed quite sure of what was happening; I didn't need to elaborate. She seemed sort of excited about it, but also a little scared."

"Scared? Why?"

"I don't know. Maybe scared isn't the right word. Almost... almost like it gave her a little thrill or something."

"So then she took you to see Finvarra?"

Hannah nodded. "We went straight to the North Tower, and she was waiting for us there."

"What's she like?" I asked, as my voice involuntarily hushed. I couldn't help it. I felt much the same way about Finvarra as Keira did about Hannah being a Caller. The High Priestess was shrouded in mystery, a figure who seemed to dwell with one foot drifting along in a legend-and-fairy-tale world and one foot planted firmly in real life.

Hannah didn't seem to think my tone was strange, though. On the contrary, she was looking around the room as though trying to find the right description written on the walls somewhere. "She seems like one of those people that no one ever really gets close to. I don't mean she wasn't nice or anything. She smiled at me and shook my hand, and wanted to know how I was settling in; but she was still very... distant."

"Okay. So what happened?"

"She asked me the same sorts of questions Keira did, and then she asked me if I could try Calling a spirit right there in her office. I wasn't really expecting that, so it made me nervous, but I tried anyhow. I closed my eyes and sensed someone right away, which isn't surprising in this place. There was a spirit of a woman passing by the base of the staircase. And then I pulled her right into the room with us."

I shook my head incredulously. "That must've freaked them out."

Hannah actually giggled. "Yeah, it did. Finvarra couldn't believe it. I think she thought Keira was exaggerating or something. I told her it was really easy to reach out to them, but she obviously wasn't expecting it to be that easy."

"So what did she say?"

"She said that Keira was right. I'm a Caller."

"Wow, that's... how do you feel about that?" I asked.

"I'm excited, I guess," Hannah replied, with her eyes shining. "I want to find out more about it, of course, and Finvarra said that there will be work to do to control it."

"Control it?"

"Yes. She said that it's likely that I've been Calling spirits to me for years without even realizing it."

I frowned. "That doesn't really make sense, though. You knew what you were doing when you brought those spirits into the Circle."

The smile faded from her face. "Actually, it probably does make sense. When I was younger and I was lonely or didn't like the place I was staying, I would sometimes wish for ghosts to find me. I called it wishing, but I guess what I was really doing was Calling them. I always thought of it like an answered prayer when ghosts suddenly appeared to me in those places, but now I think I brought them there myself."

"You actually wanted ghosts around you? On purpose?" I asked.

"Yes."

I cringed. "Some of those places must have been really bad if you preferred Visitations."

"They were," Hannah said quietly. She didn't elaborate.

"But you must have better control over it now," I said, to break the silence. "You're not doing it unconsciously, like when you were little. Why would you want to suppress a gift like yours? It must come in really useful sometimes."

I thought back to the trouble I had finding Evan when I needed to talk to him, thinking how convenient it would've been to just pluck him from wherever he was at the time for a little chat. But then I thought about how much I wished I could still talk to him, and came dangerously close to tears. I shook my tears back and focused on Hannah, who was already answering me.

"They didn't say anything about repressing it. I don't think they meant it that way. I think they just want me to get a better understanding of how it works. Finvarra said they would try to arrange for a new mentor for me."

"A new mentor? Is there actually another Caller here at Fairhaven? I thought you said there've only been three in the last century?"

"I don't know, they didn't say. Maybe it's just someone who knows a lot about it. I guess I'll find out when they reassign me." Hannah let out a long, low sigh. "There was one thing about the conversation that bothered me, though."

"Oh yeah? What was it?"

"Well," Hannah said, squirming uncomfortably. "Finvarra kept asking questions about our father."

I was completely brought up short. "Our father? Why in the world would that come up?"

"I don't know. She seemed to think it might have something to do with why I had this particular gift."

"But the Durupinen are all women. It wouldn't even make sense for our father to have anything to do with it."

Hannah frowned. "That's what I thought too, but she kept asking. She didn't seem to want to take my word for it when I told her I didn't know anything about him. You don't know anything, do you?"

I shook my head. "That was the one subject mom would never budge an inch on," I answered, with a touch of bitterness. "She would really freak out when I asked about it. She just said it was a horrible, horrible mistake, and to never bring it up again. It was usually followed by a really bad drinking binge, so I learned to avoid the subject like the plague. He's not even listed on our birth records. No name, nothing."

"Do you think maybe she just... didn't know who it was, and she was too embarrassed to admit it?" Hannah asked. She didn't meet my eye as she suggested this.

"No," I said sharply, bristling at the implied judgment. I saw Hannah flinch at my tone and felt instantly ashamed of myself. I adjusted my tone and said, "I used to think that sometimes, when I was younger, when I was really mad at her. But not now... her reactions were just too intense, too emotional. No, she definitely knew who he was, but she didn't even like to think about him."

"And you don't think Karen knows anything about him?"

I shook my head. "I asked when I first went to live with her. She said she never even knew Mom was seeing anyone. She couldn't believe Mom had hidden it from her; they were really close back then."

Hannah shrugged dejectedly. "Well, it seemed important to Finvarra. Maybe she'll try to investigate for herself. If she could find me, she might be able to find him, too."

We sat together for a few minutes, both contemplating the possible repercussions of such a thing. My father had always been a blank space, a hole that I felt no urge to fill. It's hard to miss or care about something you never had to begin with.

Finally, Hannah sighed gently. I looked up and saw that she was smiling again. "A Caller and a Muse in the same family. Who knew we were so talented?"

I smiled back. "It would've been a lot nicer to be talented at something normal. Why couldn't we have been ballet dancers? Or star basketball players?"

"Or spelling bee whizzes?" Hannah suggested.

"Or rodeo bull-riding champions?"

"Is that really more normal than this?" Hannah asked with a laugh.

"I don't know," I said, shrugging. "But I think if I had to pick between eight seconds on a bull or another freaking ghost popping out of nowhere and scaring the shit out of me, I might just pick the bull."

8

BOUND

THE NEWS THAT HANNAH WAS A CALLER SPREAD through Fairhaven like wildfire during a windstorm, but it did little to change our outcast status. In fact, Hannah's gift only seemed only to add another layer of mistrust between ourselves and the other Apprentices. This, Mackie explained, was probably because most of the Apprentices had never heard the term *Caller* before, and didn't really understand what it meant.

"I had to ask Celeste to explain it, and she didn't know much about it either," Mackie told us. "Sounds like a pretty handy gift to have, though. Sort of the opposite of what the Caomhnóir can do, you know?"

"Too bad you couldn't learn how to reverse it and use it on the living, Hannah. Then maybe we could get rid of Mr. Personality," I said as I rolled my eyes.

"Jess, you have to give him a chance. Maybe Finn's just... nervous. Coming to Fairhaven for his Caomhnóir training must have been a big adjustment for him, too."

I thought Hannah was being entirely too reasonable, but I kept this notion to myself. Like I could ever get used to our having a personal knight in shining armor—especially one who was such a jerk.

The next day, Karen came by to have lunch with us. She seemed relieved to learn that Hannah's talent had a name, and that her power wasn't unprecedented.

"I have to admit I was nervous," Karen said. I'd never heard of anyone being able to do what you do. I'm glad you'll have the chance to understand it better now." I couldn't help but notice that the smile on Karen's face didn't quite reach her eyes as she spoke, and I wondered if she were less relieved than she was letting on. I thought I'd try to coax some information out of her later, but Karen informed us that she had to fly back to Boston for a couple of weeks to help with a case at work.

"I was hoping to stay at least until the Initiation," she said, "but my firm is drowning without me, and I'm afraid I'm going to jeopardize any chance I have of being made partner if I don't go back and help bail us out. I'm going to try to get back in time for the Initiation, though."

The Initiation, as Siobhán had explained in class, was the ceremony during which the Novitiates and the Apprentices were officially pledged to each other. As I'd listened to her that morning, I glanced repeatedly across the aisle at Finn and his ever-brooding expression; the thought of the Initiation filled me with nothing but dread.

"You must've had a Caomhnóir assigned to you and Mom when you were Apprentices. What was that like?" I asked Karen.

"Oh, it was pretty awkward," she replied, and then laughed at the look on my face. "Look, I know the Caomhnóir are hardly pleasant to have around, but they do a good job of blending into the background, for the most part. And they really are an important resource to have if a dangerous situation arises. Most of the time, though, you won't even have to acknowledge each other's existence."

"But it just seems so unnecessary!" I cried. "I mean, Siobhán even said that many of the circumstances that necessitate the Caomhnóir don't even exist anymore! What are we supposed to... do with him?"

"Do with him?" Karen asked.

"Is he just going to follow us around all the time like a shadow with a mood disorder?" I asked.

"No, of course not," Karen said. "The truth is that you'll rarely see each other. Caomhnóir aren't needed on a regular basis as they once were. Think of him as an emergency contact—someone who will be on call if you need him to deal with a ghost-related situation. In the short time your mother and I were assigned to ours, we probably only saw him a dozen times outside of classes."

"But he'll still have to move wherever we are. He's English, but when we go back to America he'll have to move there too, won't he?"

Karen's smile faded. "Yes, he will. There are rules about geographic proximity."

"So he will have to uproot his entire life and move across the ocean to sit around and wait for an emergency?" I asked. "No wonder he hates us."

"I'm sure he doesn't..." Karen began, but trailed off delicately when I glared at her. "You will all adjust, including him. The Caomhnóir know what they're getting into."

"The longer we're here, the more I realize I had no idea what we were getting into," I replied.

"That's probably how Noah's feeling right about now," Karen said with a sigh.

"What do you mean?" Hannah asked. "He doesn't know why we're here, does he? I thought you weren't allowed to tell him."

"No, he doesn't know why we're here, and that's the problem," said Karen. "I've never had to say a word to Noah about the Durupinen, because it's never been a part of my life since I've known him. When your mother performed the Binding, my Visitations stopped; there was never any reason for him to know about my gifts. But now that our Gateway is open and I'm seeing spirits again, I'll have some explaining to do."

"Are you actually allowed to tell him?" Hannah asked.

"Over the centuries, the Durupinen have learned that certain concessions have to be made if we are to live normal lives." Karen saw the incredulous look on my face and laughed. "Okay, somewhat normal lives, then. The point is, I have permission to fill him in on a very basic level, enough so that he won't go looking for answers himself and find out what he isn't supposed to know... sort of like what Jess has been able to do with Tia and Dr. Pierce. We don't want Noah stumbling onto this information by accident."

"You mean like Grandpa did?" I asked.

"Yes. That's exactly what I mean," Karen said a bit hoarsely. She kept her eyes on her food, probably to hide a sudden welling of tears. "Our mother chose to reveal nothing to him. He was a very religious man, and she was afraid of losing him. I'll never understand why she married him in the first place, knowing how deeply he would abhor everything we stand for... but I guess you can't choose who you fall in love with. Anyway, we all know how that turned out. Secrecy is important, but so is the survival of the bloodlines. We can't preserve them if all of our personal relationships fall apart because of lies."

"What do you think he'll say?" I asked.

"I have absolutely no idea," answered Karen. "But ready or not, I'm going to find out." She pushed her plate away as though her food suddenly repulsed her. She put an arm around my shoulder and gave me an affectionate squeeze; I ignored the impulse to shake her off. Then she walked around the table and did the same for Hannah, who returned it with a smile. "You know how to reach me if you need me. I'll be back in two weeks, three weeks at the most."

And so we were abandoned to the wolves, but we barely had time to notice. Classes instantly became so intense that we were buried up to our necks in reading. There was so much to learn and so much to digest—I found I could barely spare a thought for the silent treatment and dirty looks we were still receiving at every turn. I could safely say that by the time I finally returned to St. Matt's, I would have written enough papers and taken enough tests to graduate twice.

Celeste piled book after book on us. We read volumes upon volumes chronicling the history of the Durupinen—from the earliest records to the present day. The first book, which we read the first week, covered the original organization of the clans, beginning with the initial attempts by the Durupinen to identify and organize themselves, including the formation of a rudimentary Council and the selection of a High Priestess. The election process was a bitter one, fraught with much infighting and political intrigue, and it was even suspected that one of the candidates was poisoned. The story of our past was just as intense and full of conflict as any ethnic or religious group in history, which piqued my curiosity.

"I can't understand how we've been able to stay so secret," I said as I raised my hand during Celeste's Friday lecture. I was clenching and unclenching my other hand, which had seized up from the intensity of my note taking. "All of the religious texts out there, yet not one of them mentions the Durupinen. How is that possible?"

Celeste looked up from the notes she was using and leaned forward on her lectern, eager for a discussion. "How do you mean, Jessica?"

"I mean, why haven't any other major religious text mentioned us? We've been around at least as long as some religions, and much longer than others, and we've had run-ins with them all over the world. How is it possible that we've escaped mention?"

"Anyone have any thoughts on that?" Celeste asked, looking around encouragingly.

"It's our code of secrecy," Peyton said at once, her tone indicating that this should've been obvious—and that, by extension, I was an idiot. "We have a foolproof system in place that prevents the world from knowing about us."

"A good point, Peyton," Celeste said, "but is it really foolproof? It's comprehensive, certainly, but there have been breaches, sometimes devastating ones, as we will be learning."

"And it's not true that we don't get mentioned," said a girl with long, dark hair in the front row. "There are references to witches and paganism all throughout religious literature. Just because they didn't know the specifics doesn't mean that they didn't discover us sometimes."

"But those aren't necessarily the Durupinen," Brenna said. "The references are vague, like you said, so we can't know if they were talking about Durupinen or Druids or some pagan group. They may not ever have known about us."

"People are afraid of the unknown. It's one of the reasons people cling to their religious belief systems so strongly," Celeste said. "I'm not passing judgment here," she added quickly. "Many people in this room probably identify with a religious group, isn't that true?"

Several people nodded, glancing self-consciously around as they did so. The dark-haired girl was fingering nervously at a gold cross around her neck.

"Perhaps I ought to clarify something for you all, as I think it bears repeating," Celeste said. "We are not a religious group. We have emerged under many names all over the world throughout the centuries. We include women of many different faiths, and many who subscribe to no faith at all. I think Jessica's question can best be addressed by posing a different question: What is the quintessential difference between us and the people who have written every major religious text in history?"

No one answered. We all looked at each other. Finally, in the pressing silence, Hannah raised her hand.

"Yes, Hannah?"

"We're women," she said, her voice barely above a whisper.

Celeste smiled. "Yes, indeed. History has been written and interpreted almost exclusively by men. Every apostle, every great prophet and soothsayer and philosopher, from the dawn of recorded time and almost without exception, are all men. It is staggering and unjust, but there it is. Very few women have ever been accorded a place of real importance in religion. At best, we are the helpers and the nurturers. At worst, we are the temptresses and the root of sin. Is it so very hard to believe, then, that we should be excluded from the annals of spirituality for this most important role?"

No one spoke. The weight of this the truth settled on all of us, like a mantle we couldn't shrug away.

"We do not exist in defiance of any religious tradition." Celeste continued. "We exist alongside it, and so if any of you consider yourselves to be women of faith, I hope you will not feel that you must give up this identity in favor of your new role. In fact, you may find that your faith is the one thing that helps you to get through the more trying times that you will face as one of us." She turned to me with one eyebrow raised. "Does this in any way answer your question, Jess?"

"Yes, thank you," I said—although I was left with far more to digest and consider than my original question had even allowed for.

Celeste changed the subject. "Now, today we will be introducing a topic which dominated much of our early history and was the source of most of the conflicts that threatened our continuation. As you have read, before our systems of concealment were in place, we operated more or less in the open. We did not promulgate our role, but we did not strive to hide it either—especially from those closest to us. We used our abilities to help those around us, to comfort and to provide closure in the most difficult times. We used our gifts as they were meant to be used, for the good of the spirits we served.

"But abilities such as ours breed various responses in the people who learn of them. Some people are afraid. It is natural to fear, and therefore demonize, what we cannot understand; that fear has underscored many of the persecutions the Durupinen have faced over the centuries. But fear is not the only—or even the most dangerous—response to our gifts. There were those who looked at us and our powers, and what these people felt was not fear, but greed—greed for the possibilities of what could be if our powers were harnessed, twisted, and used for means other than those for which they were intended. I speak, of course, of the Necromancers."

I had another one of those increasingly frequent moments when

I felt like I was having an out of body experience as I watched Celeste write the word *Necromancers* on the blackboard behind her. I'd read enough to recognize the term, even if it was usually used in fictional settings. Oh, who the hell was I kidding, my life was one big fictional setting now. I copied down the word and braced myself for more unpleasantness.

"The records of interaction between the Necromancers and the Durupinen begin early in the 10th century, although it is safe to assume that they were around before such records were created. At their inception, the Necromancers were quite harmless... they were merely men interested in understanding the true nature of our souls, and what happens to them when we pass from this world. For centuries, the Durupinen coexisted with the Necromancers—we watched them carefully, although we were equally careful not to interact with them.

But as the Necromancers' knowledge grew, as they collected more and more philosophies from around the world and began pooling the ideas of great thinkers and religious writers, they became bolder in their inquiries... and more of a threat to us. As the Enlightenment dawned, they were among the first to consider the idea that scientific principles could be applied to matters of spirituality. With the introduction of this idea, they began to experiment well beyond the simple séances and other methods of spirit communication for which they were known.

"Their advances at first, were, again, fairly harmless. They practiced rudimentary forms of paranormal investigation and exorcism. But when these experiments yielded little conclusive evidence, they delved further, combining scientific knowledge with spiritual practices. They toyed with grave robbing and reanimation. They first studied the myth of, and then endeavored to create, successful zombification rituals."

I looked over at Hannah. She was scribbling furiously, but had a troubled expression on her face. She looked up at me and frowned. My head was flooded with images of Dr. Frankenstein and his monster, mixed together with a smattering of gruesome details from Hitchcock movies and various news stories about serial killers. I suddenly found myself wishing I hadn't eaten such a hearty breakfast.

"The term *Necromancer* has been used in a variety of ways over the centuries. It has been generalized to refer to anyone who practices witchcraft or 'black magic.' More specifically, it refers to one who attempts to communicate with the dead, often in order to gain knowledge of the future. Both of these definitions are inadequate to describe what the true Necromancer does. A Necromancer is one who seeks to reverse death. He seeks dominance over the realm of spirits, to exert his control over these spirits and use them for his own ends. Once the Necromancers learned more about the Durupinen and our abilities, their goal became more focused and specific: To take control of our Gateways and their power."

"But why?" Mackie burst in. "What's the point of trying to do any of that? It's so..." She came up short; her mouth gaped open as the appropriate word eluded her.

"Morbid? Disturbing? Pervy?" Savvy suggested. I was surprised to see that she was, for once, paying attention. The gossip magazine she'd brought along for entertainment lay forgotten in her lap; she was leaning forward in her seat, staring at Celeste.

"Well, yes," Mackie said, nodding. "But the word I was looking for is *pointless*. You can't access a Gateway without the Durupinen's cooperation, and even if you did, you can't reverse it. It doesn't work like that."

Celeste didn't speak right away, but her silence was deafening in itself.

"Wait, can you? Can you reverse a Gateway?" Mackie asked, horror-struck. Her expression was mirrored all around the room.

"A Gateway has never been reversed," Celeste said, and I couldn't help thinking that she hadn't quite answered the question. "But that did not stop the Necromancers from trying. Their attempts to interfere with the Durupinen during the 16th and 17th centuries were so persistent that these assaults necessitated the formation of the Caomhnóir system."

Hands all over the room scribbled down this information. So it was the Necromancers' fault that I was stuck with Finn for the rest of my life. If there'd been a Necromancer in the room, I would've have punched him.

"So where are they now, eh?" Savvy asked. "Should we be worried?" Her tone was playful, but her grin was somewhat forced.

"Focus your worry elsewhere," Celeste replied. "The Necromancers were disbanded and their infrastructure destroyed in the early 18th century. They were utterly routed, and their library of research was burned to the ground. This castle houses a number of artifacts preserved from those times, relics of the Necromancer scourge of 1726. We will be taking a little field trip to visit them after you've completed your reading for this week, which will cover the history of the Necromancer/Durupinen relationship. And on that note, here is your assignment for the weekend."

Celeste dismissed us after unleashing upon us a crippling amount of homework; this left Savvy muttering a number of choice British phrases which I wasn't familiar with, but could deduce were inappropriate for polite company.

"She can't really expect us to read all this by Wednesday," Savvy said, shaking the fat new volume in our faces. "She's barking if she thinks I'm going to spend my whole weekend buried in this."

"And you're barking if you think you can pass her class without doing the reading," Mackie said.

"Yeah, well, I wasn't aware this whole Apprentice thing would be quite so much like... school," said Savvy. "If I wanted to learn history, I would've gone to university."

"It's pretty crazy history, though, isn't it?" I pointed out. "What about all that Necromancer stuff today?"

"Yeah, the Necromancers are properly creepy. Wait till you see the stuff downstairs," said Mackie. "My aunt told me that there's artwork and robes down there, and these masks that look like skulls. And there's all kinds of equipment they used to experiment on bodies with—like medieval torture devices."

"Sounds like a great field trip," I said.

"I don't know, I think it makes sense," said Hannah thoughtfully.

"What makes sense?" I asked.

"To want to know how it all works," she said, shrugging in an offhand sort of way. "It's the universal question, isn't it?"

"Yeah, I guess so," I said. "But their methods just sound so... unnatural."

"Yes, that's true," Hannah agreed. "I'm just saying that I understand why they were so fascinated. I mean, don't you wonder what's on the other side of the Gateway? Doesn't it bother you that we are in charge of something we don't fully understand?"

Mackie looked a little uncomfortable. "Yeah, sure. Everyone wonders about it. But it's just how it is. No one finds out what's on the other side until it's their turn to go."

"I'm just saying I understand the fascination the Necromancers had with it, even if they did go too far," Hannah said. "It's tempting to think that we might have the power not just to send people over, but to bring them back. Imagine never having to say good-bye to people."

No one said anything—Hannah's thought had landed on us hard. I thought of all the people I'd said good-bye to—my mother, Evan—and what I would've given to have them back. Maybe the Necromancers weren't as crazy as they sounded. I shook my head, expelling such thoughts like so many irksome flies. It wouldn't do me any good to dwell on things like that, especially here.

§

Later that evening, the Apprentices would be gathering in the courtyard to do their First Crossings. Since Hannah and I had already done a Crossing back on Karen's roof in Boston, Celeste told us that we were exempt from this particular ceremony—which Hannah seemed a little disappointed about, but I found to be a huge relief. I was already sick of ceremonies, and all the pomp and circumstance that went along with them.

"Have you two decided what you're going to do tonight, since you don't have to come to the First Crossing?" Mackie asked us as we walked back to our rooms after Celeste's class.

I shrugged. "Get started on this mountain of reading, I guess."

Even though the alternative to the First Crossing Ceremony was a doing a staggering amount of homework, I would face it cheerfully. I was actually looking forward to homework; what had Fairhaven done to me?

"I can't believe you get to bunk this off," Savvy said.

"We're not getting out of it," I said. "We've just already done it."

"I know, I know," she groaned. "I'm just nervy as all hell."

"Me too," Mackie admitted. "I haven't eaten a thing all day. I think I've lost the ability to swallow."

"You'll be fine," I said, patting Mackie on the back and recognizing, as I did so, the irony of the situation: Usually it was Mackie talking me down off the ledge when I was freaking out about some new aspect of our life at Fairhaven Hall.

We reached the door to our room. Savvy, Mackie, and Brenna followed us in, peppering us with questions about what it was like to do a Crossing; apparently, they didn't trust Siobhán's descriptions of it in class or Keira's step-by-step Crossing walk-through, which had taken up an entire double session the afternoon before.

Between the two of us, Hannah and I tried to put into words our First Crossing experience; the thrumming buzz of connection as we joined hands; the sense that something inside us had opened; the disconcerting feeling as life after unfamiliar life flashed through us.

We were so caught up in our conversation that I didn't even notice the two girls standing in the doorway until Hannah said, "You can come in if you want."

They started and backed away from the door. I recognized one of them as the dark-haired girl from class, the one who was wearing the cross necklace.

"I... sorry. We didn't mean to eavesdrop," she said hastily.

"No, it's okay," I said. "Really, you can—"

But they were gone, scurrying off down the hallway.

"That was Róisín Lightfoot and her sister Riley," Mackie said quietly. "Their mother Clara is one of the Council members, and she and Marion are very close. They wouldn't want to get caught being friendly with either of you. It would upset dear mummy, not to mention all of their other Council-family friends."

"That's too bad for them, then," Savvy said, and got up from one of the chairs. "I, for one, feel a right bit better about what I'm getting into tonight. I'm sneaking out for a fag before we have to meet."

"By sneaking out, do you mean going to your room and cracking the window?" Brenna asked.

"I do, indeed," Savvy said with a theatrical bow. Brenna and Mackie followed her out.

"You'll all be fine!" I called after them as Mackie, with a resigned grimace, shut the door behind her. Then I turned to Hannah, who was wearing an expression eerily similar to Mackie's; Hannah had already buried her nose in the new book Celeste had given us.

"Might as well get down to it," I said, and we settled in for a long night of reading.

Three hours later, my head was pounding and I was seriously contemplating chucking my book into the cheerfully roaring fire in our fireplace. I tossed it onto the floor instead.

"I can't do this anymore," I said. "I'm giving up for the night."

Hannah nodded absently, but kept reading. I went to my desk and shot off a quick email to Tia, asking if she'd made any progress with tracking down Annabelle or any of Pierce's other team members. Of course there was still no word from Pierce himself. I briefly considered starting my own research into Neil Caddigan, but the thought of more work made me slightly nauseous. I would have liked to spy on the many Gateways, which by now must've been opening all over the courtyard, but our window didn't afford a view of the ceremony.

I grabbed my sketchpad instead, and started doodling; the doodle eventually turned into a sketch of Hannah. At least, it was trying to be sketch of Hannah, but even with her right in front of me, something about her refused to be captured. It might have been the eyes, or maybe her mouth; I couldn't put my finger on it. Frustrated, I crumpled the drawing up and threw it into the wastebasket. Then I flipped back through my finished sketches.

The little girl in the flames. I hadn't looked at it since the day I drew it.

How could I find out who she was and what she needed if she couldn't find a way to communicate with me? Was this drawing supposed to be a clue? I don't know why I drew those flames—perhaps she had found a way to get the idea to me subconsciously? That had sort of been the case when I'd drawn the Psychic Sketch of Lydia Tenningsbrook; I hadn't even been aware that I'd been drawing it, but her face had come to me.

I thought about showing the sketch to Fiona, in the hopes that she might understand what it meant, but I cast off the idea at once. Fiona was one of the last people I would ask for help. I suppose I could have asked one of the other teachers, but something indefinable was holding me back. I looked down at the little girl in flames again; she didn't want to be shared... not yet, anyway. So who could I ask for help?

The idea came so suddenly and easily, it was like it had been waiting in the wings for its cue. "Hannah, do you think you could call Milo for me? I need to ask him about something."

"Of course," Hannah said, looking surprised. She lifted her face into the air and closed her eyes. "Hey, Milo!"

"Call, and I shall answer!" he trilled, as he appeared above the fireplace mantle and looked, for a brief moment, as though I'd shot, stuffed, and mounted him there. I wish.

"I need you to do me a favor." I said.

"Why, yes, Jess-Jess, I'd be glad to burn your wardrobe! Where are the matches? Ooh, can we do s'mores? I've always wanted to toast marshmallows over a fishnet fire," he said, clapping gleefully.

"Sorry, fresh out of marshmallows," I replied, barely able to keep a straight face. Damn it, Milo was really was funny sometimes, even if it was usually at my expense. "Actually, I was hoping you could find something out about one of the spirits here."

"Ugh, *très* boring. The dead contingent here is not exactly riveting. I mean, most of them have been dead longer than America's been a country."

"Have you met most of them?"

"I've made the rounds, yes. I was hoping to find someone I could at least gossip with while you all are doing boring, living things, like sleeping."

"And?"

"Pickings are slim, although there is one former servant, Nancy, who likes to dish. Sadly, her idea of gasp-worthy news is a woman walking around without a corset," he said. "So, basically she thinks you're all a bunch of whores."

"Have you seen a ghost of a little girl anywhere around?" I asked.

Milo dropped the drama queen act and frowned a bit. "A few. You'll need to be more specific." Even he didn't joke much where kid ghosts were concerned, probably because he was practically a child himself.

"Really skinny and grubby, and wild-looking, with long hair. She wears a white dress, kind of like an old-fashioned nightgown."

"Oh, yeah," he said, nodding sadly. "Yeah, I've seen her."

"Do you know who she is? Has she said anything to you?" I asked, sitting up straighter in my eagerness.

"No," Milo said. "No one knows who she is. She doesn't seem to be able to communicate with anyone."

"Oh," I said, and slumped back again, disappointed. "Yeah, I noticed that, too. I thought maybe it might be different with other spirits. Have you ever met a ghost like that? Who couldn't speak?"

Milo shrugged. "You get all types on my side, honey, especially in the places Hannah and I used to be. Ghosts who were drugged-up in life, and still out of it in death. Crazy ones, shy ones... there's all kinds of reasons why a spirit won't talk to you."

"Yeah, but there's something really weird about it," I persisted. "She tried to talk to me. She kind of attacked me, actually."

"Seriously?"

"Yeah, she flew right at me the first day we were here, then she found me again after my first mentoring session. But something's wrong. It's like she's in this bubble, like there's a wall up between her and the rest of the world. She's trying to communicate, but she can't get past it. Like she's trapped or something."

Milo folded his arms. "Huh. I've never heard of anything like that before. And honestly, I haven't gotten close enough to her to notice it for myself. She keeps her distance from just about everyone."

"Would you mind just asking around a little bit? See if you can find out anything?"

Milo heaved a long-suffering sigh, but nodded his head. "Fine, fine."

I smiled at him. "Thanks."

"Whatever," he huffed. "I see how it is. You think I'm just your little afterlife messenger boy. You snap your unmanicured fingers and I do your bidding."

"Actually," I said, waving my right hand in his face, "I am totally manicured today. Savvy was practicing on me."

Milo gasped. "Be still my heart! And they aren't even black! Girl, there's hope for you yet!"

§

A quick sharp knock on the door cut Milo's berating short. I didn't think anything could shut Milo up, but instantly we all knew this was no friendly visit—hell, we didn't even have enough friends for a friendly visit. Hannah, alarmed, looked up from her book, but I hopped up from my chair.

"I've got it," I told her. "Coming!" I added as the knock—more firmly than before—came again. I wrenched the door open to find Celeste standing in the hallway and looking uncharacteristically stern. Peyton stood just behind her, with her arms crossed and a smug little smirk on her face. And I'd so been hoping some ghost would just drag her on through the Gateway and end our misery. Oh well. Maybe next time.

"Jessica, I need to inspect your room," said Celeste.

"Huh? What for?" I was inexplicably nervous, even though I couldn't think of a single thing we had in our room that would get us in trouble.

"Peyton has informed me that, as she was passing by here a few minutes ago on her way back from the First Crossing, she heard a male voice issuing from this room. As you and Hannah are well aware, we have very strict rules about interactions between Caomhnóir and Apprentices, and..."

I actually laughed aloud in relief. "And you thought we were harboring boys in our room?"

Peyton narrowed her eyes at me. "I definitely heard a male voice in here," she said firmly.

"Yeah, because the Caomhnóir are so very fond of us all, we just can't get enough of each other," I snorted. "Well, you can call off the dogs, Celeste, because it's just Milo."

I opened the door widely to reveal Milo, who was still lounging on the fireplace mantle. I watched with satisfaction as the smug expression dripped off Peyton's face, but it was Celeste's look of shock that prompted me to speak. "Celeste? What's wrong?"

"He... how did he get in here?" she gasped.

"This time? Through the fireplace," Milo answered, with a limp gesture toward the stonework behind him. "Doors are more traditional obviously, but they're kind of unnecessary in my current state."

"But... but he can't... there's no possible way to... there are Wards!" stammered Celeste, pointing to the eye carved into our door.

"Oh yeah, Karen mentioned those," I said with a shrug. "It keeps other spirits out, but it doesn't seem to affect Milo... I guess because he's not hostile."

"Well, that's true of the Wards surrounding the boundaries of the grounds, but the Wards on your bedroom doors ought to keep every spirit out, hostile or not!" Celeste exclaimed.

"But I want him here," Hannah said quickly, sliding off the bed. She practically ran over to Milo, who immediately sunk down from the mantle to stand level with her. "Can't he stay, please?"

"No! This is... I don't even know how this is possible, unless..." Celeste's voice trailed away as she looked back and forth between Hannah and Milo with a dawning comprehension. She turned back over her shoulder. "Peyton, thank you for alerting me to your concerns. You may go now."

"But what's going on? Is there something wrong with the Wards?" Peyton asked, clearly fishing for information.

"No, the Wards are fine. I'll handle things from here. Please return to your room. It's nearly curfew and you've had a big night tonight," said Celeste.

Peyton managed a shadow of a respectful smile and walked toward her room.

"Milo, Hannah, I need you to come with me to Finvarra's chambers," Celeste said.

"What? Now?" Hannah asked in a panicky voice. "Why?"

"Because she will need to know that Milo can enter here. It may be a very significant fact, and I'm sure she will want to speak to you both about it."

"Well, if they're going, so am I!" I insisted.

Celeste seemed about to argue, but then changed her mind. She nodded solemnly. "Yes, I think you should, Jessica. This will affect you as well."

"What will affect me?"

"Are we in some kind of trouble?" Milo asked.

"No," Celeste assured us. "No, you aren't in trouble."

"So then why—"

"Finvarra will be able to answer your questions far better than I. Please come with me." She started briskly down the hallway without another word of explanation.

Milo, Hannah, and I looked warily at each other and then followed her out in anxious silence. Whatever Celeste had said to the contrary, it certainly felt like we were in trouble. I had a flashback to St. Matt's, when Professor Marshall had ordered me out of her classroom and straight to Dean Finndale's office. I had felt just the same way then as I felt now—nervous and completely wrong-footed.

I glanced sideways at Hannah. Her face was utterly drained of color, and her fingers were searching the air next to her for the cold comfort of Milo's hand. However much I couldn't stand Milo, I was grateful for the calming effect he had on Hannah. They'd been through so much together, and I cringed at the thought of Hannah trying to cope at Fairhaven without him.

As we followed Celeste up the tightly winding staircase of the North Tower, the loaded silence was broken only by our echoing footsteps and panting. Just as I thought I couldn't trudge up another step, we reached a small circular landing that faced an arched wooden door; the door was covered from top to bottom in beautifully carved and painted runes. I just had time enough to recognize the same eye symbol that adorned our door before Celeste grabbed the brass knocker and sent three loud thwacks resounding through the tower.

Before the echoes had even faded, the ghost of a man floated through the door and planted himself firmly before it. I knew at once he had been a Caomhnóir in life; he appeared in the same uniform as the sworn members—his dark coat and pointed leather boots were immediately recognizable even in his transient state. He glared at Celeste, arms crossed, but his expression melted into one of surprise when his eyes fell on us.

"What can I do for you? Finvarra is occupied with her correspondence," he said.

"I'm sorry to disturb her Carrick, but there is a situation here I think she needs to be made aware of quite immediately," said Celeste, gesturing to us. I tried to calm my breathing as Carrick looked us over. I recognized him as the spirit who that had been with Finvarra during her welcome speech on our very first night. He had been tall and imposing in life, with a prominent nose and long, dark hair that was tied back in a ponytail. He was staring at me with such intensity that I had to look away.

"These are the Ballard girls, aren't they? What's going on, then? What kind of situation?" Carrick's voice, still professional in tone, betrayed a hint of something else; was it alarm? He shifted his weight slightly and blocked the door from our sight more completely.

"It is not so much a situation with the girls, as it is a situation between Hannah and this spirit. This is Milo, and he arrived with them. It seems that Hannah and Milo might be... Bound," explained Celeste.

Carrick's sternly crossed arms fell to his sides. "Oh, I see. Well, that's... Celeste, do go through. I think you're quite right, the High Priestess will want to see them immediately."

Celeste stepped forward, yanked forcefully on the heavy wooden door, and disappeared behind it. We stood awkwardly in the hallway under Carrick's piercing gaze as the seconds ticked by. I could just make out the cadence of the conversation on the other side of the door.

"What are you... that is to say, how are you both?" Carrick asked.

He looked uncomfortable, like most of the Caomhnóir did when one of them spoke directly to us.

"Nervous," I said, shifting from foot to foot. "I don't suppose you can tell us what's going on? Or at least if we're about to get thrown out of here?"

"Why would you be thrown out?" he asked.

"I don't know, Celeste won't tell us anything." I said, a bit more loudly than I'd intended.

"What did she mean when she said Milo and I are Bound?" Hannah asked, with a plea in her voice.

Carrick fixed on her with a look that I knew well. It was full of sadness and pity, a look that clearly said he knew all about Hannah's history. "I am very sorry, but it's simply not my place," he replied. "Finvarra will explain, if it really is true."

My eyes darted anxiously around and fell on the door to the office again, where the same rune that adorned our door caught my attention again.

"Wait, she's got that rune on her door, too!" I said, pointing.

Finvarra's office is protected by many runes. To which do you refer?" Carrick asked, looking over his shoulder.

"The one that stands for the Wards—that creepy one with the eye that's supposed to keep ghosts out."

Carrick nodded in acknowledgment. "Yes."

"But you just came through that door," I pointed out.

Carrick nodded again.

"Well, it obviously doesn't do what Celeste thinks it does, if Milo can get through our door and you can get through that one!"

"It isn't quite as simple as that," Carrick said, and he smiled at us. The expression looked strange on his face, as though his muscles didn't quite know what to do. It was the first time I'd seen any of the Caomhnóir smile. "Just be patient. I'm sure they will be right with you, and then all will be made clear."

We waited. Standing guard before the door, Carrick looked almost alive, but for an odd shimmer around his outline that I had come to recognize as one of the hallmarks of a ghost's appearance. It was like looking at a picture of something astonishing, only to realize that it had been Photoshopped—that something about the image's light and the shadow didn't quite match up, and so created a slightly surreal appearance.

"We were all... pleased to see your clan represented here again," said Carrick. Something about his features was familiar; I thought it must be the way he kept his eyes trained away from us when he spoke, which seemed to be another Caomhnóir trademark. "You have a long and illustrious history at Fairhaven, as I'm sure you will learn."

"Pleased is not the general vibe we're getting, actually," I replied. "People around here seem much more interested in recent history than anything else."

Carrick nodded grimly. "Yes, quite so. Still, I was glad to hear that all was properly resolved. I'm sure it will get better."

"Right. Thanks," I said. Carrick looked relieved—this awkward attempt at conversation with two unknown Apprentices had obviously gone better than he'd expected—and lapsed into stodgy silence.

Finally, after a few more agonizingly long minutes, the door behind Carrick creaked open and revealed a candlelit office.

Finvarra stood silhouetted in the moonlight that was streaming in through the window, her hair a silver cascade down her back. I was struck, as I had been the first time I'd seen her, with the power she exuded—an indefinable aura that demanded respect, even awe. We hesitated in the doorway, but she gestured to us.

"Please, come in," she said.

Carrick stepped back to let us through. Still feeling like an unruly eight year old in the principal's office, I shuffled in, with Hannah and Milo just behind me. Hannah and I sat down in the chairs to which Finvarra was gesturing; Milo hovered by Hannah's shoulder like a bizarre ghostly parrot.

"I've been meaning to talk with you both," Finvarra began. Her face was obscured by the long shadows that the moonlight was throwing across her. "Hannah, we have spoken briefly, of course, regarding your gift. But everything has been so busy, preparing for the start of the fall term, that I was quite overwhelmed with other matters. Jessica, I apologize for not having met you sooner."

"That's okay," I said, when Hannah proved incapable of speaking. She was watching Finvarra as though the woman were pointing a weapon at her.

"First, I wanted to say that I am very sorry about the circumstances under which you discovered your legacy. You have both suffered needlessly, especially you, Hannah. I hope you will believe me when I tell you that we did everything in our power to find you both, and to rectify the situation." As Finvarra walked toward us, the shadows passed across her like long, caressing fingers.

I didn't trust myself to say anything polite to her about our "situation" since I was still too angry about everything we'd been through. Luckily, Finvarra didn't seem to require—or even expect—a response, and went on.

"I had to make many difficult decisions where the two of you were concerned, and I know that the consequences have been trying for you to deal with. But we knew that the most important thing was to find you both, and to restore the order to the Gateways and to the Durupinen at large. Only when you've been trained and educated can you truly learn to use the gifts you've inherited. I hope you both are settling in nicely?"

An honest answer to that question would have taken too long, so instead I trusted myself to reply with a stiff, "Yes, thank you."

"It is a big adjustment, I know, but you will grow accustomed to our ways and to your new responsibilities. It simply takes time," Finvarra said. She smiled for the first time—a subtle but pleasant expression. "We are here, though, to discuss another matter. That matter, as I'm sure you gathered, is Milo."

Hannah squirmed in her chair. "What about him?"

"We need to talk about why he's here, and why he can get through the Wards into your room. He shouldn't have been able to follow you to Fairhaven to begin with, not without great difficulty, and he most certainly should not be able to enter the Warded areas of the castle," Finvarra explained.

"But there are lots of ghosts here," Hannah said, as her voice rose to a panicked squeak. "Hundreds of them—some of them have been here for centuries, and you've let them stay here. Please don't make him leave!"

"I'm not leaving her, so if that's what you want, you can just forget it," Milo said, wrapping an arm around Hannah's quivering shoulders. "Where she goes, I go. That's just the way it is."

"Exactly," Finvarra said, still smiling. "Put yourselves at ease, both of you. We are not asking you to separate. In fact, it seems that that would be impossible at this point."

"Damn straight," Milo muttered.

Finvarra went on as though she hadn't heard the profanity. "I'd like to discover the nature of the connection between you. You do agree, Hannah, that you feel more connected to Milo than you do to the other spirits with whom you come into contact?"

Hannah seemed to relax for the first time since entering the room. "Yes. But it's different. I didn't just know him when he was a ghost. We were friends when he was alive, too."

"Best friends," Milo added.

"Yes, you certainly have more of an emotional connection, that's natural," Finvarra said. "But I want you to think for a moment about the way your connection *feels*. Try to separate, if you can, the history you and Milo had together in life, and concentrate instead on the physical and mental sensations of interacting with him now."

Hannah's brow furrowed. "I... oh! Yes, I think I understand what you mean."

"What? What is it?" I asked.

"Well, with the other ghosts, I only feel their presence when they're near me. I mean, physically near me. But with Milo, it's like I can always feel him." She looked up at Finvarra. "Is that what you're talking about?"

"Precisely. And has it always been that way between the two of you, ever since Milo has taken this form?" Finvarra asked.

"Yes."

"I see," Finvarra said, with her finger tracing her lips thoughtfully. "And you, Milo. This may seem intrusive, as what I am about to ask is of a very personal nature. I apologize about prying into what may be quite painful living memories, but I must do so in order to illuminate this situation further."

"That's okay," Milo said with a shrug.

"Would you please tell me the nature of your death? How it came about, and also any role that Hannah may have played in it?"

I sat stiffened upright in my seat. "What do you mean, any role she played in it? Hannah didn't have anything to do with Milo's death!—Did you?" I directed this question at Hannah, in a much more accusatory tone than I had intended.

"No! Of course not," Hannah said decisively. Clearly she was as disturbed as I by the turn the conversation had taken.

Finvarra held up a hand. "I do not mean to suggest that Hannah killed Milo, or assisted in his death in any way. But the moments leading up to Milo's death were very significant in shaping the relationship the two of you now share. It is important to understand how Hannah factored into his thoughts in those moments of his death. Milo, would you please share with us what you can remember?"

Milo shifted from foot to foot. The sudden absence of his usually confident air seemed to dull his very existence, as if a light of inside him had gone out. When he spoke, it was in a voice very unlike the one that usually danced from his lips. He suddenly looked very young... and very small.

§

"Growing up in my house was hell," Milo began. "My parents are from China, and my dad has a very traditional view of the world. He had my path all laid out for me before I could walk; private schools, Ivy League college, medical school, and a respectable marriage to a nice Chinese girl. We never discussed it; it wasn't up for discussion. I would bring honor to the family and be grateful for every decision that had been made for me."

The room had gone completely silent as we all listened. I'd barely ever heard Milo say two unsarcastic words in all the time I'd known him.

"So, naturally my childhood was a real barrel of laughs, especially when I started realizing I wasn't the manly son my father had expected. Dressing up in my mother's high heel shoes and asking for princess tiaras and Barbie dolls weren't exactly on my approved-activities list. Every time he turned around, I was doing shit like painting my toenails or making dresses out of my bedroom curtains like a friggin' Von Trapp. My father blamed my mother—He said she wasn't being strict enough with me. He threw every pink and frilly thing out of the house, even my little sister's stuff. When that didn't work, he thought he could beat the gay out of me. Clearly," Milo hissed a bitter little laugh, "that didn't work either, although not for a lack of trying.

"I was a really good student, you know. I totally could have pulled off the Ivy League acceptance, the med school workload, all of it. But none of that mattered anymore. My father didn't care if I brought home straight A report cards if I was also bringing home a boyfriend. My mother would've been okay with it, but she didn't dare show any sort of acceptance around my father. It got so bad that I stopped eating, started popping pills, even flirted with suicide. A failed attempt or two later and I was locked up.

"The weird thing was that when I was in treatment, I was okay. It was actually the happiest I could ever remember being. The doctors understood and accepted me. They tried to help me, but they weren't trying to change me the way my father was. They wanted me to be happy and healthy—they wanted to treat the depression and the behaviors, not change who I was on the inside. But no matter what they did, no matter how much they helped, I always had to go home to him. And, to my father, as long as I was still gay, I was still sick, still wrong.

"New Beginnings was the last place they sent me to be 'fixed.' That was where I met Hannah, and we became best friends. I was the only person there that she told about the ghosts, except for the doctors. Just as she accepted me, I accepted her. I knew she wasn't lying, even though I couldn't see the people she could see. I trusted that she was telling me the truth, because it was so obvious that we were in the same boat. Each of us had an innate part of us that we couldn't change, that we couldn't do anything about, but it made functioning outside of institution walls impossible: As long as we were who we were, we could never be happy out there. We used to joke that if we formed a band, we would be called the Unlovables. We would've had a string of great albums that no one would buy."

Here Milo paused, and sunk into the chair with Hannah. She pulled her body close to him, as though she drew comfort from his coldness the same way that others would draw comfort from the warmth of a living body. I shivered unintentionally and struggled against an unbidden jolt of jealousy; it should have been Hannah and I who that were that close.

"Then, after about eight months, they told me the 'good' news—I was going home. But I just couldn't do it again. I couldn't walk back into that house, and face the expectations that I would be an entirely new person, the son my father thought he deserved. I couldn't face my father's disappointment—or the wrath that would follow when he realized that I was still me, still the same disappointing fucked-up 'she-male' he'd locked away. And so I made the decision that I wasn't going to go. I was going to kill myself instead."

Milo said, "I was going to kill myself." with a shocking nonchalance. Maybe that was a benefit of being a ghost; you could look at your life, and even the decision to end it, with an analytical detachment. I didn't think I'd ever want that particular ability.

Milo went on with the same disconcerting insouciance. "It wasn't that hard of a decision to make, really. When I considered the alternative, dying seemed like an excellent option. I'd be free of him, free of his expectations. The only hang-up I had, the only thing that really gave me pause, was Hannah. She needed me; I was the only one who believed her about the ghosts, the only one she could talk to about it. But at the same time, it was knowing her that made me realize I might have another option—an option between living and dying. Maybe, if I died, I could escape my father but still stay with her. Maybe I could be a ghost. It felt like the perfect solution. I would never have to go home, and the two of us could stay together, no matter where else they sent her. It didn't have to be death or life, black or white; I could have a life of gray.

"I wrote Hannah a letter, just in case it didn't work. I mean, let's face it, I had no idea what it took to become a ghost; what if I'd screwed it up? I'd been tonguing my meds for weeks, hoarding them in my mattress. I also stopped eating; the less of me there was, the fewer pills it would take to kill me. I think she suspected something, but I never asked her." He stroked Hannah's cheek. "Did you know?"

"I knew you didn't want to go home. I thought that was why you were backsliding, but I didn't think you were getting ready to kill yourself. I would've been so mad at you," Hannah said, with tears in her eyes.

"I know, sweetness," said Milo with a sad little smile. "And I couldn't have that, could I? So finally, the night before my release was scheduled, I locked myself in the bathroom and took all the pills. I wasn't totally sure if I had enough, but I figured that even if I didn't, the attempt would keep me in the hospital long enough to figure something else out. Then I lay down on my bed and waited for it to happen. In the letter I'd written to Hannah, I explained that I would stay with her if I could, but that, if I couldn't, I was really, really sorry for leaving her alone."

Milo fell silent, his hands picking absently at the specter of his jeans. Finvarra gave him a moment before prompting, "And at the moment you died? What happened then?"

Milo seemed to find each phrase on his jeans, picking each carefully up and examining it before saying it aloud. "At first it was like falling asleep... I could feel myself slipping into sleep, but then... I was slipping further away than sleep, away from myself... It was like someone had cut my strings and I was floating off... And I remember feeling really relieved when that started to happen.

"It would've been very easy to let go, and most of me did, but there was this little part that was thinking about Hannah... I just kept clinging to that tiny part of me, telling myself to let go of me, but to hold on to her. And I did," he finished.

We were all shocked, utterly saddened; the emotion Milo hadn't been able to put into his words had instead bled onto all of our faces; even Finvarra was affected. I realized my mouth was hanging open, so I closed it. As I did so, another description of death bobbed up from the recesses of my mind—a description at once so similar and yet so different from Milo's story.

"I just remember I could feel a pulling, and part of me wanted to go, but part of me didn't. Everything was telling me to just let go and follow whatever it was that was taking me away, but that little part of me just kept clinging on, and then, just as I decided I was going to let go... it had passed. I missed it."

If my eyes weren't already damp from listening to Milo, they would have welled up as Evan's voice floated back to me. How strange to think of someone knowing they were about to die and actually longing for it. How strange to think that someone would choose this imitation of life, this half-life, over a real one. Evan had become a ghost out of a desperate desire to live, but Milo... Milo had shed his life like a snake sheds its skin. I could barely process it, but Finvarra was nodding as though she were hearing a familiar tale.

"We've been together ever since," Milo said. "Not that she was happy about it at first."

Hannah gave him a petulant look. "He could've had a really good life... it wasn't like with me. I was never going to get better, I knew that."

"Honey, please. Even dying couldn't make me less gay. Do you really think another year of therapy would've helped?" Milo said.

"Stop it, you know what I mean!" Hannah cried. "You could have had a normal life if you just could've gotten away from your dad. You were almost eighteen, and then you would've been an adult. You would've been free to be yourself. You could have moved out on your own and found a boyfriend, someone who loved you for who you were."

"Yeah, well, some people can wait for things to get better, and some people can't," Milo said. "Besides, like you said, I may have been able to get out eventually, but you certainly weren't, sweetness, not with your special flavor of crazy."

I opened my mouth to protest, but Hannah giggled.

"So," Finvarra said, "You undertook your own death with two specific intentions. You meant to become a spirit, and you also meant to stay with Hannah. Is that right?"

"Pretty much," Milo said.

Finvarra stood up and walked a complete circle around her desk before continuing. "What you did was very significant, Milo. It would have been significant with any living person, but because Hannah is one of the Durupinen, your choice to stay with her was far more complicated than either of you ever could have realized. The two of you," she said, coming to stand before them, "are now Bound."

"What does that mean, Bound?" I asked, before either Hannah or Milo had the chance to speak.

"I'll explain. Carrick, would you come here, please?" Finvarra called.

Carrick materialized instantly at Finvarra's side, standing as though a military officer had just ordered him at ease; any time I'd ever seen someone stand like that, I was struck with the enormity of the misnomer—he couldn't have looked less "at ease."

"Carrick was a Caomhnóir in life," Finvarra said, and Carrick nodded respectfully. "He was assigned to my sister and me for our protection on the day we were Initiated, and remained with us until his death. But, as he was dying, he made a choice to stay with me, out of a desire to continue in his role as my protector. In doing so, he Bound himself to me."

Carrick drew himself up nearly to full attention. "And would do so again, High Priestess, in a heartbeat."

"Thank you, Carrick. I know it," said Finvarra, inclining her head toward him. "When a spirit and a Durupinen are Bound, there is no breaking their connection. As long as the Durupinen lives, the spirit in question is tied to her. You will find, Hannah, that you will be able to call Milo to you, and that he will be unable to stray very far from your presence without your permission. He has, quite unwittingly, it seems, entered into an ancient and sacred pact: He will stay with you and protect you until your own time comes to Cross—at which point Milo, too, may finally do so."

"You mean, he has no choice?" Hannah asked, horrified.

"No, Hannah. He did have a choice. He has already made it," Finvarra said.

"But that's not fair," I said. "He didn't know what was happening!"

"He's standing right here!" Milo said, throwing up his hands. "He might be dead, but that doesn't mean we can talk about him like he isn't here!"

We all fell silent, even Finvarra.

"I knew what I was doing," Milo insisted. "I could tell when it was happening that it was... a big deal not to go. I could feel it. I stayed anyway. End of story."

Hannah just kept staring at him, looking close to tears. Carrick, on the other hand, was looking at Milo with something akin to respect blossoming in his expression.

"The circumstances are, forgive me, irrelevant at this point," Finvarra said. She must have realized that she sounded insensitive, because she continued in a softer tone. "What has been done cannot be undone, and so you must all learn to make the best of it, including Jessica."

"Me? Why me?"

"Because Milo is Bound to your Gateway. You will share, at least in part, in the connection he has with your sister."

"What?" Milo and I exclaimed together.

"You mean she'll be able to order me around like I'm some kind of servant?" Milo yelled.

"Hey, I don't order you around like a servant!" Hannah said.

"I don't mean *you*!" Milo told her.

"I know, but—"

"Are you telling me I'm stuck with Milo for the rest of my life?" I asked, jumping up out of my seat.

"It is unclear how exactly this connection will manifest itself. My sister and Carrick, for instance, do not need to stay in close proximity to each other, but can communicate over great distances. It may take some time for the nature of your specific connection to become obvious," Finvarra said. "But to answer your question,

Jessica, no, you are not stuck with Milo for the rest of your life, necessarily. You are stuck with him for the rest of Hannah's."

Milo and I stared daggers at each other. We both knew that amounted to basically the same thing.

"Now," Finvarra said, as she walked back around her desk, seated herself, and took up a pen. "Milo, you will need to become a formal part of the Initiation. It is customary, on the rare occasion that an Apprentice is Bound, for the spirit to be Initiated as well. You will take on the official role of Spirit Guide to the clan."

"And what does a Spirit Guide have to do?" Milo asked.

"It is merely a formal title for the connection you already have. You will take a vow, just as Finn and the other Novitiates will do, to protect the Gateway, and to serve as a companion and protector to the girls," Finvarra said.

Milo swallowed hard and raked a hand through his hair. "Protector? Jesus, pressure much?"

Finvarra smiled at him. "It requires no special skill on your part, nor anything beyond what you would surely do as a friend and someone who cares about Hannah and Jessica. If they were ever in any kind of danger, wouldn't you do all you could to help them, even in the absence of an oath?"

Milo shrugged. "Sure, I mean... if you put it that way. Right. Yeah, okay, I guess I can do that."

"Carrick can talk you through the ceremony and make sure that you are ready to participate. He can answer any further questions you have."

"It is a great honor to be a Spirit Guide," Carrick told him. "In time, I think you will come to see it this way. Just remember the reasons you chose to stay behind—you wanted to protect your friend, to make sure she wasn't alone. And that is what you shall continue to do."

Milo glanced at Hannah. They smiled at each other as their eyes met. "Yeah. I would have done that anyway," he said. "Now it'll just be official."

"Yeah, official and permanent," I mumbled. "Great."

9

THE SILENT CHILD

IT TOOK NEARLY TWO WEEKS until I got another update from Tia, who was buried in work preparing for summer-session midterms. I was so swamped myself that the days flew, although they were punctuated with guilty stabs every now and then when I realized that another day had gone by and I still didn't know where Pierce really was. When Tia and I finally Skyped again, the guilty stabs turned to a twisted, agonizing knot of worry.

"There's no way to contact anyone at the Deer Creek Inn," Tia told me. "Their website says they're closed for renovations. We called the contact number, but they've set up a recording saying the same thing, and to keep checking their website for details about when they will be reopening. They even have an auto-response set up for their email."

"And no one from St. Matt's has tried to get in touch with Pierce? Don't any of them see how sketchy this all is?"

"I can't imagine anyone has had to get in touch with him yet. He's only been gone a few weeks," Tia pointed out. "A lot of them are still on break and haven't even been back to campus yet. I bet most of his colleagues don't even know he's gone."

"I guess that's true. We wouldn't even know about any of this if you weren't such an overachiever."

Tia stuck her tongue out at me, but resumed a sober expression almost at once. "There's more, Jess. I found Annabelle's shop. Or I should say, I found what used to be Annabelle's shop."

"What do you mean, used to be?"

"It took a while with no name, but eventually I found it online. It's called the Gypsy Tearoom. I went to the address, but it's... well it's there, but... something happened to it," she said, with all the appearance of someone withholding unpleasant details.

"Out with it, Tia! Just tell me!"

"There was a fire. The place is all boarded up, the windows are smashed, and the whole facade is charred. It's been cordoned off and condemned."

"Shit," was all I could manage. My head, suddenly heavy and swimming, fell into my hands. I tried to take a deep breath, but my lungs clamped down, refusing point-blank to expand.

"I asked some of the other shop owners. The guy who owns the bookshop next door says the police suspect arson—they've been interviewing people to try to find witnesses. He said it happened in the middle of the night, and that no one has seen Annabelle since the day before the fire."

"When did it happen?" I asked, without looking up.

"Three weeks ago."

I laced my fingers into my hair. "Oh, Tia, this is bad. This is really, really bad."

"I know. That's what I thought, too."

"Any luck tracking any of the others down?" I asked.

"No. I'm sorry, but I just don't have that much information about them," Tia said. She sounded tearful. I looked up in time to see her brushing the moisture off her cheeks.

"Don't, Tia. Don't cry. I'm sorry, I'm just so worried," I said. "It isn't your fault. You've got almost nothing to go on. Thank you so much for helping me."

"I wish I had better news for you," she said, eyes downcast. "I'm getting nervous though, Jess. Something really weird is definitely going on. It might even be dangerous."

"Yeah, you're right. Back off of it, for now. I'm going to try to track down Neil, if I can, since he's the only other one we have a last name for. I'll let you know what I find. In the meantime, tell Sam thanks for me. You guys are the best." I glanced down at the clock and leapt up. "I've got to run, Ti, I'm going to be late for class."

Tia and I said good-bye. I was left with an ever-deepening pit in my stomach and a whirling in my brain that took up much more of my attention than Siobhán's lecture about the origins of the *Book of Téigh Anonn*. It was one thing for Pierce to go missing, but Annabelle too? Who could possibly be responsible for something like this, and was there any way that it could be linked to me? It seemed too much of a coincidence that they should both go missing within weeks of finding out what I was.

But no. No, it wasn't possible. Karen had promised that the

destruction of Pierce's evidence was more than sufficient to cover my tracks, and Pierce had promised not to go asking any more questions. No, there must be something else going on, something I didn't know about. I wouldn't stop digging, not yet: Pierce was so important to me. And Annabelle—well, we weren't exactly the best of friends, but if it hadn't been for her, I might never have found out about the Durupinen at all.

"Jessica?"

I snapped back into the present, where my pen was hovering over my completely blank notebook. "Hmm?"

"Are you with us? Siobhán said severely.

"I'm sorry, I didn't hear what you said. I'm a little distracted this morning," I replied, as a heat of embarrassment crept traitorously up my neck and reddened my face.

"Yes, I can see that. I asked if you could please tell me the three categories of spirit experience."

I took a deep breath. Thank goodness I wasn't too distracted to recall the previous night's reading. "Yes, I can. The three categories of spirit experience are sensory, extrasensory, and emotional."

Siobhán nodded, but I knew I wasn't redeemed yet. "And can you explain them?"

"Yes," I said again. I laid down my pen, acutely aware that all eyes were on me. "Sensory experience is interaction with a spirit as perceived with the five senses and is by far the most common form. Extrasensory experience is information picked up through intuition or a form of non-sensory communication, such as Psychic Drawing. Emotional experience is the least common, and occurs when a spirit's emotions are transferred and felt by the person as if those feelings were their own. The Empath is the most obvious example of this."

Siobhán smiled at me, my distraction forgiven; the class turned their attention back to her now that the potential show of humiliation was over.

"None of you will find yourselves limited to one of these forms of communication. Most likely, you will experience all three at one time or another in your lives. Spirits, like people, have different personalities and abilities, and therefore they channel their energy in different ways. Some will be hesitant, even timid in their attempts to communicate with you; others with more forceful presences will find more powerful ways to get their points across.

We may find ourselves, at times, deeply affected by spirit communication, but remind yourselves that these experiences are the only chance a spirit has to find the help it needs."

Olivia raised her hand. "Is there any way for us to block spirit communication, if it gets too intense?"

Before she answered, Siobhán's eyes flicked briefly toward our table. "It is possible—temporarily and in extreme circumstances—to block spirit communication. It is rare, though, for such a circumstance to arise."

"But they do happen sometimes?" Olivia asked.

"Yes, on occasion," said Siobhán.

"So then, what can be done, in those rare circumstances?"

Siobhán glanced at us again, and suddenly I knew what she was going to say before she said it. "There is a Casting called a Binding, which will temporarily block all spirit communication from a Gateway, and which we will cover more extensively in a later class."

I looked at Hannah, whose expression had become frozen yet impassive. She was staring at a spot somewhere in the heart of the fireplace, giving every indication of someone who was not paying attention; a tiny muscle twitching in her jaw gave her away.

"But surely," Peyton began in an affected tone, "that can't be allowed. Isn't the whole point of our existence to be accessible to the spirits that need our help?"

Siobhán seemed to realize she was walking into a trap, but she also knew that ignoring the question would only have made Peyton's intentions more obvious.

"A Binding is certainly allowed as a last resort, when all other means to help the spirit in question have been exhausted, but, even then, a Binding is allowed only for a short period of time. There are several types of Bindings and various situations in which using one would be entirely appropriate, as long as it is removed promptly."

"What happens if someone performs a Binding and just leaves it in place?" Peyton asked. Her voice was dripping with an avid curiosity that I knew she did not feel: She knew the answer to this question. Everyone in the room knew the answer to this question, with perhaps the exception of Savvy and Phoebe, who didn't yet know the full story of our family's fall from grace.

Siobhán sighed but answered. "A prolonged Binding can result in great turmoil for the spirits who are being denied access to the Gateway. They build up, like a traffic jam, with nowhere to go. It can cause a ripple effect through the Gateway system and create great unrest and instability."

"Wow," Peyton sighed. With an obviously loaded tone, she turned to Olivia and continued her playacting. "I can't believe anyone could ever do such a thing, can you?"

"I can't imagine," Olivia said, nodding gravely, but with a malicious light in her dark eyes, "that any one of us could be so selfish as to jeopardize the entire system like that."

"I agree, but," Peyton's eyes lit up as though she had only just remembered something, "isn't that exactly what Jess and Hannah's mother did?"

"That's quite enough, ladies. I will tolerate no harassment in this class. You are passing judgment on a matter about which you understand little, and you are getting us off topic," Siobhán said gravely before continuing on with her lecture. She was now saying something about Empaths, but all I could hear was the blood pounding in my ears. Olivia and Peyton were smiling smugly now, basking in the smirks and giggles coming from their surrounding entourage of lemmings.

If my face had been pink before, it was a flaming scarlet now. I could've flung my notebook straight at one of their faces.

I was still seething when the bell sounded. I threw my stuff into my bag and stood up. Hannah hadn't moved.

"I have to book it if I'm going to be on time for Fiona," I said to her. "Are you going to be okay?"

"Yes," she said tonelessly.

I didn't believe her, but there was nothing I could do about it now. I turned to shuffle up the aisle and almost walked into Finn.

"Can I help you?" I asked, in a tone that actually said, "Get the hell away from me and mind your own damn business."

"No," he said. "I just wanted to know if you..." he looked at my face and seemed to lose his nerve, "if she was holding up." He jutted his square chin in Hannah's direction.

"She's fine," I said. "She's tougher than she looks."

"Good," he said. "You should probably get used to it. They're not going to let up."

"Very encouraging, thanks," I said.

He stalked away without another word. I watched his retreat, feeling even angrier. Finn's social skills were so abysmal that I honestly couldn't tell whether he'd been trying to show concern or add insult to injury.

I turned toward Hannah again and saw, with surprise, that Siobhán was packing up her things as though to leave the classroom.

"Aren't you having your mentor meeting now?" I asked.

"I'm not going to be Hannah's mentor anymore," said Siobhán.

"What? Why not?" I asked.

"As I was just telling her, Finvarra was able to secure her a new mentor, now that her gift as a Caller has been discovered. Hannah needs to be with someone who can help her to explore those abilities."

"But she said that there have only been three other Callers in the last hundred years," I raised my eyebrow. "Who is her new mentor?"

"Call the devil, and the devil shall appear," said a silky voice from the doorway. I turned and saw Lucida lounging languidly against the doorframe.

"You?" I cried, with an undisguised animosity in my voice. "No! Why does it have to be you?"

"Now now, Jess, calm down," Lucida said, as an amused smile toyed with the corners of her full lips. "I might start to think you aren't fond of me."

"You know perfectly well I'm not fond of you," I shot back.

"Jessica," Siobhán said sharply, "That is no way to talk to your elders."

"This elder," I said, turning to Siobhán in outrage, "broke into my house in the middle of the night and turned my life upside down."

"The window was open, dear; it was as good as an invitation," said Lucida. "And it wasn't me who turned your life upside down. Your life already was upside down—I simply... alerted you to the situation."

I turned away from her and addressed Siobhán. "Why does she have to be Hannah's mentor? Why can't they get someone else?"

"As I've just explained to you," Siobhán said curtly, "Hannah needs someone who can help her with her gift, and Lucida is the only person who can do that. She is the only other known Caller alive today."

My mouth dropped open in shock. Hannah, who had been silent through the entire exchange, spoke for the first time.

"You're a Caller? Like me?" she asked, with wonder in her voice.

"That's right, love," Lucida said, smiling at her. "Two of a kind, we are. You could've knocked me flat with a feather when Finvarra told me."

I looked back and forth between the two of them, shaking my head.

"Finvarra has asked Lucida to step away from her other Durupinen duties and consent to take on the role of Hannah's mentor, and she has most kindly agreed to do so," Siobhán explained. "I'm sure that she and Hannah will get along just fine. Hannah will benefit greatly from Lucida's guidance."

Lucida gave Siobhán an elaborate bow of sorts. "Cheers for that vote of confidence, Siobhán. I think we'll be great chums, me and Hannah. Lots to talk about, eh?"

"Oh yeah, I suppose you'll get all your juicy details now, right Lucida?" I spat.

"What details?" Hannah asked, frowning. "What do you—"

"Does Karen know about this?" I plowed on.

"I believe she's been told, yes," Siobhán said.

"And what did she have to say about it?"

"Nothing that will make the slightest bit of difference to the necessity of the situation," Siobhán said quellingly. "Now I must insist that you reconsider your attitude toward this arrangement, Jessica, as it shan't change in the face of your disapproval. Lucida is by far the most qualified and appropriate mentor your sister could have. I would think you'd be pleased, for your sister's sake, that she will have the chance to develop and learn about this most rare of gifts."

I bit my lip. I looked at Hannah, and thought there was a hint of something accusatory in her eyes. An instant later I was convinced I had imagined it. "Of course I am."

"Well, then," Siobhán said, "let's have no more of these objections. Now, I believe you have your own mentor meeting to attend."

"Off you trot," said Lucida, with a Cheshire cat smile.

There was nothing else I could do. I turned on my heel and walked out of the room as Lucida sauntered further into it. My feet carried me all the way to Fiona's tower automatically, while my mind seethed. Of all the people to subject Hannah to, why did it have to be Lucida? Hannah needed support and encouragement;

she needed to be handled gently so that the tenuous grasp she had on this new world wasn't shattered before it had a chance to strengthen. But instead, she was going to be mocked and made to feel like a freak by someone who had no regard for her feelings or her mental well-being. I felt so helpless I could've screamed.

Instead I yelled, "Milo!"

"Yes?" His voice came from so close behind me that I shrieked.

"Don't do that!" I cried.

"You're the one who called me!" said Milo, with a not-so-innocent smile on his face. "If this is the thanks I get for being a prompt and attentive Spirit Guide, I'll just ignore you next time."

I decided not to play into his banter, as I was already late. "I need you to go keep an eye on Hannah."

My words wiped the smile cleanly from Milo's face. "Why? What's wrong?"

"They assigned her a new mentor today. Her name is Lucida, and she's an absolute bitch. I'll explain more later, but they're meeting right now in Siobhán's room. Can you please just go down there and make sure Hannah's okay?"

"Of course," he said, and vanished at once. He reappeared an instant later. "Thank you for alerting me," he said quite seriously.

I nodded. "You're her best friend. If I think she's in trouble, you'll always be my first call."

He smiled at me—a genuine smile, without a trace of irony or attitude... which, I noted, was a first.

He started to shimmer out of view when a sudden thought occurred to me. "Milo, one more thing."

"Yeah?"

"Have you had any luck figuring out who that little girl ghost is, the one I asked you about?"

Milo sagged a little. "No, and I've been trying, I swear. She's been here longer than all the ghosts I've talked to, so none of them know who she was when she was alive. I've seen her a few times, but she scampers away every time I try to talk to her."

"Okay, thanks," I said. "I appreciate it."

"No problem. I'm off to check on our girl," he said, and vanished again. I relaxed a little bit—enough, at least, to move Hannah to the back of my mind and concentrate my energy on what was sure to be another strange and mildly terrifying mentor meeting with Fiona.

§

I'd had three more classes with Fiona since we'd met. In the first, she had ignored me for the first half an hour while she stared, muttering, at a partially formed sculpture. Then she'd handed me a pad of paper and a pencil, pointed at a bowl of fruit set up in the corner, and said, "Have a go at that." I had spent the rest of the class attempting a still life of the fruit while she chain-smoked and carried on her one-sided dialogue with the sculpture.

During the second meeting, I handed in the still life. She had taken one cursory look at it, snorted, crumpled it up, and tossed it on the floor. Then she had stalked over to the bowl of fruit and knocked the whole thing over. The bowl shattered; fruit rolled in every direction. At this point she had bent down, scooped up a single apple, and put it back on the table in front of me. "Just this," she said, and started to walk away. Then she turned back, snatched up the apple, took a huge bite out of it, and replaced it. She didn't talk to me for the rest of the class, but instead had alternated between eating bruised fruit off of the floor and chiseling away at her sculpture, which was starting to take the shape of a woman in long, sweeping robes.

During the third class, she had forced me to sit, with my eyes closed and pencil and paper in hand, in front of a huge oil painting of a woman. No matter how many times I asked her what I should've been doing, she just shushed me and said, "Just listen to what she's got to say to you." But with no further illumination on how exactly to do this, I had sat there like an idiot for a full hour, trying to sense someone or something that absolutely refused to be sensed.

Finally I had given up, shoved the paper into my bag, and stood up. "This is pointless," I told her bluntly. "I'm getting nothing. Absolutely nothing."

Fiona then looked up from the painting she had been restoring, with her eyes bizarrely magnified from behind a pair of restoration goggles. "Good. You can go."

"Good? I just sat there for a whole hour and got nothing. How can that be good? What am I supposed to be sensing? Who is she?"

"She's nobody," said Fiona, her nose an inch from the canvas. "There's no spirit attached to that painting."

I threw my hands up in exasperation. "So what the hell did you have me do that for?"

"To keep you honest," she said. "Congratulations. You aren't full of shite."

That day, I was the one who had come dangerously close to throwing furniture.

At the end of each class, I was sure Fiona would tell me to leave and not come back, but each week, just as the door was about to creak shut behind me, she'd say, "Next week, same time."

I left Fiona's studio each week relieved that I had a whole week ahead of me before I had to see her again—as well as somewhat surprised that I had, in fact, survived the encounter without grievous bodily harm. But, as always, "next week" came surprisingly quickly.

This meeting was our fifth session. I knocked on the tower door and opened it without waiting, as Fiona rarely bothered to open it herself. At first glance, it seemed she wasn't there. Then my gaze fell to the floor.

I gasped.

Fiona was sprawled across the bare stone floor. She was twitching from head to foot, and her eyes had rolled back into her head.

"Oh my God! Fiona!" I dashed to her side and fell to my knees. My hands hovered helplessly above her for a moment, as I racked my brain trying to decide what to do.

I saw with relief that Fiona was obviously breathing; her chest was rising and falling, and her mouth was moving rapidly in a silent stream of words.

I reached down and shook her shoulders. "Fiona? Can you hear me?"

No response.

I rocked back on my heels and ran a frantic hand through my hair. Should I go get help? What if she swallowed her tongue or something while I was gone?

I shouted straight into her ear, "Fiona! FIONA!"

Her expression changed; her eyebrows contracted. My pulse quickened. She must have heard me. I looked around for something, anything, to rouse her. I ran over to the nearby desk and grabbed a large bowl of water that was beside some drying brushes and splashed it over her face.

With a sputtering, coughing gasp, Fiona sat up. Her eyes flew open; her hands swiped furiously at the water streaming down her face, then she pushed her sopping hair out of her eyes. She looked up and saw me.

"What the bloody *hell* do you think you're doing?" she shouted.

I backed away from her in surprise. "I... you... you were having some kind of seizure!"

"And so you thought the appropriate course of action was to drown me?" she yelled.

"I didn't know what to do!" I said, backing involuntarily away from the livid look on her face. "I thought you needed help! I was trying to wake you up!"

"Well, I'm good and awake now!" she cried. She jumped to her feet, a little unsteadily, and looked around, as if she had lost something. "Dogs!" she shouted.

"What are you looking for?"

"I'm looking to see if I managed to draw any of it before you blundered in and ruined everything!" she shot at me. She shook her fist combatively at me, and I saw a charcoal pencil clenched in it.

"Draw any of... huh?"

"Look! Use your bloody eyes, will you?" Fiona snapped, darting forward. She grabbed my upper arm, yanked me to my feet, and dragged me back to the spot where I'd found her. There on the stone, clearly unfinished, was a drawing.

I knelt down and examined it. It was hard to make out. The shapes in the background could have been trees or perhaps buildings, but they were obscured by the dark cloud of smoke rising from what was unmistakably a large and raging fire.

"What is this?" I asked.

"I'm not likely to find out now," Fiona grumbled, toweling off her hair with a spare smock.

"You were drawing this during that... seizure, or whatever it was?"

"It wasn't a seizure, it was Psychic Trance," Fiona said slowly and deliberately, as though this should have been obvious. "Spirit communication was being channeled through me."

"Well, how the hell was I supposed to know that?" I cried. "I walked in the room and you were thrashing around on the floor! I thought you were dying!"

Fiona opened her mouth to retort, but apparently there was a little too much logic in what I had just said; instead, she let out a frustrated sort of growl and stomped over to her desk. I decided the safest course of action was to stay where I was and not make any sudden movements until she calmed down. I watched as she rummaged around in an open trunk behind her desk and pulled out a dry, paint-spattered shirt. Finally she turned to me, and although her face was still a storm cloud, her voice had calmed down.

"It happens that way sometimes," she said, and, without warning, pulled her damp shirt over her head. She was wearing nothing under it. I quickly spun around and looked back at the strange, partially finished drawing. "If the vision is really strong, it blocks everything else out, and I collapse. Usually I can feel it coming, and can get to the floor safely first. Sometimes not, in which case I wake up with a bastard of a headache."

"And when you come to, you've drawn something?" I asked.

"Yes," Fiona said. "I don't remember a thing, though. The only clues I have to anything a spirit may have said or done or shown me is whatever I've managed to create… which, in this case," she added with a frown, "is almost nothing."

I chanced a look back at her. She was clothed again. "Look, I said I was sorry. But you at least should've warned me that might happen."

She ignored my apology. "So what did I get, then? Anything discernible?"

"It looks like a fire. A bad one," I said. "Do you know who the spirit was? Is this how they died?"

"I have no idea who it was, it just came on me. It isn't necessarily the way they died, no," Fiona said. She stood behind me, staring at the drawing. "Sometimes it takes several encounters or drawings for the meaning to become clear. Sometimes the meaning never becomes clear."

It was as though she flicked a switch in my head. "Is it possible this spirit is trying to communicate with more than one person?" I asked.

"Of course," Fiona said vaguely, still poring over the image on the floor. "Why?"

"Because I've got something to show you." I rose to retrieve my bag, which I had dropped unceremoniously in the doorway. I fished out my sketchbook, found the image I wanted, and thrust it at her.

It was the drawing I had done of the mute little girl who'd been following me; the wall of flames leapt around her on the page.

Fiona's sharp, dark eyes darted over the page. It took her a moment to absorb what she was seeing, then she snatched it from my hands.

"When did you do this?" she asked.

"A little over two weeks ago."

Fiona rounded on me ferociously. "You had a Psychic Drawing experience two weeks ago, and you never told me? Why the hell are we even bothering with this mentor bollocks if it takes you two weeks to show me something like this?"

"I didn't think it was a Psychic Drawing, not at the time, anyway. I was drawing the little girl from a clear visual—she was standing at the edge of the forest bordering the north garden. But then I realized that the forest I thought I'd been drawing was actually..." I gestured to the sketch again.

"The seventh circle of hell?" Fiona suggested.

"Something like that, yeah," I said.

"Hmm, fascinating," Fiona started wandering across the room with her face still buried in the picture. "Any idea who she is?"

My heart sank. "No. I was hoping you might. She follows me all over the school."

"Hang on," Fiona said slowly, and placed the sketchpad on her desk. She then, with surprising ease, retrieved a magnifying glass from her overstuffed desk drawer. "That's the Silent Child, isn't it?"

My pulse quickened with excitement. "Who's the Silent Child?"

"She's one of the resident spirits," Fiona said, still gazing her through the magnifying glass. "Been here for centuries."

"Why is she called the Silent Child?" I asked.

"She's never spoken a word to anyone. Never even tried to, as far as I know. That's where the nickname comes from, I expect."

"But do you know anything about who she was in life?"

"No one really does," Fiona said. "She's always kept to the shadows. She hides from anyone who tries to get near her. You say she's been following you around?"

"Yes! And trying to communicate with me, but she doesn't seem able to."

"She's probably lost the ability to communicate," Fiona said. "That can happen, you know. Their energy can weaken over time, and she's been here quite a spell."

"I don't know. She doesn't seem weak to me," I said, remembering how the little girl had barreled me over with the sheer force of her being.

"I wonder what's suddenly drawn her to you, after so many years of silence?" Fiona asked, looking at me with a budding interest—almost as though she'd only just noticed I was there.

"I'm sure she would tell me, if she could," I said.

"And you say the flames were unintentional?"

"I thought I'd drawn the forest behind her. I didn't even recognize that I'd drawn the flames until Hannah looked over and pointed them out to me. I was focused so intently on her face that I didn't concentrate on anything else very much."

"Fascinating," Fiona said again, tracing a finger along the tips of the leaping flames. "Quite fascinating... Well, what you describe is common to the Psychic Drawing experience, so I suppose first I ought to say congratulations. I think we can safely say that you are indeed a Muse."

This lifted me out of my brooding. "Really?"

"Oh yes, I think so," Fiona said. "Which means that we are definitely stuck with each other for the rest of your time here."

I don't know exactly what in my expression betrayed of my thoughts about this, but Fiona seemed amused by it. She certainly smiled for the first time since I'd arrived. "We'll have to spend our time exploring this aspect of your artistic penchants for now, and get back to the basics later—however badly you may need them."

"You mean no more fruit?" I asked.

"No more fruit."

"Hallelujah."

§

"I don't know what the problem is," Hannah said as we climbed into bed that night. "Lucida was really nice to me."

"As long as she keeps being nice to you, then I guess there isn't a problem," I replied.

"But why do you hate her so much?" Hannah persisted. "She was the one who tracked me down and told you where I was."

"I know that," I said. "And for that reason, I guess I'll always owe her. But you don't understand what she was like when I met her. Karen and I were both so upset and she just seemed to... enjoy it a little too much."

"Why would she do that?

"I don't know. Why does anyone do anything?" I said, my voice rising. "She just rubs me the wrong way, okay? I know that she's your mentor now, but that doesn't mean I have to like her, does it?"

"I guess not," Hannah said. Her voice sounded especially tiny, hurt.

I sighed. "I'm sorry. I'm not trying to… I want you to be happy that she's your mentor. If she's being nice to you now, that's all I really care about. As long as she's helping you, the rest doesn't matter."

We lay for several minutes in the dark. I thought Hannah had fallen asleep.

"How was your mentor session?"

"It was… fine," I said, after a moment's hesitation. "Fiona didn't throw anything at me, so I guess that's progress. And she didn't crumple up my drawing this week."

"That's great," Hannah said. "See? Maybe both of our mentors will turn out better than you expected."

"Yeah, maybe," I said.

I wasn't sure why I didn't tell Hannah about the Psychic Drawing and Fiona's trance. Maybe I didn't want to scare her. Maybe I needed a little more time to process it myself before I was ready to share it with anyone else. Whatever it was, I promised myself that I would only give it until the next day to work its way out of my system. Not telling Hannah felt like lying; the last thing I wanted to do was widen the space between us, even by the micro-width of a small lie.

I rolled over and dozed off within minutes. When I awoke abruptly, several hours later, I was sure it was because my tangled web of thoughts had spawned a terrible nightmare.

But it wasn't a nightmare at all.

The hands that grabbed my arms and forced them behind my back were real. So was the fabric stuffed roughly into my mouth. And before I could make out more than a mass of dark, moving shapes, a bag was forced over my head and everything was darkness.

10

HAZING

FOR A MOMENT, I was a flailing mess of sheer animal panic. Then my brain detached from my panic and started trying to identify any details that could help me figure out what the hell was going on.

The hands that were binding my wrists together were small and soft. Long hair was brushing against my leg. Several voices hissed sharply at each other; they were definitely female voices. Young female voices.

"You're tying it too tight!" one of them rasped.

"No, I'm not!" snapped another, as I felt a sharp tug on the fabric now twisted around my wrists. "We don't want her to get out of these, do we?"

The girl nearest my face was laughing. Her breath smelled of cheap wine. I'd know that smell anywhere—I associated the odor with a warped sort of nostalgic comfort, like the way others experienced the smell of campfire smoke or Christmas cookies. I inhaled it as if it were a calming aroma, and I composed myself enough to figure out what was happening. We weren't being kidnapped or murdered by random lunatics. These were some of the other Apprentices, and we were being hazed—hazed like pledges in the most disturbing sorority of all time. Worst of all, this was a sorority we didn't even want to join. Even as hatred for these girls coursed through my veins, I had to admit they had flair; I had no idea what twisted traditions Fairhaven had for this kind of thing, but I could pretty much guarantee that the night wasn't going to include keg stands or naked streaking across the sprawling lawns.

I could hear Hannah struggling and whimpering beside me. I tried to make some sort of reassuring sound for her, but it was all I could do not to gag on the wad of fabric in my mouth, which was very rough and tasted like cardboard.

Hands were all over me, grabbing me under my armpits and around my legs. I tried to kick out, but one of them laid herself across my legs while another tied my ankles together. My feet immediately started to tingle from the restricted blood flow. I twisted back and forth, trying to throw them off, but there were too many of them.

"Just stop struggling," one of them breathed in my ear. "We're going to do it anyway, and you'll just hurt yourself."

If she, whoever she was, were trying to reassure me, she was doing a terrible job. I was filled with a renewed flutter of panic as I contemplated all the horrors that "we're going to do it anyway" might entail.

Someone pulled me clean off the edge of the bed and I landed hard on the floor.

"Shit, ouch! I thought you said you had her?"

"I do have her! You're the one that dropped her. Get her arm!"

Our captors lifted me off the rug and began—with difficulty—to half-carry, half drag me out of our room and down the hallway. I kept struggling in earnest until we reached the stairs, and then calmed myself, afraid that one wrong move would throw my kidnappers off balance and send us all toppling down to the stone floor below.

Our pack of kidnappers continued out the front doors and across the lawns. The night air carried no residual warmth from the damp, clammy day; the heat had drained from the world with the sunlight, and I shivered violently in my thin T-shirt and shorts as we made our awkward, painful way across the lawns. I had little sense of direction even in the best of circumstances, but now—trussed up and hauled around like this—I had no idea which way we were going until their footsteps took on a muffled, shuffling quality. I knew they were now dragging us through the thick, mulch-like layer of fallen leaves that covered the forest floor.

Finally, we came to a halt. Our captors continued to whisper. I heard a crackling, then the almost-sweet smell of smoke found its way to my nose. I was roughly lowered to the ground, landing hard on a rock. Ignoring my cry of pain, my captors pulled me up and forced me into a kneeling position. Then all the girls' hands fell away, and all around me I heard retreating footsteps. Then nothing. For one long moment, there was no sounds at all save my own ragged breathing and Hannah's whimpering beside me. Then the bag was whipped off my head and the fabric pulled from my mouth.

I looked around me. Hannah had been forced into the same kneeling position as I was. She was rocking back and forth, self-soothing, and I realized that her whimpering was actually a quiet song. We were in the woods on the grounds, in a sunken clearing. All around us were ruins of what might once have been a walled enclosure or small building. Around the outskirts of the clearing stood a dozen figures, clad in long, dark, hooded robes and carrying torches. Each face was hidden behind a mask. Each mask was identical—blank and porcelain-doll-like, with wide blank eyes, rosy cheeks, and perfect pouting lips.

If I hadn't already suspected who was behind those masks, I might have died of fright right then and there. Hannah was so pale in her terror that she looked as though she had died already.

I swallowed hard and spoke, hoping my voice would sound steadier than my nerves felt. "What the hell is this, *Valley of the Dolls*? Congratulations, you scared the crap out of us, and you are officially the creepiest fucking things I've ever seen. Now enough already, okay? Joke's over."

All around us, the masked faces shook back and forth in silence. I could actually feel a phobia of dolls forming in my psyche.

For what felt like an eternity, the figures stared down at us as the firelight played on their fixed, waxen features. Then a voice rang out from a masked figure to our right.

"You find yourselves, sisters of the gift, within the walls of the ancient Fairhaven *Príosún*. You have been brought to this place because it has been determined that you must answer for the transgressions of your clan."

"We don't need to answer for anything! Untie us now!" I demanded.

"You have not been granted permission to speak," the same voice said.

"We don't need permission to speak!" I shouted. "Let us out of here now. This isn't funny!"

The figures didn't move, but from somewhere to our left I heard two of the girls sniggering. Then the same voice began speaking again.

"Your clan has shirked its duties. You have shamed the Durupinen and abandoned the spirits. As your peers, we invoke the ancient right to call judgment down upon you and sentence you to retribution on behalf of the many souls who have suffered at the hands of your clan's negligence."

"We haven't done anything!" Hannah called out in a cracked voice. "It wasn't our decision. Our mother was the one who—"

"It doesn't matter," I said to Hannah. "They know all of that, and they don't care. This is just their sick way of keeping the upper hand."

The same voice went on as though we hadn't spoken. The more she said, the more I was pretty damn sure who the ringleader of this stunt actually was. "Because your clan has hidden in such shame, it's probable that you don't know what this place is for. The Fairhaven *Príosún* was the site of trial and punishment for the Northern Clans for many centuries. Within these walls, many prisoners, Durupinen and enemies alike, have faced terrible fates at the hands of the Elemental."

An expectant silence followed these words. Hannah and I looked blankly at each other.

"Did you hear what I said?" the voice demanded.

"Oh, are we allowed to talk now?" I asked. "Are we supposed to react to this? We don't know what an Elemental is."

"The Elemental is an ancient being, older than mankind itself," another voice chimed in from behind us. She sounded like she was reciting from a textbook. "It is fear and horror and anger. It is beast and spirit. It dwells within those very walls, and what it may do to you, none of us can tell."

A few more scattered peals of laughter. One of the figures stumbled, snorting and giggling. "Shh! Shut up!" the girl beside her hissed.

"If you survive the night," the first voice said, "Your penance will be paid and you will be released at dawn. If not... well, your penance will still be paid."

More titters met these words. A few of them attempted a spooky "Woooooo!" but the effect was spoiled by their inability to control their laughter.

By this point, my fear had transformed completely into anger. It was obvious that no one here actually thought this so-called Elemental was real, and that the real intention was to leave us both to freeze our asses off in the woods for the night.

"A Casting has been placed around the borders of the *Príosún*.

You cannot leave until the sun comes up," the second voice said. She raised her hands above her head. "So it is decreed."

"So it shall be," the others responded, slightly out of sync.

I looked around. In the wavering torchlight, I could just make out runes, drawn in a white powder, all along the outside of the stone enclosure. I recognized a few runes from class, and my heart sank as I realized we probably really would be stuck out here all night. Well played, sorority sisters from hell: Well played.

Then came renewed laughter. Several of the voices called out to us.

"Nighty-night!"

"Sweet dreams, girls!"

The circle around us started to break up into groups of two and three, each group chatting quietly with each other. A few had actually turned to leave when the first voice rang out again.

"I will now complete the Casting to call forth the Elemental," she said, pulling a small leather book and pouch from the folds of her robe.

Everyone stopped. All of the figures turned to look at her.

"Peyton, what are you doing?" one of them said. Every trace of amusement had drained from her voice, and I noticed her slip—Peyton was indeed the ringleader. Peyton said nothing, but began rummaging in the pouch. All around her, the other girls' voices were rising anxiously.

"Wait, what is she doing?"

"She's not serious, is she?"

"Okay, Peyton, very funny, now let's go."

Peyton pulled a black candle from her pouch and lit it with the flame of the nearest torch. "We said they needed to be taught a lesson."

"Yeah, and we all agreed it would be funny to leave them here," another girl said. As she turned away from us to face Peyton, her hood fell back and I recognized Róisín's raven-colored hair. "We never said anything about Summoning the Elemental."

"I'm improvising," Peyton said, flipping open her book and searching for the right page.

The tension was palpable now. The girls who had been laughing a moment ago were shifting uncomfortably from foot to foot, or else standing frozen with their eyes glued on Peyton.

"We shouldn't mess with the Elemental," Róisín said, with an even greater anxiety in her voice. "Seriously, no one has Summoned it in a really long time. We don't know what will happen."

Peyton began chanting quietly, dropping small stones to the ground around her.

Róisín turned tail and fled. Her retreat sparked a full-on panic, like a fire that starts as a tiny smolder and builds into a raging inferno. The other girls called out to one another.

"She's not really doing it, is she?"

"It's not going to do anything, is it? It's a myth, right?"

"I don't know, but I don't really want to find out."

"Someone stop her!"

"I'm getting out of here."

"Me too, let's go!"

Peyton continued to chant. One by one, the other girls fled from the clearing and were swallowed immediately by the darkness of the forest. Soon, only one figure—evidently torn between escaping and witnessing what, if anything would actually happen—remained behind; finally, Olivia tore off her mask and scampered over to Peyton.

I looked over at Hannah, who was working her feet and hands desperately against the fabric, trying in vain to loosen her bonds. Her expression spurred me into action—I scooted over to her on my knees and positioned myself so that we were back-to-back. I found her hands with my own scrabbling fingers and squeezed them.

"Stop moving," I said as calmly as I could. "Let me try to untie them."

Hannah instantly went as still as a rabbit that had spotted a predator. I began to work blindly at the knots.

"What's happening?" Hannah asked quietly.

"I don't know," I said, tugging at a loose loop of fabric. "Maybe nothing. Maybe something really bad."

Peyton's voice suddenly rose to a wail and then stopped. She raised the candle and circled it over her head three times before blowing it out. We all froze, waiting.

The torches flickered. The breeze rustled the trees. Nothing else whatsoever happened.

Peyton dropped her hands to her sides, looking for a strange moment like a depressed doll in an abandoned dollhouse. Then she gathered up her stones and turned to Olivia.

"It was worth a try," she said. "I just wanted to scare them anyway."

"I did too, but that's no reason to mess with stuff like the—"

"Oh shut up, Olivia. It was just a joke," Peyton said dismissively. She turned back to us, and with a twisted glee hidden in her voice, she bade us goodnight. "Sleep tight ladies. We'll try to remember to come back for you in the morning."

The two of them turned and walked away. The wind carried snatches of their laughter back to us for several minutes after they vanished.

I let out a low, long sigh and turned my efforts back to Hannah's bonds. I had broken out in a cold sweat, which made it that much harder to work at the knots. Luckily, the other Apprentices were no Boy Scouts, and after a few more minutes I felt the fabric become loose and fall away.

Hannah let out a cry of relief and sniffled loudly. She untied her own legs quickly, and, as she turned to help me, I saw that her face was glazed with tears.

"Are you okay?" I asked.

"I hate her!" she cried.

"So do I. But every school has someone like Peyton. She's just a trumped-up little queen bee who can't—"

"I'm not talking about Peyton."

"Oh? Who are you talking about?"

"Never mind. It doesn't matter."

I opened my mouth to press the question, but at that moment my own hands came free; I let the subject drop and got to work on untying my ankles.

"Do you think we're really trapped in here until morning?" Hannah asked, as she stood up and began walking to the edge of the Circle.

"It's definitely possible if they did it right. This is probably one of the protective Castings we read about last week for Keira."

I stood up unsteadily. My legs felt like they were crawling with countless tiny, burrowing insects as the blood began to circulate freely again. I joined Hannah, who was examining the nearest rune by torchlight. I recognized it as the one Finn used during our first communication Circle. I was pretty sure the rune symbolized a lock, having recorded it on a flashcard a few nights ago—along with about a hundred other runes we were supposed to have memorized by the end of the next week.

"What do you think would happen if we tried to walk out?" Hannah asked.

"Only one way to find out," I said. I picked my way along the border of stones until I found a gap. I took a deep breath and tried to step across the Circle.

All sense of where I was and what I was doing melted away. My vision spun and my ears were filled with a deafening, rushing sound. The very air I was trying to breathe turned solid around me, crushing down on me from all angles. I was filled with a fear so absolute that I could not master it: Terrible, terrible things would happen if I left this space. I could not go on. I could not face whatever was out there. I wrenched my foot away from the gap and fell backward.

"Jess! What happened?" Hannah cried, coming to kneel beside me.

"I don't know." I shook my head to clear it, but the moment I had stepped back into the Circle, the chaos had all stopped. "That was really weird. I think it's a psychic barrier, not a physical one. It felt like it was my own fear keeping me inside here."

Hannah stared at the spot where I had tried to cross. "Do you think I should try it? Maybe from the other side?" She half-rose, but I grabbed her arm.

"No," I said firmly. "No, that was... you really don't want to experience that, trust me. I think we are stuck here until morning, like they said. Unless—" I said, with sudden inspiration, "can you find Milo? He could go for help!"

Hannah bit her lip. "I don't think I can. I was trying to when we first got here, but I can't find him. Everything is really fuzzy and unfocused. I think it might be part of that psychic barrier. I'm sorry, I should have connected with him while they were dragging us out here, but I was just too panicked. I wasn't thinking straight."

"Don't. This isn't your fault. I was panicking too," I said, but my heart sank. "So, what about Calling other spirits?"

I held my breath as Hannah closed her eyes and went perfectly still with concentration. Thirty seconds later, her eyes fluttered open and she shook her head. "I can't pick up on a single one. It's all a big haze."

Hannah seemed to deflate. She sunk back onto the ground and

pulled her knees up under her chin like a small child. The moonlight highlighted the many scars on her wrists and forearms as she wrapped her arms around her legs and hugged them to her chest.

We sat together in the dark and the cold. It was probably good that we were stuck here, because if we could make it back to the castle now, I might just kill someone. When was it going to end? Were we ever going to be accepted here? Would we ever stop being punished for transgressions we didn't even understand? It was probably too much to hope that all would be forgiven once we came out on the other side of this sick ritual. I couldn't imagine Peyton or any of the others getting in trouble for this; they'd just hide behind the skirts of the older Council members and claim it was a harmless joke, a nod to an ancient, twisted tradition. The more I thought about the injustice of it, the more I seethed.

I didn't say any of this to Hannah. There was no point in bothering to articulate what I knew we were both feeling—anger and despair, sadness and helplessness. It was... *absolutely delicious*.

I bolted upright. The thought had not been mine. I had no idea where it came from.

"Did you feel that?" I asked.

Hannah looked up. "Feel what?"

"That... *something*. I was just thinking about how pissed off I am and then... something was there. It was like another thought dropped into my head!"

Hannah lifted her chin from her arms. "Who's thought? What are you talking about Jess?"

"I don't know." My eyes scanned the *Príosún*. "I was just thinking about how angry I am, and suddenly..." I couldn't describe it. This thing, whatever it was, was a strange, indefinable violation—a hijacking of my train of thought. My heart began to race and my pulse quickened.

"We can hear it, faster and faster, the galloping beat of it..."

I leapt to my feet. "What the hell?" I spun on the spot, probing the darkness with my eyes, my ears, my thoughts. Nothing.

"Jess you're scaring me," Hannah said, her voice becoming shrill. "What is it? Do you sense a spirit?"

"It scares the other, how delightful."

"We taste it, the cresting, the breaking."

This time it was Hannah who jumped up. "Who said that? Who's here?"

But I'd heard it too, as a seamless part of my own thoughts. "What did it say? What did you hear?" I asked.

"Something about breaking and cresting, or..." Hannah's voice shivered and died away as she looked at me. "Is that what you heard?"

"Yeah," I said. "It... it must be a ghost, right?"

"I'm not sure. I still don't sense one, do you?"

"No," I admitted. "But maybe it's using another form of communication? Maybe this is an emotional spirit experience? I've never had one before."

"I have," Hannah said. "Plenty of times. That was... different."

"It builds and, ah! The intertwining tendrils of it, it finds us, it feeds us.

"We longed for it so. It fills us, it feeds us."

A sudden wave of dizziness swept over at me. I stumbled into Hannah, who grabbed onto my arm to steady me even as she began to sway dangerously herself.

"I feel weak," I said. I swallowed back the urge to be sick.

"I can feel it, too. What's going on?"

"Ah, sustenance! Shall we dance with them? Shall we play?"

"Oh, let's indeed! To dance, to walk, to feel and feed."

I exhaled sharply, and felt an indefinable something ride away on my breath, a something I didn't know had been there until it suddenly wasn't. Hannah gasped, then wretched beside me.

One cracking footstep in the leaves. One quiet whisper of laughter.

We looked up at the creature before us. Instantly, every element of the night seemed to go utterly still; motes of pollen hung in the motionless torchlight, and the constant hushed murmur of the living forest instantly extinguished. The most unnatural of silences.

At first glance, the figure was a woman, and for a split second I was very relieved to see a form so familiar and human—the long pale legs, the wisps of hair, the suggestion of garments hanging from her body—but in the next moment, I knew that I'd never seen anything less human.

The figure emanated its own light, which pulsed and undulated fluidly as it moved. Images rippled over the planes of its limbs and through the glittering hints of its garments. The images were so quick, so fleeting, that my eyes couldn't decode them; instead, I felt them. Each image was a disconnected flash of pain and fear and every powerful negative emotion I'd ever experienced... plus a few I'd only imagined.

Whatever this creature was, it had a face. Many faces, actually. A constantly morphing collection of features—some of them human, some of them bestial, some of them something else entirely—flickered and melted and reformed themselves constantly. It was the most terrifying thing I'd ever seen.

A fear filled me that no scream could ever express. I didn't need Hannah's whispered words to understand what had entered into the Circle with us.

"The Elemental."

It walked toward us with the very real sound of live footsteps, but the Elemental never actually made contact with the ground. Frozen by my own fear, this creature could have continued forward until it was upon me, but it stopped a few feet away from us and tilted its head, considering us with its ever-changing faces.

From some previously untapped spring of courage, I retrieved my voice and spoke. "What do you want from us?"

"We have what we want. You are giving it to us. We feast upon it."

Its voice, like its face, was multi-faceted—at once singular and yet made up of a strange cacophony of voices and sounds. I understood its words with my brain rather than my ears.

"I don't understand," I said. "What are we giving you?"

"It beats under your skin. It floods your thoughts and your form. Can't you feel it getting stronger? We can. Oh yes, we can."

I chanced a glance at Hannah, who, even in her terror, looked just as confused as I felt. I didn't want to press the thing into explaining itself—What if it got angry? I tried another question.

"What are you?"

The Elemental moved a few paces closer, with the sound of its footsteps slightly out of sync with its movement. For the merest trace of an instant, the Elemental was not a woman, but a creature... but before I could commit a single detail to memory, it was a woman once more.

"Many believe we were here first, and perhaps we were." With a sidestep, the Elemental began to circle us slowly, prowling. "We do not know how we began, for we are so many parts, and ever-changing. But we truly began to be with the first of the screams."

"What screams?" I asked.

"The screams." The Elemental waved its flickering arm, which flashed suddenly into something like a bat's wing and then back again. "The screams of this place. There was a time when we gorged ourselves—a time of glorious gluttony. So many prisoners, so much pain. So delectable."

Some part of it lashed at us, like the flicking of an enormous spectral tongue. And I felt something ineffable pulled from me, a theft that left me dizzy and breathless.

"Such familiar nectar."

The Elemental glowed a bit brighter as we gasped and staggered. As we cried out, it heaved with an animalistic moan of pleasure.

"They thought they had enslaved us, to punish and torture us. They did not know that they were nourishing us, creating this form with their beautiful cruelty."

The Elemental lashed at us again.

"Stop that!" I cried. "Leave us alone!"

"Hear how it pleads—positively dripping with it. Cannot. Will not. We will not return to the darkness and the famine. We must feed."

Hannah grabbed my arm. "It's FEAR!"

"What is?"

"It's... it's made of fear! Look at it. Listen to it!"

I looked back at the Elemental, trying to focus on the images that continued to flash through it. Most of the images were too muddled, but the longer I concentrated, the more I was able to discern. A hand trembling. A woman cowering, hiding her face. A pair of wide, terrified eyes. The same was there in the Elemental's voice too; the very fabric of its voice was woven from the screams and pleadings and whimpers of centuries of victims, all of which were all bound together in the Elemental itself. Realizing all this, my own fear heightened, and the Elemental lapped at me with an indecent relish.

"Oh my God."

"It's feeding on our fear!" Hannah said. "That's what it meant when it said we were giving it what it wanted. We were already afraid."

"Oh great," I whispered. "As long as we're afraid, it will keep feeding and getting stronger?"

"I think so," said Hannah.

"Swell," I said through clenched teeth. The Elemental lashed at us again. "So all we have to do is stop being afraid. No problem."

It was the ultimate endless loop of torment. A being that created and sharpened—by its very presence—the fear that it fed on. And we were trapped in the cycle.

"Okay. Okay, Hannah, let's think here. I know you can sense spirits and bring them to you. Have you ever tried to... send them away?" I asked.

Hannah frowned. "What do you mean? Like, expel them, like the Caomhnóir do?"

"Yeah, sort of like that."

Hannah shook her head. "I can persuade them to do the things I ask, sometimes. You've seen it; those ghosts at the hospital attacked the nurses because I asked them to. But I don't think the Elemental will be interested in any requests, do you?"

As though in response, the Elemental lashed out again. The force of it brought us both to our knees. My blood rushed loudly in my ears, thudding along with my racing pulse. The Elemental purred in terrible delight.

"If you were ever going to try, don't you think this would be the moment?" I asked breathlessly. "What've we got to lose?"

Hannah bit her lip and closed her eyes. I watched her anxiously, with my vision growing hazy around the periphery. After a few moments she opened her eyes again. "It's no use. I don't know exactly what the Elemental is, but it isn't a spirit. It was never human."

"They are sinking, sinking in it. Soon it will swallow them up, and so shall we."

And with the echoing joy of this thought, the Elemental's hair began to blow around its nightmare of a face; the tendrils came alive—floating toward us and riding on the currents of our own terror until they reached us. They snaked around our limbs, tightened around our throats, and knotted into our hair. We screamed and clawed at them, but they were as insubstantial to the touch as wisps of smoke. Yet the pain of them... Oh God, the pain.

I knew this was it. We would never see the morning. The Elemental would feed and feed upon us, its very presence spawning a steady supply of fear that would only increase until there was nothing left of us but empty shells, sucked dry to the last. I felt Hannah slip to the ground beside me, unconscious.

I wished, for the first time in my life, to die, and I could feel the Elemental smile at the taste of it. It tilted its head back and basked in its own power, drunk with it.

I closed my eyes. "Please just let us die," I thought.

"Despair is the sweetest of the sweet, my sweet."

Please...

§

"Jessica! Hannah!" Another voice was calling to me, a familiar one. But I was so deeply and firmly lost to the Elemental's grip that it was a moment before I knew the voice wasn't coming from inside my own head.

"Hannah! Jessica! Can you hear me?" it said.

"Yes!" I called out.

"It's Carrick! Finn is here with me!"

I opened my eyes. The edge of the clearing was blurred but visible. Two figures, one dark, one bright and wavering, stood between the torches. The reality of them fell like a heavy weight into my brain.

"Help us! Help us, please!" I cried. "It's the Elemental!"

"I know!" Carrick called back to me. "Finn and I are going to expel it, but we can't do it while it's feeding on you. Listen very carefully. It is latching onto your negative emotions. You've got to force it out with positive emotions."

"Are you telling me," I cried, panting with the incredible effort of focusing on him, "that I need to think a happy thought? This isn't fucking never-never land, Carrick! You've got to do something!"

The Elemental tightened its grip, perhaps sensing that my attention was focused elsewhere. Cradled in the curve of its terrible tentacle, I screamed again.

"There's nothing I can do yet!" shouted Carrick. "As long as you're focused on your pain and fear, it won't release you! All we need is a moment, one moment of positive energy, and it will weaken enough for us to expel it. You've got to try, Jessica!"

I rose onto trembling knees. I didn't think I had a single positive thought or feeling left in my body. I dug down into the empty pit in myself and came up with nothing but handfuls of darkness.

"I can't," I cried. "I can't do it. I've got nothing left."

"You *have* got something left!" Carrick shouted firmly. "And you will lose Hannah if you don't do this! Look at her! Look at your sister!"

I turned to Hannah; she lay curled on the ground just inches from me. With a greater effort than anything had ever cost me, I reached across to her and clasped her hand in mine. An unbidden, unsummoned love for her rose up in me so powerfully that I couldn't breathe.

We would not lose each other again.

The icy grip holding me slackened.

"Now!" Carrick shouted.

A dreadful echoing scream filled the night, mounting to the skies, and a powerful gust of wind swept the clearing. Then, with a rustle of settling leaves, warm, throbbing life flooded back into the Circle again.

The relief was instant and all encompassing. The pain that had been crippling me moments before vanished, leaving not a trace behind; as I clambered to my feet, I felt steady.

I turned to see Hannah pulling herself into a sitting position. "I think I passed out. Where did it go?"

"You did, but it's okay. The Elemental's gone."

She looked frantically around the Circle for a full thirty seconds before she seemed to accept my words. "How in the world, did you—"

"I didn't." It was Finn and Carrick." I pointed to the Circle's boundary, where Finn was crouched on the ground, hastily scrawling something in the dirt. Carrick stood over him, instructing. Then the torches around us all went out at once, plunging us into pitch darkness.

"It's quite alright!" came Carrick's measured, soothing voice. "That was us. The breaking of the Circle put out the torches. Just stay where you are a moment, we're coming to get you."

There was the distinct snap of a match and a tiny flare of firelight, and then I saw Finn stepping over the stone wall with one of the relit torches in his hand. Carrick floated along behind him. They reached us just as I bent to help Hannah to her feet; Finn caught her under the elbow and lifted her with me.

"Are you both alright?" he asked gruffly.

"Yes, I think so," Hannah said. There was a wonder in her voice as she said it, as though she couldn't quite believe that she was safe.

Finn looked at me expectantly. I nodded curtly. While the Elemental had been menacing us, I would've given anything for help to arrive in any form; now that I'd been freed, I felt nothing but mortification at Finn being one who had found us. Why, why did it have to be him, this protector I didn't want... but apparently needed?

"Where's the Elemental now?" Hannah asked.

"It won't be able to approach this place for a good while," Finn said. "The expulsion Casting will take days to wear off."

"How did you find us?" I asked. I was too embarrassed to look Finn in the eye, so I addressed my question to Carrick instead.

"I've been keeping an eye on you," Carrick said, and then added hastily, "at Finvarra's request, of course. Fairhaven has a long history of welcoming rituals, not all of them very welcoming in nature. We had a feeling that something like this might be in the works. Although," and he shook his head, "I must admit I never imagined they would have the nerve, or indeed information enough, to attempt Summoning the Elemental."

"That wasn't part of their plan," I said. "At least, they hadn't agreed on it. That part was Peyton's extra special touch. The rest of them went running when they saw what she was trying to do. Peyton didn't think it had worked... there was a few minutes between her Summoning and its arrival. But, yeah, the Elemental makes a quiet entrance."

"That doesn't surprise me," Finn said flatly. "Peyton has always had a flair for the dramatic. It's only gotten worse as she's gotten older."

Carrick glanced sharply at Finn. "Finn, I realize Peyton is your cousin, and so there's a certain degree of familiarity, but it is not in our code to speak ill of the Durupinen."

Finn hung his head. "Yes sir."

Carrick turned back to me. "You see, I saw the others emerging from the wood and had a hunch about what might be afoot. By the time I reached this place, the Elemental had already begun to feed. There was nothing I could do to help you without a true physical form, so I went for Finn. Protecting you is, after all, his duty now.

But he was already on his way. One of the girls had panicked and went to fetch him."

"You're kidding!" I said. "Who was it?"

"Róisín Lightfoot," answered Finn. "She pointed me in the direction of the *Príosún*, then went back to the castle. I think she was too scared to come back here. Then Carrick found me at the edge of the wood and showed me what to do."

"Right" I said, somewhat stiffly. "Well... thank you."

"Yes, thank you," Hannah added. "I don't want to think what would've happened if you hadn't showed up."

Finn just grunted and waved us off. We all trudged up out of the clearing together and onto the path, with Finn lighting the way ahead of us with the torch.

"I don't want you to have a false impression of what the Elemental would have done to you," Carrick said briskly as we walked. "The Elemental is a physical manifestation of negative emotions—specifically, pain and fear. It feeds on these emotions, as you have unfortunately learned firsthand. But it cannot really harm you, not in a physical sense, unless you allow it."

I scowled at him. "I was feeling pretty damn harmed."

Carrick very nearly smiled. "I don't mean to minimize the horror of your experience. But the pain was an illusion. How do you feel now?"

I considered. "Completely fine. Tired, but fine."

"Hannah?"

She nodded. "The same."

"The Elemental was used to force confessions many centuries ago. It was an ideal form of torture. The cycle of terror it both created and feed upon meant the prisoners always gave in—and since the Durupinen knew how to intervene, the Elemental did no lasting damage. Prisoners were always able to participate fully in the rest of the penal process."

"That's barbaric," I said.

"The medieval ages generally were, I understand," said Carrick. "My point in telling you this is to help you understand that you were never in any real danger."

"Really? Because it sounds like you're trying to make excuses for what those girls did," I snapped.

"I do not make excuses for them," Carrick replied. "I merely wanted you to fully understand what just happened."

"Yeah? Well, why don't you go a few rounds in the ring with the Elemental, and then talk to me about how much danger we were in."

Carrick definitely smiled this time. It only elevated my temper.

"Is something about this funny to you?" I asked.

"No, not at all," Carrick said quickly, although the smile lingered almost imperceptibly around the corners of his mouth. "You just reminded me of someone."

"Who do you—"

But Carrick was no longer paying attention to me. We had reached the front of the castle. "Finn, I'll see the girls safely to their room. You should head back to your quarters before someone misses you."

"Yes sir," said Finn. He gave an odd sort of slouchy nod in our direction. "Good night."

"Good night Finn," Hannah said. "Thank you again."

He turned without another word and loped off in the direction of the Caomhnóir quarters—a long, low stone building that I'd mistaken for stables during our first week.

We trudged back up to our room in silence. Fairhaven's staircases had never seemed so long or hard to climb. Despite what Carrick claimed about there being no lasting damage, I felt utterly drained from the experience and desperate for sleep.

We reached the door to our room. "Just one thing before I leave you here," began Carrick in a hushed voice. "I would appreciate if you didn't mention my role in your escape tonight to anyone. I told you I was watching out for you on Finvarra's orders, but the truth is she doesn't know I have been doing so."

"Why would you lie about that?" I asked.

"It was for Finn's benefit. Strictly speaking, I am not supposed to interfere in situations like this, and I don't want it known that I got involved without Finvarra's consent," he replied.

"Well then, why did you do it?" I pressed.

Carrick didn't answer right away. He seemed to be weighing his words carefully. "I see and hear much in my current state that I was not privy to when I was alive. I may be Bound to the High Priestess, but that will not stop me from seeing to it that all the Durupinen are protected, whenever it is in my power to help."

I opened my mouth to question him further but Hannah cut me off. "We won't say anything. Thank you again."

Carrick clicked his heels together like a soldier, then faded from the spot. I put my hand on the door handle, but Hannah reached out and pulled it back.

"What?" I asked.

"I think we might be missing an opportunity here," she said. She was looking at the shadow of the graffiti that no amount of scrubbing had quite been able to remove. Then she looked at me; I was shocked to see that she was grinning.

"Okay, I'll bite," I said, smiling a little myself. "What opportunity?"

"Peyton and the rest of them obviously think we're going to be stuck out there until they come to get us in the morning," Hannah began. "And Carrick doesn't want us to reveal how he helped us get out."

"True."

"So, why don't we just let them think we did it ourselves?"

My smile widened. "I like where this is going. Keep talking."

"There should've been no way for us to get out of that Circle, even if the Elemental hadn't turned up. Let's give them a little dose of fear, too."

Hannah told me her plan.

"Can you actually do that?" I asked in awe.

"Yup."

I bowed and stepped aside for her. "Lead the way. I'll take my cues from you, oh devious one."

Hannah giggled—a most welcome sound after the night we'd had—and crept across the hall to the door of Peyton's room.

"Oh, hang on," Hannah said. "Let me get Milo. He won't want to miss this. He's wanted us to get back at these girls since we first laid eyes on them." She closed her eyes; after a quick moment of silent conversation, Milo popped into the hall between us.

"They did what to you?" he shouted.

"Shh! I'll give you details afterwards. I just thought you'd enjoy watching this."

"Watching what?" he asked.

"You'll see," said Hannah. Without hesitating at all she knocked forcefully on Peyton's door. Milo faded from view, but I knew he was still there—he was drawn to drama like sharks to the scent of blood.

The sounds of a muffled commotion came from inside the room.

After a few moments, the door opened a crack and Peyton poked her head out.

Her jaw dropped.

"Hi there!" Hannah said cheerily.

"What's the matter, Peyton?" I asked. "I'd say you look as though you've seen a ghost, but well… that cliché doesn't carry the same kind of meaning around here, does it?"

We pushed our way into the room. Olivia and several of the other girls were sitting around; I spotted liquor bottles and hastily stashed paper cups poking out here and there. One girl was still holding her cup half-concealed behind a throw pillow. I noticed Róisín and her sister Riley were not among them.

"Oh sweet, you guys are still drinking?" I strode across the room, snatched a cup from behind the vanity's mirror, peered into it, and gave it an experimental swirl. I shrugged and swallowed the contents in a single gulp. Then I spotted another cup, scooped it up, and offered it to Hannah. "Cheap wine, sis?"

"Don't mind if I do," said Hannah, taking the cup from me. She, too, emptied the drink in one gulp. "Although I could use a stiff drink after that little excursion."

"Yeah," I agreed. "You haven't got something with a bit more kick, do you Peyton? Maybe a nice Scotch?"

"Or Absinthe? That's what the really hardcore kids drank in the last mental hospital I was locked up in," Hannah added. "Y'know, when they weren't high on stolen pills."

No one spoke. The girl sitting closest to the fireplace looked like she might cry.

"No real booze?" I said. "Okay then, we just wanted to stop by and congratulate you on a prank well pulled."

"Yes," Hannah said. "A very good try, honestly."

Peyton finally became the first to recover the power of speech. "How did you get back? That Circle should've held." Her tone was boldly accusatory for someone so obviously in the wrong.

"Oh, that?" Hannah said, and snorted with laughter. "That was the easy part. Seriously girls, was that really the best Circle you could produce? Keira would be horrified. I'd get studying if I were you."

"We'd have made it back for more of your little party if that had been all we had to deal with," I said, peering into an empty cup and tossing it aside. "The Elemental was the interesting challenge."

Everyone froze, as though the Elemental itself had silenced them with its approach.

"The..." Olivia swallowed something back and cleared her throat. "The Summoning worked?" She shot a terrified look at Peyton. "We didn't think it worked."

"Oh yeah," I said. "Yeah, it showed up a couple of minutes after you left. I'd be lying if I said we weren't freaked out. Anyone stuck in a Circle with that thing would've had the longest and most horrifying night of her life."

Hannah nodded solemnly. "Oh, yes. I wouldn't wish that on my worst enemy." We both paused to admire the effect of these words. The pall of their guilt was palpable. "But," Hannah added, "there's one thing you girls really need to take into account before you go trying something like this."

The other girls all looked warily at each other; each clearly wanted to ask what that 'one thing' was, but none of them had the guts to do it. We let the silence spiral; finally, the girl sitting closest to the fireplace asked in a breathless voice, "What's that?"

"A Caller," Hannah began, in a voice that was at once quiet, forceful, and haunting, "is never alone." With this, she pointed to the windows.

All the girls turned to look. A few screamed. Those nearest the windows scrambled away in terror. Even though I'd been expecting it, my heart thudded at the sight: A hundred ghosts, with their faces pressed against the glass, covered every inch of the room's two floor-to-ceiling windows. The overwhelming cold that accompanied them seeped into the room like a gas, extinguishing the fire.

"And those are just the ones she found while we've been chatting," I said brightly.

"So I guess what we're saying is, nice try girls." said Hannah. "You might think you run this place, but you really have no idea what you're dealing with," She flicked her arm to the right. Every ghostly face behind her turned to follow her movement. Hannah's tone was entirely friendly, but the effect—with a hundred hypnotized spirits under her control—was terrifying.

Finally, Hannah clenched her hand then quickly flicked it open again. The horde of ghosts vanished instantly.

"Ooh, snacks!" she said, grabbing a bag of potato chips from one of the beds. "Thanks! I'm starving."

At this, she turned and practically skipped out of the room.

"Sweet dreams, girls. Really fun night. We should do it again sometime," I said, and followed my sister out. As I closed the door behind me, I laughed at the stunned expressions we were leaving in our wake, but also because—however damaged she might have been—my sister was a hell of a lot tougher than she looked.

II

MISSED CONNECTIONS

K ARMA SHOULD HAVE DICTATED that we emerge from our
room the next morning fresh-faced and full of confidence in
our new reputation as the badasses of Fairhaven Hall. By
rights, we should have left our room with a new swing in our step,
tossing our artistically styled hair as we bounced down the hall.
Instead, we both caught monstrous colds and spent the next four
days coughing and sneezing miserably.

We did our best to look as un-miserable as possible at breakfast
the next morning—although I, for one, would almost rather have
spent another hour with the Elemental than give Peyton the
satisfaction of knowing her prank had any lasting negative
impact... even if that impact were only a cold. The only thing that
lightened the wretchedness of our congested morning was the wary
looks plastered on many of the faces in the dining hall. Hannah
even took a break from blowing her nose to give Peyton's table
a casual wave, which caused many of the girls there to become
intensely interested in their cornflakes.

Savvy, Brenna, and Mackie listened to our story with their
mouths hanging open, although Mackie's initial response was not
so much one of horror, but rather guilt—all of this had unfolded
on her watch as First-Year Head. It took us nearly ten minutes to
convince her that there was nothing she could've done to prevent
it.

"I can't believe they left you there with the Elemental," Mackie
said, shaking her head. It was rare for something in the Durupinen
world to elicit more from her other than a nod or a knowing smile.
"No one's done that in about a hundred years, at least. I didn't even
think it was real. I thought it was one of those stories you make up,
to frighten people into behaving themselves, like the boogeyman."

"Well, we can definitely confirm that it's not only real, but every bit as scary as the stories claim," I said. "If I were in charge around here, my first act would be to figure out a way to get rid of that thing."

"You going to report them?" Savvy asked.

"What would be the point?" I said. "They kept those freak doll masks on the whole time, so even though we know at least a few who were involved, we can't really prove it. It would be their word against ours. And besides, who on the Council is going to punish them?"

"Well, Celeste would try, but she'd likely get overruled," Brenna said.

"Yeah, by Marion and her crew—and you know she was probably the one that put them up to it in the first place," added Mackie.

"Well that's complete crap," Savvy said, slamming her hand down on the table and knocking over the maple syrup. "I've gotten punished twice already just for breaking curfew. Meanwhile those toxic mannequins kidnap you and unleash a demon creature from hell on you, and they don't even get a proper slap on the wrist?"

"Tradition is the best defense for anything that happens here," I said. "They're just going to insist that they were following the old customs. No one would even bat an eyelash."

"With the bizarre shit classified as tradition around here, it's no wonder people have been persecuting your lot over the years," said Savvy. She was applying a shocking pink lipstick while using the back of her spoon as a mirror.

We all looked at her in mutual surprise.

"Does this mean you've started staying awake in History and Lore?" Mackie asked.

"Not if I can help it," Savvy replied. "But I have accidentally learned a few things, despite my best efforts. Alright mates, what's the verdict, does this color work for me?" She pouted her full lips seductively.

We all shook our heads; my "no" somehow turned into a cough.

"Bollocks," she grumbled, and wiped the lipstick away with the back of her hand. "Guess I'll return it to Phoebe's purse, then."

True to our word, we hadn't mentioned Carrick's role in our rescue, but instead made it sound as though Finn found his own way to the *Príosún* on Róisín's information.

"I'm surprised Róisín did that," began Brenna. "She's always been close friends with Peyton, but much more of a follower. I wouldn't have thought she'd have the guts to defect like that, especially if she might've gotten them all in trouble."

"I'm not surprised," Mackie said. "I liked her a lot until a couple of years ago, when she started following Peyton around like a puppy dog. She's obviously the only one with any sense in that whole group." Mackie turned to me and Hannah. "You're lucky Finn agreed to come. He could've been in a lot of trouble if he was caught out unchaperoned with Apprentices. He's certainly committed to his job, even though he hasn't even officially been Initiated yet."

"Yeah, we were lucky alright" I said. I felt a pit in my stomach every time I thought about Finn and the Initiation. Everything about it felt wrong, but there was no way out of it. It was a helpless feeling, like being sentenced for a crime you never even realized you'd committed.

"I know you don't like him much, but at least you know he can do his job, eh?" offered Savvy, shaking my shoulder bracingly. "Poor old Bertie looks like one stiff breeze would knock him over. He actually screamed out loud when we got that first spirit to approach our communication Circle last week. What a tosser. Looks like Phoebe and I will be doing our own protecting for a while."

"Yeah, well at least he tries. Isaac is so busy trying to look imposing that he forgets what he's supposed to be doing half the time," Brenna said. "All brawn and no brains."

"Well, let's keep the hope alive, shall we, girls?" Mackie said, looking every bit the First-Year Head. "We've all got a lot of learning left to do. We're not much better at our own jobs yet." Brenna stuck her tongue out at her sister.

"The exception to that being Hannah, of course," I said, ruffling her hair. "She's got ghosts lining up at the snap of her fingers."

Hannah blushed, and grinned shiftily. "I never thought I'd say it, but it has its uses."

"No kidding. I would've paid good money to see the looks on their faces when you Called all those spirits," Mackie said. "I'll bet it was absolutely priceless."

"Yeah, it was pretty great," said Hannah. "I just hope the mystique lasts long enough for them to make a habit of leaving us alone."

The first bell chimed loudly; Peyton and her friends left so quickly that the bell might have been signaling a fire rather than the end of the breakfast hour.

So far, Hannah was getting her wish.

§

After a miserable two hours of Ancient Celtic Languages, during which I fought to stay awake and butchered my pronunciation even more than usual, I decided a nap was the best use of my time. I crossed the courtyard, where Finn and the other Novitiates were doing some sort of martial-art combat drills. They were set up in pairs, throwing punches and kicks at each other while attempting to block the blows from their opponents. I saw just enough to tell that most of them were very good, with the glaring exception of poor Bertie. I realized for the first time that the Caomhnóir took their physical training very seriously. I guess that should've made me feel safe or something, but it didn't. Instead, I was left contemplating what possible situations I could find myself in that would require my own personal ninja.

Deeply troubled by these thoughts, I nearly ran headlong into Róisín in the hall.

She stared at me for a moment, then stepped around me without a word and kept walking.

"Róisín, wait!" I cried, turning to follow her.

She pretended not to hear me and lengthened her stride.

Róisín, stop! I want to talk to you!"

She stopped and spun around so suddenly that I almost walked into her again.

"What?" she hissed, as she glanced nervously around. There was no one in sight.

"I just wanted to thank you," I said.

"For what?" she asked, crossing her arms.

"Finn told us you went to find him last night."

"So what?" Róisín said tartly. "You obviously didn't need the help, from what I hear, so forget about it."

"You couldn't have known that."

"I told you to forget it. It was nothing."

She turned to leave again, but I caught her arm. She shook it angrily out of my grip.

"It wasn't nothing!" I said.

"Yes, it was," Róisín hissed; there was an edge of panic in her voice now. "And if you ever tell anyone about it, I'll deny it."

That pulled me up short. "Why?"

"Because I'm not getting dragged down in this!" she whispered. "I know how things are around here, and I'm not winding up on the wrong side. My mother is on the Council, my friends are all—I'm just not going to do it. And I'm sorry, okay? But please, just forget about it."

"Fine," I said. "I won't say anything. But we know what you did, and we're grateful. I just thought you should know."

A softened expression flitted across Róisín's face for just long enough to give her away. Then her eyes hardened again and she gave a derisive laugh. "Whatever. I wouldn't want you thinking it was out of concern for you, okay? I was just trying to save our own skins. My friends may not want you here, but I don't think the Council would've been very happy if you and your sister had died."

With that, she walked away, her long, dark hair swinging behind her. But I wasn't fooled. There was some shred of comfort in knowing that—even in the inner circle of resistance—there were those who, if they'd had the courage to make up their own minds, might've accepted us. It wasn't much, but it was something.

I trudged back to my room and flopped onto my bed; I was sure I'd be asleep in seconds. Instead, I lay there wide awake—my body was exhausted but my brain was buzzing with a hundred different things. After thirty minutes, I gave up any hope of sleep and decided to spend the time on something else that seemed impossible: Tracking down Pierce.

With no new clues about where he could be or why he'd vanished, I decided to focus on locating the last person that I knew had definitely seen him: I opened my browser and Googled Neil Caddigan.

I began to sift through the results. There was an astrophysicist by the same name, but he had been dead for ten years. There was also a thirty-something aspiring actor named Neil Caddigan; he had a toothy headshot and a resume consisting mostly of community theatre, plus one deodorant commercial. Finally, I spotted a link that looked promising and clicked on it.

It was an article debating whether historic buildings should be opened to the increasing requests for paranormal investigations. The author had interviewed a number of sources on both sides of the argument. I scanned for Neil's name and read the section.

Few have been as vocal in the quest for this open door policy as

Dr. Neil Caddigan, a noted scholar in the field of theology and a self-styled para-historian. "What you must understand," Caddigan insists, "is that this trend is only growing. We are missing a crucial opportunity to learn more about the history of our country's most iconic places and events. There's only so much that artifacts and documents can tell us; we must push the boundaries of science and technology, as well as the limits of our own beliefs, if we are to learn more. Imagine the wealth of primary-source information we might have access to if spirits could be reached! There have been many significant technological advances that could, if embraced, quite possibly lead to some startling new discoveries."

I went back and read the entire article carefully, but although Neil was quoted twice more, there were no details shedding any light on where I might find him. I went back to the search page and tried typing, "Caddigan theology."

Bingo.

The very first link was to a course catalog for a college in London where students could take theology classes with a Dr. N. Caddigan. A thorough search of the college's website gave me Neil's faculty email address. It was a long shot, given that it was now summer, but I sent a message to him anyway. It took a surprisingly long time to write, considering that my message really wasn't very long. I was careful to leave out all mention of my own whereabouts, and kept the tone very light and friendly. I tried not to sound too anxious, and invented an excuse for needing to get in touch with Pierce. I also requested any contact information Neil might have for any of the other team members, so I could follow up with them if Neil turned out to be a dead end.

Next, I shot off a quick email to Tia to keep her in the loop. I would've loved to vent to her about the events of the previous night, but that was definitely too much classified information to share. Instead, I picked up the phone and called Karen. Karen obviously wasn't my first choice for a confidant, but I thought she ought to hear about the Elemental from me, rather than from someone else.

Predictably, Karen launched into mama bear mode. "Those little shits!" she spat, after I'd given her all the twisted details. "There's not a chance in hell they came up with that plan on their own, no matter how vindictive they are."

"That's what we figured, too. Mackie said they wouldn't have been able to find that Summoning ritual without an adult's help."

"Yeah, and I know exactly which adult helped them," Karen replied. "That's it. Screw this case, I'm coming back there."

"No," I sighed. "Don't bother. It's over, and they're not likely to try anything like that again, now that they're all scared to death of Hannah."

"Are you sure? I can hand this work off to another partner. There should be an adult there who's on your side." Karen suddenly sounded as if she were holding back tears. "Damn it, I never should've left in the first place."

"Karen, stop. This isn't your fault." I only barely stopped myself from adding, "It's mom's." I bit that back and continued, "If we need help, we can go to Celeste. She's been great. Siobhán seems alright, too. And if push came to shove, Fiona would probably help us. We'll be fine."

"Well, okay... but only if you're sure."

"We're sure," I repeated. "I promise. Look, I've got to go. I'm going to be late for Meditation and Bonding." This wasn't strictly true; I had plenty of time to get to class, but listening to Karen fuss was making me feel worse, not better.

"Right. Well, call me if there are any other incidents. I mean it, Jess, I want to know about it."

"I know you do," I replied. "That's why I called. I'll talk to you soon."

I hung up, grabbed my bag and a handful of tissues, and headed down to the courtyard. It was completely deserted except for—

Finn was sitting in our Circle—we had intentionally left them intact from the day before—with his face buried in his usual journal, scribbling away. I stopped abruptly at the sight of him, and was just about to turn and flee when he looked up and saw me. I cursed inwardly, knowing it would be rude to leave now that he'd seen me. I started for the Circle. Finn stared at me as I crossed the courtyard, as if some bizarre apparition were approaching instead of just me and my ball of wadded-up tissues.

"Hey," I said as I sat down, being careful to stay outside of the Circle lest he fault me for familiarity.

"Hey, yourself," he replied curtly, finally taking his eyes off of me and returning to his book.

"You're early," I said.

"So are you." He crossed out a word vehemently and kept writing.

"Yeah. I didn't think anyone else would be here."

"Me too," he replied. His tone implied that he wished he'd been right.

I decided to stop talking and leave him to his... whatever he was doing. I thought about pulling out my sketchpad, but I didn't like the idea of Finn seeing my work—it felt too personal. So I just sat, letting my mind wander and sniffling occasionally. But then I glanced in his direction and noticed that he was staring at me again.

"What?" I snapped, a little too harshly.

He looked startled. "I, uh... I was going to ask how you're holding up—you know, after last night."

"Oh," I said. "I'm fine. I mean, we both caught this nasty cold, but otherwise we're okay."

He looked surprised. "Oh, I see. You're ill."

"Yes, of course I'm ill," I said, holding up the tissues. "What did you think I..." I broke off as I realized what I must've looked like—runny nose, puffy eyes, expression of general misery. "Did you... did you think I'd been crying?"

Finn shrugged, looking back down on his book.

"I heard you told Peyton that Hannah got you both out of there last night," he said, picking at a patch of grass that had sprung stubbornly up from between the cobblestones.

"What? Oh yeah, we did," I said, frowning.

"What did you do that for?"

"Are you offended?" I asked.

"Why would I be offended?"

"Well, you were the one that got us out of there. Wouldn't it boost your Caomhnóir street cred if everyone knew about it?"

"Will it boost my what?" Finn asked, scowling.

I shook my head, half-laughing. "Nothing. It was just a joke."

"Oh," he said, not even cracking a smile—and I thought how odd his face would've looked if he had actually managed a grin. "It doesn't matter to me if you tell them I was involved or not. Come to think of it, it might make things easier for me if Peyton and Olivia don't know that I helped you. I just wondered why you lied about it."

"We thought it might help keep them off our backs if they

thought Hannah was powerful enough to get us out of there herself."

Finn nodded. "Right, I expect that will work for a while."

We sat in silence for a minute or so before he spoke again. He was so abrupt that his voice startled me and I dropped my tissues; they started tumbling gently across the ground in the breeze.

"So is she?"

"Is who what?" I asked, snatching at a passing tissue. Finn reached a hand out automatically for it. "Don't touch that!" I shouted at him. "I already... that's not clean. Please, just... I'll get it."

My face was scarlet with mortification; the idea that this guy was actually going to rescue my used tissue from a blustery fate was almost more embarrassment than I could handle.

"What did you ask me?" I asked, when all of the tissues were clutched safely back in my fist.

"I wanted to know if your sister—"

"Hannah."

"I know," he said brusquely. "I wanted to know if Hannah really is powerful enough to do that."

The question surprised me; I was torn about how to answer it. But I decided that Finn would shortly see far too much of our spirit interactions to keep any sort of lid on Hannah's abilities, and—as much as I hated to admit it—our abilities were actually his business.

"She couldn't get out of that Circle, and she can't break other people's Castings or anything like that, but when it comes to Calling, she's really powerful. The spirits can't seem to resist her when she Calls them."

"What does that mean for you?" he asked.

That pulled me up short. "I don't really know," I said. "I guess I hadn't thought about it much."

Finn nodded and then returned to his book. It was true that I hadn't really thought about this, but I was sure as hell thinking about it now: What would Hannah's being a ghost magnet mean for me? Would our lives be a constant stream of unwanted Visitations and emergency Crossings?

Since I'd first started seeing spirits, I'd had days when I'd felt haunted and days without a ghost in sight—days when I could pretend I was normal. But for Hannah, who'd never known life any other way, normal was a life among the dead. Was my twin sister's constant communion with the dead about to become my new normal? I pressed the palms of my hands against my eyes and sighed. I was too sick and too exhausted to ponder big life questions today.

I heard Finn's tentative voice. "Are you?—"

"Still not crying," I muttered.

"Right."

The rest of the class trickled in until the courtyard was full again. Hannah arrived and we took our place inside the Circle. She plopped down beside me looking half-dead.

"How is it only two o'clock?" she whimpered.

"I don't know, but I'll be adhering to a senior-citizen schedule tonight," I said, handing her one of my clean tissues as she sneezed loudly. "Early bird special for dinner and asleep by seven."

"I'll be joining you," Hannah agreed, wiping her nose. "Hi, Finn."

Finn didn't even look up. He raised a hand in acknowledgment and continued with his scribbling.

Hannah leaned in and whispered to me. "What do you think he's doing with that book?"

"Penning his memoir? 1001 Awkward Social Interactions by Finn Carey?" I suggested. Hannah burst out in a giggle that quickly disintegrated into a hacking cough. I patted her arm in sympathy.

"Settle down, settle down, everyone, please," Keira said, and the class came to order. "Today we will be starting our foray into true spirit communication. As you know, our grounds play host to an impressive number of spirits. Our resident spirits are particularly useful for an activity such as this, which depends on spirit proximity to be successful."

"Unless, of course, you're a Caller and can just pluck a spirit out of thin air from a hundred miles away," I whispered to Hannah.

"I can't do it from a hundred miles away," she said dismissively.

"Yet," I said.

"Our relaxation and concentration exercises thus far have built the foundational skills needed to establish clear and detailed spirit communication. It is now time to put these techniques into effect and see how well you can commune with the dead. These books, which I am now going to hand out to you, are spirit journals. You are to document—in as much detail as you can—your conversations with, and observations about, the spirits you encounter. The quality of your interactions will improve with concentration and practice."

Keira handed me a book with a plain blue fabric cover. I flipped through the blank white pages, marveling at the idea that I was about to start filling them with details about ghosts that I'd communicated with *on purpose*. Seriously, what was my life becoming?

"Caomhnóir, your task during these sessions will be to practice your mood reading," Keira went on. "A big part of your ability to protect your Gateway is being able to sense danger before it happens. A spirit's energy, when correctly read and interpreted, can be an important clue to the nature of an interaction, even before first contact occurs."

Finn had finally tucked away his book and pen. He was listening intently to Keira's instructions.

"Novitiates will allow spirits to approach and enter the Circle, please. Only when you sense hostility should you expel. Apprentices, it is important that you work together with your Caomhnóir. Talk to each other. Listen to each other. Only when we are clear and honest can we work together successfully."

Finn caught my eye. He wore the stoic but determined look of someone about to face an oncoming enemy horde. Irrational resentment flooded through me. Of course I didn't want to work with him either, but... did he need to look *that* miserable?

"Excellent," Keira said, clapping her hands together. "Apprentices, you will need to work one at a time in your Circles. Two Durupinen presences within a Circle may muddle the strength of your connection or confuse approaching spirits. Decide who will go first in each pair, and let's begin. Casting instructions are on page 394 of your textbooks."

Hannah and I looked at each other. "You can go first," I told her.

"Okay," she shrugged, and I scooted out of the Circle to give her space. I followed along in the textbook as she worked through the steps of the Casting, which was more complicated that many of the others we had attempted thus far. Hannah carefully drew six different runes around the perimeter of our Circle; each gave off a queer shiver of energy as it was completed. Then she carefully pronounced the six necessary lines of ancient Gaelic as she took three round, agate stones from her Casting bag and placed them in a neat row in front of her. Keira hovered nearby, listening and nodding her head.

"Very nice pronunciation, Hannah," she said, with an approving smile.

Hannah smiled, and turned slightly pink. Then she closed her book and turned to Finn.

"I'm ready to start, Finn. Are you all set?"

Finn grunted his readiness. Hannah closed her eyes. Within seconds, she was murmuring to someone and Finn was shaking his head.

"She's quick, I'll give her that," he muttered.

I looked around the courtyard. Although many of the Apprentices' eyes were closed in concentration, Hannah was the only one who had made contact already. Those Apprentices who were waiting for their turns were staring aimlessly around or else flipping through their textbooks.

One by one, the Apprentices in the Circles began murmuring to companions unseen. Here and there, a figure shimmered into view or materialized into a fully visible apparition, but for the most part the spirits remained invisible. A hard-to-define energy built in the courtyard, like a mental vibration—almost like a high buzzing beyond the range of actual hearing.

After thirty minutes or so, Keira called out softly, "Time to switch places. Apprentices, please end your communications; Novitiates, prepare for expulsion by mutual consent."

Hannah's spirit said something that made her laugh softly, and then I heard her murmur, "*Beannacht leat go bhfeicfidh mé aris thú,*" before she opened her eyes. She collected her three agate stones, dropped them back in her Casting bag, and grinned at me.

"Tag, you're it!" she to me playfully, and tried to stand up. "Ouch, my foot's asleep!"

I helped her out of the Circle. She sat on the cobblestones, trying to massage some feeling back into her numb foot. I took her place in the Circle. The runes were already drawn, so I flipped my textbook open to the Casting and looked for the next step.

I read the instructions carefully, then fished around in my own Casting bag for my agate stones. They were smooth and polished, layered with brown and gold stripes that reminded me of the rock formations from our road trips through the Southwest when I was young. I laid the stones in a straight line on the edge of the nearest rune; I knew from my reading that this rune was called *ansuz*, and that it helped facilitate communication, revelation, and knowledge. *Ansuz* looked a bit like a letter "F" that had been bent at strange angles. Then I stumbled through the words of the Casting. I knew I was butchering the pronunciation, but both my brain and my mouth were refusing to cooperate.

I looked up and saw Hannah's mouth twitching as she wrote in her journal.

"You better be laughing at something in that book," I teased. She smiled more broadly, but kept her eyes trained on her journal.

I turned away from her and saw Finn staring at me as well.

"Can I help you?" I snapped.

"I can't start my Casting until you've properly finished yours," he said. "Are you done?"

It took two more cracks at the ancient Gaelic before I pronounced the Casting correctly enough to open the Circle. I felt the moment when the Circle buzzed to life, as did Finn, who immediately began his own work. Finally, we were ready to start. I closed my eyes and cleared my mind, reaching into the mental space around me and searching for a spirit.

I searched. I searched some more. Nothing.

Even though I knew I shouldn't, I opened my eyes and looked around the courtyard. Every Apprentice within a Circle was deep in communication now; everyone, that was, except for me. It was like being the last one picked in gym class—a social stigma I'd had quite a bit of experience with since I was always the new kid. I closed my eyes again, pushed aside my middle school emotional traumas, and reached outward. The minutes ticked by. Nothing.

Disconcerted, I opened my eyes again and consulted my textbook. Had I missed a step? Was I doing something wrong? I couldn't find anything obvious.

"Is there a problem here?" Keira, in her wanderings, had arrived beside me.

"No, I think I've done it right," I said as quietly as I could, not wanting to draw attention to myself. "I just haven't gotten anything yet and I'm not sure why."

"Sometimes it takes a bit more time when you are starting out. When was your first Visitation?" Keira asked.

"Last year," I replied, as my heart began thudding a confused rhythm from the emotion of the memory.

"Your gift is among the newest here," said Keira. "How would you say you feel about Visitations?"

"How do I feel about them?"

"For instance, are you excited about the idea of a Visitation? Nervous? Frightened?" Keira prompted.

"Oh," I said, and tried to find a tactful way of expressing myself. "The Visitations... haven't been a positive experience for me, generally. I guess if I had to pick a feeling, I'd have to go with unenthused."

Keira actually smiled, which surprised me. "You didn't have an ideal introduction to your gift, which is, of course, unfortunate. Try not to be discouraged. You are also not feeling well, which often has an effect on communication in the beginning. You will all improve with practice. As impossible as it seems, you will get used to it." Then she gestured broadly at the other Apprentices. "Many of the connections being made here today are very weak, lacking detail and clarity. Each and every one of you has plenty of work to do."

"Okay," I said. I closed my eyes again and repeated the exercise for another twenty minutes with no success. I was nearly ready to throw in the towel and accept defeat when Hannah spoke.

"Hey, isn't that your Silent Child?" she whispered.

I opened my eyes and followed Hannah's gaze. The Silent Child stood barely visible in the shadow of the North Tower. Her penetrating stare was concentrated on me with an intensity that ought to have burned a hole straight through me.

"Yes, that's her," I said, and quickly closed my eyes again. I tried feeling out and searching for her energy, almost sure that she must be trying, as she so often was, to communicate with me. I could find nothing. Then an idea struck me.

"Hannah, can you try to Call her?" I whispered.

Hannah frowned. "Are you sure? I don't want her to attack you again."

"It's fine," I assured her. "We've got a Caomhnóir ready to expel her, remember?" I hitched my thumb over my shoulder at Finn, who was watching our whispered conversation with a storm cloud of an expression. "Please? I really want to know why she's been following me. Maybe Calling will help her communicate."

"Okay, if you want me to," Hannah replied, although she still looked wary. Her eyelids fluttered closed and I watched her now-familiar ritual of Calling. My eyes darted back and forth between

Hannah and the Silent Child; the girl hadn't moved or made any indication that she sensed what Hannah was trying to do.

"That's really strange," Hannah said after a few minutes. "I can't even sense her out there."

I gaped at her. "You're kidding! Has that ever happened before?"

"Not with a ghost," Hannah said firmly. She was looking at the Silent Child now with a fearful new fascination. "I know right where she should be, but when I reach out for her something is... in the way."

"It's not like last night, with the Elemental, is it?" I asked. "You couldn't sense that thing, either." I glanced back at the Silent Child; she was crouched and motionless, like a spooked cat.

"No, it's not like that," said Hannah, chewing thoughtfully on a stray wisp of hair. "It's hard to describe. I know she's there, but something is preventing the connection. I can't get the mental grip on her that I need to Call her; she's behind some kind of wall."

The booming tower bell made us jump. We'd gone over time. There were several scattered shrieks around the courtyard as connections were broken accidentally. A gust of frightened energy blew across my back, ruffling my hair. Savvy started cursing loudly at Bertie, who had panicked and expelled the spirit Savvy had been communicating with.

We looked back in the direction of the Silent Child, but the bell had driven her away from us and back into obscurity.

That night, I dreamed of the Silent Child for the first time. She stood before a wall of fire, with her mouth open in a scream that no one could hear.

12

LEECHES

A S PREOCCUPIED AS I WAS WITH THE SILENT CHILD, I was
far too busy trying to keep up with classwork and other
responsibilities to dwell on her constantly. Two days and one
more abysmal attempt at a communication Circle later, I was still
no nearer to making contact with her—or, it seemed, with any spirit
at all.

"I don't understand!" I cried, as I shoved my Casting Bag and
book back into my bag at the end of the next lesson. "Why can't
I do this? There are ghosts everywhere here! Literally, there goes
one right now!" I pointed across the garden; the pearly figure of
a chambermaid was hovering on the front steps, shaking out the
specter of a dustrag laden with the grime of ages past. "I see them
all day long, I've spoken to them in the halls. I have one in my room
that I can almost never get rid of! But as soon as I enter that Circle,
nothing! It's like a black hole of spirit activity as soon as I get in
there!"

"You'll get the hang of it," Mackie said bracingly. "I'm still really
only getting vague emotional impressions."

"At least you've got something to start with, though," I said.
"Your spirit journal isn't completely blank, is it?"

"Well no, but we've all got a lot of work to do!" said Mackie.
"Keira doesn't seem concerned, so I don't think you should be."

Savvy swaggered over to join us. A cigarette dangled from her
lips. "Alright?"

"Savvy, did you get much in communication today?" asked
Mackie.

Savvy opened her purple spirit journal with a flourish and read
dramatically, "Ghost was a bloke with angry energy and possibly
a white shirt. The only two words I got in answer to any of my
questions were unclear, but they sounded like 'battle axe.'"

Savvy closed her journal with a snap. "Well, that communication was definitely worth thirty minutes of my life. I knew I should have stayed in bed today, but after last night I thought skipping class might be pushing my luck."

"What are they making you do this time?" I asked.

"Kitchen duty," Savvy said. She'd been caught in the entrance hall in the wee hours of the morning, sneaking back to her room after a crazy night at a house party. "That Marion is a right pain in the arse. You'd think I murdered someone, the way she was going on. Think I'll spit in her food!"

"Fine by me. Just don't spit in mine, mate," Mackie said. "Are you all going to go to the courtyard for the Crossing tonight?"

"Yes, we'll be there," said Hannah.

"It might be better if you don't bring me, Hannah," I said, starting back for the castle. "The spirits will probably take one look at me and head for another Gateway."

"That's not how it works and you know it," Hannah replied. "Stop being so dramatic. You'll get the hang of it soon enough. And besides, all this negative energy you're creating isn't going to help you establish communication."

I stuck my tongue out at her, but I knew she was right. I was starting to psych myself out about the entire communication Circle process; I would need to get out of my own way if I were going to improve.

That morning, Agnes had informed us that there would be teachers on hand in the courtyard at nine o'clock tonight if anyone wanted continued guidance or supervision for their next Crossing. Hannah and I hadn't performed a Crossing since our very first experience on Karen's rooftop back home, although we had practiced the steps many times for Siobhán's class.

Crossings, we had learned, were divided into two categories: Crossings by necessity and Crossings by lunar cycle. Crossings by necessity were performed at the request of—or, in some cases, by the desperate demands of—spirits who sought out the Durupinen for help. Our first Crossing was the ultimate example of a Crossing by necessity, as the backlog of trapped spirits had become highly dangerous and volatile by the time we were able to perform it. Crossings by lunar cycle were also sometimes called maintenance Crossings, and were performed at regular intervals to provide periodic opportunities for spirits to decide to Cross. The lunar cycle, according to generations of Durupinen, was the most constant and reliable method of ensuring that these Crossings happened on a regular basis.

As of this afternoon, the full moon had already risen, pale and swollen, in the summer sky; the time for this month's lunar cycle Crossing had arrived. I was not nearly as nervous about this Crossing as I'd been about the first, mostly because I did not anticipate meeting any ghosts with whom I was emotionally involved. I felt even calmer about it when I learned that the Caomhnóir, otherwise engaged with a training exercise, would not be present... which meant that I wouldn't have Finn scowling over me.

We went back to our room, where Hannah dumped out her bag. She then repacked it with different books and a faded, musty quilt from the chest at the end of her bed.

"I told Milo I'd meet him on the grounds. Do you want to join us?" she asked.

"Sure, I just need to check my email first."

"Okay, see you down there. We'll be over by the fountain with the statues of those three dancing girls."

"Great," I said, waving absently over my shoulder. My email was already open and the first thing I saw was a message from Tia, with the subject line "URGENT!"

With my heart in my throat, I clicked on her message and began to read.

Hi Jess,

I really hope that everything there is getting better, and that you and Hannah are doing okay. I've attached an article from our local newspaper that I think you need to see. I think this whole situation might be much more dangerous than we thought. Sam and I have backed off, like you asked, but it sounds like the police are now getting involved.

Love and miss you,

Tia

I clicked on the link and began to read the article, which was dated two days prior.

LOCAL FIRE RULED ARSON: STORE OWNER DECLARED MISSING

Police have confirmed today that last month's devastating fire in the downtown shopping district on Elm Street has indeed been ruled arson. The fire completely destroyed one store, The Gypsy Tearoom, which sold books, herbs, and other novelty items used in occult practices such as fortune telling. The fire also caused mild to moderate smoke damage to neighboring businesses.

In a new twist, the owner of the shop, Annabelle Rabinski, 39, has been reported missing. It seems that Ms. Rabinski has not been seen since the evening of the fire; all attempts to contact her have been unsuccessful. A routine visit to her residence revealed that the apartment had been broken into and many items were missing or stolen. Police are asking anyone with information about Ms. Rabinski's whereabouts to come forward.

I leaned away from the computer, as if my proximity to this disturbing new information made it more true. First Pierce, now Annabelle. What the hell was going on?

Filled with an aching desire to do *something*, I went back to my inbox and looked for a reply from Neil, but he still hadn't answered me. I knew three days wasn't an excessively long time to wait for a reply, but the news about Annabelle had left me shaken; I decided to cast another line. I pulled up the original article in a Cambridge-based newspaper where I'd first come across Neil's name. I hopped onto the paper's site and emailed the reporter who'd written it, asking for any contact information he might have for Neil. I sat staring at the computer for another ten minutes, racking my brain for another lead, but could think of nothing. I grabbed my bag and went to meet Hannah and Milo.

We spent most of the afternoon out on the grounds, slogging through a pile of homework for History and Lore. It was my favorite kind of summer day—sunny and breezy without a trace of humidity in the air. We didn't even go back in the castle for dinner, opting instead to eat on Hannah's quilt, soaking in the last of the warmth before the English countryside absorbed it along with the setting sun. The work was a good distraction, but terrible "what-ifs" kept popping up in my head like weeds in a garden—unbidden and damn near impossible to get rid of.

Finally, as twilight fell, we gathered in the central courtyard for the Crossing. I hadn't been here since the Welcoming Ceremony, except to cut through on my way to Keira's class. The stone *Geatgrima* loomed in the center, exuding its strange, seductive energy. I averted my eyes from it; the pull felt dangerous somehow.

A reverent hush hovered over everyone as they silently created their Circles and lit their candles. Hannah and I joined in the quiet ritual. Finally, when all the Circles were finished, Finvarra herself—accompanied by Celeste, Siobhán, and Keira—swept into the courtyard, with Carrick marching soundlessly along behind her. They weaved among the Apprentices, examining our work and suggesting an adjustment here or there. They then took their places at the center of the courtyard, fanning out along the base of the arch.

"I have been told," Finvarra said, addressing us with her arms flung wide open, "that you all did very well with your first Crossings. I am sorry that my responsibilities as High Priestess had me otherwise engaged that evening. I look forward to watching tonight as you continue to embrace your calling and honor your heritage. Please begin."

I fumbled to extract my copy of the *Book of Téigh Anonn* from my bag. I took a deep breath.

"Ready?" I asked Hannah.

"Ready," she replied.

Hannah took her place beside the green candle, while I stood beside the yellow one. A quiet murmuring of spirit voices began as soon as we took our assigned places. I had been expecting this, so it didn't startle me as it had the first time. It was also a much gentler hum than on that first night, since we weren't opening the Gateway for nearly two decades' worth of trapped souls.

We said the Incantation together, speaking slowly and carefully:
"We call upon the powers endowed to us of old.
We call upon the connection that binds us together.
With the joining of hands and the joining of blood,
The Gateway we open, the spirits we Summon."

Hannah lit the white Spirit Candle in the center of the Circle, and then we joined hands. I felt the Gateway, ready to burst open, flowing through us. We began to chant.

"Téigh Anonn. Téigh Anonn. Téigh Anonn."

Flash.

A hot and smoky kitchen with stone walls and a dirt floor. A baby screaming in a wooden cradle nearby. Running through a sea of wild grain, sunlight gleaming in my golden hair. The smell of livestock as I struggle with a pail of fresh steaming milk. The sound of sobbing as I lift a scabbed and oozing hand in front of my face.

Flash.
Light shattering into a rainbow across a tiny, dimpled hand. The smell of a freshly starched shirt sliding over my braids. Crying over a torn and bloody hole in my new stockings. Climbing out over a peeling white windowsill to the boy below on his red bicycle.

One by one, the memories flooded through me, at once foreign and familiar. The sensation was disorienting, and beneath the current of the spirits' thoughts, I found myself worrying that I would lose my balance and break the connection.

Flash.
Astride a galloping horse, the wind filling my lungs with the heady scent of lilacs. Clinging for dear life onto a bedpost as a grim-faced maid tugs mercilessly at my corset strings. Lying beneath a barrel-chested man in a down bed, tears streaming down my face.

Flash.
A butterfly trapped beneath a glass jar, beating its wings frantically against the walls of its prison. Running along beside a train, waving and crying, at the man in uniform. Crawling through the sucking mud as explosions rain down overhead. Dragging the terrible dead weight of a friend across a wasteland of barbed wire and mangled corpses, sobbing my curses at the leaden sky.

I lost track of how many lives passed through us, but before I could process the flood of emotions, it was over. Much more quickly than I had expected, I felt the Gateway close tightly. I opened my eyes as my own consciousness flooded back through me. Even though I was full of my own thoughts and memories, I felt weirdly empty. I brushed someone else's tears from my cheeks.

Hannah, with her right hand still grasped tightly in mine, was pale and trembling. I watched as her sense of where and who she was flickered back into her eyes. Then she seemed to see me again, and smiled gently.

"That wasn't as bad as last time," she said quietly.

"No, it wasn't," I agreed. "But it's still very…" I put my fingers to my chest, struggling to retrieve the right word. But Hannah didn't need it.

"Yeah. It is," she replied. "I don't think that will change, no matter how many times we do it."

I dropped to the ground, pulled my knees to my chest, and gazed around the courtyard. Nearly everyone had finished; the quiet surrounding us was punctuated by an occasional sob. Most of the girls looked the way I felt—windswept and emotionally depleted. Then I saw Peyton and Olivia several Circles away, quietly talking as they packed up their candles. There was something odd about their appearance: They looked refreshed, almost glowing.

Finvarra didn't address us again, although she had a satisfied expression on her face as she conversed quietly with the teachers—we must have met with her approval. Mackie and several other students were wending between the groups with tall, silver pitchers of water and washing the Circles away.

"So how did your Crossing go Hannah?" a voice said.

I turned and saw, to my astonishment, Peyton talking to Hannah. Peyton's tone and expression were perfectly friendly.

Hannah answered warily. "Fine. Much faster than last time."

Peyton nodded. "I'm told it gets easier. I would think it must be even smoother for you, with the power of your gift."

Hannah frowned slightly. "Yes, I suppose so."

"Some of the girls and I were going to meet in the library tomorrow to start researching that Necromancer paper for Celeste. Would you like to join us?" Peyton asked, looking at us both.

I could barely think past my surprise to answer. "Are you serious?" I finally blurted out.

"Yes, perfectly. Many hands make light work," Peyton said brightly.

"Why would you want us to come?" Hannah asked.

"Will there be an ancient creature bent on our destruction lurking in the stacks?" I asked, mimicking Peyton's bright tone.

Peyton looked unconvincingly confused for a moment, then laughed airily. "Oh, I see. I hope you aren't going to read too much into our little prank the other night," she said. "It was all in good fun, I promise you."

"Oh yeah, I for one had a blast," I said. "Hannah?"

"Yes, we should definitely do that again this weekend," said Hannah.

Mackie walked over, splashing water over our expired Circle. "Everything alright over here?"

"Oh, yes," Peyton said. "I was just inviting Hannah and Jess along to a study session, but I'm afraid they don't seem very interested. Still a bit touchy about our joke the other night."

"If that's your idea of a laugh, your sense of humor is complete rubbish," Mackie replied.

"If you say so," Peyton said, smiling. "I'm just trying to extend the olive branch. If you ladies aren't ready, I certainly understand. Perhaps another time."

"Don't hold your breath," I said.

"You've got a lot of nerve even talking to them, you know," Mackie said sternly. "In fact, you've got a lot of nerve talking to any of us right now."

"I don't know what you mean," replied Peyton.

"Leeches never do," Mackie spat with contempt.

Peyton's face tightened slightly at the word, but quickly relaxed into a smile. "I'm just going to let that unfounded accusation pass, and choose to accept the implied compliment."

"Whatever helps you sleep at night," Mackie said.

Peyton smiled ingratiatingly and flounced across the courtyard to her waiting pack of minions, who began whispering excitedly at once. Mackie continued to look daggers at them until they vanished into the castle.

"She can't possibly think we'd want to have anything to do with her," I said.

"All I wanted to do was scare her off with that Caller stuff," Hannah said, "but now it sounds like she wants to be best friends or something!"

"I'm not surprised," Mackie offered. "Peyton's kind always flocks to the talented and the impressive. You've achieved celebrity status around here with your gift; they can't stop obsessing about it. That's probably why they want to hang out with you now."

"Why did you call her a Leech?" Hannah asked, stealing my question before I could ask it.

"Because that's what she is. Her and her mother and the whole lot in the Council's inner circle."

"Yeah, but what does it mean? I can think of a few choice words I'd like to call her, but *leech* isn't one of them," I said.

Mackie trained her eyes on us, then shook her head like a dog shaking off water. "Sorry, I forget how much you don't know."

"Thanks for rubbing it in," I said.

"No, not like that. Sorry. I just mean that I probably say all kinds of stuff around you that you don't know about yet, without properly explaining myself."

"That's okay," I said, waving her apology away. "We're used to playing catch-up around here. Usually we just nod and smile until we can figure out what the hell is going on."

"Yup," Hannah agreed. "You're looking at two expert nodders and smilers."

Mackie motioned for us to follow her as she finished washing away the Circles. "Right. Well, have you noticed that Peyton's mother and her flock are a bit… well, gorgeous? Like, weirdly so?"

"Yeah, I did. I just figured they all indulged in a lot of plastic surgery," I replied.

"Well, they are indulging, but surgery doesn't play a part. Let's see, how to explain it." Mackie bit her lip. "Look, you know how when you're doing a Crossing and you can see the spirits' lives flash before your eyes?"

"Yeah," Hannah and I said together.

"And you know how you experience things almost as though they are happening to you, as if you're living their memories?"

"Yeah," I said again, with a shudder. The sensation was still fresh in my mind and body.

"The reason we can feel and see those things is called an Aura Flow. Because of our abilities, we're wired to be receptive to the feelings and energy of others, as long as they're dead. It's a little tricky to explain, but I expect Siobhán will be covering it in Ceremonial Basics pretty soon," Mackie said, scratching her chin thoughtfully.

"I think I'm with you so far," I said. "We're programmed to experience their memories."

"Right," she went on, "but it's more than that. Their lives, when they flash past us, are like an electric current, a live feed of energy. We're supposed to act solely as conductors, letting the energy pass through uninterrupted—that's the whole point of the Gateway. But some of us," and here she cast a dirty look toward the castle entryway where Peyton had disappeared, "can't help but take a little for themselves."

"How do you mean?" Hannah asked.

"*Leech* is a term for a Durupinen who siphons spirit energy from the ghosts as they Cross through the Gateway. They pull the energy from the spirits and take it into themselves."

My mouth dropped open. "Why? Why would someone do that?"

"Just look at them," Mackie said bitterly. "It's like a fountain of youth. They can use the energy to perfect themselves, correct flaws, and enhance their looks."

"Okay, I know I'm new at all this stuff, but that sounds seriously wrong to me," I said.

"It is," Mackie said. "The ability to siphon is a latent one, and not meant to be used except in dire emergencies."

"What kind of emergency could ever possibly require that?" Hannah asked.

"Like, if a Durupinen was too sick or injured to conduct a Crossing on her own, she could siphon a bit of spirit energy to give herself the strength to complete it," Mackie said, pouring out the last of the water into the grass and placing the pitcher on a stone plinth. "You use the spirits to strengthen yourself, but only to help them, see?"

I nodded my head slowly. "I think so. Are we likely to be in a situation like that?"

"Not really anymore. Being a Durupinen used to be a lot more dangerous, back when people considered witch burning a recreational sport, and also when the Necromancers were still around. But somewhere along the line, someone figured out that the siphoning had some beneficial side effects, and started using it for her own means. It caught on in certain clans, and since then it's become a rather common practice here."

"But it's so obvious who's doing it," I cried, dropping onto the seat beside her. "They aren't exactly being subtle about it, are they? I mean, they look like freaking supermodels for God's sake!"

"It's one of those things we aren't supposed to do, but everyone sort of turns a blind eye to it. Finvarra's been especially lax about it since she came to power... but then, she's looking pretty young and attractive herself these days," Mackie pointed out.

"You mean she does it, too?" Hannah said, shocked.

"Either that or she hasn't aged in about fifteen years," Mackie said darkly. She pulled an apple from her bag, examined it, and took a huge bite. "The point is, a lot of the women around here have started to view it as one of the perks of the job. They think the spirits owe it to us for devoting our lives to helping them."

"But we aren't helping them if we're draining their energy. Are we?"

Mackie continued through a mouthful of apple. "That's the most ironic part. They're taking this energy as though it's some kind of just reward, but actually it's quite dangerous. The spirits need that energy to fully Cross beyond this world, and all it takes is someone being a little too greedy for that spirit to get trapped in the Aether."

"What the hell is that?" I asked.

"It's the space between worlds. We don't know what lies deep beyond the Gateway, what the final destination is, but we do know there's an in-between space, a realm immediately beyond the Gateway but before the next word. A spirit can become lost there. That space is the Aether, also called the Fifth Element; when we open the Gateway we are, in part, Summoning the Fifth Element. But if Marion and the others aren't extremely careful, the energy they're sapping could cause a spirit to become disorientated and weak—so weak that it could become trapped between worlds, unsure of who it was or where it's is meant to be. It may never reach the final destination."

We sat in silence as the weight of this settled on us.

"That's horrible. How could they risk that?"

"They placate their worries by telling themselves how unlikely it is. They convince themselves that they're careful and controlled—and therefore that the risk to the spirits is minimal. Like an acceptable margin of error."

"That's disgusting," Hannah said with a shudder.

"That's Leeches, mate. That's why they've got the name, and why the rest of us feel so strongly against what they do."

"Well, that and the fact that we're probably jealous as hell of how they look," I said with a smirk.

Mackie grinned. "Yeah, that's most likely part of it, too."

"How can Marion rake our family over the coals for breaking one rule when she and her friends are so obviously breaking another? Isn't she supposed to be all hard core about Durupinen law?"

"Only when it's convenient for her," Mackie snorted. "Don't forget, her family only came to its position because your family fell into disgrace. Of course she's going to blow your issues out of proportion... look where it's gotten her. But like all power-hungry fundamentalists, she's a hypocrite at heart. They shout the loudest at other people's transgressions so that no one will call attention to their own."

I swallowed back the urge to punch something. "You know, Mack, I was really trying to give these people the benefit of the doubt. I told myself that I'd try to understand where they were coming from with all this hostility. But now, between our date with the Elemental and this whole Leech thing, I'm thinking I'm just going to screw that plan. Thoughts on that?"

Mackie chucked her apple core over her shoulder. "Brilliant! Come on, let's head in. That took longer than I thought, it's nearly curfew."

We trudged back to the castle and started up the stairs. I felt fatigued, like I'd run full speed through all those lifetimes; my legs ached in protest as we climbed the stairs.

"I wonder why that last ghost didn't Cross," Hannah said.

"What last ghost?"

"Didn't you sense him? He was sort of off to the side, like he wasn't sure yet if he wanted to go."

"That's not so surprising. It's a big decision to make. Some of those spirits felt hundreds of years old," I said.

"I couldn't get a really clear sense of him. I just kept hearing drumming," added Hannah.

"Drumming? Like, music?"

"No, more of a steady, repeated knocking sound."

I shrugged. "Well, he knows where to find us, whoever he is. Maybe he'll Cross next time. I'm sure he'll let us know if he needs something."

"I guess so. Anyway, that was much easier than last time, wasn't it?"

I nodded. "Yup. Much less of a traffic jam. I'm just glad the feelings pass with them. Some of those were really intense."

"Yes," she said. "Mackie, is it more intense for you, being an Empath?"

Mackie shrugged. "I've never done it any other way, so I don't know. But I think it must be. Brenna has felt fine within a few minutes both times we've performed a Crossing, but it takes a few hours for the effects to wear off for me. It's almost like residual mood swings. If you hear someone sobbing in the bathroom later tonight, don't worry about it. It's just me, bawling my eyes out about someone else's break up or tragic end."

She laughed it off, but as we parted for the night, I thought Mackie's usually buoyant stride was sagging a bit. Being an Empath, I thought, was probably a lot harder than she let on.

It was difficult to believe that a practice like Leeching could actually be going on, but as the day of Initiation crept closer, the evidence mounted. The signs were subtle at first; if Mackie hadn't pointed them out, it would've taken me a long time for me to pick up on them. At first, Peyton, Olivia, and several of the other girls merely seemed to have a healthy glow, as though they had gotten a really good night's sleep or spent some time outdoors in the fresh air. Then it became more pronounced; their skin seemed smoother and more even—almost lit from within—and their hair seemed thicker and shinier. And now that I knew why Marion and the others looked the way they did, I couldn't stop staring at them when they were around.

Peyton was persistent in her attempts to befriend Hannah, and although Hannah continued to refuse, she did so more and more reluctantly. When the morning of the Initiation finally arrived, I came down to breakfast late, having slept in after another restless night of Silent Child dreams. I stopped short in the doorway to find Hannah sitting with Peyton, Olivia, Róisín, and Riley. They were all chatting animatedly.

Olivia looked up and saw me standing there, and quickly rose. "We should get going. I've got to finish my paper before the Initiation tonight."

The others took her lead, said good-bye to Hannah, and flounced past me out the door.

Hannah could barely meet my eyes as I slid into the chair Peyton had just vacated.

"What's going on, Hannah?"

She shrugged guiltily. "Nothing. They asked if I wanted to sit with them, and you weren't here."

"Are you all going to wear pink on Wednesdays?" I asked.

"Huh?"

"Never mind," I said. "I just don't want to see you get hurt, Hannah. Don't forget what those girls did to us."

"I haven't forgotten," said Hannah. "But they all apologized.

Everyone makes mistakes. And you know, it might not be so bad, making friends with them."

"Yeah, if you want to fraternize with the enemy and get tips on morally repugnant anti-aging regimens."

"I just mean that it might make life easier around here, if we can all just get along."

I looked at Hannah carefully. Her voice was casual, but she couldn't disguise the hint of longing in it; for the first time in her life, the popular girls wanted to hang out with her, and that was no small thing after a lifetime of rejection and marginalization.

I phrased my reply carefully. "I think we just need to be careful around them. That's all I'm saying. We shouldn't take it for granted that their intentions are good."

"You didn't like Lucida either, but she's turned out to be a great mentor."

I didn't answer. Every week, Hannah came back from her mentoring sessions with Lucida raving about how nice and helpful and encouraging she was. I was glad Hannah was happy, but I was just waiting for the other shoe to drop—or in Lucida's case, the other designer stiletto. I didn't trust that woman as far as I could throw her, no matter what Hannah said. And the same was true of Peyton.

After a minute, Hannah, in a quiet but firm tone, said, "It's just that it would be nice to have friends."

Ugh. Dagger right to the heart, with a firm little twist to make sure it went in nice and deep. "You've got Milo. And you've got me."

"Milo's a ghost. We can't be friends the same way living people can."

I snorted. "Don't tell him that, he'll kick your ass."

Hannah smiled. "And you don't count either."

"Excuse me?" I crossed my arms, affronted.

"You're my sister, you have to like me."

"That is not true! I don't have to like you! Genetics is no guarantee of friendship... look at Savvy and Phoebe! They're first cousins and Savvy would cheerfully throttle Phoebe if she could get away with it. But I do like you, and I want to be your friend, sister or not."

Hannah's smile broadened into a grin. "I like you, too."

§

Karen had taken the red-eye and arrived bleary-eyed but smiling a couple of hours before lunch. Despite her exhaustion, she went right into lawyer overdrive and interrogated us mercilessly about how the other Apprentices had been treating us since the Elemental slumber party. She took my stance when she heard that Peyton and her friends were trying to get on our good side.

"If that Peyton is anything like her mother, you should watch her like a hawk," Karen advised. "And from what I've seen so far, the rotten apple didn't fall far from the tree. When I alerted the Council to what those girls did to you, do you know what Marion said? Nothing but"—and here Karen affected an excellent imitation of Marion's condescending tone—"'Girls will be girls.' Marion didn't even sound surprised, which confirms that she probably suggested the whole thing."

There wasn't a lot of time to discuss it. Karen went off to meet with our mentors—sort of like the Durupinen version of parent-teacher conferences—and Hannah and I went to get into our ceremonial whites and clan garb for the Initiation.

When we arrived in our room, Milo was doing his own paranormal version of pacing, which involved popping in and out of material form in rapid succession in a bunch of different locations.

"Stop doing that!" I cried at last, after he materialized directly behind me in the mirror, making me jump. "You're freaking me out. I never know where you are."

"What are you so nervous about, anyway?" Hannah asked. "Carrick talked to you about being a Spirit Guide. It doesn't sound like anything too difficult."

"I know that," Milo said, wringing his hands. "I just don't like going up in front of all of those people."

"Since when have you been shy?" I asked. "I always thought you considered a moment out of the spotlight a moment wasted."

"Maybe with you ladies, but with the Caomhnóir? They're so..."

I didn't need to hear the word that was eluding him. "Yeah, they are. And I can't believe we're going to have to spend the rest of our lives with one."

"Finn's really not that bad, you know. And he is really good at his job," Hannah said.

"I know, I know," I said. "I'm not saying he's not a good

Caomhnóir. I just hate the way he talks to me—like he's being forced to do something painful."

"I don't blame the guy. I feel that way every time I talk to you," Milo sneered.

"The feeling is mutual," I replied.

Hannah paused from braiding her hair and put her hands on her hips. Her expression was unusually fierce. "Are you two even going to try to get along? We're less than an hour away from the ceremony that's going to tie us all together for life!"

Milo caught my eye. His face reflected my own sheepishness. "Sorry, sweetness," he said to Hannah. "I'm just messing around, honest. Jess knows I'm kidding, don't you, Jess?"

I nodded. "We're fine. We just don't know how to interact without torturing each other."

Hannah continued to scowl at us, but went back to braiding her hair. "Don't think I'm going to spend all my time breaking up your arguments."

"Yes, Mom," Milo and I said at the same time. We looked at each other and burst out laughing.

Hannah tried—but failed—not to smile. "That's better."

The Initiation was to take place in the Grand Council Room, which, according to Mackie, was like the great hall or the throne room in other castles. It was the most opulent room in the castle, with intricately carved Gothic arches, massive candle-filled chandeliers, and two-story stained glass windows depicting historic High Priestesses. I noticed after a few minutes of gawking that our own ancestor, Agnes Isherwood, whose tapestry Mackie had pointed out to me on the first day of classes, was included among the priestesses. For some reason, the sight of her serene face, illuminated by the setting sun, calmed me.

The Fairhaven bell rang the eight o'clock hour; right on cue the Caomhnóir marched in, followed by the Novitiates. Each Novitiate wore a black silk sash over a white button-down shirt; their tan trousers were uniformly tucked into their tall boots.

"Mixing brown and black? Tragic," Milo whispered to us. We both attempted unsuccessfully to stifle our snickers, which earned us a dirty look from Siobhán.

Each of the Senior Caomhnóir was wearing a sash that corresponded with one of the clans. I looked carefully at each and realized that our clan wasn't represented.

"Karen, why doesn't our family have a Caomhnóir? Is the one who was assigned to you not here?"

Karen's expression became grim. "No, he's not. His name was Liam. He died in a car accident not long after your mom ran off."

"He died?" Hannah asked in surprise.

"Yes," Karen said. "It was really tragic. Lizzy and I never got along with him very well—you've seen how the Caomhnóir are trained to treat us—but obviously I was very upset when he died. It was the same car crash that killed Finvarra's Caomhnóir, Carrick."

"That's awful," I said. I looked over at Carrick, who, as usual, was standing at attention by Finvarra side. "What happened?"

"Carrick was Liam's mentor. When your mother first vanished, Carrick offered to help Liam look for her. It was just an accident—a slippery road at night. I'm told Finvarra took it very badly."

"That's awful," I said again. We lapsed into silence and watched the Novitiates approach the raised platform at the front of the room.

"Where's Finn?" Hannah whispered.

I scanned the two lines of marching figures as they climbed the stairs and faced the crowd. There was an obvious gap in the line beside Isaac; Finn was nowhere to be seen.

Other people had noticed, too; whispers were rippling through the rows of seats. Siobhán had slid out of her chair and gone to the doorway, where Braxton stood deep in conversation with another Senior Caomhnóir. After a moment, Braxton jogged from the room.

"They all look confused," said Hannah. "They must not have realized he was missing."

"Well, they've certainly realized it now," I said. It struck me as very strange that Finn wouldn't be here. He personified the Caomhnóir's commitment to duty—how could he miss a ceremony like this?

Minutes ticked by. The Novitiates continued standing at attention, but were sneaking more and more frequent glances toward their instructors, unsure if the ceremony was going to proceed. The scattered whispers had blossomed into a low hum of conversation; Olivia, I noticed, looked particularly concerned. She had flagged down Marion, who was talking to her in a soothing, but nonetheless carrying, voice.

"Not to worry, Olivia, dear, I'm sure he was merely delayed.

These things happen. No doubt he will have a reasonable explanation for his absence."

Finally, after about fifteen minutes, Celeste climbed the steps to the platform and stood in front of the Novitiates.

"Our apologies everyone, but there has been a delay in locating one of our Novitiates. We've decided to postpone the Initiation until tomorrow so we can—"

The doors banged open. Braxton entered, followed by Finn. Finn's expression was defiant. He spared not a single glance for the crowd of onlookers, but marched straight up onto the platform and took his place in the front row. He was not wearing a sash.

"It appears that I spoke too soon!" announced Celeste with an apologetic shrug. "If everything is now in order, we will begin."

Braxton nodded, and a drum began playing from the back of the hall. I watched as three Caomhnóir marched toward the platform, each with an enormous flag; the central flag was purple with a large golden Triskele on it. The other two flags were black, and depicted, in silver threading, the now-familiar rune of protection. It was the same symbol that each of the Caomhnóir wore on the shoulder of his sash.

As the drum beat, each of the Novitiates stomped his right foot in time and pounded his chest with his left hand. They then all began chanting something which, to my still-untrained ear, sounded like Old English. It was at once primitive and powerful. The flag bearers marched to the staircase at the left of the platform, mounted it, then set their flags into the stands behind the Novitiates. The bearers then took their positions among the others. The drumming rose to a thunderous crescendo and then stopped.

Braxton stepped forward. "These men today begin their sacred duty as protectors of the Gateways. The Caomhnóir have a long and glorious history as Guardians of the Durupinen. Our commitment to the Durupinen and the spirits they serve is vital to the continuation of our ancient calling. We the chosen, salute you, our Brothers."

Here the Senior Caomhnóir turned to Novitiates and gave them a specialized salute—three sharp strikes against the chest followed by a bow.

Braxton went on, turning to the Apprentices, "When I call your clan name, please come forward and join your Caomhnóir on the platform.

Róisín and Riley Lightfoot were called first. They ascended the platform and stood beside their Caomhnóir, a strapping man named Patrick who looked about ten years older than the others. He thrust forward a large, veined hand, and Róisín and Riley placed their hands on top of it. Braxton raised a long, ancient-looking leather strap, which was branded with runes. He placed the strap on the three joined hands and wrapped it once, twice, three times around.

"And thus you are Bound to the service of the Gateway. Gatekeepers and Guardian united as one, until the beacon is passed to the next generation."

Braxton unwound the leather strap, and then one of the Senior Caomhnóir stepped between Patrick and the Lightfoot girls. He faced Patrick and removed his own bright scarlet sash. Patrick bowed and the Senior Caomhnóir placed the sash over Patrick's head; he adjusted the sash carefully then pinned to Patrick's shoulder.

The crowd broke into applause, under the cover of which I asked Karen another question.

"What happens to that older Caomhnóir now?"

"He has completed his duties. He's done," Karen replied.

"So what, he's... unemployed now?"

"Yes, I suppose so," Karen said with a laugh. "But the Durupinen aren't just going to kick him out to fend for himself. They will ensure he finds a good job and a comfortable home. He may even want to stay here to teach and train the Novitiates. That's what many of them do. And there's also diplomatic positions he could take. Don't worry, he's got plenty of options."

I looked across the line of Senior Caomhnóir waiting to turn over their sashes. How strange it must be to train your entire life for something, and then be told you can't do it anymore. But at least they were free to choose their own paths now.

One by one, the Novitiates were Bound to the Apprentices. Finally, with only three clans remaining, it was our turn.

"Clan Sassanaigh." Braxton's voice boomed.

Hannah and I mounted the platform. We were accompanied by Milo, who'd been instructed to follow us.

"To this clan we Bind not only a Caomhnóir, but also a Spirit Guide. Milo Chang, do you swear to defend these Apprentices as they carry out the sacred duties of the Durupinen? Do you promise to do your utmost to guide them and protect them from harm?"

"I swear by the body I have left behind me, and by the form in which I now exist," Milo recited carefully. Upon completing the vow, his form lit up with a momentary glow so bright that it forced us to shield our eyes. When we dared to look again, Milo was himself once more—although he had an upright, prideful air about him.

"Very well. And now, Finn Carey please step forward," said Braxton.

Finn did not move immediately. His face was absolutely inscrutable, but his hands gave him away—he was clenching and unclenching his fists at his sides. With a deep, low breath—as though he were preparing for something dangerous—he stepped forward at last and thrust out a hand.

Hannah and I placed our hands on top of Finn's. As my skin came to rest on top of his, I felt him twitch; I thought for sure he was going to pull away. He kept his eyes carefully trained on a spot somewhere over our heads.

Braxton wound the strap around our hands. He did it very loosely, but I still felt the alarming urge to break free from the strap and run. Finn's eyes were closed; he was breathing very slowly and deeply through his nose, as though fighting the urge to be sick.

Braxton's voice rang out. "And thus you are Bound to the service of the Gateway. Gatekeepers and Guardian united as one, until the beacon is passed to the next generation."

Before the strap could be completely unwound, Finn pulled his hand away. When he opened his eyes again, they bore—for the briefest moment—into my own, and they spoke of a pain that took my breath away.

The rest of the ceremony continued around us, beyond my notice. All I could do was wonder: Why had Finn been late for the ceremony? Had he been trying to avoid being placed with us? Could he really have been dreading the Initiation even more than I had? And what in the world was causing him the kind of pain that I'd seen in his dark, fathomless eyes? Perhaps—at some point in the many years we would now be compelled to spend together—I would find the courage to ask him.

13

A CANDLE IN THE DARK

THAT NIGHT, I DREAMED AGAIN OF THE SILENT CHILD. She stood before a towering inferno, with flames rolling and churning behind her. She made no attempts to escape the fire; she did not run, or scream, or call for help. She simply raised her hands helplessly, perhaps in supplication. The smell of smoke was overpowering; it scratched at my throat and stung my eyes. I began to cough.

I didn't remember having woke up, but suddenly, I was sitting upright, racked with a spasm of real coughing. Although the dream had faded, the acrid smell of smoke remained.

"Hannah, wake up! I think something's on fire!" I gasped between spasms.

Hannah did not stir. I looked around the room, but everything was still and quiet. The fire in the grate had long since burned down to gently glowing embers, and the few candles we owned sat cold and unlit in their holders.

I continued to cough. Was it just the aftermath of the dream? I could still smell smoke. I slid out of bed and crossed to the door, where the smell grew more pungent. The door handle was warm to the touch. I hesitated; I was pretty sure I had a vague memory of a public service announcement that warned children to stay away from such doors. I opened it anyway, then leapt back with a yell.

The Silent Child stood perfectly still just outside the door, alight like a human torch.

My first instinct was to look frantically around for something to smother the fire, but my reason caught up with me—I remembered that a spirit couldn't burn. I shielded my eyes from the intensity of the flames. The Silent Child didn't appear to be in any pain at all; she simply looked at me with a very serious expression visible through the conflagration.

"What do you want?" I asked her.

She beckoned for me to follow her, and turned to walk down the hallway.

I looked back over my shoulder. Hannah was still sound asleep, and Milo was nowhere to be seen. I threw on the black sweater that was hanging on the back of my chair, quickly slid my feet into my slippers, and followed the Silent Child out into the hall. As if this were a real fire, I closed the door behind me to keep the flames from spreading.

She made no sound as she guided me through the corridors—a grisly little beacon bent on an unknown destination. Her light undulated over the stone floor and casted long, pointed shadows all around her.

On and on I followed. We climbed yet another staircase and entered a wing of the castle I'd never seen before. We turned a corner; the statue of a robed woman loomed. The Silent Child stopped.

I froze several feet behind her. She turned back to me and pointed a small, trembling finger toward the end of the hallway. I could see a sliver of light escaping around the edges of a slightly ajar door.

"Is there something in there you want me to see?" I asked.

She shook her head, sending sparks twirling into the air above her. She pointed again, and then put a finger to her lips. Then she vanished in a puff of smoke that hung for a moment in her shape before dissipating, leaving me in almost total darkness.

I crept down the hallway, my heart pounding like mad, toward the partially open door. As I inched nearer, I could hear muffled voices coming from the room—at least three different voices, one much lower than the others. I pressed myself up against the wall as I approached the door, blessing the thick old carpet that deadened the sound of my footsteps. I leaned in as close as possible and listened.

"...don't quite understand why this needed to be brought to my attention, and at such an hour," said the first voice, which I recognized at once as Finvarra's. "Honestly, Marion, I don't see what there is to be concerned about."

"Did you not read my notes properly?" came Marion's voice, with a sharp edge of impatience.

"I would venture to say that my literacy skills are as good as ever they were," Finvarra replied, her own voice growing sharp now.

"Well then, perhaps you are interpreting things differently, but I found Lucida's report to be very disturbing indeed."

"Disturbing in what way?" said the third voice, a deep one. Carrick, never far from Finvarra's side, had accompanied her to this late night meeting.

"The girl's skills are clearly far more advanced than any other Caller we have record of," Marion said. "She has not only the ability to Call spirits to her, but she's able to Call many spirits at once... and with impressive speed."

I fought to calm my breath. They were talking about Hannah.

"This is not unheard of," Finvarra said calmly. "Lucida herself can Call multiple spirits at once, and there's no great delay in their appearance."

"Lucida has had years of training," Marion snapped. "But this is not the most disturbing detail. This girl also seems to be able, in some circumstances, to influence the spirits' behavior."

"The gift of Calling is very rare," replied Finvarra. "We have very little precedent with which to compare the girl's abilities, and the documentation is scattered at best. It is impossible to say if her abilities are unusual for a Caller. It could very well be a normal part of the gift."

"No part of this gift is normal!" Marion cried, and there was a blunt knocking sound, as though she had rapped her fist against something hard in frustration. "And given the other unknown factors in the girl's life, I think we need to give the Council this information and open the issue for discussion."

"Calm down, Marion," said Carrick. "You forget yourself."

There was a pause. Marion took a deep breath. "I apologize, High Priestess," she said, although her tone was still sharp. "But I must ask you to consider this request. We have monitored the situation carefully for years. The gift is only the most recent—though in my opinion the most significant—piece to a puzzle that points more and more clearly to—"

"I disagree, Marion," Finvarra said firmly. "You have made no efforts to hide your disdain for their entire clan since the girls have arrived here. I will not allow prejudice and suspicion to cloud our fair treatment of them. What you have shown me thus far is not conclusive proof, but biased speculation. We will watch and we will wait. That is my final word on this matter."

"I wish for my objections to this course of inaction to be noted," said Marion.

"So noted," Finvarra said.

Several seconds of loaded silence followed these words. Then, without warning, the door flew open and Marion stormed out. I flattened myself against the wall as the door came swinging at me; I just managed to stop it from hitting me by using my foot as a doorstop. Marion was so intent on her own dramatic exit that she didn't notice.

I waited for her to turn the corner, then I skirted along the wall as quickly as I could and ducked behind the robed statue just as Finvarra and Carrick emerged. Finvarra closed the door behind them. I wedged myself tightly between the wall and the stone plinth, crouching awkwardly, until they too disappeared around the corner. Despite my discomfort, it was several minutes before I climbed out.

I don't know how I found my way back to my room; I was so distracted that I was barely paying attention to where I was walking. I knew Hannah was special—I'd known it from the first day we'd met. Her connection to spirits was something altogether more mysterious and powerful than anything I'd ever experienced; she had such an affinity for them, such an intuitive understanding of their energy and their communications. I thought at first this was merely the result of practice, since she'd been interacting with them for her entire life. But I knew now—and so, it seemed, did everyone else—that Hannah's gift was unique. But was it dangerous? Was it something for the other Durupinen to be worried about?

The Silent Child certainly seemed to think so. Why had she showed me that conversation? To warn me? Did she understand more about the exchange than I did? My head was spinning by the time I lay back down; I dozed fitfully until morning.

§

I decided not to say anything to Hannah or Karen about what the Silent Child had shown me; I didn't know what it all meant, and there was no reason for all three of us to obsess over it. Karen left the next evening, off to bury herself in more legal briefs. We wouldn't see her again until her next trip out—another month at least. I didn't want to add to her already-crippling worries about us. And Hannah was so happy about the progress she was making in her mentoring sessions; I didn't want to ruin that for her.

"Lucida says my gift could be a real asset in the future," Hannah said enthusiastically after the following Monday's session. "She says I may be of real use to the Durupinen, and maybe even on the Council one day!"

"Do you want to be on the Council?" I asked her.

"I don't know," she replied. "Maybe not, but it's still nice to know that they might want me."

I didn't respond. I, for one, wouldn't set foot on that Council if they begged me on bended knee—not that I thought that was likely. My own mentoring sessions were getting slightly better; at least Fiona now acknowledged my existence most of the time, but the tasks she set me to were increasingly difficult. No matter what I produced, she was never satisfied with my results. On one hand, her unattainable standards drove me to work harder in her class than I did anywhere else; on the other hand, I was usually left feeling inadequate and frustrated.

This feeling was likely to infect my other classes as long as the Silent Child kept haunting my dreams. I now spent every night in her company. It was always the same dream... and in every dream I called to her. I begged her to show me something, anything, new that might help me understand what she was trying to tell me. Was she showing me what had happened to her? Was she showing me something that was going to happen in the future? She never replied.

I scoured the library for books on dreams and dream interpretation, but they yielded little. I asked Siobhán in class, hoping she could shed some light on how spirits might communicate in dreams, but other than confirming that spirits do sometimes choose to appear in dream-form, she could offer little help.

"Are you having dream Visitations?" she asked, with her voice full of academic interest.

"I... no, not recently," I said. "But I have in the past. I was just curious."

I wasn't entirely sure why I lied. But there had to be a reason that the Silent Child had chosen me; talking with others about our interactions, however unfathomable they were, felt like a betrayal of her trust.

The cherry on the top of the aggravation sundae that week was yet another dead-end in my search for Pierce. The reporter who had written the story about Neil sent me the contact information the paper had on file for him, but it was the same email address I already had. I was at a complete loss for what to do next.

Friday rolled around at last, and all I could think about was how happy I'd be to get through the day so I could fall into bed and sleep in on Saturday morning. I hadn't been this tired since my first few weeks at St. Matt's, when I'd been plagued by nightmares. Back then, I hadn't known what the nightmares meant, or what was causing them; this time I knew exactly who was causing the nightmares, but I was no closer to making them stop. At St. Matt's, I'd been able to rely on really strong coffee to get me through—now that I was in England, there wasn't enough tea in the entire school to give me the caffeine jolt I needed.

That afternoon, I stumbled into the courtyard for Bonding and Meditation with a sense of relief... just two more hours and I could hang out with my new best friend: Unconsciousness. Then I saw how Keira had drawn the Circles for class.

"Crap."

Finn was sitting on the edge of our communication Circle, with his face buried in one of his battered notebooks. Hannah saw the look on my face and put a reassuring hand on my shoulder. "Don't worry, it'll be fine. We'll be done really soon."

"Easy for you to say. All you have to do is snap your fingers and the spirits come running. It'll be all Finn can do to line them up single-file and make them play nice."

Hannah smiled. "Want me to send some over to you?"

"I don't need your pity ghosts!" Hannah giggled in response.

"Come along, everyone," Keira called, her voice echoing through the courtyard like a whip-crack. "The hour is about to start, and you all need appropriate time to meditate if you are going to have any meaningful communication! I want those spirit journals filled today, no excuses!"

There was a general flurry as the class hurried to their Circles and settled on the ground, which was still damp from the previous night's rain. I pulled off my hoodie and folded it under me in a feeble attempt to keep my jeans dry.

"Hi," I said to Finn.

He didn't look up from whatever it was he was writing, but nodded his head in grudging acknowledgment of my presence.

"Castings for connections should now be underway," Keira said. "I will be coming around to make sure your runes are correctly drawn."

I pulled my chalk out of my black velvet bag and held out a piece to Finn, who was still scribbling in his notebook. I cleared my throat loudly.

"I'm not getting marked down because you want to be the next Shakespeare," I said.

Still without looking at me, Finn snapped his journal shut, shoved it deep into his backpack, and snatched the chalk from my hand.

I pressed my hands against my eyes so hard that the black behind my eyelids popped with white lights. What the hell were the runes I was supposed to use? I didn't dare glance at the other Circles or take out my textbook, lest Keira notice and call me out in front of everyone for being unprepared. I visualized the page from the book that contained the instructions for this Casting; I forced myself to see first the heading, then the illustrations. The runes emerged from the fog of my brain, and I opened my eyes and scratched their shapes onto the rough cobblestones. When I had finished, I turned to Finn, who had already set down his chalk.

"Are you ready to start?" I asked.

"Yes."

We both closed our eyes and began to concentrate. I knew what to expect, so I didn't waste time doubting myself and instead concentrated all my energy on relaxing my body. After a few minutes of this, I had to reroute some of my energy into keeping myself awake. I started to repeat the Incantation Keira had taught us, doing my best not to massacre the pronunciation. I'd barely gotten through it twice when a voice broke in.

"Are you Jessica Ballard?"

I jumped in alarm, and my eyes snapped open. I couldn't see anyone. I looked over and caught Finn's eye. He'd clearly sensed something as well.

"You've got something?" he asked.

"Yeah, I think so."

"Me too," he said. "The spirit doesn't seem terribly happy, but he's not properly hostile. I think you can try to communicate."

"Okay," I replied, and closed my eyes again. I tried to find the mental place I'd been in when I heard the voice, but before I'd even gotten my mental bearings back, the voice broke through again.

"Hello? I really don't have all day here. Are you Jessica Ballard?" It was a man's voice, and he sounded... annoyed.

"Yes, I'm Jess Ballard," I thought, trying not to move my lips with the words. "Who are you?"

"My name is Lyle McElroy. I have a message for you."

His tone completely threw me off. It was like being on the phone with a telemarketer who resents his job. I scrambled for the next thing I was supposed to say.

"I mean you no harm, Lyle. I welcome your presence."

"I don't care whether you welcome my presence or not!" said Lyle, and I felt Finn shift his weight protectively. "I really couldn't care less! I just want to deliver my message so I can get back to my flat. I've been trying to communicate with you for days, but every time I've seen you out here that kid keeps me and all the other ghosts away."

"What kid?"

"The creepy one. The one in the nightdress. Looks like a street urchin from a Dickens novel."

The Silent Child again. So that was why I couldn't get any connections. She was keeping the spirits away, trying to keep the lines of communication between us clear and unfettered from interference. At least I knew now it wasn't me.

"It took me days to convince her that I needed to see you. Doesn't talk much, but she certainly gets a point across. Kept lighting herself on fire every time I got too close. Now, can I give you the message or what?" Lyle said.

Finn's voice cut across Lyle's. "His negative energy is rising. Should I expel him?"

"No," I whispered. "He's not hostile, he's just... grumpy."

"Grumpy?"

"Yes, grumpy!" I snapped. "I'll let you know if he needs to go! Now would you please leave me alone so I can concentrate? I don't need another bad grade in this class."

I felt for Lyle again and found him quickly. "What can I do for you, Lyle?"

"What can you do for me? What can you *do* for me? I'll tell you what you can do for me! You can tell your friend that I don't appreciate being used as a messenger boy! I might be dead, but I have things to do and places to be! Well, one place really, but I'd like to get back there as soon as possible!"

I tried to force Lyle's energy to form a picture in my mind; slowly, the hazy form of a balding, middle-aged man appeared. He wore heavily-framed glasses and an ill-fitting, crumpled suit. He also had a bad comb-over that I had thought only existed in cartoons.

I tried to remember the next thing I was supposed to say, but Lyle's wheezy breathing distracted me. I decided to drop the official text and go off-script. "Did you say you have a message for me?"

"Yes," Lyle said with a sigh. "She wants you to meet her tomorrow night."

"Who wants me to meet her? Who are you talking about?"

"She didn't tell me her name, in case anyone else intercepted her message, whatever that's supposed to mean," Lyle said, shrugging in a resigned sort of way. "I don't know who's going to bother trying to intercept a message from me. I haven't spoken to anyone living at all since I died. Well, except for my brother, but he's still pretending he can't hear me."

"How am I supposed to know who I'm meeting if you don't know her name?"

"She told me the first time you met her was in her tent, and that you brought a fish. She said you'd know who I meant."

"Annabelle!" My heart began to race. She was alive.

"If you say so," said Lyle. "Whoever she was, it was quite rude of her to insinuate that I had nothing better to do than run her errands."

"Why does she want me to meet her?" I thought-spoke as hard as I could.

"I don't know why, I only know where," Lyle said, his voice rising with impatience.

"Jess," Finn murmured, "I really don't like his energy right now. If you can't calm him down, I'm going to expel him."

"I said he's fine! Will you just trust me, please? I can handle this," I replied, a little more loudly than I meant to. I heard some movement around us, and I knew without opening my eyes that some people had paused in their own meditations to eavesdrop on our Circle.

"Well handle it then... or I will!" Finn said firmly.

"Sorry about that, Lyle," I thought, as politely as I could. "Could you please tell me where I'm supposed to meet her?"

"Tomorrow night at eleven o'clock. She wants you to meet her on one of the benches outside of the Tate Modern in London. She'll be waiting for you there, and she urges you not to be late and to come alone. She also begs you not to tell anyone here that you're meeting her, because it would be very dangerous if they knew she was contacting you."

I repeated the instructions over and over again inside my head. "Okay, I will. Can you please tell her that I will be there?"

"Oh, another errand, is it?" Lyle said, his voice rising. "Just because I'm dead, my previous engagements don't matter?"

"I'm sorry, I didn't mean to..."

"I won't stand for it! Do you understand? I have no intention of spending my afterlife as an errand boy! I delivered the message—not that she gave me much of a choice—and now I intend to—"

But I didn't find out what Lyle McElroy intended. Before he could shout another word at me, his presence was swept with decisive force from our Circle and expelled beyond my range of communication. Furious, I opened my eyes and snapped at Finn.

"Why did you do that?"

He opened his eyes as well, and turned to face me in surprise. "He was getting properly hostile. I did my job."

"I told you I could handle it!" I cried.

"It didn't feel that way to me!"

Hannah, agog, cast a distressed glance at me, but didn't speak.

"I don't give a damn how it felt to you!" I said, jumping to my feet and knocking one of the candles to the ground in the process. "What matters is how it felt to me, and I told you that I had it under control!"

"And I didn't believe you!"

"You didn't believe me? So what... I'm a liar now? Suddenly it's your job to decide whether or not I'm telling the truth?"

Finn got to his feet as well. "It's my job to protect you!"

"No, it's your job to trust me, and you suck at it!" I shouted.

Finn opened his mouth to retort, but Keira stepped in, her face scarlet with anger. "Will the two of you please stop this display at once!"

"Gladly!" I said, and, without another word, I snatched up my bag and stormed from the courtyard.

I could hear Keira and Hannah calling after me; I knew I'd probably be in trouble, but I didn't care. I strode out of the courtyard and into the gardens, searching mentally as I did so for any sign of Lyle, but I could sense no trace of him—I was way too angry to concentrate on spirit communication. I tried to forget my burning desire to beat the hell out of Finn and instead focused on my new information: Annabelle was in London and she wanted to see me. It was at once exhilarating and terrifying news.

On the one hand, I was quite sure that Annabelle wouldn't travel all the way to London and send a clearly reluctant ghost to find me if all she wanted was a casual catch-up. Her shop had nearly been burned to the ground and she had vanished without a trace only to turn up in the same country as me: Obviously, she wasn't enjoying a relaxing vacation. She had information about Pierce, I was sure of it. On the other hand, that information could bring a terrible realization to all of my fears.

Almost as if this thought had an influence on the weather, the misty drizzle gave way to a heavy sun shower. I broke into a run and took refuge beneath the slate eves of a garden gazebo just as it began to rain in earnest.

I couldn't ignore Annabelle's summons, which meant that I had to find a way to meet her without anyone at Fairhaven finding out. And if I were going to sneak out under cover of darkness and find my way around a strange city without getting caught, there was only one person I could trust to help me pull it off.

I caught up with Savvy just after dinner. I needed her help, but I was also careful to keep the information sharing on a need-to-know basis. As I predicted, Savvy was thrilled to take me under her wonderfully louche wing.

"Excellent!" Savvy said, grinning from ear to ear.

"Shh!" I hissed, and cast a panicked glance around the corridor. Although I saw no one, I could hear a few scattered voices—though if living or dead, I couldn't tell. "So, I take it that's a yes?"

"Of course it's a yes! I've been trying to convince you to have a bit of fun for ages! What changed your mind?"

"I didn't change my mind. I'm not interested in hitting one of your friend's parties," I said. "I got a... message from a friend who's going to be in the city tomorrow."

"Oi, what friend is this now? Is this a male friend?" Savvy waggled her eyebrows suggestively. "No," I replied. "Your seeing me in the shower is the only action I'm likely to get for a while. So how do we do this?"

"Simple enough," said Savvy. "Leave it all to me. What time do you need to meet this friend?"

"Eleven o'clock tomorrow night outside of the Tate Modern."

"Right then. We ought to leave by eight-thirty at the latest. We could fuss with train schedules and the Tube and all that, but since you have a specific schedule, I think we ought to skip all that and hire a car. But I have to warn you, a hackney will be pricey—probably ninety pounds, anyway. Can you swing that?"

"Yeah yeah, whatever. I don't mind forking out some cash as long as we can do this without getting caught. I just need you to come with me, because I have no idea where I'm going. I've never been to London before. I've driven through it, but that doesn't really count."

"Of course I'm coming with you! You think I'd organize this whole thing but not take advantage of a night away from this place? There are plenty of pubs in Southwark. I'll drop you at the Tate and then find myself a pint."

"If you can get me there and back without getting caught, I'll buy you that pint," I said.

"Don't you worry love, I've never had trouble finding some bloke to bankroll a night of drinking," Savvy said with a dismissive wave of her hand. "How long do you think you'll need in the city?"

"I have no idea. I don't know why she wants to meet me. I think, to be safe, we should assume we'll be there a couple of hours. I can text you when I'm done and then meet up with you for the ride back?"

"Sure you don't want to stay in town awhile? If we're going to be there anyway, we might as well make a night of it, hit some clubs—"

"Sav, I promise, if we get away with this, I'll join you on your next field trip and we'll hit as many clubs as you want. I'll let you drag me on a debauchery tour of London, okay?"

"It's a deal. Leave it to me," Savvy said.

"Thanks," I said. I turned to go, but she caught my arm.

"Debauchery tours of London." said Savvy, with a thoughtful expression. "That might just be a million dollar idea you've got there. I bet someone could make a fortune on that, eh?"

"If anyone could do it, I'm sure you could," I told her. "You're the most debaucherous person I know. Now get planning."

I didn't want to tell Hannah what I was going to do, but I didn't really see any way around it. It was a little too much to hope that she wouldn't notice my being gone all night. I considered telling her a half-truth—that I was going into London with Savvy, but that we were just having a girls' night out. I nixed the idea as quickly as I thought of it; the only person less likely than myself to participate in that kind of girls' night was Hannah, and we both knew it. Plus, Hannah and I had to trust each other totally and completely if we were going to make it here. So, on Saturday afternoon, during a well-earned break from a mind-numbing mountain of history homework, I climbed up onto her bed.

"I have to tell you something, but I don't want you to freak out."

"Oh God, what is it?" she asked as her eyes widened.

"I said don't freak out!"

"Well, then don't start a conversation like that. If you imply there's going to be something to freak out about, I'm going to freak out!"

"Good point. Okay, starting over... I'm just letting you know that I have to go out tonight."

Hannah's eyebrows contracted. "Oh. Where are you going?"

"To London."

She stared at me expectantly. When I didn't volunteer anything else, she asked, "Aren't you going to tell me why you're going?"

I took a deep breath. "You know how I'm trying to find out what happened to Pierce?"

"Yeah."

"Well, a mutual friend of ours is in London this weekend, and I want to meet up with her to see if she knows anything. It's Annabelle, that medium I told you about, remember?"

"The one with the tarot cards?"

"Yeah."

Hannah furrowed her brow. "How did you find out she was in London?"

"She sent me a... message," I hedged.

"If she got in touch with you, why didn't you just ask her about Pierce? Why do you have to go all the way to London to ask her?"

I squirmed a little. "It wasn't that kind of message. She sent a spirit to find me. That's who I made contact with during meditation yesterday, the one Finn expelled from the Circle."

"She can send spirits to bring messages?" Hannah asked in surprise.

"Apparently."

"I didn't realize there were people besides the Durupinen out there who could do that sort of thing," she said, forgetting her worry for a moment and perking up with a very Tia-like curiosity.

"Me neither. But the spirit wasn't very happy about being sent to find me, so I didn't really have a chance to get many details... especially with Finn butting in and expelling him mid-conversation." I took a deep breath and forced my aggravation at Finn out of my mind. "Anyway, she wants to meet me tonight night, and I think it must be important if she's sending afterlife messengers to track me down."

Hannah bit her lip. "How are you going to get there?"

"I've enlisted our resident escape artist."

"Savannah? You're letting Savvy do this?" Hannah cried.

"She's the only one who sneaks out of here regularly. She's my only chance."

"Jess, she's always in trouble! She can't be that good at sneaking out if she's always getting caught and punished for it!"

"Actually, she's really good at the sneaking out part. It's the sneaking back in part that usually gets her in trouble... and that's usually because she's been partying too hard to do it right," I replied. "I'm won't be doing any partying, so I'm sure I'll get back in without a problem."

"Why can't you just get permission to go to London and talk to Annabelle?"

"She doesn't want anyone to know she's meeting me... and to be honest, neither do I. You know how the Council is about outsiders knowing too much. All I need is for Marion or someone to get wind of this. Then Annabelle could be in trouble, too."

Hannah opened her mouth to argue again but I held up a quelling hand.

"It doesn't matter whether I get caught or not. This could be really important and I have to go. I wasn't even going to tell you, but I didn't want you to wake up, find me gone, and send out a search party."

"I still don't like it," said Hannah.

"I don't either," I said, reaching out and squeezing her shoulder. "But you know how much Pierce means to me. If Annabelle knows something, I have to find out what it is."

Hannah sighed. "You're right. But you'd better keep Savvy on a tight leash or you'll both get caught anyway."

I smiled. "Good point. Consider her leashed."

§

I was so distracted for the rest of the afternoon that I wrote what was probably the worst history paper of my life—middle-school-level bad. But I didn't care—two thirds of my brain was focused on the clock as I watched the minutes crawl by. Finally, Savvy tapped briskly on our door at quarter past eight.

"You ready?" she asked.

"Yup. Let's rock this, Catholic-boarding-school style."

She nodded to Hannah, who was curled up in her pajamas in one of the armchairs by the fire.

"Don't worry about a thing, wee one. I'll have her back in one piece in a tick."

Hannah scowled. "I don't think I'll be sleeping much."

"I'll have my phone with me," I told her, holding my cell up before stashing it in my back pocket. "You can text me every five minutes if you want to."

"You'll have something even better than that with you," Hannah said, and closed her eyes. "Milo? Can you come here for a second?"

Before she had even opened her eyes, Milo was lounging in the chair next to hers.

"You rang, sweetness?"

"It's right creepy the way you do that," Savvy said, shaking her head.

Hannah ignored her. "Milo, Jess needs your help."

I could almost literally see the storm cloud form over Milo's head. "It's starting already, isn't it? I knew this Spirit Guide gig was going to suck."

"Okay, fine, *I* need your help." Hannah said. "Do it for me, okay? And anyway, I think you'll be more than willing when you find out what it is."

"Still listening, but refusing to look at you," Milo said, crossing his arms.

"Jess has to go to London tonight and I want you to go with her."

Milo dropped his arms and his jaw simultaneously. "London? Seriously?"

"Seriously," replied Hannah.

"Wait a minute!" I cried. "What's the point of that? What possible good will it do for Milo to come with me?"

"I don't know what good it'll do you, but it will make me feel better," Hannah said. "And besides, now I'll be able to communicate with him and make sure you're okay."

I held up my phone again. "I have a cell phone. The obnoxious Spirit Guide is superfluous."

Hannah smirked. "You could lose your cell signal. I never lose my Milo signal."

"Lucky us," I grumbled. "Well, whatever, he doesn't want to go anywhere with me, do you?"

"Of course I don't want to go anywhere with you," Milo answered. "But I do want to see London, so if you're going, I'm tagging along."

"You've got to be kidding me." I dropped my head into my hands. Of all of the moments for Milo's contempt for me to fail! "Hannah, I know you're nervous, but can't you just give me a break here? I've got enough to worry about without Milo floating around and criticizing my wardrobe, okay?"

"I know," Hannah said. "That's why he's going to promise not to do any of that tonight."

Milo whipped his head around and stared at her. "Come again?"

"You two are going to be around each other a lot, so you might as well get some practice learning to live with each other," Hannah said, before passing a stern look between us as though we were a pair of toddlers tugging on the same teddy bear. "Milo, I know you want to travel, so here's your chance. You can go with Jess to London and have a look around—now that you're Bound to both of us, you should be able to travel that far away from me as long as she's with you. But you also need to be nice to her and stay in touch with me so I know everything is okay."

Milo stuck out his bottom lip in a cartoonish pout. "Can't you and I just go together?"

"I hope we can, eventually, but I don't know when that will be. In the meantime, don't you want to take a stroll through the shopping districts? I bet Savvy would know where to send you."

"Sloane Street," Savvy said at once. "It's like walking down a runway during London's fashion week."

Milo's eyes lit up like a kid's on Christmas morning. Savvy had said the magic words.

"And anyway," she went on, "we need to use a spirit to get across the Wards. This will simplify things."

"What do we need a spirit for?" I asked.

"You'll see," replied Savvy.

Hannah jumped in before I could demand a better explanation. "See? It all works out! So Milo, all you need to do is come if Jess calls you, but otherwise you can window shop to your heart's content. What do you say?"

Milo glanced over at me and tried to reassume a nonchalant air. "Well, I guess I could find something to occupy myself while she's there."

"Jess? Any more objections?"

I had plenty, but none that wouldn't sound petulant. "Fine, I'll bring him."

Hannah smiled at last. "Great. Have a nice time, and please try not to get caught."

"Right." I grabbed my bag, slung it over my shoulder, and followed Savvy out.

"You don't look as nervous as I thought you would," she said, clapping me on the back as we started down the hall. "You've got some faith in ol' Savvy then, eh?"

"I've got faith in your wardrobe choices," I said. "Miniskirt and four-inch heels? At least I know we won't be shinnying down drainpipes or climbing over hedges."

"Says you," Savvy replied. "Have you got your drawing stuff?"

I patted my bag. "All in here."

"Brilliant. Now, we split up. Take the main staircase, then meet me in the northwest corner of the courtyard in ten minutes. We need stay along the edge of the woods if we're going to get off the grounds without being seen. Milo, you can come with me."

"Fab," said Milo.

"See you in a few," I said, and started for the main entrance hall.

We had decided that I would use my sketchbook as a pretext for getting out onto the grounds. The grounds were big enough that, if anyone were looking for me, I could claim to have been tucked away in some forgotten corner whole time. It also gave me an emergency excuse if I got caught sneaking in after curfew—I could say I had dozed off while sketching. I might still get reprimanded, but probably not punished.

As I rounded the last landing to the entrance hall, luck was on my side; Celeste was just coming out of the dining room.

"Hi, Celeste," I called with a wave.

"Hello, Jess," she said with a smile. "Where are you off to?"

"I thought I'd do a little twilight sketching," I said, lifting the flap on my bag so that my sketchbook was clearly visible. "There's a full moon tonight. The shadow play should be pretty spectacular."

"Wonderful," Celeste said. "Karen tells me you draw beautifully. I'd love to see some of them sometime—if you wouldn't mind showing me, of course."

"Why would I mind?" I asked, pulling my sketchbook out.

"Well, I know how some artists can be about their work," she said, with half a glance behind her. Fiona was sitting on a bench by the far wall, hunched over a book and a soup bowl. Her posture promised that she would pounce on the first person who disturbed her ruminations.

"We're not all quite so... well, we're not all like that," I said, flipping the book open to a sketch of one of the fountains.

"This is just splendid!" Celeste said as she took my sketchbook. "Karen was quite right to brag." Then she lowered her voice and whispered, "How is it going with Fiona?"

I grimaced. "She still lets me come to classes, and last week she didn't throw anything the whole session. That's about the best thing I can say about it."

"Don't take it personally. She's the castle curmudgeon, always has been." Celeste handed the sketchbook back to me. "Have fun then, but don't lose track of time out there. Curfew starts at 10:30 PM."

"I've got my watch," I said, raising it up for her to see. "See you later."

"Don't forget you also have a paper due Monday!" Celeste called after me.

"Finished it!" I called back as I slipped out the door. No need to mention that she would probably make me rewrite it.

I walked casually along the gravel path that led to the courtyard, stopping here or there to examine a flower or a statue, just in case anyone was watching me from the windows. I ran my hand along the smooth, weathered stone of the castle wall, turned the corner, then picked up my pace in the shadows of the cloister's ivy-covered roof. By the time I reached the spot where Savvy and Milo stood waiting for me, I was jogging.

"Alright?" she asked.

"Yeah, good," I said a bit breathlessly. "I saw Celeste and told her I'd be out sketching."

"Well played," Savvy said. "Right, let's go then."

We skirted along the castle wall, keeping to the shadows, and snuck into a nearby fringe of trees. We put a few yards of foliage between us and the lawns before we turned and started for the far end of the grounds. Savvy covered the ground unnervingly fast in her heels, and I started to wonder if we would indeed be scaling walls or climbing trees. After about fifteen minutes, we reached the furthest corner of the grounds, where the trees thinned to a smattering of bushes. Finally, we reached the road.

Savvy checked her watch. "The cab should be here any minute. We should try to cross the Wards before it gets here or it's going to look dodgy."

"Don't we just... walk across?" I asked. "It's not an electric fence or anything."

"Sure, we could just step through, but they'll know," Savvy explained, as she cocked her head in the direction of the castle, the top towers of which were just visible over the trees. "That's how I got caught the first two times I snuck out. The Wards will let us through, but they also alert the Caomhnóir to our crossing. Two of them were waiting for me right here when I got back."

"Great, so how are we supposed to leave without being detected?"

"With a little help from the dearly departed," Savvy said, pointing first at Milo, and then into the trees, where a ghost I'd never seen before was emerging from the woods.

"This is Martin," she said by way of introduction. The spirit named Martin gave a sweeping bow in my direction. He was dressed as if he were on the cover of a trashy romance novel, and looked as if he'd just dismounted from a white steed and was ready to clasp Savvy in his burly arms.

"And what do we need Martin for, other than undressing us with his eyes?" I asked, edging away from him.

"He can undress me with anything he wants," Milo said.

"Down boy," I said, rolling my eyes.

"I started trying to figure out if there were other way across," Savvy began. "I noticed ghosts going back and forth all the time, as though the Wards didn't exist. Spirits can cross the Wards whenever they want as long as they aren't hostile. Then in class, Siobhán told us about Corporeal Habitation, and it came to me... I realized we could likely use the spirits to secret ourselves across without being detected. When I found Martin swaggering about the woods here, I decided to... experiment."

Milo and I looked at each other. He looked at least as wary as I felt.

"You mean you let Martin... possess you?"

"Well, it sounds mental when you put it like that!" Savvy cried, throwing her hands up in the air.

"It is mental!" I said. "I've had the serious displeasure of Corporeal Habitation, and I really don't want to repeat the experience—especially not for something stupid like sneaking out for a beer!" A shiver rocked its way through my body as I remembered, all too vividly, that night in the library bathroom: William flying at me; the madness in his eyes; the crippling agony that followed as he inhabited me.

"I'm not just doing it for a beer!" Savvy said. "I'm doing it for my freedom! And anyway, I remember you telling us about that, and this ain't the same thing. That spirit forced his way in and then tried to prise the Gateway open. That's why it was so painful—it wasn't a Habitation, it was an assault. I'm talking about inviting a spirit in. Completely different experience."

I hesitated. "Okay, I'm listening."

"You just have to give them permission, like," Savvy said. "Just sort of... make room for them, yeah? It's a bit disorienting, but not painful. And once the spirit is in there with you, you can just stroll across the Ward. The Ward senses the spirit, but doesn't seem to notice that the ghost has borrowed a body. Problem solved!"

I could still feel my doubts etched onto my face. Apparently, Savvy could see them too, because she gestured to Martin, who came over to her immediately.

"Watch, I'll do it first," she said, and turned to Martin. "You ready, then?"

"Oh yes, if you wish it," Martin said, in a much softer voice than I expected. It was like watching a lumberjack open his mouth and sing soprano. Milo stood transfixed, his eyes darting rapidly between the two of them.

Savvy closed her eyes, and stood very still. Martin strode forward with a hungry expression, and stepped into Savvy as if she were an open doorway. She inhaled sharply, then opened her eyes.

I clapped a hand over my mouth and spoke in a muffled voice from behind it. "Savvy? Are you okay?"

"Yes, I'm fine. It's still me," she said with a trace of impatience. "I could let him speak, if I wanted to, but I've got the control. I can hear what he's thinking though, the cheeky bugger."

She turned, smirking at whatever Martin was thinking, then walked purposefully across the Wards. The only tiny betrayal of the Wards' existence was a hint of an undulation in the air, like the dull shimmer of a heat-haze.

Savvy stood with her back to us, completely still for a moment, and then Martin appeared beside her, smiling broadly.

Savvy turned and grinned at me. "See? Easy as you like. Feels a bit funny is all. Go on, then, before the cab gets here."

I looked at Milo, who was still eyeing Martin with unabashed interest. "I'm supposed to let *Milo* do that?"

"I don't want to be seen in that outfit, it's against my religion," Milo said, crossing his arms. "And I don't want her to know what I'm thinking."

"I'm sorry, but when have you ever not said exactly what you're thinking?" I snapped.

"Huh," Milo said, cocking his head to one side in consideration. "Good point."

"Look, you don't have to use him if you don't want to. Martin can do it again," said Savvy.

I took one look at Martin, who was waggling his eyebrows at me, and turned back to Milo. "Okay, okay, fine, just make it quick."

I closed my eyes and braced myself. With a sensation that reminded me of an undertow at high tide, I felt Milo cross my threshold. My mind spun with a dizzying sensation as twice as many thoughts as usual flew across it.

Milo's next thought drifted across my brain as though I'd thought it myself, "Whoa... this feels really funky."

"No kidding," I said, opening my eyes. My vision was slightly misted, as if I were looking through a foggy windshield. "And I really don't like it, so I'm crossing now."

"The sooner the better," Milo said. "I feel like I'm being flattened by a steamroller in here."

I walked carefully forward. The movement had a dizzy, heavy feeling, as though I'd just woken up from anesthesia. I concentrated all my effort on moving toward the Wards without falling on my face. As I did so, a humming started to buzz in my ears.

"Do you mind not humming?" I thought-spoke, as I shook my head to clear it. "I'm trying to concentrate here."

"I'm not humming," came Milo's voice; the humming continued softly under it. "I thought that was you."

"No, it's not me. Why would I be humming?"

"I don't know, why would *I* be humming?"

I stopped walking and listened. The voice was soft, and the melody was lilting and familiar.

"Who the hell else is in here? Do we have a stowaway or something?"

"No, it's just me in here. Well, and you, obviously," Milo said.

"Hello?" I thought. The humming went on unbroken.

"Who are you?" Milo thought-spoke suddenly. His voice echoed inside my head and made it ring like a church bell.

"Shh!" I said. "Calm down, it hurts my head when you shout like that!"

"Sorry," Milo replied, more calmly. "But I don't see anyone else, and I can still hear it, can you?"

"Yes!"

"Oi! Get a move on, Jess, the cab is coming!" Savvy called.

With the gentle song still echoing through my head, I shuffled forward the last few steps. I felt the Ward wrapping my body with its gentle pressure as I walked through it, before twanging away from me like an elastic band.

"Out, out, out!" I thought-spoke.

"My pleasure!" Milo was gone from me in the same instant. The humming stopped at once.

I rubbed my watering eyes as my sight readjusted. "That was…"

"Bizarre," Milo finished for me.

"Come on, let's go!"

I looked up. Savvy was standing next to the cab, tapping her foot impatiently. The driver leaned one elbow out of the window; his mouth hung slightly open as he watched me have a spirited conversation with thin air. I smiled awkwardly at him as I slid into the back seat after Savvy, and tried not to come across as crazy.

"London then, please mate, Queen Victoria Street, as close to Millennium Bridge as you can get," Savvy said, then slid the plexiglass partition firmly shut before whispering, "What was that all about, then?"

"I have no idea. Milo and I could hear someone else while he was inhabiting me—a girl, I'm pretty sure, who was singing. Any idea what that's about?"

"Not a clue," Savvy said, frowning. "I've only ever used Martin, and he's the only one I've ever heard. Mind you, his thoughts are properly distracting, but I think I would've noticed a totally different voice."

"Let's talk about it later," I murmured, as I caught the avid gaze of our driver in the rear view mirror.

14

REVELATIONS BY THE THAMES

THE DRIVE TO LONDON TOOK WELL OVER AN HOUR, and at first I had no interest in the bucolic scenery flashing past me on either side of the M11. But as we moved into the city, the tourist in me couldn't help but gawk a bit at the sights of a city I'd always wanted to experience. I couldn't help but geek-out over our proximity to the British Parliament, St. Paul's Cathedral, the Tower of London, and about a dozen other places I'd only ever seen on postcards or in movie screens. I was obviously betraying my feelings of awe on my face, because Savvy kept chuckling at me.

"You'd do the same thing if we were in New York," I said, as I pressed my hands to the window, gaping at Buckingham Palace.

"I suppose," Savvy said, still laughing.

At long last, we pulled sharply to the side of the road on Queen Victoria Street, and I looked again at my watch, which I'd been checking obsessively since the moment we'd gotten into the car. It was just after 10:30 PM.

"Is it a long walk from here?" I asked as I handed five crumpled twenty-pound notes to the driver.

"No, not at all," Savvy said, checking her reflection in the dark tinted windows. "We could have had him drive us across the river, but since you've never been here before, you've got to at least walk across the *Millennium Bridge* and see London from the Thames."

I smiled in spite of my mounting nerves, and we set off down the street. The night was balmy with few feathery clouds, through which the stars were beginning to wink shyly in the dark night. The city was like its own wonderful, anachronistic jumble—at once modern and historic. It was alive and thrumming with an energy that only lives in a cosmopolitan city on a weekend night; we wove our way between knots of late night revelers.

"Hang on a minute, Hannah's calling," Milo said.

We stopped and pressed ourselves up against the facade of a pub with low-hanging baskets of geraniums dangling from its eaves and mellow acoustic guitar music wafting out of its open door. Milo didn't pull out a cell phone, of course, but closed his eyes and flickered a bit as he connected with Hannah. His form, so clear moments before, took on a dimmer, washed-out quality while they talked.

"Yes, the ride was fine," he said, sighing. "Yes, I was good. Not a word, I promise. Yup, she's right here." He opened his eyes and rolled them before turning them on me. "Hannah says hi."

I laughed. "Hi, Hannah."

"She says hi," Milo said, closing his eyes again. "Yes, we're almost there, and then I'm off duty, right? Okay, sweetness, I'll check in later." He opened his eyes again and smirked at me. "Mom says to behave ourselves and be careful."

"Okay okay," I said. "Can we keep going, please? I don't want to be late."

"You can do whatever you want. I was promised couture window-shopping," Milo said, crossing his arms and pouting like a small child.

Savvy gave him directions to Sloane Street, and with his face alight in anticipation, he vanished. We set out again along Queen Victoria Street for another block and then took a left toward the Millennium Bridge.

The south bank stretched out along the Thames, which glittered in the darkness. The London Eye rose above the scene like a glowing cog in a massive urban clockwork. We stepped out onto the narrow metal footbridge; Savvy's heels clicked cacophonously. The breeze off the Thames caught at our hair and whipped it over our shoulders. I stopped only long enough to gaze back at the shore we'd just left to see the great dome of St. Paul's cathedral capping the city like a crown, before charging across the bridge toward the other bank. Ahead to the left, the thatched roof and whitewashed walls of the Globe Theatre poked out, a fantastic anachronism. I couldn't believe I was here—and I couldn't believe that I didn't have even the briefest amount of time to just appreciate it all.

"The Tate is just there," Savvy called over her shoulder to me, pointing completely unnecessarily across the water, where the stark brick building dominated the skyline with a single, thrusting tower. The Tate didn't simply draw one's gaze, it demanded it. My pulse sped up, and so did my pace. I checked my watch. It was ten minutes to eleven.

At last we descended the gently sloping ramp and onto the sidewalk. Savvy turned to me. "Alright, mate. So you're here. Do you want me to stay with you a bit, or what?"

I shook my head. "No. You've earned a night out in the city. I'll just wait here for Annabelle, and you go have some fun. I'll text you when I'm done here and we can meet back up, okay?"

"Brilliant. See you, then," she said, and—with a smile that seemed to radiate to the ends of her curls—turned on her heel and sauntered off down the sidewalk. I watched her go into the night, and just caught the tiny red glow of her cigarette bouncing along before she turned off the sidewalk and disappeared.

I looked around. The area in front of the Tate Modern was wide and open, flanked by an unexpected expanse of green lawn to the right. There were any number of benches that Annabelle could have been referring to, but I trusted that she would find me. I settled myself on the bench nearest the water. Almost instantly, Lyle McElroy was sitting beside me. It took every ounce of my self-control not to shriek out loud.

"Lyle, you scared the crap out of me!" I hissed through clenched teeth, uncomfortably aware of the group of giggling girls walking past us.

"To apologize would insinuate I care," Lyle said, crossing his arms. "And anyway, I'm not staying. She wants to know if you were followed."

"She's here?" I asked, craning my neck for a glimpse of Annabelle's wild hair. Lyle merely glared at me, so I answered, "No, I don't think so. No one knows we're here. We were able to sneak out without raising any alarms, and I can't see how they could possibly know where we went."

"Very well, I'll tell her," he said. "And then do me a favor and give her your phone number, because I won't be doing this again, no matter how she threatens me, understand? I can't leave my flat unattended for any length of time. Somebody might try to clean it out, and I can't allow that."

"Sure," I said. "Uh, thanks."

Lyle merely heaved a farcical sigh and faded away. A minute later, Annabelle emerged from around the corner of the Tate, walking briskly; her hands were thrust deep into the pockets of her jacket and she had a scarf wrapped around her head.

"Jess, thank God!" she cried as she dropped onto the bench beside me and flung her arms around my shoulders.

I froze. My interactions with Annabelle up to this point had been cordial at best, but were more often antagonistic—bordering on hostile. That she was now hugging me like a long-lost sister was terrifying. I pulled away from her and looked her in the face.

"Annabelle, are you okay? What's going on? Tia told me about the fire at your shop, and I didn't know what to think."

Annabelle looked terrible. Her usually fiery eyes were dull and glazed, with bluish rings under them. Her cheekbones jutted sharply out from the hollows of her cheeks, as though she'd recently lost a little too much weight. Her lips trembled as she took in my features.

"I'm okay. The fire was... well, it was good excuse to make a quick exit, so I took it. I'll explain that in a minute, but first, are you absolutely sure you weren't followed?" she said, her voice quietly urgent.

"As sure as I can be. I wasn't exactly keeping an eye out for a tail," I said.

"I'm sorry for all the secrecy, but we need to be careful. I'm glad to see that you're alright. Lyle was not the ideal way to get a message to you, but I had to try something and he was the best I could do on such short notice," said Annabelle.

"Where did you find him?"

"In the apartment above mine." The first of my many, many questions must have been written on my face, because she clarified quickly. "I'm renting a place just a few blocks from here, and I found Lyle almost at once. He died a few months ago, but he won't leave because he's obsessed with his collections."

"Collections?"

"Yes. Don't ask me what he collected, exactly. I think it's more of a hoarding situation than real collecting. He keeps going on about his magazines and how they mustn't disturb the piles, because they 'might be worth a lot of money someday.'" She rolled her eyes. "I told him I'd pick the lock and start throwing his collections away if he didn't do what I asked."

"I was wondering why he was so angry. But enough about him, what's going on? What are you doing here?"

Annabelle dropped her head into her hands. "Oh Jess, I don't even know where to begin."

"Why don't you start with how the hell you knew I was here," I said. "How did you find me? No one is supposed to know about Fairhaven Hall."

She said nothing, but pulled at a loose string on the cuff of her jacket.

"When you found me in the bathroom, after William attacked me," I began, finding her eyes with mine, "you knew what had happened to me. You started to say words over me in another language. And when I woke up in the hospital, you knew what I was. You knew my aunt would be able to help me. Why did you know all of that?"

Annabelle sighed. "I knew you were trouble the second you walked into my tent; I knew what you were the moment I saw you, although I tried to convince myself otherwise. But after the investigation in the library, I couldn't deny it anymore. I was face-to-face with a living Gateway, something I'd only ever heard stories about from my grandmother. She learned them from her grandmother, who had lived them firsthand."

I waited in rapt silence for her to continue, listening to the rapid tattoo of my own pulse.

"You grew up without a clue about your family's legacy. I grew up immersed in every detail of a family legacy I'll never get to experience for myself. Generations ago, the women of my family were just like you. We were one of the oldest and most powerful Gateways in the world. Our clan hailed from the mountains of Romania, and at one time we even presided over the Council there. But then my great-great grandmother produced just one daughter, and her sisters none at all. The Gateway could not continue into the next generation, and so it was closed. It has remained closed ever since."

"You're... a Durupinen too?"

"No. There are no more Durupinen in my family, not true ones, anyway. I'm the only one of my family who shows any trace of a spirit connection—it's simply the genetic vestiges of an inheritance I will never come into. My grandmother could sense spirits, and even converse with them on occasion. But my mother never saw a ghost in her life. She convinced herself that my grandmother was crazy—that her stories were nothing but ancestral folk tales. My abilities are the most pronounced my family has seen in decades, but it still will never mean the reopening of the Gateway, not as long as I'm the only one."

"I can't believe you knew all of this and you didn't tell me."

"Can't you? Haven't you had enough experience with the Durupinen by now to know why I stayed silent? What if I'd been wrong about you, and told you ancient secrets you had no right to? I pointed you in the direction of your nearest female relative and trusted that she would help you, if she could. It was the only safe thing to do."

"Do the Durupinen know about you?"

"Oh, yes. They keep a watchful eye on any former Gateways, if only to monitor the possibility that they might be reopened. No one from the Northern Clans has anything to do with us directly; we have our own Council whose job it is to oversee things. But I don't doubt that they were aware of our happenings, just as we were aware of theirs."

"So that's how you knew where to find me?"

"Fairhaven is not the only school of its kind, you know. It took a little digging, but I was able to figure out where it was."

"So why are you so scared they might have followed me? You're allowed to know what I am, and you didn't interfere or tell me anything you shouldn't have, so what's the problem?"

Annabelle hesitated. "The situation is... complicated. There are still a lot of unanswered questions, so I want to lay low until I've figured them out."

This mention of questions flipped a switch in my brain. "Are you talking about Pierce? Is that why you're here?"

She looked momentarily stunned. "How do you know about David?"

"My roommate from St. Matt's told me. You met Tia, remember? You read her tarot cards that night at the fair. She told me Pierce had suddenly gone on sabbatical, but I saw him right before I left... and he never said a word about a sabbatical. Tia got the details about where he's supposed to be, but we can't get in touch with him. Annabelle, please tell me you know where he is and that he's okay."

Annabelle closed her eyes a moment, and when she opened them again, they were shining with tears. "I have no idea. Nobody does. He just vanished. We talked a couple of months ago, the same week you went to see him, and we made plans to meet up a few days later to talk about another potential paranormal investigation. But he never showed up, and no one's been able to get in touch with him since."

"Did you call the police and file a missing persons report?"

"No, we can't involve the police in this. It's only going to make matters worse."

"But he's missing, Annabelle! Who could be better to help than the police?"

"Don't be a fool, Jessica," Annabelle snapped, with a momentary flare of her old spunk. "In the first place, the false trail is too convincing. No one's going to start a search for a man who has properly filed paperwork explaining exactly where he is and how long he will be gone! I went to his office trying to find him, and his department head told me all about this so-called sabbatical. Any paranormal investigator worth his salt knows that the Deer Creek Inn is a hoax. They've been planting those stories for years to attract customers, and they don't let investigators in because they don't want to be exposed as frauds. And the new owners are even worse—planting lies about unexplained injuries and deaths. It's true that David might want to get in there, but only to debunk the rumors—and he'd certainly never waste his time writing a book about it. But from an outsider's perspective it looks like the perfect place to set up a long term project."

"So you don't think Pierce is actually there?"

"I know he's not. I decided to make absolutely sure and drove up there myself. The address he's supposed to be staying at is an abandoned motel, and his room is empty except for some broken furniture, a family of rats, and an answering machine plugged into an extension cord in the middle of the floor."

I hid my face in my hands and started to rock back and forth. "Oh, God. Oh my God. Annabelle, what's going on? Why would he just take off like this?"

"I don't think he *did* take off. I don't think he would have done this of his own free will."

"So, you think he's been... what? Kidnapped?"

Annabelle didn't answer right away. She seemed to be struggling with how to say what she wanted to say.

I stared at her in horror. "It's because of me, isn't it? It's because he knows what I am."

"This isn't your fault," she said, almost grudgingly. "But... yes, I think it may be because he knows what you are."

"But the Durupinen wouldn't do this! They can't, not after everything he did for me! He saved my life, Annabelle! They took his evidence away—Karen promised that would be enough, that he would be safe! They erased everything that could've given us away! He knows how important this is, and he promised not to ask any more questions!"

"I'd like to think the Durupinen wouldn't have done this, although I can't be sure. They certainly have the resources, and they have gone to incredible lengths to keep their secrets over the years. And one of the reasons I admire David is because of his persistence when it comes to getting the answers he wants. I'd like to think he kept his promise to you, but he might have been too tempted to resist a little more snooping."

I groaned. Hadn't I told him how important it was to just leave it all alone? Why couldn't he have just listened to me?

"There is another possibility, though," continued Annabelle. "I've been wondering about it for a while..." She stood up, walked a few paces away from me, and leaned against the railing. Staring out over the river, she asked, "What do you know about the Necromancers?"

"The Necromancers? We talked about them in class. They were the enemies of the Durupinen centuries ago. But they don't exist anymore, Celeste told us that they were disbanded and destroyed."

Annabelle smiled wryly. "We all remember history differently, depending on what side we're on. The Durupinen did indeed topple the Necromancers at the height of their power, but that doesn't mean the Necromancers ceased to be. They had to start again, and secretly, or risk another battle."

"So the Necromancers aren't gone?"

"No, they aren't gone. You can wipe out the infrastructure of an organization like that. You can eliminate their resources and force them into hiding. But you can't kill their ideas. The philosophy is too tempting, too alluring. People have been drawn to the idea of raising the dead since the dawn of time. It makes absolute sense—it's human nature to want to overcome death, so societies like the Necromancers will always find followers and they will always exist."

"So let me get this straight. You're not only saying that the Necromancers still exist, but they might have kidnapped Pierce?"

"Yes."

"Even if that were true, why would they want Pierce? What possible use could he be to them?"

"If the Necromancers are trying in earnest to organize again, they will need as much information about the current state of the Durupinen as they can get. If one of them somehow knew that you and Pierce had contact, they might try to use him to get information."

I pressed my hands against my temples, as though they could force this new information into a coherent picture in my brain. It didn't work. "I'm sorry Annabelle, but this just seems so... unlikely. It sounds like a crazy conspiracy theory."

"I'm sure the idea of the Durupinen sounded crazy when you first heard it. Aren't you the girl who entered in my tent and scoffed at the idea of spirits?" Annabelle countered.

I opened my mouth to argue and closed it again. One group that helped the dead to Cross, another who sought the power to bring the dead to back to life. Was one really so much more feasible than the other?

"Well, you better hope this particular conspiracy theory is right, because if it isn't, you're up to your neck in the organization that kidnapped our friend," Annabelle said.

We sat in silence for a while as I let this horrible thought sink in.

"Is that why you came all the way to London? To warn me?" I asked finally.

"Not just to warn you, no," Annabelle replied. "After David vanished, it seemed like the safest thing for me to do would be to disappear too. So I left some strategically placed candles burning in my shop, bashed in a few windows, and hopped a plane."

My mouth dropped open. "You did that to your own shop? Aren't you afraid the police are going to figure it out?"

"Jess, I've told you already, we've got bigger problems than the police right now!" Annabelle's words were a little too loud, and several people gawked at her as they walked by. Lowering her voice, she went on. "When it comes right down to it, there are two possibilities. Either the Necromancers are back in operation and hunting down information at any cost, or the Durupinen are dealing pretty harshly with the loose ends you left behind. Either way, we are both in the kind of danger that law enforcement can't help with. I don't care what conclusions the police come to about my shop. But I'm hoping that whoever came looking for David won't know where to find me."

"Do you think Pierce is dead?" I asked. I tried to sound calm, but my voice hitched and broke.

"I don't know. I really hope not."

"So what do we do?"

"We keep our eyes and ears open, and our heads down," Annabelle said. "You will need to be very careful about who you trust over there. Your High Priestess might give the orders, but she's not the only one to be wary of. She'll be influenced by the people who have her ear, so be careful of her advisors as well."

"Yeah, I can already think of a few Council members who might fall into that category," I said darkly.

"Find out what you can about the Necromancers. Use the resources you have there at Fairhaven. I'm sure they have an extensive library, and you may even be able to squeeze some better answers out of your teachers, if you feign some academic curiosity."

"Okay. And what about you? Are you going to be safe here?"

Annabelle took a deep breath. "I suppose we'll see, won't we? In the meantime, I'm going to keep looking for David. You mentioned that your roommate back home was helping you look for him too?"

"Yeah, and our friend Sam. He was Pierce's work-study student," I said.

"Get in touch with her right away and tell them to stop, okay?" Annabelle said. "We don't want any more collateral damage than we have already."

The nervous pit in my stomach grew, if possible, even deeper. "We already agreed they should back off when it looked like something bad had happened to you. They've stopped digging."

"Good." Annabelle said. "Now you should get back to school before anyone notices you're gone." She stood up abruptly. "Do you have a cover story for where you've been, if they ask?"

"Yes. If I get caught alone, I'll tell them I fell asleep sketching in the gardens. If we get caught sneaking in, we'll tell them we were out at the pubs. Partying seems like a plausible cover for a night in the city, don't you think?"

Annabelle's face spasmed with panic. "Who else is here with you? I thought you came alone?"

"No, I came with my friend Savvy. She's another one of the Apprentices."

Annabelle raked a frantic hand through her hair. "Jessica, I told you to come alone! None of them can know you've been meeting with me!"

"I did come alone! Savvy just helped me sneak out and find my way here. I couldn't have gotten here without her help."

"But how do you know you can trust her? She could easily tell—"

"Calm down, Annabelle! It's not like that; Savvy isn't from an old Durupinen family, she's a new Gateway. She's the first one in her family to do this, and she couldn't care less about their rules and politics."

Annabelle still looked unconvinced. She chewed at her bottom lip, with her eyes darting nervously around us. "And you think she'll cover for you, if they ask her what you were doing?"

"She doesn't really know what I've been doing. I just told her I needed to meet a friend from home. She's off drinking somewhere in the neighborhood. But even if she did know the details, I'm sure she'd keep it quiet if I asked her to. She's having a hard time adjusting to Apprentice training, so her loyalty isn't exactly with the establishment. She's from the city and she sneaks out all the time... that's why I asked her to help me."

The wrinkles in Annabelle's forehead relaxed away. "Well, there's nothing we can do about it now. Don't tell her more than she needs to know, alright? And that goes for anyone else you might want to talk to about this."

"Of course," I said. "How do I get back in touch with you?"

"You don't. I'll send another spirit to you if I get any more information. In the meantime, please remember what I've told you. Keep your head down and your eyes open. Assume nothing."

"Okay. I'll be careful."

Annabelle gave me one last, long look. Her expression was almost resentful, but softened into half a smile when she spoke. "I knew you were trouble, I just knew it." Then she turned, pulling her scarf back over her hair, and walked away.

15

PURSUIT

I DON'T KNOW HOW LONG I SAT ON THAT BENCH. My eyes were focused on the Thames, but my thoughts were focused deep inside my mind. At last, the cool night air penetrated my contemplation and a shiver brought me back to reality again. Annabelle had left me even more worried and confused than I'd been before I'd seen her, and my questions, rather than being answered, had multiplied. I stood up, pulling my cardigan tightly across my chest, and pinned it beneath my folded arms for warmth. I started walking in the direction Savvy had gone, and pulled out my phone. She had texted me. I opened the message.

At the King's Arms on Roupell Street. Come get pissed with me.

A quick internet search told me the pub was not even a ten-minute walk from the Tate Modern, so I enlarged the map and started down Hopton Street. I glanced at my watch. It was 11:55 PM. Hopefully Savvy hadn't had enough time to get too wasted. I mean, how drunk could the girl get in an hour, after all?

The answer was very drunk. Magnificently drunk.

Savvy was waiting for me in the small, crowded pub on the corner. I could see her through the slightly steamy windowpanes. She was sitting on the bar and surrounded by a small crowd of men, pounding her fists on the bar as they each dropped a shot glass into a pint of beer, then drank them both down in one long gulp. A red-faced man on the end finished first, slamming his glass onto the bar and raising his arms in triumph. Savvy laughed raucously, then grabbed the man by his collar and kissed him on the mouth.

"Ah shit," I said as I sidled in, squeezing myself between the tables until I'd reached the bar.

"Jess!" Savvy shouted when she saw me. "A pint for my friend, here! Come on boys, cough up! Who's going to buy this gorgeous girl a drink, eh?"

Several hands were reaching into their pockets for wallets, but I shook my head. "Thanks, boys, but I'm all set. Sav, we need to go now." My words were met with a chorus of groans.

"Now now, love, let's not spoil the fun!" the man on the end said thickly. He was wearing more of Savvy's lipstick than she was.

"I'm sure you will all have plenty of fun without us. You're big boys, you can manage," I replied, and held my hand out for Savvy's; she grabbed it and clambered with difficulty down from the bar.

"That meeting of yours was a lot shorter than I'd hoped," she said, jutting out her bottom lip like a baby about to burst into tears.

"You seem to have made the most of it, though," I said, jerking my head back toward the group of men who were still begging, with varying levels of coherence, for us to stay and have another drink.

"I always do," she replied with a dazzling smile. "Do we really need to go already?"

"It's a long ride back to Fairhaven."

Savvy pouted a bit more, but nodded and followed me out of the pub, blowing kisses over her shoulder as she went.

We started back for the Millennium Bridge. Savvy threw her arm chummily around my shoulders, which caused us both to weave a bit.

"Sorry I'm so pissed," Savvy said.

"That's alright," I said, sighing. "I had a feeling you might be, by the time I went to find you."

"Thought I'd have a bit more time to sober up before you showed up," she went on, trying—and failing—to walk in a straight line.

"Honestly, I don't mind," I said. "My mother was perpetually pissed. I'm pretty used to it."

"Oh. Mine too." I looked at her and she smiled sadly at me. We stumbled along in silence for a block or so, concentrating on not falling over.

"I never said sorry," Savvy said suddenly and loudly in my ear.

"Yes, you did," I told her with a laugh. "You just apologized a minute ago. I already told you, it's fine!"

"No, no for that!" she said, punching my arm in what she obviously thought was a playful way, but which actually felt more like assault.

"Ouch! What for?"

"Oi. Do you forgive me? Really, truly, forgive me? Say you forgive me mate, or you'll break my little heart right in two," she moaned, clasping both arms around my neck and practically toppling me with a hug.

"What am I supposed to be forgiving you for?" I asked, grunting with the effort of keeping us both on our feet.

"For gate-crashing your shower the first time we met! And you were so nice, covering for me, even though you were naked as the day you were born and had no idea who I was," Savvy gushed.

"I forgive you," I replied, as I managed to get my neck out of what was now more stranglehold than hug.

"No you don't. You're saying that to make me feel better, yeah? See, you don't even want my hugs."

"Of course I do," I said. "Your hugs are wonderful. You can give me lots of hugs later, when your balance is better, okay?"

"'Kay," she said, and attempted to straighten up. "Can I make it up to you?"

"You don't need to. I forgive you, I promise."

"Yes, I do need to. I *need* to, Jess!"

I stopped walking. With an exasperated laugh, I asked, "Okay, fine. How are you going to make it up to me? You better make it good—I don't want a half-assed apology."

Savvy's face scrunched in thoughtful consideration. Then she said, "Wanna see my tits?"

"NO!" I cried.

"You sure? They're fit," she said, reaching for the buttons on her shirt.

"No... *no!*" I said, wrenching her hands from her shirt before she could start removing it. I tugged on her elbow and started to pull her forward again. "I'm sure they're lovely, but I don't want to see your tits right now."

"You sure?" Savvy asked.

"Positive. We'll come up with another way for you to make it up to me."

"'Kay," she said with a shrug. Then, after a moment's silence, she added, "But everyone loves 'em. I've never had a complaint."

"I bet."

"It's true! I bet anyone here would like to see them. I bet he would," she said, and cocked a thumb back over her shoulder.

"Who?"

"That guy that's behind us. He's been following us since the bar. Keeps taking our picture."

"Huh?" I stopped and whirled around. About thirty feet behind us, a man in a black hooded sweatshirt and dark trousers stopped in his tracks. He was holding a cell phone out in front of him and pointing it in our direction, as though he'd just taken our picture with it.

"Say cheese!" Savvy said, flinging an arm back over my shoulders and posing. "How 'bout it, mate? Don't you want a pic now that we're looking?"

The man said nothing but continued to stare at us as he pressed a button on the phone and put it to his ear.

"Not interested? Oh, I get it, you're an ass man, eh?" Savvy said. She turned and shook her rear end in the man's direction. "There you are, have a good look, then."

My heart began to race. "Come on, Sav, let's go." I pulled her along, walking as quickly as I could.

"'Smatter with you?" Savvy asked. "Why are you walking so fast?"

"I don't like the look of that guy behind us." I chanced a glance over my shoulder. The man, still on the phone, was keeping pace with us but maintaining a steady distance.

"Ah, come on. Don't go all country mouse on me, Jess!" Savvy said. "We're city girls, you and me, we know how to handle ourselves. He's probably just looking for a good time, yeah?"

"I'd rather not find out what he's looking for," I said, as we rounded the corner onto Blackfriars Road. I took a deep breath as I walked and tried to reason with myself. This guy could be anyone—a random creep, a drunk idiot. He could be a total pervert, cruising for vulnerable girls to attack. None of these things frightened me much. Savvy was right; I was a city girl, and unfortunately I'd dealt with this sort of thing before. And not for nothing, but I was pretty sure that Savvy could beat the hell out of any guy who messed with either of us. What scared me much more was the idea that this guy might not be a random encounter at all. Maybe he'd been following me since we'd gotten into the city, or even before. He wasn't dressed like a Caomhnóir, but then again, he might have dispensed with the formal attire in hopes that I wouldn't notice him. I couldn't tell if I recognized him or not; his face was too obscured by the shadowy recesses of his hood.

And then there was Annabelle's warning. There could be others out there besides the Durupinen who might want to follow us...

"Savvy, keep walking, but listen to me for a minute. If you needed to run right now, could you do it?"

"What are you on about?" Savvy giggled at first, but then caught sight of my face. Whatever she saw there wiped the grin off her own, and her eyes, as she looked into mine, seemed to instantly sober up through sheer force of will. "What's going on?"

"I don't know, but I think we might be in trouble. Can you run?"

"Yeah, I can run. Want to tell me what I'm supposed to be running from?"

I hesitated. I hadn't planned on telling her anything about my meeting with Annabelle, but it looked like I didn't have a choice.

"A friend of mine found out too much about the Durupinen and now he's missing. I'm afraid that guy following us might have something to do with it."

"Is that why we're here tonight? Because of your friend?"

"Yeah. I was hoping to find out what happened to him, but instead I think I landed us in a dangerous situation."

"That bloke behind us?"

"Yeah."

Savvy moved to look back, but I grabbed her arm. "Don't look! I don't want to draw any more attention to us."

"I got you. Hang on," she said, and started digging around in her purse.

"What are you—"

"Play along," Savvy muttered, pulling her phone out of her bag. Letting out a high-pitched laugh, she squealed, "Selfie on girls' night out!" Then she pulled my head against hers as she raised the phone high in front of us and snapped a picture.

She pulled up the picture. "Oi! Let's take another one, my eyes were closed." she said to cover ourselves as we examined the picture, in which the tops of our heads were barely visible. Behind us, the man was still there, staring right at us, and was much closer to us now than when we'd first noticed him. He couldn't have been more than fifteen feet away.

"No, let me do it, you take the worst pictures!" I said loudly, pulling the phone out of her hand as we continued down the sidewalk. Then I added in a whisper, "Right, we run for the bridge on three and see if we can lose him on the other side."

Savvy didn't even bat an eyelash. "On three, then."

"One. Two. Three!"

We broke simultaneously into a run, hands clasped together, and sprinted as fast as we could for the bridge. I heard the man curse loudly, then his footsteps began pounding against the sidewalk as he too broke into a run behind us. I chanced half a glance over my shoulder. He was still on the phone, and was talking into it as he ran.

"Milo!" I called between my ragged gasps. I felt the connection open, like a tiny window in my brain.

"Don't bother me, Jess. This Gucci trench coat and I are having a moment."

"You need to meet us on Queen Victoria Street where the car dropped us off. *Now!*"

"What, you're done already?"

"Yes, and we're in trouble. Some guy is chasing us."

"What the hell—"

"Just do what I asked, please! We've got to get out of the city now!"

"Okay, okay!" said Milo.

I broke the connection and we flew up the ramp onto the Millennium Bridge; our footsteps clanged loudly. Small knots of people were strolling along the bridge and stopping to take pictures of London in the starlight. Savvy barreled through them, knocking several people into the railings as we pelted across the bridge.

"We'll have to try to lose him on the other side so we can call our driver," said Savvy. With this, she shoved a man with an enormous camera out of our way, shouting, "Clear off, you!"

As we tore off the end of the bridge and onto the sidewalk, one of Savvy's shoes caught in a crack in the concrete and the heel snapped off, sending us flailing to the ground in a heap. We scrambled back up just as the hooded man reached the sidewalk. He ran toward us, with his arm outstretched as though to grab us, but Savvy pulled off her broken shoe and flung it, as hard as she could, at his head. Cursing, the man ducked for cover behind a trash barrel as she reached down, yanked the other shoe from her foot, and threw that as well. We took off again and dodged straight into traffic; a cab driver slammed on his brakes as he beeped loudly at us.

We had just made it to the other side of the street when we heard a loud cry. "Oi! Watch where you're going! What are you chasing after girls for, eh?" said a booming male voice.

We turned and saw that our pursuer had run smack into a group of men, all of whom were now shouting vulgarities at him while intentionally blocking his path. The man struggled to get past, but the group closed around him, jeering and laughing.

"I don't think they fancy you!"

"How about I rearrange your face? They might like it better that way!"

In a bizarre display of alcohol-and-testosterone-fueled chivalry, the men continued their taunts, provoking our pursuer with pokes and jabs. The hooded man struggled, but couldn't get around them. I could hear him cursing angrily over the laughter.

Nearby, a car skidded to a stop with a deafening screech.

"Jessica! Savannah!"

I turned at the sound of my name. My mouth dropped open—Finn was leaning out of the window of one of the Caomhnóir's black SUVs and motioning at us frantically to get in.

Savvy gasped. "What the—"

There was no time to think about it. "Come on!" We dashed for the car, flung its door open, and jumped inside. Finn peeled away from the curb before we'd even shut the door.

We'd barely had time to reach for our seatbelts when Milo materialized between us.

"Forgetting someone?" he asked.

I ignored him and turned to Finn instead. "What are you doing here?"

"What are *you* doing here?" he insisted.

"Trying to become a big city statistic, apparently," Savvy said, as she struggled to catch her breath, sounding every bit the smoker as she hacked and wheezed. "Wow, that was way too close for comfort. Thanks mate, you really—"

"I'm not your mate," Finn practically growled. And what's happened to your shoes? I think I saw Bertie's gym bag in the back—see if you can find a pair of trainers." Then Finn's eyes found mine in the rearview mirror. "What are you playing at?"

"What do you mean?"

"What the hell are you doing here in the middle of the night?"

I pulled my eyes from his penetrating stare and fumbled with my seatbelt. "None of your business."

"Of course it's my business! Everywhere you go and everything you do is my business!" he said. He turned the corner too quickly and the tires squealed in protest. "I've sworn an oath to protect you, and I can't do it if you're sneaking off in the middle of the night!"

"How'd you even know I was here?"

"I saw you on the grounds heading for the woods with your bag."

"And so you decided to spy on me?" I said. I sounded like a tween who'd been caught climbing into her bedroom window after a night of drinking wine coolers in the woods. This realization only made me angrier.

"I just wanted to see where you were going. And it's a good thing I did, or who knows what would've happened when that guy caught up to you," Finn said. "Who is he?"

"I have no idea," I replied, which was only a half-lie.

"And you don't know why he was chasing you?"

"No. We were walking along the south bank, minding our own business, and he just started following us."

"Did he say anything to you?"

"Not a word," Savvy answered. "Just started snapping pictures, the bloody pervert."

I could tell from his expression that Finn didn't believe a word of this, so I quickly changed the subject. "How did you get here?"

"I saw you get into that cab and head south, so I borrowed one of the Caomhnóir vehicles and took the front entrance road. I knew I'd catch up with you eventually; there's only one road that goes by Fairhaven."

"But how did you find us in the city?" Savvy asked, as she laced up a black tennis shoe that was obviously two sizes too big for her foot.

"I've been waiting since the car dropped you off. I just parked a block behind him and waited until you came back. Then I saw you running and followed you."

"Are you allowed to take these cars out?" I asked.

Finn gave a humorless bark of a laugh. "Does it matter? I needed it to do my job. I don't think anyone will take issue with that, and if they do I'm not bothered."

Silence fell in the darkened car. I watched the lights of the city pass over Finn's stormy features.

"You still haven't told me why you're here in the first place," he said at last.

"I know."

"Well?"

I hesitated, throwing a sidelong glance at Savvy. "We needed a night out. You know, just to unwind and have a little fun."

Finn's brows contracted so tightly together that he looked for a moment like a giant bird of prey. "A little fun?" he repeated, his voice dripping with contempt.

"Yes, fun. Maybe you've heard of it. It involves laughing and socializing and other such foreign concepts."

"I don't believe you," he said baldly.

"Believe it or not, I don't really care."

"That's all the explanation I'm getting? After I stole a car and risked my neck tracking you down after curfew?"

"I don't owe you an explanation," I said, staring out the window so that I wouldn't have to meet his gaze in the mirror. "I never asked you to do any of this. Look, I appreciate your concern, but I don't always need your protection. I can take care of myself."

"Is that so? Didn't look like it from where I was sitting."

I said nothing. Of course he was right, and we were damn lucky he'd decided to follow me, or who knew what might've happened when that man caught up to us. On the other hand, there was no way I was going to admit this... it would only encourage his habit of treating me like a damsel that he had to constantly, but grudgingly, rescue from varying degrees of distress.

"Sorry to interrupt this really awkward silence," Milo broke in, "but there's been an SUV behind us for the past couple of minutes, and whoever is driving it just blew through a red light to stay on our tail."

We all turned to look out of the back window. Between the darkness and the tint on the vehicle's windows, it was impossible to make out anything about the driver.

"Let's not panic," Finn said. "Plenty of people ignore traffic lights. Everyone turn around and pretend you've not noticed, just in case. I'll see if I can't shake them off."

Finn took a few side roads that pulled us away from what would have been the most direct route out of the city. The SUV stayed unobtrusively but undeniably on our tail. We came to a traffic circle. Finn started around it, and put his turn signal on as though he were going to take the first exit. The SUV did the same. At the very last moment, Finn pulled the car sharply back into the flow of traffic, eliciting several angry honks from the cars around us, and confirming Milo's suspicion—the SUV veered away from the exit at the last moment as well. In the process, it almost sideswiped a small blue hatchback and caused another volley of beeping. We had all turned to see what the SUV would do, in spite of Finn's warnings, but we were now all facing frontward again. The mounting panic was tangible, a toxic fume that permeated the car and was threatening to suffocate us all.

Finn caught my eye in the mirror. "Are you still going to tell me that you have no idea who these people might be?"

In my panic, I nearly told him my suspicions, but I kept my mouth shut. I nodded instead. "I really don't know who they are."

Finn shook his head at me, clearly frustrated, and then floored it. We were all pressed back into our seats as the car picked up speed alarmingly fast. Finn wove through the traffic recklessly. I clutched at the door handle as we peeled around the next corner, while thinking of those video games where you careened wildly through digital landscapes and, more often than not, end up in a fiery wreck behind a flashing red "Game Over" screen. I swallowed back the urge to scream.

"Finn mate, you've got to shake them off before we hit the M11 or we'll never be able to—" Savvy began.

"Don't you think I know that?" Finn shouted. "I'm driving like a maniac!"

As though to prove his point, Finn veered onto the wrong side of the road in order to pass the car in front of us; he came very near to colliding with the oncoming traffic. We all screamed.

"Bloody hell," Savvy hissed through clenched teeth as we watched the SUV behind us barrel halfway onto the sidewalk and take out the front of a shabby newsstand. This barely slowed the SUV down; it emerged directly behind us again.

"Shit," Finn began muttering under his breath. "Shit, shit, shit!"

Soon the city began to fall away and we merged onto the M11 at breakneck speed; the SUV surged and caught up to us quickly.

"I don't know what to do!" Finn said, his knuckles white on the steering wheel. "It's open road, there's nowhere to go." We wove from lane to lane, dodging cars like traffic cones, but the SUV followed, closing the distance second by second.

"Brace yourselves, he's going to hit us!" Savvy suddenly shouted.

With a shattering crash, the SUV slammed into ours. Everyone shouted, and as we fishtailed wildly; Finn struggled to get control of the steering wheel and stop us from spinning out. I reached right through Milo and grabbed Savvy; Milo vanished.

"Milo!" I called frantically. "Milo, where are you?"

CRASH!

The SUV collided with us again, clipping our rear corner. We swung wildly around, spinning completely out of control. Everything was a blur. But then for one perfectly clear instant, I saw Finn's face in the rearview as the guardrail reared up and crashed through the windshield.

Finn's eyes found mine, and in that tiny—but seemingly endless—moment, they said they were sorry. Then he closed his eyelids, almost gently.

We were crashing, rolling, and sliding all at once. The car tumbled down the embankment, with glass exploding from every window and needling through the air. I threw my hands above me as the roof of the car crunched inward. Everything was a blur of pain, confusion, and heart-stopping terror.

Then it was nothing but silence.

§

I lost time. I didn't pass out—I don't think—but I was so stunned by the sheer terror and utter pandemonium that it was a few moments, at least, before my brain could register anything. The first thing I registered was that I was not dead. The second was that I was upside down, with my face and hands pressed against the surprisingly soft roof of the car. I could feel my seatbelt cutting into my thighs, holding me suspended. I turned my head and saw Savvy staring back at me. Her eyes were wide, but very alive, and they blinked several times. They were almost all I could see in the darkness.

"Are you okay?" I asked.

"I dunno," Savvy said, blinking again. There were several small cuts on her cheek, and a trickle of blood was snaking its way into her hair. She raised her hand and felt the blood. "I feel like I ought to be covered in this. You alright?"

"I don't know," I said, making a rapid mental inventory of my body. I could feel everything, and although I was sore and aching, nothing was in terrible pain. "I think so."

"What about Finn?" she asked.

"Finn?" I called into the broken, smoking darkness. I held my breath through an agonizingly silent few seconds, and then called his name again. "Finn?"

Nothing. A new fear began to flood through me, rising inside me, threatening to drown me before I could do anything to stop it. He came here to save us, and if he were dead, it was my fault. All my fault.

"I can smell petrol," Savvy said. "I think we should try to get out of here as fast as we can." She was already trying to wedge herself out of her seatbelt.

I felt around and found my seatbelt's buckle; I tried to undo it, but it was jammed. I clenched the buckle tightly between both hands and squeezed as hard as I could. Finally, it popped apart with a muffled click and I crumpled into a heap on the roof of the car. A moment later, Savvy also fell with a loud curse.

"Finn?" I called again, and my voice broke with fear at the answering silence. "Savvy, we have to get to him. We have to get him out of the car and get help."

"There's no way we're getting out this side," she said, gesturing to her own window. She was right. The car had slammed into a tree, leaving only a few inches of space between the shattered window and the splintered trunk.

With difficulty, I twisted my neck and examined my window. The glass was gone, and there was a clear five or six feet between the car and the nearest tree. "We should be able to escape on this side," I said. "Hang on, let me get out and I can help you."

I grabbed the window frame and braced my other hand against the back of the passenger seat, using my legs to push off against the seat above me. I cried out in pain as my back slid across the glass-strewn roof beneath me. I pushed my head and shoulders through the window frame, and then I was able to brace my hand against the frame of the car and push myself out the rest of the way. I landed with a thump on the cold, wet grass, where I gladly could have lain for the rest of my life. Instead, I got to my knees and reached my arms back through the window. Savvy grabbed hold of them and together we pulled her out, panting and groaning.

"You alright?" I gasped.

"Dizzy," she said faintly. "I think it's the fumes from the petrol. Just need to catch my breath."

"Are you sure you don't have a concussion?" I asked.

"Mate, I'm barely sure I'm alive."

"Stay here, I'm going to check on Finn," I told her, and stumbled to my feet.

It seemed to take forever to reach him; my vision was strangely tunneled. I rounded the front of the car and reached his window.

Please don't let him be dead. Oh, please, please don't let him be dead.

Finn's eyes were closed. His mouth hung slightly open, and his head rested against the steering column. The air bag had deployed; air now hissed quietly from it. His face was covered in small abrasions, but he didn't seem to be bleeding anywhere else.

"Finn, can you hear me?" I asked in a hoarse whisper. He didn't stir. My eyes blurred with terrified tears.

"Jess, there's fire back here!" Savvy called. "Is he okay? Can you get him out?"

"I don't know!" I called back. "I'll try!"

I wedged my head into the window frame and reached across Finn's body to release his seatbelt. I pulled his limp arm through the strap, grabbed him under his armpits, and pulled as hard as I could, bracing my leg against the door. He slid out onto the grass as I tumbled backward; his head come to rest on top of my thigh. I vaguely remembered something about not moving accident victims in case of head injury, but it was too late for that. I bent over him and brushing his hair out of his face.

"Finn? Finn?"

I bent so close to his face so that his lips brushed my cheek. With a surge of relief, I felt his warm breath against my skin.

"He's alive, Savvy!" I called, my voice hitching over a sob.

Savvy gave a strange whoop of relief. The sound of it seemed to rouse Finn a bit, and he groaned quietly in my lap.

"Finn?" I asked again, pressing a hand to his forehead to wipe away a trickle of blood before it dripped into his eyes.

His eyelids fluttered and opened. He looked straight up into my face but seemed for a moment not to know me. Then he reached a trembling hand up and stroked my cheek. It was such a gentle touch that my heart gave a strange flit in response.

"Are you okay?" he mumbled. "Are you hurt?"

I actually laughed with relief. "You're the one lying on the ground, barely conscious and bleeding from the head, and you want to know if *I'm* hurt?"

"Yes," he said, as though the question confused him.

"That's a Caomhnóir for you, never off duty," I said.

"Answer me. Are you hurt?"

"No, I'm not hurt."

His eyes bore into mine as though looking for something that might contradict what I'd said. We held each other's gaze in that one strange moment, as if we were in a bubble of silent intensity within the smoking, burning chaos. We were so close that I could feel the heat from his face rising in waves and breaking against mine. My breath caught in my throat. Then Finn seemed to satisfy himself that I was telling the truth, and, in that same moment, realized that he was still touching my cheek. He snatched away his hand as though he had burned himself, and his softened expression hardened into its usual stoic mask. He immediately started trying to sit up.

"Where's the other car? Did it drive away?" he asked.

"Yes," They're gone, whoever they were." I said. "You were knocked out for a good while."

I tried to help him into a sitting position, but Finn batted my hands away, looking almost angry. "I'm fine. We need to get out of here." He got shakily to his knees and almost keeled back over.

"Finn, I really think you should—"

"I said I'm fine! Get out of it!" he snapped. He gained his footing, steadied himself against a tree trunk, and focused on the mangled car for the first time. His mouth dropped open.

"Oh my God."

I craned my neck so I too could see the remains of the car. It was a twisted wreck, the kind of thing they pry bodies from with the Jaws of Life.

"Oh sweet Jesus, it's a miracle," Savvy moaned from the grass nearby.

"I know," I said. "I can't believe we're alive."

"What? Oh, well yeah, I guess that's a miracle, too," Savvy said. "I was talking about these."

I turned to her. She was holding up a crumpled pack of cigarettes and a lighter, both of which had landed in the grass along with the rest of the contents of her purse. She pulled one out, straightened it slightly, and lit it with near-euphoric relish.

"I have never needed one of these more in my entire life," she said, taking a drag.

"Savvy, do you want do that just a little further from the leaking gas?" I said in exasperation. "It would suck pretty bad to survive a crash like that only to blow ourselves up because you needed a nicotine fix."

"Good point," Savvy said, then crawled several yards further away to a nearby tree. Finn limped around the car, absorbing the extent of the damage. "You both sure you're alright? No broken bones?"

"I guess I could still be in shock, but I really think I'm alright," I said. With the exception of some cuts and scrapes, and some glass shards that I was pretty sure were still lodged in my back, I was uninjured. My overriding emotion was one of stunned relief, although I was pretty sure that—given a few minutes to fully absorb what had just happened—I would soon be a sobbing, retching disaster.

"Me too," Savvy said, exhaling a plume of smoke into the night.

"Did anyone see what happened to Milo?" I asked. "I know he can't get hurt or anything, but one second he was in the car with us and then suddenly he was gone."

"Can you call him?" Savvy asked.

"I don't know," I said, and closed my eyes. The world began to spin behind my eyelids, and I couldn't focus on his energy. "I think I'm still too dazed. Either that, or he's too far away. I've never tried from more than a few miles."

"Hello? Is everyone alright down there?" said a deep voice.

Finn leapt into a defensive stance and I scrambled to my feet, ready to run if the driver of the SUV had come back to finish us off. But the face that peered down at us from the other side of the twisted guardrail was very old, and he was standing beside a rusty Peugeot.

"We're okay," Finn called back, waving.

The man shined his flashlight toward us. "What happened? Did someone hit you?"

"No, our tire hit something on the road. It blew out, and I lost control of the car," Finn replied, without so much as a moment's hesitation.

"Do you need me to ring the police? I've got a mobile for emergencies," the man offered.

"No!" Finn said sharply, then calmed his voice. "We've already called them. They're on their way now." As though to drive his point home, he pulled a cell phone from his back pocket and held it up for the man to see. "I've called my dad as well. Honestly, we're fine, sir... although we won't be when my dad gets here. This is his car, and he'll go crackers when he sees it." He hung his head.

"Nonsense. He'll just be glad you're alright," the man said.

"I hope so. I've never had a wreck before. Thanks for your concern."

"Right, then. Well, if you're quite sure you're alright, I'll be going then. Best of luck to you," the man said, and returned to his car.

Finn took a deep breath and blew it out slowly, as he started to pace, favoring his left leg. "Right. That man won't be the only one to stop. We've got to get in touch with someone at Fairhaven to come clear this all up, before the police get involved."

"Why?" Savvy asked. She pulled a second cigarette out of the package and lit it right from the first one, which she flicked into the grass. "Why wouldn't we want the police to come? You haven't been drinking, and we need to report the prick that hit us."

"Haven't you learned anything? It's always better for us to clean up our own messes, without the authorities," Finn said. "We want Fairhaven to stay as far off the grid as possible." He held up his phone and tried to dial, but seemed to be having trouble focusing on the numbers. He pressed his palms into his eye sockets.

"So that arsehole, whoever he was, is just going to get away with it, then?" Savvy asked.

"Probably, unless you or Jess can tell us anything else about him," Finn said, glancing up from his phone and shooting a dark look at me.

The longer we stood there, the more aches and pains were surfacing through my shock, and along with them came the panic of earlier that night. I couldn't be sure that the man who had been following us was connected to the Necromancers, but I didn't want anyone at Fairhaven to know about him until I could find out more. What if the Durupinen decided my loose ends were too much of a liability? What if I put Pierce or Annabelle in even more danger? What if I managed to reignite a battle that had lain dormant for hundreds of years? Or what if—and this possibility was perhaps the most disturbing—someone within the Durupinen was responsible for the attack? Annabelle certainly didn't trust them... like she said, they had the means, motive, and plenty of opportunity. There were certainly many on the Council who resented our family—I couldn't rule out the possibility that one or more of them might be trying to clean up the mess we'd created, whether the other Council members knew about it or not. Until I could rule this out, I had to conceal from all of them, as much as possible, the truth.

"We can't tell them about this!" I said.

"What do you mean, we can't tell them?" Finn snarled.

"We can't tell them about the man who was following us," I said.

Finn's expression was incredulous. "And what are we supposed to tell them? How in the hell are we supposed to explain this?" he said, gesturing to the smoking wreck of the car.

"The story you just told that guy up there sounded pretty good to me," I said.

Finn laughed derisively. "That was rubbish! That would never work on anyone who actually took the time to look at the car, and I can promise you that my superiors will be going over it with a fine-tooth comb. They're not going to accept the story of a blowout when the tires are just about the only things on the car that aren't destroyed. And we were obviously hit from behind!"

"Can't we just tell them it was..." I cast around in my brain around madly for a lie. My eyes fell on Savvy, who was now vomiting into a nearby bush. "Tell them it was a drunk driver, some random idiot with road rage, anything! Please, Finn, it's really important!"

"And you still aren't going to tell me what's going on?" he asked.

"I can't. I just need you to trust me."

Finn snorted. "Yeah Jess, because you are proving to be properly trustworthy."

Before I could respond, Milo blazed into the space between us, causing us both to leap backward in shock.

"Milo! Where did you—"

"Holy shit, thank GOD you're alive! I went for help! I thought that maniac was going to kill you all!" he cried. He took in all three of us and the smoking wreckage of the car. "It's a freaking miracle you aren't all floating deadside with me right now!"

"What help? Who's coming?" I asked.

"I went to Hannah, and she told Celeste, and Celeste called in the Caomhnóir. There are about ten of them on the way."

"Milo, what do they know? How much did you tell them?"

"Hannah told them Finn was driving you and Savvy back from

London and that someone hit your car. She was too hysterical for long explanations, so they didn't press her for any more details."

"How long do you think it will be before they—"

As if on cue, screeching tires and sweeping headlights converged on the other side of the guardrail above us and rendered the rest of my question unnecessary.

"Connect with Hannah, now!" I hissed to Milo, as car doors slammed and figures started appearing above us. "Tell her we're okay, and to play dumb about why I was here and what we were doing, please! I'll explain everything later, but right now—"

"Jess, there's something else. I saw who was—" Milo said.

"Tell me later, Milo! Go! Now!"

Milo faded from view just as a deep voice called, "Finn? Jessica? Savannah?"

"Here!" Finn called back. "We're down here! We're okay!"

There was no time to say anything else. With one last pleading look at Finn, whose expression was completely unreadable, I turned and faced the team of Caomhnóir now climbing down the embankment.

16

CRIME AND PUNISHMENT

"WELL, THAT WAS ONE MASSIVE COCK-UP," Savvy said. "Next time, I'm planning girls' night, yeah?"

We were sitting on a bench outside of one of the Council's conference rooms, awaiting a disciplinary meeting, as if we were a pair of pranksters sent to the principal's office. It was humiliating.

"I'm sorry about all of this, Sav," I said. I kept my eyes on my knees, which were covered in grass stains and smears of dried blood. "I had no idea I was getting us into a situation like that. Seriously, I never would have asked for you to come."

"Nah, don't apologize," she said, nudging my knee with her own. "I'm only playing around. I know you didn't plan any of that."

"No, I definitely didn't."

"And I've got to say, that was a damn sight more exciting than any night in town I've ever had, even if it was a bit heavy on the mortal danger. You're a real badass, eh?" She grinned.

I couldn't help but smirk a tiny bit. "Yeah, that's me. Bad to the bone."

Somewhere nearby, a clock was ticking ominously. Savvy put a reassuring hand on my knee, which was bouncing up and down with manic, nervous energy in time to the clock.

"You've got to take a breath," she said. "It's going to be fine, you know. I've had, like, five of these meetings already."

"Yeah, but you didn't wreck a car and nearly kill yourself and two other people, did you?" I asked.

"No, and neither did you. It was an accident! They may be cross about our sneaking out, but even they know you can't control everything."

I found a tiny shard of glass still caught in the web of distressed threads on my jeans and picked it carefully out with my fingers. No,

I couldn't control everything. In fact, I couldn't control anything, it seemed. Everything was spinning horribly out of control, and there was nothing I could do to stop it. I didn't know who I could trust, who I could talk to, or even what was unfolding in the room behind me.

We weren't the only ones who had to endure a disciplinary meeting. Finn had been in there for fifteen minutes, and I couldn't hear a single word that was being said—although not for lack of trying.

Our rescue by the Caomhnóir had been cold and efficient. In fact, other than brusquely ensuring we weren't hurt, not one of them had spoken a single word to us. Before I could say anything else to Finn, before I could beg him—even with one last look—to stick to my story, Savvy and I were led up the embankment, ushered into a car, and driven away. My last glimpse, as we peeled out into traffic, was of Finn walking around the still-smoking wreck and pointing to various parts of it as one of the Caomhnóir scribbled in a small, black notebook.

Had he told them everything? Would they guess what was going on? And what would happen to Annabelle, or Pierce, or Tia if they did? My stomach was churning: I was suddenly fighting the urge to be sick.

"Thanks for sticking with my story," I whispered to Savvy when it felt safe to open my mouth again.

"You got it," Savvy said with a wink. She winked more than anyone I'd ever met. The fact that she could still pull off such a flawless wink, despite what must still have been her still-sky-high high blood alcohol level, was impressive. "I'm no snitch. Besides, no one's going to have a problem believing I went out in search of a good time."

"Psst! Jess!"

Milo was hovering just around the corner, beckoning to me.

"What is it, Milo? I can't talk right now, I have to—"

"This is really important!" he said.

I half-stood to go over to Milo, but just then the door beside us swung wide open and Finn stalked out. He brushed by us without so much as a glance of acknowledgment. As he disappeared around the corner, a voice from inside the room called, "Jessica, Savannah, come in, please."

I turned back to Milo. "Wait for me here," I said. "I'll be right back, if they don't kill us. In which case I will probably be right back anyway."

He made an impatient noise, but nodded in accent. We stood up—Savvy a bit unsteadily—and turned to face our doom. Marion stood before us, her face pale with rage. She leaned forward and started drumming her fingernails on the polished wood of the conference table.

I groaned inwardly. Of course it was Marion. Because that was exactly the kind of luck that I had.

She pierced us with the kind of icy glare meant to make mere mortals squirm. "Well, I'd like to say that I'm surprised to be standing here, but that would be categorically untrue."

I returned her glare. Savvy, on the other hand, was actually smiling in an amused sort of way.

"I need hardly tell you why you are here, so let me rather begin by expressing my deep, deep disappointment. Do you have any appreciation at all for the seriousness of this situation?"

I said nothing, unsure of what, exactly, Marion thought the situation was. Savvy however, chose that moment to pop her gum loudly, which we all took to mean, "No."

"You should both be ashamed of yourselves. Savannah, you have shown nothing but the most blatant disregard for every single rule and regulation we have, despite the fact that most of them are for your own safety and the safety of others. I'm just not sure at this point what we can say or do to make you realize the gravity of what you agreed to in coming here." Marion paused and raised an expectant eyebrow.

Savvy snapped to mock attention. "Sorry, was that a question?"

Marion's eyes narrowed. "What do you have to say for yourself?"

"Only this," Savvy said, crossing her arms. "If it had been made clear to me that I was going be cooped up here in the middle of this godforsaken wilderness with nothing to do and nowhere to do it, I'd have said thanks, but no thanks."

"Your responsibilities were made clear to you," Marion said with a dismissive wave of her hand.

"Sure, they explained about the spirits. I know I've got to Cross 'em over, and I've agreed to learn how to do it. I know how bad it is for them to be trapped here, and I know how important it is for me to step up and do this job. But no one told me about the boundaries and the lectures and the bleeding curfews. Hell, we're not children!"

"Your behavior thus far contradicts that statement," replied Marion. "The rules here are the rules here, and you will abide by them or you will be shown the door."

"Oh, I know where it is, thanks, and I'm about ready to walk out of it myself!" Savvy said, stepping aggressively forward. I grabbed her arm and pulled her back beside me, and although she twisted herself out of my grip, she stayed where she was.

"I'm sorry to say that threat is empty," Marion said. "You've begun the journey here, and we must tolerate you until you finish it. But until that happy day, you will abide by our rules or suffer the consequences."

Savvy rolled her eyes but did not retort.

Perhaps seeing that she would get nowhere with Savvy, Marion turned to me.

"Jessica, you owe us all an explanation for the considerable trouble you've put everyone through tonight. I've already spoken to Finn, as you very well know, and he has informed me that this little excursion was all your idea."

Damn it, Finn.

Marion walked around the table, closing most of the distance between us; I took an involuntary step back. "I must say that I was not expecting to hear this, seeing as Ms. Todd is our resident party animal. I thought surely she must have talked you into one of her outings. I've taken you for many things, Jessica, but a party girl was never one of them."

I squirmed but kept quiet, fighting the impulse to shoot down her accusations. Sticking to my own cover story in the face of someone like Marion was harder than I'd imagined.

"Well? What possible explanation can you give?"

I cleared my throat a bit and found my voice lurking in the back. "We're all under a lot of pressure here. I just needed a night to unwind, without any responsibility."

"Well, responsibility is certainly one thing you've completely ignored, I think we can both agree on that point," Marion said with a tittering little laugh that put my teeth on edge. "You led a fellow Apprentice, however willing, to sneak off campus and engage in the worst kind of excesses, and for what? A good time? And did you have a good time, Jessica? Was it fun being harassed by inebriated men? Did you have a laugh at being run off the road and nearly killed by a driver who, most unfortunately, shares your complete lack of self-control in the face of alcohol?"

I started to answer and then halted, completely wrong-footed. "I... what?"

"Perhaps you are still having too much fun to understand me?" Marion suggested, her voice sagging with the weight of her own sarcasm. "I asked if a car wreck with a drunk driver qualifies as an appropriate activity with which to 'unwind?'"

"Did Finn tell you that?"

"Of course!" Marion said. "You didn't think he'd try to cover for you, did you? I must say, your understanding of the Caomhnóir/ Durupinen dynamic is sadly lacking. Finn Carey is under no obligation to lie for you, or to make excuses for your abominable behavior. His one and only job is to protect you. You might give thought to him before you make that job quite so difficult."

I couldn't believe it. I'd been convinced he would tell them everything. I tried to pull myself together before I blew my own cover story and rendered Finn's unexpected loyalty pointless.

"How is Finn?" I asked.

"Your concern is too little, too late, I must say. His Caomhnóir superiors will deal with him and his own questionable decisions. You should be worried about yourself at this point, and what your late-night jaunt will mean for your future at Fairhaven."

I cast my eyes down and tried to look contrite; there were plenty of appropriate moments to show my general contempt for Marion, but now was not one of them. At this moment, she had the power to make my life measurably more unpleasant than it already was, and I knew it.

"Have you anything else to say in your defense?"

I took a deep breath, more to give an impression of penitence than anything else. "We just wanted a night out. Had things gone the way we had planned them, I think it would've been a pretty harmless excursion. We might've been caught and reprimanded, but no one would've been hurt or really even inconvenienced. We might be able to see spirits, but we aren't psychic—never in a million years could we have predicted how the night would turn out. If we had, we certainly never would've gone through with it. I'm really sorry for all of the trouble we put everyone through, especially Finn and the other Caomhnóir."

Marion kept silent but stared at me expectantly, as if I'd stopped speaking midsentence.

"I... don't really know what else to say. We're sorry, we really are." I found Savvy's foot with mine and kicked it. She started and added, "Yes, very sorry indeed. Yeah."

"Very well, if that's really all you have to say for yourselves," Marion began, as she retreated around the table and flipped open a file folder. She started writing in it as she spoke, "I'm sorry that you both find your duties here so taxing, and that you can find no constructive way of spending your free time without endangering people's lives. To that end, I will be recommending to the Council that you both be put on work detail for the next month during free periods. Perhaps if you are more constructively engaged, you will better appreciate your roles here. We shall also have to determine how you will make reparations to the Caomhnóir for the loss of their vehicle."

Savvy opened her mouth, presumably to argue, but I kicked her again, harder this time, and she closed it with a snap; she proceeded to fume is silence.

Marion set down her pen and ran one long, perfectly-manicured finger over her mouth before speaking again. She seemed to be weighing her words carefully, no doubt torn between what she ought to say to us as an administrator and what she'd like to say as a person who hated us on principle. She then smiled, which was a strange phenomenon on a face that did not seem to crease regardless of expression; it made her mouth look oddly disembodied.

"It really is too bad. There are some among the Council who would have all clans on equal footing. They would suggest that history, tradition, and service should have no weight, that each clan should be treated with the very same level of respect and given the same opportunities. Yet here you stand before me, proving them absolutely and incontrovertibly wrong. How very disappointed they'll all be. I really ought to be thanking you for proving my point."

"Glad to be of service," I said.

Savvy curtsied elaborately. "Is that all?"

"Yes, that is all. You will be notified of the details of your punishment as soon as they have been decided. In the meantime, you should both tread carefully from here on out. Another breach of this nature will not be lightly tolerated."

"Is that a promise?" Savvy asked. I grabbed her arm and pulled her out the door before Marion could berate us any further.

Outside the door, we found Milo bobbing up and down with a manic sort of energy. I let out a long sigh of relief.

"Still alive, I see," he said.

"Yeah, thanks to Finn," I said. "He covered for us. I can't believe it."

"Well ponder his charity later, I have something important to tell you!" Milo said, throwing his hands in the air in his characteristically dramatic fashion.

"Right, sorry. What is it?"

"I saw who was driving the car that hit us!" Milo cried.

My jaw dropped. "You're kidding me! How did you manage that?"

"He was ramming our car, and I suddenly thought that maybe I could just pop into his car and freak him out! Scare him or distract him, you know, so that you guys could get away. So I tried it. He couldn't see me at all, even though I was trying to manifest, but I sure as hell saw him. He hit you guys and I went for help, and—"

"Who was it? Was it someone we know?"

"It wasn't anyone I'd ever seen before, but I think I could show him to you."

"How?"

"We could use your gift. I could try to send his image to you and see if you can sketch it."

"Milo you're a genius!" I cried.

Milo shrugged. "This I knew, but I'm glad you're coming around."

"Let's go!" I said. "My sketchpad is right here in my bag."

I arrived in my room out of breath, with Milo in tow. Hannah was practically in a state of nervous collapse. I sat her down and explained everything that had happened, assuring her that we were not going to be kicked out and that everything was okay.

"Jess, I was so scared. I thought you were dead," she sobbed into my shoulder.

"I'm not even hurt, just bruises. Seriously, Hannah everything is okay." I looked over the top of her trembling head to see that she had obsessively organized the entire room in my absence—something she hadn't done hardly at all in weeks. "I'm so sorry. I'm sorry we scared you."

"It's okay," she said with a shuddering sigh. It's okay, I'm glad you're safe." She rubbed at her streaming eyes with her sleeve.

"Right now we have to try something," I said, extracting myself from her grip. "Milo saw the driver, and I want to see if I can get a good drawing of him." I spread several sheets of paper on the floor around me and fished a charcoal pencil out of my bag.

"Okay, Milo. I need you to concentrate as hard as you can on just one image of him, the clearest one you can remember. Try not to get distracted, and concentrate on the details. I'm going to focus myself and see if we can get anything down on paper."

I took a deep breath. I half-wished Fiona was here to oversee this and make sure I was doing it right, but she'd probably just yell at me and rip up the results anyway.

"Ready?" I asked.

"I don't know," Milo said. "I don't really know how to do this."

"Neither do I," I admitted. "Anytime it has happened before, I wasn't even aware of it. But Fiona said that the harder you concentrate on sending an image, and the more I concentrate on receiving it, the better the odds that I'll get something on paper."

"Okay, I'll try," Milo said.

I closed my eyes and rested the tip of the charcoal pencil on the paper. Then I cleared my mind and tried to reach out beyond myself to where Milo was, opening myself to him and what he wanted to show me.

The next thing I knew, the pencil dropped from my hand, which had cramped itself into a fist. I clutched at the seizing muscles and tried to pull my fingers straight.

"Jess! Are you okay?" cried Hannah.

I groaned, massaging my hand. "It worked didn't it?" I asked. "Damn it, that hurts!"

"That was one of the coolest things I've ever seen!" Milo cried. "Your hand was moving so fast it was a blur! Don't you remember doing it?"

"Not a stroke," I said, looking around for the result. My eyes fell on the paper to my right and I gasped.

"Neil!"

It was Neil Caddigan, there was absolutely no doubt. He stared up at me from the floor with his cold, pale eyes as if he were looking up through a window. His expression was hungry and fierce, unlike any expression I'd ever seen him wear; he had always appeared so calm, so scholarly.

"Do you know him?" Hannah asked, stunned.

"Yes," I breathed. "This is the guy I've been trying to get in touch with, the team member I told you was from England. And he was walking in to Pierce's office on the last day I saw him—the last day anyone saw him."

"What is that symbol there on his shirt?" Hannah asked sharply.

I followed her gaze to a small insignia near Neil's throat.

"It wasn't on the shirt, it was a pin or something," Milo said.

I stared at it. The symbol was familiar, but I couldn't place it. It looked like an arch with a ring encircling both sides of its threshold.

"The Necromancers," Hannah whispered. "It's the symbol of the Necromancers. I recognize it from class."

I stared at it again. She was right. My head swam and my stomach heaved; I closed my eyes and put my head down between my legs. Neil Caddigan was a Necromancer, and he had found me... in fact, he had probably tracked my ISP address from the email I'd written him. I'd led him right to me, and he had tried to kill me. And if he had been the last one to see Pierce alive...

"I'm going to be sick." I jumped up and ran across the hall to the bathroom. I skidded to my knees in front of the toilet and was violently ill, retching and heaving until there was nothing left in me but crippling fear and worry.

Hannah knelt behind me, stroking my hair. "They're supposed to be gone," I said. "They're supposed to be dead and gone. Why are they suddenly back again, and what would they want with us?"

"I don't know. Jess, we have to tell someone," Hannah said gently.

"Who? Who do we tell? No one's going to believe us, and even if they did, what can they do?"

"They can use their resources. They can help you find Pierce. They know so much more about the Necromancers than we do, they might be able to help. And they'll want to protect us, Jess. If the Necromancers are really back, they need to know."

"I can't think, I need to sleep," I said. "We can talk about it later. We need to be careful who we talk to, and I don't want to do anything rash."

"Half the Durupinen in this place already want you both out of here," Milo said. "If they know the Necromancers are after you, they might throw you to the wolves just to protect themselves."

"They would never do that," Hannah said harshly.

Milo shrugged but looked unconvinced. "So far I haven't seen a lot of loyalty in this happy little sisterhood, especially toward you."

"I need to lie down. I need to sleep," I repeated.

"It'll be okay, Jess. It will be okay," Hannah intoned, still stroking my hair.

But she couldn't know that. Nobody could.

That night, my usual dreams had one disturbing difference. The Silent Child stood where she always stood, before the wall of flames. But now a second figure stood beside her, with his hand resting on her shoulder and a malicious smile narrowing his blanched, nearly silvery eyes.

17

KNOCKING

MARION, IT SEEMED, didn't want the other apprentices to know about my adventure with Savvy, because I received not a single unusual glare from any of the other girls the next day. I couldn't have cared less either way. I had far too much on my mind to give even the slightest of damns what Peyton or anyone else thought of my behavior. There were much bigger, much more dangerous problems to deal with now.

When Savvy saw us at breakfast, I decided to fill her in. She was a part of all this now, whether she wanted to be or not, because Neil had seen her with me. I decided she had to know the details for her own safety.

She listened to everything I had to say with an uncharacteristically serious look on her face. When I was finished, she said, "Damn, mate. If I knew you were going to be this much trouble, I'd have jumped in someone else's shower that first day."

"I'm sorry, Sav," I said. "I had no idea any of this was going to—"

She held up a hand. "I know that. Stop apologizing. You're my mate, and if it weren't for you and your sister, I never would have lasted here as long as I have. Mates stick together, come whatever, you got me? Now is there anything I can do to help?"

I blew out a long, slow breath. "I don't think so. Well yeah, you can stop sneaking out while Neil is still out there looking for us. Just lay low here and keep safe."

Savvy rolled her eyes. "Suppose I'll have to. I don't fancy another run in with that car. I don't think we'd be lucky enough to walk away from something like that twice. Anyway, plenty here to keep us busy." She handed me a slip of paper bearing Marion's handwriting. "That's your punishment. Two weeks of cleaning and restoring artwork every night with Fiona. Ought to be a barrel of laughs, that."

I groaned. "I barely survive one class a week with that woman. Every night for two weeks? That's going to be a nightmare. When am I going to get my work done?"

"No idea, but if you figure it out, let me know, will you? I'll be trapped in the library, filing and stacking books."

Savvy could whine and moan all she liked, but I had no doubt my punishment was worse than hers—and that Marion had taken great pleasure in ensuring it was cruel and unusual.

"I was just thinking, if this Necromancer guy is trying to kill you, it doesn't look good for your professor mate, does it?" Savvy said.

"No," I said grimly, "it doesn't."

§

That afternoon, on my way to my first torture session with Fiona, I spotted Finn on the grounds. He was standing shin-deep in a hole, heaving large shovelfuls of earth onto a pile on the grass nearby. Just behind him was one of Fairhaven's beautiful fountains; this one depicted a woman in Grecian robes carrying a pitcher of water on her shoulder. Coming to a spur-of-the-moment decision, I walked toward him until I stood on the very edge of the ditch. I waited for him to notice me, but he didn't look up; I cleared my throat.

"Hi," I said tentatively.

He said nothing with the exception of a grunt that could have been directed at me, but could also have been a result of the physical exertion of digging.

"How are you feeling?" I asked.

"Tired," he said, wiping his shining forehead and smearing it with dirt in the process.

"No, I mean, after the accident. Were you hurt?"

"Mild concussion, a sprained ankle, and a few stitches. It should have been a lot worse," he replied.

"Good," I said. Finn's head snapped up and he glared at me, so I clarified. "I mean, it's good that you weren't badly injured. I was really worried there for a few minutes, before I got you out of the car."

He shrugged, as though he didn't want to dwell on the memory. I looked down at his callused, work-blackened hands—I must have imagined how soft his touch had been on my cheek because those hands couldn't possibly have been so gentle.

"I'm fine, too. Not even any stitches," I said after a few moments of ringing silence.

"I know," he said.

"You know?"

"I went to Mrs. Mistlemoore in the infirmary for a full report on your injuries."

"Oh," I said. "Right."

"It was the most direct means of ascertaining your physical condition," he said stiffly.

I nodded. It did not escape me that going to Mrs. Mistlemoore was also the best way to get the information without having to interact with me. And whatever happened to patient confidentiality?

"What are you doing out here?" I asked.

"What does it look like I'm doing?" He heaved a shovelful of dirt onto the growing pile. "I'm digging. If you're wondering where to find me for the foreseeable future, I'll be right here—digging."

"Is this your punishment for the car?"

"No, this is my punishment for leaving the premises without alerting a superior. Those," he said, pointing to a wheelbarrow full of large square stones, "are my punishment for the car."

"Oh," I said. "I... did you get in a lot of trouble?"

He looked at me, and then pointedly at the wheelbarrow. "There are six more of those behind the shed when I've finished with these. So yes, I think it's fair to say that I'm in proper trouble."

"I'm sorry."

"Save it."

"Save it for what?" I asked.

"For someone who gives a damn," he replied. He raked a filthy arm across his face, depositing much more dirt onto his skin than he wiped away. "I tried caring, but it's only ever turned around and bitten me in the arse—I'm done."

"But I think you do give a damn," I said quietly.

He didn't answer, but merely continued to dig.

"Just stop that for a minute and listen to me, would you?" I said, wrenching the shovel from his grip and tossing it to the ground. It landed with a crunchy thunk on the gravel walk.

"Give that back to me."

"No."

"Give it to me before someone sees that I'm not working and I wind up with another ditch to dig."

"Not until you stop and listen to what I have to say."

Finn glared at me, and for a moment I thought he might lash out, but instead he shook his head, climbed out of the pit, and sat himself, grudgingly, on the fountain's edge.

"I know that you didn't have to lie to them. I know you had no good reason to do what I asked you to do, because I didn't give you one. So why did you do it?"

He still wouldn't look at me, but instead just stared intently at his fingernails as he picked, picked, picked the dirt from under them.

"I don't know. I was going to tell them everything, and then I just... didn't. I still can't properly explain it to myself, and now I wish I hadn't done it."

"I kept telling you that you needed to trust me, but I had no right to ask that of you. Trust has to be earned, and I haven't been nearly honest enough with you to earn it."

He stopped picking at his nails and sat very still. I took this as a sign that he wasn't completely ignoring me.

"I know we haven't gotten along. I don't know why we can't just suck it up and coexist. Maybe we're both too stubborn to depend on someone else. I know I am. I hate depending on people—probably because I could only depend on myself for most of my life. Self-reliance is kind of my thing. But now I'm here, trying to figure out what the hell is happening with my life, and almost everyone is awful to us... and all I want to do is go home."

I chanced a glance at his face, but he still wasn't looking at me. I still couldn't tell for sure if he was listening. I looked away again, and watched as the water from the stone woman's pitcher bubbled upward before tumbling over itself in a rush to reach the pool below.

Finn still said nothing, but I had more to confess. "I'm trying my best, but it's hard to commit to something that tore apart my family and ruined my life. I'm trying to buy into the idea that this is my duty, but I can't help feeling like the Durupinen owe a hell of a lot more to me than I owe to them. So in the end, I'm not here for the clan or the Council or whatever other bullshit. I'm here for the spirits, because I've seen what can happen to them if we aren't here to help." I paused before adding with a bitter laugh, "I don't even know why I'm telling you all of this. You grew up in the middle of all this Durupinen and Caomhnóir stuff; it probably just feels like second nature to you."

He snorted. "Yeah, I grew up in the middle of it—every minute of every day. Believe me, that comes with its own problems."

I nodded. "Fair enough. But still, you lied to them. You could've told them about the guy who was chasing us, but you didn't. I can't imagine what reason of your own you would have to do that, so I can only assume you did it because I asked you to."

He looked away—unwilling, I supposed, to acknowledge this.

"I just needed to say thank you for that. Thank you."

"You still aren't going to tell me why I had to lie for you?" Finn asked grudgingly.

I took a deep breath. "No, I'm not. But it's not because I don't trust you. That may have been true before, but it's not true now."

He frowned at me. "So why then?"

"Because I don't know the truth yet, not all of it. I have some more digging to do before I really know what's going on," I explained.

"Is that supposed to be a joke?" he asked, with just the merest hint of an upward tilt to his lips.

It took me a moment to realize what he meant, but when I did, I burst out laughing. "No! No, I'm sorry, that was totally unintentional wordplay, I promise."

"Do you also promise your 'digging' won't land you into another situation like yesterday's?" he asked, serious again before I could even register how his smile had, momentarily, changed his features; it was so very foreign to my perception of him.

"I can't promise that," I said. "But I do promise that I won't disappear again, not on purpose anyway. And if I find the answers I'm looking for, and if I can confirm them, then I'll tell you everything."

Finn looked momentarily stunned. "You will?"

I smiled at his shock. "Yes, I will. We're going to be stuck with each other for a good long time. We might as well make the best of it... and I think a little bit of trust is a good place to start."

He wasn't happy—I could see that much. But the nod he gave me, devoid of satisfaction, was at least accepting. He stood up, and I handed him his shovel. Finn took it without a word and went back to his work. I left him to it.

§

Three nights in a row of cleaning grime off of paintings with Fiona gave me a lot of time to think, but I still couldn't convince myself to tell any of the other Durupinen about Neil. It wasn't that I felt bereft of people to trust—I was fairly sure that Celeste or Siobhán would do everything in their power to help me. But I was also fairly sure that their idea of help would be to bring the information straight to the Council, and I wasn't prepared for that. Hannah didn't push me, either. She seemed to think that—as long as we stayed safely tucked away at Fairhaven, surrounded by Caomhnóir—there was no immediate danger. And every time I saw the Caomhnóir making their rounds or practicing their martial arts on the grass, I had to admit that Hannah was probably right.

When I arrived back in my room Wednesday night, Mackie and Hannah were in front of the fireplace, bent over the night's heap of homework from our Ancient Celtic Languages class, my least favorite subject. My eyes were aching and tired, so I made myself a cup of tea. I'd just settled into the chair beside them when Savvy, with a triumphant expression on her face, burst into our room like a whirlwind. I jumped so badly at her sudden appearance that I spilled hot tea all over myself.

"Damn it, Sav, you have *got* to stop doing that!"

Savvy ignored me and strutted into the middle of the room. "What's the one thing you've been wondering about for ages?" she asked.

"Why you always have to scare the crap out of us every time you enter a room?" I muttered, shrugging out of my tea-soaked sweater and crossing to the closet for a dry one.

"Go on. What's the one thing that's been driving you absolutely bollocking crazy?"

"Just tell us what you're on about or sod off," Mackie grumbled as she crumpled up another sheet of paper and chucked it into the fire. "Hannah, can you please show me how to do these conditional tenses again?"

"Sure." Hannah slid closer to Mackie, and pulled a pencil from somewhere in her hair as if by magic.

"Oi!" Savvy shouted, stamping her foot. "I'm trying to tell you I found something important! Is someone going to ask me what it is or not?"

"Aren't you just going to tell us anyway?" I asked.

Savvy sighed an exasperated sigh and walked into the middle of the room. She extracted an enormous leather-bound book from her satchel and dropped it with a resounding thunk onto the floor between us. It generated an impressive cloud of dust.

"What is that?" I choked out.

"Do you remember that first week here, when Peyton brought your mother up in Siobhán's class?"

"Yes," Hannah and I said together. Not that we needed reminding.

"Well, she made that snarky comment about Bindings, and then Siobhán said that there was more than one kind of Binding and different circumstances for using them. I read it in my notes last night—yes, I take notes when I fancy it—and it got me thinking about the Silent Child."

I stopped blotting my sweater and looked up at Savvy. All of the worry about Neil and the Necromancers had driven the Silent Child to the perimeters of my mind in recent days. "What about her?"

Finally getting the undivided attention she was hoping for, Savvy plopped herself down on the floor beside the decades-old book and went on. "Well, I started thinking, didn't I? I mean, what if Bindings could be used in reverse, right? What if, instead of putting the Binding on herself to keep the spirits away, a Durupinen could put a Binding on a particular spirit to keep it from communicating?"

Even Mackie looked up from her work. "That sort of seems like the opposite of what we're meant to do. I mean, we're here for them to communicate with, aren't we? Could we... even do that?"

"That's the big question!" said Savvy. "So after class I went to the library—"

"Right, I'll stop you there," said Mackie. "Let's all just appreciate, for a brief moment, that Savvy not only knows where the library is, but entered said chamber voluntarily."

"Of course I bloody well know where it is! Spent the last few nights of my life in there alphabetizing them little catalog cards, haven't I? And I didn't go there voluntarily, I've still got detention hours to do. Anyway, after no small amount of searching, I tracked down this book." She slapped the cover of the monstrous book and another cloud of dust blossomed from it. "And it told me everything I needed to know. I have officially solved the mystery of The Silent Child!" Savvy looked at us as though waiting for applause.

"Well, get on with it!" Mackie shouted. "What've you found out?"

"It's here, listen." Savvy flipped to the middle of the book where she had marked a page with a torn Cadbury wrapper, and started reading aloud.

In the common course of dealings with the spirit world, the occasion may arise when a spirit who will not Cross must be silenced. This is only to be expected, as spirits are often trapped in great turmoil, and cannot or will not channel their energy in a positive manner. The silencing of such a spirit may only be done in good faith, and only if the spirit is using its presence among the living to torment or otherwise inflict harm. It must be borne in mind, however, that silencing a spirit will cause it great distress; silencing should therefore be done only as a last resort, and only for the amount of time needed to discover another means of banishing the spirit from the presence of the living with whom it is in conflict. If, and only if, these conditions are met, a Caging may be performed.

The Caging will sever the direct connection between the spirit and the living world. Although the spirit will still be of the living world, it will no longer be heard. All attempts by the spirit to communicate will be lost to silence and echo, unable to penetrate the Caging.

Hannah's eyes were round with horror. "That's... terrible. We shouldn't be able to do something like that. They come to us for help and we... trap them?"

Mackie nodded grimly. "It does sound rather wrong. But it does say a Caging should only be done in emergencies, doesn't it? Like if a spirit is tormenting someone and we can't get it to stop."

"I... I guess..." Hannah said; a shiver rocked her frail shoulders.

"So this is it, isn't it?" Savvy asked. "This is what happened to the Silent Child. Someone's gone and performed a Caging on her and that's why she can't talk to you."

"It sounds right from the description," I said. "But it can't be... Fiona said the Silent Child has been here for centuries. This Caging thing is only meant to be done for a short time, until you can find another solution to the problem."

Savvy shrugged a little too unconcernedly for my taste. "Maybe they couldn't find another solution. Maybe they never found a way to get rid of her, so they left her Caged."

"No way," Hannah said at once. "Someone would have realized and let her out, surely."

"Maybe not," I said, hopping up and starting to pace. "Fiona was really surprised when I told her that the Silent Child had attacked me, remember? As far as Fiona knew, she's never spoken to anyone; that's how she got her name."

"And there are hundreds of spirits here," Mackie chimed in. "There always have been. It's like they're part of the landscape. We hardly take notice of most of them. I've never stopped to wonder why a single one of them is here, have you? I just sort of took them for granted. We all do, don't we?"

Our silence was answer enough. Mackie was right. I'd never stopped to think about who the other ghosts were or why they had never Crossed over. Their presence seemed natural at Fairhaven Hall. If the Silent Child had never tried to communicate with anyone else before, she would've blended into the spirit masses, trapped in plain sight. It was a terrible thought.

Hannah, who'd been reading through the marked section of the book, broke the quiet. "There are instructions here for a ceremony to break the Caging."

"Yeah, I saw that, and it looks bloody complicated. You've got to do it in the middle of night when the moon is full... and on consecrated ground," Savvy said. "There's about a thousand steps to that Casting."

Hannah was still reading, but she nodded her head in understanding. "Yes, it will be difficult, but it's not impossible. We've just got to follow the instructions carefully. And it needs four of us to perform it properly, one for each of the classical elements."

"We've got to do it," I said, as I crept up behind Hannah and started reading over her shoulder. "The Silent Child is trying to tell me something and I can't just ignore her. If this really is what's going on, then someone's left this poor little girl voiceless and trapped for hundreds of years!"

"I'll help you," said Hannah at once.

"And me," said Savvy.

I turned a pleading gaze on Mackie. "Come on, Mack. It takes four. We need you."

Mackie was hesitant, as I knew she would be. She chewed on her lip, playing for time. "I really don't think it's a good idea. Consecrated ground in the middle of the night means breaking curfew and puts us out of bounds... and that's even before we've done the Casting itself."

"I know we'll be breaking a few rules, but this is important!" I insisted.

"And what if we're unleashing something dangerous?" Mackie asked.

I frowned at her. "What do you mean, dangerous? She's not dangerous, she's just a little kid."

"That doesn't mean she can't be dangerous. At some point a long time ago, a Durupinen Caged her for a reason... and never released her. That sounds like something we might not want to mess with."

Mackie's expression was wary. Savvy's face, on the other hand, was utterly enthralled. "That sounds like *exactly* the kind of thing we should mess with!"

I couldn't suppress a grin. It looked like Savvy's penchant for rule-breaking and general shenanigans was about to pay off—instead of blowing up in our faces as it usually did.

"Savvy don't be absurd," Mackie spat.

"Who's being absurd? Look, when you lot came pounding on my door and recruited me for all this, you made it sound like a right adventure. But so far it's been nothing but a load of schoolwork. I barely passed year ten, so what the hell am I doing here? I might as well have stayed home and worked in a shop—at least I'd be getting paid. But now we've got the chance to do something exciting! This is what I thought it would be like! Now you're not gonna bloody well spoil the only fun I'm likely to have by being sensible, are you?"

"This isn't about having fun," Mackie replied.

"No," I agreed. "It's not. It's about doing what's right. That little girl needs help, and I have to be the one to do it. I can't do it without all of you. Please, Mack."

Mackie continued to frown, but heaved a long-suffering sigh and said, "Give me the book. Let me see that Casting."

"Thank you," I breathed.

"I'm not agreeing to anything yet," Mackie said firmly. She flipped the book open and started to read.

Mackie took a good bit more convincing, but she eventually came around—though not without conditions. We sat up planning well into the night, because Mackie would only agree to help if we had every detail accounted for. She also insisted that we prepare ourselves for the possibility that we might need to Cage the Silent Child again, which Hannah wasn't too thrilled about. I wasn't thrilled either, but in the end we all had to agree that—despite my gut feeling about her—the Silent Child was a mystery, an unknown quantity, and that we couldn't predict what would happen when we lifted the Caging. Mackie was right; we had to at least learn how to perform a Caging, and be ready to use it if need be.

We agreed we would do the Uncaging the following Saturday night, which was the night of the next full moon. I hated to wait, but we had no choice. In a way, it was good that we had time to prepare; the Casting called for things that were not a standard part of our starter kit, and we needed time to track them down. After all, if we didn't follow the ritual to the letter, we'd risk the integrity of the entire Casting. Mackie seemed fairly confident she could borrow most of what we needed from Celeste; there was just one item she was unsure about.

"Celeste's got drawers and drawers full of every precious stone and mineral you could think of, so none of these will be an issue," Mackie said, running her finger down the list. "She also has all of these herbs—half of them grow on the grounds anyway. But I've never heard of lapis lazuli powder."

"I have," I said, and she looked at me in surprise.

"You have?"

"Yes. Fiona uses it in her restoration work. It was one of the rarer powders used to make blue pigments for paint during the Renaissance."

"Brilliant!" Mackie said. "Do you think you could get your hands on some? We only need enough to draw one rune."

"I'll find a way," I said. "I have absolutely no idea how, but I'll do it."

§

When I arrived in Fiona's studio Thursday night, she was working intently on a huge gilt-framed painting. And much to my surprise and relief, her full set of powder-filled apothecary jars was laid out on the table beside her.

I placed my bag carefully on the table, sat down beside her, and waited for her to acknowledge me. I had found that this was the best way to avoid her too-easily-awakened wrath. Finally, after about ten minutes, she spoke.

"You remember how to mix the vermillion?" she asked.

"Yes, I think so."

"You'd better know so, or you're not touching those pigments."

I refrained from rolling my eyes with extreme difficulty. "Yes, I remember how to mix the vermillion."

"Well, do it then, and add it to that palette over there for me. And bring me some of the varnish remover from the supply cupboard."

I went to the cupboard and dug out the varnish remover and a bottle of linseed oil. Then I returned to the table and set to work, while Fiona grumbled under her breath about dirty varnish layers and smoke damage.

Without consciously making the decision to speak, a question bubbled to my lips.

"Fiona, do you think it's possible that the Necromancers are still around?"

For the first time since I arrived, Fiona looked up from her work. Her face was astonished. "Of course not! What in the world would make you ask me such a question?"

I kept my eyes carefully on the bottle of linseed oil as I measured it out into a tiny glass bowl. "I've been writing a paper about them, so I've been doing a lot of research."

Fiona nodded absently and returned to her work. "Well, if you've been reading carefully, you'll know that they were destroyed centuries ago. There was nothing left by the time we were done with them. No order could survive a routing like that."

I said nothing, but began adding the linseed oil very slowly and carefully to the little mound of red powder. I could feel Fiona's eyes on me, probing me.

"Jess? Is there any other reason why you're asking? Don't you hold back on me."

I looked up at her and caught her eye. The concern in her face was completely unadulterated by its usual measure of contempt and annoyance, and I realized for the first time that Fiona could be pretty.

I almost told her. I almost let loose the floodgates and told her everything.

Almost.

"No. I just found the whole idea of them creepy, and I know we've still got the Caomhnóir, so I just wondered if that's what they are supposed to protect us from. That's all."

Fiona furrowed her brow. I couldn't tell if she believed me or not.

Finally, she seemed to decide that it didn't matter. She discarded the cotton ball in her hand and snatched up another before returning to her work.

"The Caomhnóir have many functions besides fending off enemy cults. They are indispensable in maintaining safety during spirit interactions, and also in keeping the outside world from discovering our secrets. Believe me, they've found plenty to keep them busy in the several hundred years since the Necromancers were destroyed."

I concentrated on working the powder into the oil slowly and methodically. "I hate that we have to have them around."

"Do you?" Fiona asked.

"Yes! Don't you? Doesn't it feel backwards? Here we are, this powerful, female-centric society full of strong, independent women in every type of leadership role, yet we need men for protection? It doesn't make any sense!"

Fiona didn't say anything.

"So it doesn't bother you at all?" I asked, looking up.

Fiona's face had gone slack. Her hands hung limply at her sides. As I watched, her eyes rolled into the back of her head and she began to mutter under her breath.

My heart began thudding against my ribcage. I glanced around the room, but if a spirit were present, it couldn't—or wouldn't—reveal itself to me.

"Fiona? Can you hear me?"

She continued to mutter unintelligibly. Realizing I couldn't have hoped for a more perfect opportunity, I grabbed the tiny stoppered bottle of powdered lapis lazuli and pocketed it. As I did so, Fiona's hand began thrashing around, searching through the air, and I realized she was looking for something to draw with. I jumped up, knocking my newly mixed paint to the floor, and lifted the painting she had been restoring out of her reach—she'd be inconsolable if she destroyed it with a spirit-induced drawing. I carefully lay the painting aside, then snatched a pencil and a nearly blank canvas from the table. I positioned the canvas on the easel and thrust the pencil into Fiona's still-flailing hand.

Immediately she began to draw; her hand moved over the canvas with unnatural speed. There was no logic to the strokes she made on the paper, as there would have been if she were drawing of her own free will. A line here, a curve in a corner, an oval shape over there—all of these were seemingly completely unrelated until, through the building up of more and more disparate strokes, a picture began to form.

From Fiona's lines and curves emerged a young man in an army uniform, with a friendly smile and smudges of mud on his face. He had an M-16 rifle strapped across his chest, and although I couldn't quite put my finger on it, something about this rendering made him look larger than life—almost as though he were a great American hero.

But there was something odd about the picture too. The perspective was of someone looking upwards at this man, as if the soldier were standing on a staircase, or as if the viewer were a solid foot or more shorter than the soldier.

And then there were his eyes: Although I'd never seen this man before, I knew those eyes.

Fiona suddenly dropped the pencil to the floor, but her hand, rather than coming to rest, began to knock, one-two-three, one-two-three, against the tabletop.

Something was stirring in the back of my mind, but it wouldn't coalesce into a clear memory. Why was this familiar? I knew I had never seen this soldier before, and yet there was something familiar in his face, in his eyes.

Knock-knock-knock. Knock-knock-knock.

I closed my eyes and tried to feel out into the space around me, trying to find the spirit that Fiona had connected to, but the two of them were too tightly latched together for me to identify this spirit.

I opened my eyes and looked back at the face again.

Knock-knock-knock. Knock-knock-knock.

A voice joined my thoughts, although I couldn't distinguish whether this voice came from my own memory or from the spirit himself.

"Then about a week later, two uniformed officers showed up and destroyed my mother with three sharp knocks on our battered screen door."

I jumped to my feet. "No. Please, God, no."

I abandoned Fiona there as she continued knocking absently into the silence. This could not mean what I thought it meant. I flew from the room, my eyes filling with tears as I tore down the stairs. I ran from corridor to corridor all the way back to our room. My breath was fire in my lungs. It couldn't be true.

But I knew those eyes. I knew that voice.

I flung our door open. It crashed against the wall, causing Hannah leap off of her bed and making a shocked Milo to flicker out of sight and back again.

"We need to do a Crossing. Right now."

"Jess, are you alright? You look terrible! What happened to—"

"That ghost you mentioned before, the one that was drumming or knocking, is he still around?"

"I... yes, he's been around since then. I hear him every now and then, but he doesn't seem to want to Cross. Why are you—"

"Please, I have to know. I think I know, I think it's him. I think it's—but I can't... please, we have to do a Crossing. We have to do it now!" I said, with panic sharp and bitter in my mouth.

"Okay, okay!" Hannah said, grabbing her Casting bag. "But we can't do it in here because of the Wards."

I turned and walked into the hallway. I frantically lifted the edge of the carpet runner and flung it aside, revealing the bare stone beneath.

Hannah stood in the doorway, staring at me. "You want to do it right here? In the hallway?"

"Yes! Just do it, do it now!" I shouted at her, barely suppressing a sob.

Half-consoling, half-terrified, Hannah set swiftly to work drawing the Circle in the almost-too-narrow hallway. I tried to light the candles while she did this, but my fingers were shaking too badly. Hannah pulled the candles gently from my hands, lighted each, and placed them. We took our positions and I stammered through the Incantation. I felt the Gateway open between us, felt the flow of energy, and braced myself for what I feared would come next.

At first there was nothing. Just us chanting in the flickering light, and for a moment I thought it hadn't worked at all... that we'd somehow done something wrong, or that—by some wonderful miracle—I'd been mistaken.

Then it came.

Flash.
Lying on the roof of a rusted out car, watching fireworks explode over my head as an ice cream cone dripped, forgotten, between my fingers.

Running through a field, chasing after the laughing, bobbing boy in front of me, as he turned back, gently teasing me.

It was the young man from Fiona's drawing, but younger and happier, laughing and smiling.

Watching that same man grow smaller and smaller as he waved to me from the window of a train full of soldiers... running and waving and crying until I thought my lungs and heart would burst. Sitting in my darkened bedroom, talking to that same man, aglow with happiness at his return.

Why did it seem perfectly natural for this soldier, armed and in uniform, to be in a child's bedroom at midnight?

Sitting at a scrubbed, white kitchen table. Suddenly, three sharp knocks. My mother opening the door for the uniformed officers. Watching her crumple to the ground as the officers failed to catch her before she hit the floor.

I knew this story. I knew this boy.

Watching a dark-haired, pale-skinned girl enter my office, her panic barely contained as she extended a shaking form to me, begging to be signed into my class. Standing by in helpless terror as that same girl writhed and shrieked, under attack by something I couldn't see.

I could barely keep my grip on Hannah's hand. My sobs came one upon the other, drowning me in my own sorrow.

Laying on a cold floor, watching my own blood pool against my cheek, as a figure turned in the doorway to look at me one last time—a figure with pale, nearly colorless eyes.

One last thought flickered through my head. Not a memory, but a message.

"I'm sorry, Ballard. I tried. Stay safe."

The Gateway pulled shut, locking Pierce forever on the other side. It was true, all true: Pierce was dead. Crossed over. Gone.

The blood rushing in my ears deafened me to every sound except that of my own racking sobs. I lurched to my feet, knocking over the nearest candle, and took off down the hallway. I could hear Hannah hurrying along behind me. I felt her fingers clutching at the back of my T-shirt.

"Jess! Jess, wait! Where are you going?" she cried. "Who was that? Who Crossed?"

I twisted my shoulder violently so that she lost her grip. I plowed on, stumbling on the uneven stone floors as my tears blurred my vision into a distorted haze.

He was dead. Pierce was dead. And it was all my fault.

No. Not my fault. Their fault. *Her* fault.

I hadn't known where I was going, but I did now. Changing direction with a suddenness that made Hannah shriek, I made for the North Tower, with Hannah and Milo calling after me every few steps. In what felt like no time at all, I reached the base of the staircase and took the stairs two at a time, relishing the pain in my lungs as I gasped for breath. Pain was good; pain made me angrier. Milo appeared, hovering several paces in front of me as I climbed.

"You can't just go storming up there. Just stop and think for a minute!" he cried.

"I... don't... care..." I panted. "Did they stop to... *think* before they left him exposed? He's dead now! They did nothing to protect him!"

Milo's replies were meaningless noise in my ears as I mounted the last landing to Finvarra's chambers. I hammered on her door it with both fists.

Almost instantly, Carrick materialized in front me, his arms held out in a defensive stance. His expression was at once confused and upset.

"Jessica? What is the meaning of this?"

I ignored him and pounded on the door again. "Finvarra!" I shouted hoarsely.

"Jessica, answer me! It's almost curfew! What are you doing here? What's happened to you?"

"Get out of the way, Carrick. I need to talk to her. Now!"

Carrick stood his ground. The force of his presence, like a sudden gale of wind, billowed out, thrusting me away from the door. I caught my heel on the carpet and fell backward into Hannah, who had just staggered to the top of the stairs, panting.

"Jess stop, just stop!" she begged as we both climbed to our feet.

"He's... dead!" I gasped. "He's dead and it's her fault! *FINVARRA!*"

Carrick drifted toward me. He blocked the door and demanded, "Jessica, if you don't calm down, we can't help you!"

Behind him, the door flew open and Finvarra stood silhouetted in the lamplight, her face blazing and stern.

"What is going on here? Jessica, how dare you—"

"How dare I? How dare *YOU*!" I shouted, lunging forward as Hannah grabbed my collar to restrain me.

Carrick thrust out a hand and I was lifted off my feet and hurled through the air. My back slammed into the wall and I slid down to the floor; he'd knocked the wind completely out of me.

Carrick began floating toward me, with his face full of horror at what he had done. "Jessica, I didn't mean to—"

"No!" Hannah cried, extending an arm toward him. By the force of her own hand, Carrick too was driven backward and pinned to Finvarra's open door, unable to move.

"Hannah, don't!" I wheezed.

"Everyone, stop! Stop this at once!" Finvarra shouted.

An odd, tense stillness fell over us. I leaned against the wall, still gasping for air.

Finvarra, her expression extremely wary, looked back and forth from Carrick to Hannah.

"Carrick, are you alright?" Finvarra asked slowly.

"I can't move," he said. It was painfully clear that he was stunned by this realization.

Finvarra turned to Hannah. "Hannah? Are you restraining him?"

Hannah tore her blazing stare from Carrick with seeming difficulty. When she found Finvarra's eyes, she suddenly looked terrified.

"Yes," Hannah squeaked, sounding almost surprised.

"Can you let him go now, please?" Finvarra asked, her voice a gentle lull. Hannah continued to stare at her, as though she couldn't understand Finvarra's words.

"Go on then," Finvarra soothed. "Just relax yourself. He's not going to hurt Jessica."

Hannah's hand began to tremble; she seemed on the verge of tears. "He *did*. He hurt her... He—"

Carrick inhaled sharply and cast a panicked look at Finvarra. She froze.

I suddenly realized, as I looked back and forth between them, that Hannah was actually causing Carrick pain. But Carrick was a ghost: Ghosts couldn't feel physical pain, could they?

Milo was standing so close to Hannah that, if he'd been alive, his body would've been pressed right up against her. He laid his face against her cheek.

"Sweetness, I want you to listen to me. Let's do what we always do when we get upset," he whispered. "Close those baby browns."

Hannah's eyes fluttered shut.

"Now take a nice deep breath with me, and when we let it out, we're just going to blow all those bad things away. Just send 'em out into the world and far away. And when you do, you'll let Carrick go. He's not going to hurt Jessica anymore." Milo paused and turned to Carrick. "Go on, Carrick, tell her."

"I didn't mean to hurt her to begin with," replied Carrick, his voice strained. "And I will not hurt her again—I give you my word as a Caomhnóir."

"There, see? Isn't that nice? You've protected her. She's safe. You got me?" Milo cooed.

"Yes," Hannah whispered.

"That's right, sweetness, Milo knows what he's talking about, just like always. Now, deep breath in."

With his face still pressed to hers, they both inhaled slowly and deeply. Then, in a movement that relaxed Hannah's entire being, they exhaled. Hannah's arm dropped limply to her side, and as it did, Carrick slumped forward and away from the door, apparently unrestrained once again. He traded one meaningful look with Finvarra, who nodded slowly in relief. She then turned quickly and smiled gently at Hannah.

"There now." Finvarra began. "Now that we have all calmed ourselves, please come in and sit down so we can discuss whatever it is that has brought you here tonight." She waved her hand toward her office door. I didn't need the warning look that she shot me, the one that clearly said, "Keep calm." What Hannah had just done had shocked me into submission; I followed Finvarra quietly.

Hannah walked in almost as if she were in a trance, staggering slightly. She collapsed into the nearest chair, where she closed her eyes and tucked her knees up to her chin as tears streamed down her face. Milo curled up like a cat beside her, with an expression on his face that was just-this-side of threatening.

Finvarra took her time closing the door shut, then strolled over to the windows to pull the long silk hangings closed. She seemed to be giving Hannah as much time as possible to calm down before addressing us again. Carrick hovered in Finvarra's wake like a shadow.

Finally, Finvarra sat down behind her great desk and folded her hands. "Before we address the reason for your visit, we must discuss the rather significant event that just occurred outside my office."

Carrick drifted forward so that he came to rest beside Finvarra. He was looking back and forth between her and Hannah with a worried expression.

"Hannah, I think you must know that what you have just done is extremely unusual for a Durupinen, perhaps unprecedented. Granted, we have little documentation on the abilities of Callers, as there have been so few in our history, but it is not generally in our nature to have any control over the spirits. It is partly for this reason, in fact, that we have the Caomhnóir for protection."

What little color ever resided in Hannah's face was receding rapidly. She looked like she might be sick.

Finvarra continued. "You were able to restrain Carrick and, if I am not much mistaken, to cause him discomfort. Carrick, is that accurate?"

"Yes, High Priestess." Carrick affirmed, although he seemed hesitant to admit it. I wondered if this was simply a result of Caomhnóir culture—an inability to admit weakness before the woman he was honor-bound to protect.

"Have you ever done this before?" Finvarra asked.

"No," Hannah said. "I… panicked. He hurt Jess. I just reacted."

"And can you think of no other instance in which you have had control over a spirit in this manner?"

Hannah shot me a frightened look. I shook my head as minutely as possible.

"No," Hannah said.

Finvarra studied her for a long, tense moment.

"If I may, High Priestess," said Carrick hesitantly.

She turned to him. "Yes Carrick, what is it?"

"It's possible that Hannah was experiencing a burst of a power she does not generally possess, just as other young Apprentices sometimes experience gifts that are not a permanent part of their spirit interactions. Non-Muses have been known to produce a single Psychic Drawing; non-Seers have been known to experience a single, unexplained premonition. These moments often come in times of extreme distress. Perhaps this was simply one of those moments, nothing more."

Finvarra considered this. Slowly she began to nod her head. "This is a wise observation, Carrick. I think you may be right. We will let it go and say no more about it for now. But if anything of this nature occurs again, Hannah, you must tell Lucida at once. Is that understood?"

Hannah nodded. Carrick looked as relieved as I felt, which seemed odd. I had no time to dwell on it, though, as Finvarra returned, at last, to the reason we had come.

"Now that that is settled, please tell me your reason for coming here tonight. Jessica, you are obviously quite upset."

I tore my eyes away from Hannah and looked at Finvarra; in that moment it all rushed back to me, and my anger broke through the temporary dam caused by Hannah's actions. I couldn't restrain the shuddering quaking in my voice as I was forced to say it out loud once again—this devastating, irretrievable thing.

"Pierce is dead. Someone killed him."

Unbidden, those three echoing knocks reverberated in my head.

Finvarra's face was utterly blank. She had no idea who I was talking about; she couldn't spare a tiny fraction of her memory for the man who had played such an integral role in my life. This realization only choked me with a darker, thicker anger.

Carrick, however, moved closer to me, with his brow furrowed in concern. "Pierce? You are speaking of David Pierce, your professor at St. Matthew's College?"

I was momentarily pulled up short that Carrick would know this when Finvarra did not.

"Yes."

"And how is it you know that Dr. Pierce is dead?" he asked.

"He appeared to Fiona in a Psychic Trace. I thought Pierce was trying to reach me, so we performed a Crossing, and..." Tears swallowed the rest of my sentence, but Carrick understood me clearly.

"And he Crossed. You saw his memories and you recognized him," Carrick said softly.

I nodded, wiping my still-streaming eyes.

"And why is it exactly that you think someone killed him?" asked Finvarra, in what I considered to be an unnecessarily skeptical tone.

"I saw it!" I cried. "I watched it from his perspective. He was lying on the ground and there was blood all around his face, and there was a man there... and I knew him, too!"

Finvarra and Carrick traded looks. "You're saying you know the man who killed Dr. Pierce?" she asked.

"Yes. His name is Neil Caddigan. I met him on Pierce's investigative team. They thought he was a demonologist, but he's not. He's a Necromancer."

Finvarra and Carrick merely stared at me as though I had shouted something in an alien language.

"What about the Necromancers?" Carrick asked blankly.

"They killed him! The Necromancers killed Pierce!" I said again.

Finvarra was already shaking her head. "The Necromancers have been dismantled for centuries. We have very methodically seen to their destruction as an organization. They are in no way a threat to us in these modern times."

"Everyone keeps saying that, but you're wrong! Neil's a Necromancer... he was wearing their symbol on his shirt. We recognized it from class!"

I turned to Hannah and Milo for support, and they both nodded in confirmation.

Finvarra and Carrick still looked skeptical, and so I plowed on recklessly, "And there's more. When I went to London and we were in the car accident, it wasn't a drunk driver who caused it. It was Neil. Milo saw him behind the wheel of his SUV right before we went off the road."

Milo nodded again. "He was wearing that symbol, I'm positive about that."

Finvarra came forward and placed a hand on my shoulder. When she spoke, it was with the air of someone trying to inject reason into an absurd conversation. "Jessica, you are tired and upset. I don't blame you. I know how much this man meant to you. He was there for you at a time when we were not, and we must all be grateful to him for that. But you are not being logical. This

Neil Caddigan, whoever he is, is not one of the Necromancers. It is simply not possible."

"But it *is* possible!" I cried, knocking her hand away. "The Necromancers are back. They killed Pierce, and they tried to kill me. I don't know what they want or why they've targeted me and the people in my life, but you've got to do something!"

"I think I can be trusted," began Finvarra, with every trace of warmth now gone from her voice, "as the High Priestess of this order to have a clear understanding of the dangers we face. Far clearer, I assure you, than any Apprentice—and certainly clearer than an Apprentice such as yourself, who as yet has only scratched the surface of what it means to be one of us."

"Don't you get it?" I shouted, jumping out of my seat. "People are dying! I was almost one of them! Pierce is gone! And you should have protected him! He never should've been a part of this mess, but you and your Council screwed it up, and now he's dead! If you honestly can't see past your own arrogance and accept—"

"Enough!" Finvarra said forcefully. Her whole presence crackled with authority, and I lapsed into stony silence. "I have tolerated your behavior tonight because you are upset, but I will not entertain wild theories based entirely on hysterical speculation. If you continue to pay attention in History and Lore, you will learn that the Durupinen have utterly routed the Necromancers. We have desecrated their halls. We have captured and locked away their relics. This very castle holds their only remaining traces in the bowels of its dungeons. They are gone. Let me hear no more about it."

Finvarra and I stared at each other for a long silent moment. My whole body shook with rage.

"You're wrong. Accept it and put your resources into finding the Necromancers, or the Durupinen will suffer... and you'll have no one to blame but yourself."

"You are dismissed." And just like that, Finvarra slammed the door on the conversation.

There was nothing I could say that would convince her. I turned without another word and stomped towards the door. I felt, rather than saw, Hannah and Milo following behind me.

"Jessica..." Finvarra's voice made me pause, but I did not look back. "I am sorry about your friend. I promise I will put our full investigative powers into discovering what has really happened to him. We will put your doubts to rest."

"I don't want anything from you," I said quietly. "Not ever again."

18

THE UNCAGING

I DID NOT SLEEP THAT NIGHT, AND I DID NOT go to class the next day. I didn't even want breakfast in the morning, but Hannah crept back up to our room before Siobhán's class with plate of eggs, sausage, and toast. She left the food on my bedside table, where it still sat, cold and congealed, when she returned to check on me at lunch time.

I would never have been able to accept the truth of Pierce's death if I hadn't felt—within my own body and heart—the actual physical loss of him. I couldn't close my own eyes without seeing Pierce's final moments through his eyes. I fought against sleep because I could well imagine the horrors I'd see in my dreams. Blaming Finvarra was the most satisfying outlet I could find for my pain; I gave over to it completely, seething in it. She had left me stumbling blindly through the early days when my gift first manifested itself, forcing me to seek out this man. Everything Pierce knew and suspected about me was because of Finvarra's neglect: It was Pierce's willingness to help me understand my abilities that had gotten him killed.

I was helpless. I had no way of contacting Annabelle, and even if I could, there was no way to meet with her again—it was far too dangerous. And since I couldn't do anything to help her, and since I couldn't do anything to bring Pierce back, I didn't do anything at all. I stayed in my bed for the better part of two days, getting up only to go to the bathroom, and once—after a terrible nightmare about Pierce's death—to dry-heave over the trash can near my desk.

Celeste stopped by once to check on me. Mackie did too, bringing cookies with her; Savvy ate these when she came to check on me later. Hannah spared me their sentiments and condolences, and sent them away quickly. Karen called a number of times, but I wouldn't speak to her. Hannah and Milo stayed in the room with me a lot of the time, but thankfully they didn't speak to me much. There was nothing to say.

When Hannah slipped out on Saturday night, I thought she was just trying to escape the woeful pall I was casting over the entire room. It was late—perhaps even after curfew—but I couldn't even summon the interest to check the clock on the wall. I dropped into a fitful half-doze.

"Jess?"

Hannah had crept into the room. Savvy and Mackie were right behind her.

I didn't answer, but looked back up at the ceiling as the three of them shuffled in. They approached my bed the way some people approach an open casket at a wake—hesitant and a little afraid of what they would find.

"It's Saturday," said Hannah.

"Is it?" I mumbled.

"This is the night we all agreed we would try to Uncage the Silent Child."

I felt a dull pulse of something under my smothering blanket of misery. Was it guilt? I hadn't spared a single thought for the Silent Child—or anything else really—in days.

"We've got to do it tonight," said Mackie, "or else we'll have to wait another month."

Still I said nothing. I was searching—really searching—for the part of me that still cared about things. It was doing a damn good job of keeping itself hidden.

"We've set everything up," Hannah said. "The whole Circle is cast out in the Memorial Garth in the east garden. We just need you."

"Can't you do it without me?" I asked.

"We thought about that," said Savvy. She sat herself on the bed next to me, and I turned my head to avoid her gaze. "They were all for letting you be, up here all by yourself, but I told 'em it wasn't right."

"And she has a point," Mackie said. "The Silent Child chose you. You're the one she wants to communicate with. If we try to do this without you, she may not cooperate... or even turn up at all."

"You're the best chance we have of freeing her," said Hannah. "Don't you understand, Jess? She needs you. Plus, the Casting calls for four of us... if we don't have you, who knows what will happen during the ritual. I know it's hard, but the Silent Child needs you to be there for her now."

Finally, I turned to look at them; they were three blurry shapes behind the film of tears clouding my eyes. "I don't think I can. Honestly, I am completely useless right now. I have nothing left."

Hannah sat down on the bed beside Savvy. "Jess, you have plenty left. You can't feel it right now because you're grieving, but you're still here—behind the pain, you're still here.

"I don't want to be here."

"Yes you do!" Her voice rose so sharply that I looked her in the eye for the first time. "It seems to me that your friend Pierce died trying to protect you. If that's true, the best way to honor him isn't to curl up in a ball and give up; you need keep doing what he always wanted to do himself--help the spirits."

The tears and the beginnings of a smile fought for dominance on my face. "You are just too smart for your own good, you know that?"

Hannah smiled weakly back. "I know. It's a character flaw."

I sat up and tried, but failed, to run a hand through my unkempt, matted hair. "Okay. Someone get me a hairbrush and something to eat and we'll try."

"That's our girl!" Mackie said. She pulled my hairbrush off of the desk behind her and handed it to me.

"And I've got the food covered," Savvy said, holding out a napkin containing an apple, a muffin, and a peanut butter sandwich.

Hannah gave my hand a squeeze. "It will feel better to be doing something productive, I promise."

"If you say so," I replied through a mouthful of muffin.

I pulled on my shoes and sweatshirt, and we set off together through the castle and out onto the grounds. The food helped restore my energy; the fresh air seemed to clear a film from the inside of my head as I breathed it deeply in. We didn't meet anyone along the way, which was fortunate, although Hannah told me she had a cover story that no one would dare to punish us for—just in case.

"If anyone catches us, we're going to say that we were performing a ritual of remembrance for Pierce," she said with an apologetic squeeze of the arm. "I read about it in the library, and like the Uncaging, it also needs to be done at night and on sacred ground."

"Good idea," I said quietly.

"There is one more thing we have to tell you though, Jess,"

Hannah went on, as we set off down the darkened interior of the cloisters. I could tell from her delicate tone that I wasn't going to like it, whatever it was. "What? What is it?"

"We had to invite Finn."

The sandwich I was now eating turned to gravel in my mouth. I forced myself to swallow before saying, "Why?"

"It's the only way to protect ourselves," Mackie said. "If we Uncage the Silent Child and she turns out to be violent, we might not be able to Cage her quickly enough to stop her from hurting someone. We need to have a Caomhnóir there just in case."

"So, why don't you bring Isaac?" I asked.

Mackie shook her head. "He's got rocks for brains, that one. We need someone who can think on his feet."

I groaned.

Savvy smiled at me. "Oi, aren't you going to ask why we didn't bring Bertie, then?"

"I think we all know why you didn't ask Bertie," I replied flatly.

The Memorial Garth, which was filled with dozens of flowering trees, was in the furthest corner of the east garden and was surrounded by a low stone wall. From drooping, blossomy branches hung hundreds of glass lanterns, each ready to be lit in honor of one of the hundreds and hundreds whose names were etched into the smooth white stones of the winding pathway.

I looked down at the carvings. Many of the names had faded into obscurity; others, more recent or better protected from the elements, could still be read.

Hannah read my mind. "She's not here. Elizabeth. I looked while we were setting up."

I shrugged. I was too spent to dredge up a feeling about this omission.

"Over here," Mackie called, waving us over to the Circle they had already prepared. The Circle was actually five circles—a large one at the center, with four smaller circles at each of the cardinal directions; each of the smaller circles overlapped into the main circle. My eyes widened. There were at least twenty different runes drawn carefully around the perimeter of each of the circles, with several more drawn inside their borders. The runes were all different colors, and created, I knew, from ten different minerals and stone powders—including the lapis lazuli I'd taken from Fiona's office. Scattered bunches of herbs and sticks of incense smoked gently, mingling their heady vapors with the sweet perfume of the trees. I shook my head at the complexity of it all. It must have taken hours to set up.

Without announcing himself, Finn slunk up beside us, making me jump.

"You were able to do everything, then?" he asked Hannah, nodding toward the Circle.

"Yes," she replied. "Thank you for coming."

Finn didn't grunt or scowl, or give any of his typically churlish responses. Instead, quite to my surprise, he gave a short bow toward her. "No need to thank me. I agree with you. This is obviously something that needs to be done. I'm glad to assist you in doing it."

I stared unflatteringly at him until he caught my eye; I looked hastily away.

Mackie took charge, in classic First-Year Head style. She directed us all to our positions in the Circle while handing each of us a different colored candle.

"Jess, you're the one who's going to establish communication, so you need to light the Spirit Candle last," she told me, as she thrust a white candle into my hand. "Start in the north, and then, when I tell you, light the Spirit Candle and place it in the center of the Circle, right inside the blue rune."

"Okay," I said, starting to feel nervous. "What do I need to say?"

"Nothing. Just focus like we do in Keira's class. If all goes well, the Silent Child will appear in the Circle, but she will be trapped there."

"Why are we trapping her?" I asked. "The whole point is to free her."

"Yes, but we've got to have a way to keep her in one place until the entire Casting is complete, or it won't work. When she's properly Uncaged, she'll be able to move freely out of the Circle." Mackie turned to Finn. "That's when you'll need to be ready."

"I will be," replied Finn.

"Okay, then," Mackie said, puffing out her cheeks in a nervous sigh. "Are we all ready? No turning back once we start."

No one spoke. We were all too nervous.

"Right," Mackie continued. "Here goes nothing."

Mackie spoke the Incantation, since she had the most experience with the pronunciation. As she nodded to each of us, we lit our candles and placed them in the centers of our respective circles. Finally Mackie pointed to me, then gestured to the center of the Circle.

With my heart pounding, I lit the Spirit Candle and placed it in the Circle's center. Then I crept back to my place and closed my eyes. I felt out into the darkness, searching for her, urging her to me. "Come on, Silent Child," I thought. "Where are you? We're here to help you."

A bright, red light filtered through my eyelids. To my left, Hannah gasped.

The Silent Child burned like a candle, hovering two feet above the ground in the center of the Circle. Her eyes, too, were burning... but burning with intensity as she looked at me. There was an accusation in her look. She darted to the edges of the Circle, but was repeatedly thrown back into the middle. She tried to shout at me, but her words were lost to the usual mire of echoes.

"It's okay," I told her. "We're here to help you."

She pointed frantically to the others, still shouting incoherently.

"I know. I know you don't want to talk to anyone but me. But it's going to take all of us to free you. Please, let us help."

She dropped her hand to her side.

Mackie continued to chant while waving a bunch of smoldering sage over her head. The Silent Child's light grew brighter and steadier. She held her own hands up in front of her face, as though she'd never really seen them before.

"Alright girls, on the count of three, blow out your candles. Leave the Spirit Candle lit. Finn, when the flames go out she'll be Uncaged, so be on the alert.

The Silent Child was now so bright that I needed to shield my eyes. The light breeze of the garden was rising into a harsh wind, whipping our hair and threatening the dancing candle flames.

Mackie's voice rose over the gale. "One, two, three!"

Mackie, Hannah, and Savvy blew out their candles. A wave of energy billowed out from the center of the Circle, knocking us all off our feet. I looked down in panic, afraid I'd been thrown from the Circle, but I was still safely within its boundary. Miraculously, the Spirit Candle remained lit.

The wind died out, and the intense light emanating from the Silent Child became merely a dull, pulsing glow. She crouched on the ground with her hands thrown protectively over her head. I opened my mouth to speak to her, but I faltered, unsure of what to say. Luckily, she chose that moment to lift her head and look at me.

"Can you hear me?" asked the Silent Child, and she jumped at the clear sound of her own voice.

"Yes!" I breathed.

The girl's shoulders relaxed. She gawked at me. "I'm free?"

"Yes, you are," I said.

"Blimey," Savvy murmured.

"You've been Caged," I explained. "Someone didn't want you to communicate with anyone."

The girl nodded solemnly and her expression of wonder darkened at once. "I know."

"What do you need to tell me?"

She shook her head violently. "I will speak to you alone."

"But they all want to help you. No one here will hurt you."

She shook her head again. "I cannot trust them. I cannot trust anyone else here."

"Why?" I asked.

The Silent Child began to shake with emotion; she pulled at her hair and clawed at her own skin.

Hannah's voice rang out, full of alarm. "Mackie! What's wrong with Mackie?"

I tore my eyes from the Silent Child and looked over at Mackie. She was shuddering and gasping, clutching at her own arms and hair. Tears were streaming down her cheeks.

"Mackie?" I called. She didn't seem to hear me at all.

"What should we do?" Hannah cried in a shaky voice.

"I don't know," I said. I turned back to the Silent Child. "What are you doing to her?"

The Silent Child continued tear at herself. "I will not trust them! Too much pain for too long!"

"It's because she's an Empath!" Finn declared suddenly. "She's feeling the Silent Child's pain and experiencing it along with her."

As though his words had opened a floodgate, Mackie began to writhe and scream; her agony was clearly unendurable.

"What do we do?" Savvy asked. "Cage her again?"

"No!" I cried. "She's not doing it on purpose. Mackie's just too sensitive to it."

Mackie's screams rose. She fell on the ground, her back arching.

"Do something!" I cried. "Expel her, Finn!"

But Finn was already muttering. He thrust his hands toward the center of the Circle, and the Silent Child sailed backward into the air. She landed soundlessly on all fours, like a cat.

We converged on Mackie, whose body had relaxed the moment the Silent Child had broken through the barrier of the Circle. She lay panting and sobbing.

"Mackie? Are you okay?" I asked.

"Yes," she gasped, wiping the cold sweat from her face. "I... can't believe the pain she's been in. It was... unbearable."

"Can you guys stay with her?" I asked, craning my neck. The Silent Child was beckoning to me from the edge of the garden. "I'm going to follow her. She's waited long enough to tell me what she wants me to know."

Hannah looked like she was going to protest but Mackie spoke up first. "Go. I'm fine. We'll clean up here and meet you back in your room."

Her face was so pale under her freckles that I faltered. "Are you sure?"

"Yes! That's why we did all this! Go!" said Mackie, with a touch of her usual authority.

I smiled at her, squeezed her hand, and took off in the darkness.

"Please be careful!" Hannah called after me.

I followed the Silent Child back into the castle, then tracked her tiny flickering form down several flights of stairs. Her glow was barely enough to light my way; I picked up a dusty candle from one of the stone recesses and lit it. She led me all the way down into the dungeons, leading me past the display of Necromancer artifacts—which now held a new horror for me, and which I quickly ran past. When I arrived in the next chamber, the Silent Child was nowhere in sight.

"Are you here?"

My voice, a careful whisper, exploded into echoes in the darkness.

"I came alone, like you said. There's no one here to be afraid of."

As my candle cast a fluttering light into the corners of the chamber, a tiny shadow came alive; it shivered and detached itself from the wall. The shadow glided along the floor and nestled into a niche in the wall before solidifying itself into the crouching form of the Silent Child, her scabby knees tucked up under her chin.

"What's your name?" I asked.

She thought long and hard before she remembered the answer. "Mary."

She cocked her head to one side, and her curtain of hair swung across her face like a veil. It was my move, and I knew it. I hesitated to demand any more information, in case she saw it as a threat.

"How... how are you?"

She narrowed her eyes as though the question made little sense to her.

"I do not understand you."

I swallowed. "I mean... never mind. Before we Uncaged you, you seemed to be in such pain. Are you... better?"

She raised her tense, grubby hands from the floor and wrapped her arms around her knees. "Yes. I am free now."

"Good. I'm really glad. We all hated seeing you suffer like that."

Her eyes narrowed and her hair crackled with the same strange electricity that had nearly ended our attempt to free her. "Many watched me suffer for a long time. Not one tried to help me."

"I can't speak for all of them, but I'm sure many of them just didn't understand what had happened to you. We certainly didn't, at first." As I spoke, I shuffled slowly towards her, watching for signs of skittishness or fear as I moved. Then, when only about ten feet separated us, I lowered myself carefully to the floor and sat down. I placed the candle between us like an offering. Her wide eyes watched my progress without blinking.

I sat in silence for a few moments, letting Mary adjust to my proximity. Her eyes fell upon the candle, and she watched the flame bob and dance in the drafts that whispered across the floor. As she did, her body relaxed by degrees; her knees drifted and then fell to one side, so that I could finally see her entire face. Her pointed chin was trembling; the corners of her mouth were pinched in misery.

"You aren't in pain anymore," I ventured, "but you're still not at rest."

Mary wrenched her eyes reluctantly from the flame. "I cannot rest," she whispered.

"Why not?"

"Because you must know. You must know what they did to me, for we are the same."

My heart began to race. "What who did to you?"

"Them." She raised her eyes to the ceiling as though she could see right through it.

"You... do you mean the Durupinen?"

She nodded solemnly, although her eyes remained fixed on the ceiling.

"Did they do more than just Cage you?"

She nodded again.

"Did..." I swallowed hard. "Did they... kill you?"

The words had barely parted company with my lips, when suddenly Mary was there—so close to me that I found myself staring at my own terrified reflection in her eyes. Her finger hovered between us, silencing me. I could feel the chill of her finger upon my lips.

"When they discovered what I was, I could not be allowed to live. I was an abomination. I was a terrible, terrible mistake," she whispered.

I couldn't ask aloud—the words wouldn't come. My question echoed inside my own head, where her voice somehow joined my thoughts.

"What do you mean, a mistake?"

"I should never have been. I was too dangerous."

"Dangerous how?"

"They had been warned. For many hundreds of years they had been warned, but my mother did not listen. She was one of them."

"One of the Durupinen?"

"Yes. She knew it was forbidden, but she could not help herself. She loved him so."

"She loved who?"

"My father. They were forbidden. Yet they loved each other, and so I was born in secret."

"Their relationship was forbidden? Was...was he a Caomhnóir?"

"Yes. The Guardian and the Gatekeeper must never be as one. It is their greatest fear. I was their greatest fear."

"But why? You were just a child. What could they have to fear from you?"

"The Prophecy. They feared the Prophecy would come to pass."

"What Prophecy?"

Instantly, Mary was across the room; her form was now pressed once again into the shadows of the furthest corner, where she began pulling desperately at her wildly tangled hair. Yet her voice continued to echo in my head as though she were crouching on my shoulder, like a tiny angel of death muttering in my ear.

"They do not speak of it, for their fear keeps them silent. But I must show you. I must warn you, for if I do not, you will surely meet my fate."

"But why? Why me? Why would anyone want to kill me?"

"We are the same."

I was breathing so hard and fast now that I cupped my hand over the candle protectively, afraid that my frantic breath would blow out the flame and plunge us both into darkness.

"How? How are we the same?"

"We are the same. And if they discover it, you will surely die. The Prophecy cannot come to pass. They will never allow it."

"But what do you mean, Mary? How are we the same?"

But I knew—I knew it as surely as I knew my own name. The greatest question mark in my life had been whispered away by a child ghost in the darkness: My father.

"But if you and I are the same, that must mean Hannah is, too. She must be in the same danger. Why did you choose me, and not her, to speak to?"

"The Caller is too dangerous. She is always surrounded by whispers. She is never alone. It would never be safe to speak to her with so many dead nearby to listen."

"Okay, but you still haven't told me. I need you to say it. How are we the same?"

"We are both forbidden. We are both an abomination. We must be ripped from the world lest we destroy them all. The Prophecy must never come to pass."

Something in my gut sunk within me; a trembling knot unlike any other I'd ever felt. I could barely take all this in. "But what is it? What is the Prophecy? Show it to me!"

"Once revealed, it can never be un-learned," whispered Mary gravely.

"Show it to me now! Mary, I have to know."

She cocked her head to the side again, as if she were deciding whether or not to continue. As she did, her eyes filled with spectral tears.

She nodded once. "Be it so. Mercy upon you."

And before I could draw another breath, she flew at me, flew *into* me. There was a flash of light, a rush of screaming, and everything went dark.

19

THE PROPHECY

THE ACRID SCENT OF SINGED HAIR burned in my nostrils, the odor like sandpaper against my cheek. Aches coursed through my body as if they were racing against each other to reach my fingers.

My eyes opened, but only a blurred vision revealed itself; it was like trying to see the world through a window as a deluge beat mercilessly against it. Why the hell couldn't I see? And where was that terrible sound coming from—that horrid, wailing keening? I swallowed convulsively in an attempt to dampen my bone-dry mouth, and the wailing became muffled and then stopped. It was me. I was making that wretched sound. And it was my own tears that clouded my vision. I was crying uncontrollably and I had no idea why. I blinked furiously to dislodge the tears from my eyes and tried to master my breathing.

I focused on calming down as I peeled myself off of the floor and into a sitting position. I put a hand to my throbbing head and felt something wet. What was on my face? I stared at my fingers. They were covered in blood, but it wasn't from my head. My fingers were rubbed raw to the point of bleeding, and my blood was mixed with something dark and dusty; the mixture ran in rivulets down my arms. My skin, from fingertips to elbows, was blistered and peeling away, and was coated in what looked like ash. As I looked at them, the dull aching that had awoken me exploded into a violent pain such as I'd never endured before. I started sobbing afresh.

What the hell had happened to me? What was the last thing I remembered?

A candle. A dark dungeon. Mary.

The Prophecy. She was going to show me the Prophecy.

I tore my gaze from my ruined arms and focused on the floor around me. I was in the entrance hall, just in front of the enormous stone fireplace. Bits of blackened firewood were scattered all around me—most were only smoking, but a few still glowed in their hearts. The charred remains of one piece of firewood was still clutched between two of my battered fingers, as if I'd been using it as a pencil.

A scream rent the air and my head jerked up instinctively.

Olivia stood at the gallery railing, her hands clutching the banister tightly. Within seconds, her shriek caused a commotion of slamming doors, shuffling footsteps, and answering cries of alarm.

"What's going on?"

"Is everything okay? Who screamed?"

"Olivia, are you... oh my God!"

"What is it? Who did it?"

"Someone get the teachers!"

No one was looking at me. They were instead staring into the hall, clearly horror-struck. Brushing the blinding tears from my eyes with the back of my burned hand, I looked around properly for the first time.

The entire entrance hall, from floor to ceiling, was covered in drawings. No, not drawings. A drawing. One elaborate mural wrapped around the entrance hall like the embracing arms of a nightmare. All around me, sketched figures were running, screaming, writhing, and falling; their faces were each a study in terror as they stared at the source of their torment. I followed their gazes. High above the marble mantelpiece was the image of a towering doorway. Hordes of ghastly figures burst from it, flying in every direction, intent on terrorizing the fleeing masses. And there, silhouetted all alone in the center of the doorway, her arms outstretched, was a tiny, dark-haired girl unleashing this unspeakable horror.

Although her features were obscured in shadow, I knew who that girl was.

"Jessica?"

I tore my eyes from the mural and found Celeste crouching near the base of the grand staircase, about twenty feet away from me. She raised a tentative hand toward me; I realized, with a swooping sensation in the pit of my stomach, that she was afraid to approach me.

"Jessica?" she asked again. "Are you okay?"

I shook my head, blinking back another wave of tears.

"Will you let me help you?"

I cringed at the quaver in Celeste's voice, horrified that I could be the one who had put it there.

"Can I look at your hands? It looks like you've burned them rather badly. Can I see?"

Wordlessly, I held my arms out to her. She stood up very slowly and approached me so carefully that I wondered exactly how horrifying I looked. She knelt beside me and, very gently, examined my hands and arms.

"We need to get you bandaged up. Mackenzie has already gone for the nurse. Are you hurt anywhere else?"

I calmed down enough to try to take stock of the rest of my body. One of my ankles was throbbing, though the pain barely registered in comparison to the agony in my arms.

"My right ankle, I think," I said. My voice was a hoarse croak, and I began to cough.

"You may have breathed in some smoke from the fire," said Celeste, and then turned her head and called out, "Olivia! Get a glass of water and bring it here, please. Everyone else, I want you back in your rooms immediately."

Hardly anyone moved. Many were still transfixed by the mural, but many had turned to gawk at me.

"Beds! Now!" commanded Celeste. "Wait in your rooms until further instruction. If I see anyone in the halls before permission has been given, she will find herself facing Council disciplinary action."

Whispering and huddling together, the Apprentices slowly disappeared from the gallery. Olivia appeared beside Celeste and handed her the glass of water, which Celeste tipped toward my mouth so I could drink it.

As soon as Olivia had crept back up the stairs and out of sight, Celeste placed the glass down on the rug. "Jess, what happened?"

"I don't know," I replied, struggling to think through the pain. I tried to recall what Mary had told me, but the memory was still too blurry. "I don't know how I got here."

"Did you draw all of this?" Celeste asked. She looked up at the mural; she seemed agog at its size and scope. The drawings crept up into the dark recesses of the rafters and into the vaulted ceilings, disappearing only where the shadows swallowed them. How in God's name did I even get up there?

"I think so," I said. "I think I did it with the ash from the fireplace."

"And... do you know why you did it?"

"Aunt Celeste? I've got Mrs. Mistlemoore."

Mackie stood at the base of the stairs with the old, kindly-looking nurse. Mackie was bouncing nervously on the balls of her feet, barely daring to look at me. Mrs. Mistlemoore, though, didn't hesitate a moment; she hurried forward without a trace of apprehension. She examined my hands with a businesslike efficiency.

"Well, these are quite severe," she said. "How did you sustain these burns?"

"I don't know."

"They seem to have been caused by the logs and ash in the fireplace," offered Celeste.

"But how—"

"That's all we know, Mrs. Mistlemoore. Please bring Jessica to the infirmary and get her bandaged up. Mackenzie, could you help Jessica up? Jess, do you think you can walk?"

"Yes, I think so."

"After you've done that, Mackenzie, I need you to find Fiona and have her meet me and the rest of the Council here in the entrance hall."

Mackie nodded solemnly before scooping her arms under my armpits and hoisting me onto my feet. My right ankle began to tremble madly, and I shifted my weight quickly to my left leg before I collapsed to the floor. Mackie slid her head under my right arm, being careful not to make contact with my burned forearm.

"Ready?" she asked me.

"Yes."

We began our slow and awkward trek down the corridor. I chanced one look over my shoulder back into the entrance hall; Celeste stood alone, revolving slowly on the spot, taking in the full horror of the mural. She pressed one shaking hand over her mouth.

Mrs. Mistlemoore bustled on ahead of us, muttering about salves and bandages. Not until she was out of earshot did I risk speaking to Mackie.

"It was the Silent Child."

Mackie stopped walking so suddenly that I stumbled forward ahead of her. "What?"

"Her real name is Mary. I followed her all the way down to the dungeon. She told me that Hannah and I were in danger."

Mackie hurried forward to support me again. "What kind of danger?"

"She said she had to warn me, that she and I were the same," I explained, with the words falling over each other in my mouth in my haste. "She was murdered, Mackie. Her mother was a Durupinen, and her father was a Caomhnóir. Mary said the Durupinen killed her when they found out about her parents."

"Killed her? Come on, Jess, we would never... I mean, I know those relationships are forbidden and all, but that's just for our protection—"

"Mackie, there's no time to argue about it! She told me she was killed because of the Prophecy."

Mackie's face was completely blank. "What prophecy?"

"You mean you don't know what she's talking about?"

"No, I have absolutely no idea. I've never heard of any Durupinen prophecies. Did she tell you what it was about?"

"She said she was going to show me. Then she sort of... flew into me. The next thing I knew, I woke up in the entrance hall burnt within an inch of my life, surrounded by all those drawings. Mackie, I know I must've drawn them, but I don't remember any of it. I don't know what it's all supposed to mean, but I think what I drew must be the Prophecy, or something to do with it. Now are you absolutely sure you can't think of anything you've ever read, or maybe something Celeste or one of the others said, about a prophecy?"

Mackie's face crumpled with concentration. "No Jess... honestly, there's nothing. We don't have prophets in Durupinen culture, at least not that I've ever heard of. But why are you and Hannah in danger?"

"Mary kept saying we were the same. I think..." I swallowed back a spasm of fear. "Mackie, I think she was talking about my parents. I've never known who my father was, but now..."

Mackie gasped. "You think he was a Caomhnóir?"

"He must have been! It's the only thing that makes sense. He and my mother had a forbidden relationship, and now Mary is trying to warn me because she thinks..." I couldn't even finish the sentence, but there was no need. What little color Mackie had in her face quickly drained away behind her freckles.

"Jess, no. They would never... You can't possibly believe that—"

"I don't know what to believe anymore!" I said, more loudly than I'd meant to. I dropped my voice again as we hobbled around the last corner to the infirmary. "Find Hannah. Find her and tell her what's happened... all of it. She needs to get out of here until I can figure out what this all means."

"But—"

"Just do it, Mackie! Please! Maybe I have it wrong, maybe we aren't in the kind of danger Mary thinks we are. But I can't risk it. Promise me. Promise me you'll find her and tell her to get out of here."

Mackie opened her mouth to argue, but something in my face made her snap it shut again. "Okay. I promise."

"Thank you," I whispered as we pushed open the infirmary door. Mackie helped lower me onto the nearest bed and was gone without another word.

Mrs. Mistlemoore was doing something to my arms, but my brain barely had room to register it. Whether she had administered a local anesthetic, or whether I was simply in shock, I neither knew nor cared.

I struggled to reel in my scattered, frantic thoughts. I dropped each thought into one of two categories in my brain: Things I knew, and things I thought I knew.

What did I know?

I knew that Mary had been the child of a Durupinen and a Caomhnóir. I knew that she was killed because of her parents' relationship. I knew she had then been rendered unable to communicate for centuries to cover up her murder. I knew she believed that I was in danger, and that this danger stemmed from some prophecy. And I knew if Mary were right, then Hannah and I were in serious trouble.

What did I think I knew?

I thought I knew that my father, whoever he was, was a Caomhnóir. I thought I knew the mural I had created upstairs—that awful, impossible drawing—depicted the Prophecy, and that every bloody, ash-smudged inch of it spoke of misery, despair, and apocalypse. And I thought I knew that this prophecy, whatever it was, had something to do with a child like Mary.

Like me.

Like Hannah.

A sharp stab just below my shoulder made me jump. I turned just in time to see Mrs. Mistlemoore removing a syringe from my arm.

"What was that? What are you doing?"

"Just a little something to help you relax dear," she said, pressing a small adhesive bandage over the puncture. "The pain is only going to get worse as the shock wears off, and I won't be able to do anything to help you if you're thrashing around."

"Wait, no! I can't sleep! I can't stay here, I have to—"

"You aren't going anywhere, love," she said with a chastising click of her tongue. "You're going to have a nice rest whilst I patch you up."

My head began to spin, and a strange cottony drowsiness crept through me.

"Jess?" I squinted as Finn's form swam into view. He seemed to float across the room toward me.

"Finn! You have to help me!"

"Jess, what happened to you? How did you—"

"No time. You have to stay with me," I said thickly.

"What?" He reached out to grab my shoulders but dropped his hands quickly when he saw the state of my arms.

"Oh my God, Jess," he whispered.

"Please. Stay with me. Don't let them do anything to me." My eyelids drooped; I struggled to hold them open.

"Who? Who do you think is going to hurt you?" he asked urgently.

"Finvarra. The Council. There's a prophecy... dangerous... don't tell them... don't let them... don't leave me... protect me... you promised..."

But the words were suddenly huge and marble-like in my mouth. My thoughts shuddered to a halt and then floated away from me. Finn's face, twisted with confusion and concern, was the last thing I saw before the sedative overwhelmed me.

§

When I woke up several hours later, I felt remarkably clear-headed. I didn't need a moment to get my bearings or refocus myself; the knowledge was waiting to ambush me upon the first twitch of my eyelids. My panic was instantaneous and as sharp as a blade on my skin. My body struggled to catch up.

"It's okay, Jess. I'm here. Everything is going to be okay," said a voice.

It was Finn. I took a deep, steadying breath and looked around me.

We were in the Grand Council Room. I was propped in an old-fashioned wheelchair, with a blanket tucked around my legs. My hands and my arms were encased in thick, gauzy bandages. At the other end of the long, rectangular chamber, the Council had assembled; they clustered in groups on the hall's stone benches, whispering and murmuring to each other. Just as I noticed that Finvarra wasn't present, the door behind us swung open and she swept in; Carrick followed behind her.

"Here we go," I muttered.

"This emergency meeting of the Durupinen High Council is now called to order. Please take your seats so we may begin," Finvarra called out over the dull buzz of conversation; most of the Council members hadn't realized that she had arrived. A flurry of movement followed as everyone scrambled for their assigned positions. "We have gathered here tonight to confer about the events that occurred a few hours ago here at Fairhaven Hall. I see that Jessica Ballard is here already. Where is Hannah?"

"Braxton's gone to fetch her, High Priestess. She will be here presently, I'm sure," Marion said, rising as she spoke. "He also has a man looking for Lucida, as you requested."

"Very well," said Finvarra, settling into her throne-like seat at the center of the highest bench. Carrick hovered by her shoulder; his eyes darted around the room as though he expected a catastrophe at any moment. He was flickering with a strange, nervous energy that pulsated through his form and alternately brightened and weakened his visibility.

"I think we should begin at once, rather than waiting for Hannah and Lucida to arrive," Finvarra continued. "Most usually, we would have Jessica's elder here with us, but Karen is out of the country and this matter is too vital to delay."

A dull murmur of assent met this pronouncement. Finn shifted his position so that he stood just in front of me.

"We are here," Finvarra said, her voice ringing through the hall, "because one of our Apprentices, Jessica Ballard, has experienced what we believe to be an episode of a prophetic nature, the subject of which is relevant to us all, and the evidence of which has been seen by everyone in this room. Jessica, come forward, please."

It should have been quite apparent that I couldn't "come" anywhere, but before I could even open my mouth to reply, Finn stepped behind my wheelchair and pushed me forward until I was positioned upon the enormous Triskele inlay. My heart was in my throat. I hadn't had a chance to decide what I would tell them, and I had no idea who, if anyone, I could trust.

Finvarra's first question was unexpectedly kind. "How are you feeling?"

"I'm... fine." I lied.

"We are sorry we had to bring you here when you ought to be resting in the infirmary. Are you in pain?"

"No," I answered, and it was true—at least for the moment. Whatever Mrs. Mistlemoore had given me left my arms numb and heavy at my sides. I tried not to think of what my limbs might look like under the dressings, or how the pain would come flooding back when the drugs began to wear off.

"I am glad to hear it. We will make this all as quick as possible, so that you can get the rest and recovery you need," Finvarra said. She turned to Finn. "Thank you for your assistance in escorting Jessica. You are dismissed now with our thanks."

Finn didn't move. "High Priestess, begging your pardon, but I will be staying with her."

Finvarra raised a single eyebrow. "Your services are not required any longer, Caomhnóir Carey."

"My services are always required if Jessica asks for them. She has asked me to stay with her. I will stay." He shifted his weight subtly, setting himself just a bit closer to me. It was the tiniest gesture of defense, but Finvarra didn't miss it.

Marion stood up, glaring at Finn with the utmost contempt. "How dare you talk back to your High Priestess! You are bound by the sacred oath you took to obey her commands and you dare to—"

"My oath is to Jessica and the Clan Sassanaigh. I am honoring it."

Finn's voice rose like a clarion over Marion's words, drowning them out.

Marion looked too shocked to go on, and a full few moments of ringing silence followed his words before she spoke again.

"You are here to serve the Durupinen. The word of the High Priestess is your highest law," she proclaimed.

"He is not here to serve anyone," said a new voice. Every head in the room turned in surprise to Carrick, who had come forward from beside Finvarra. He inclined his head respectfully to her before again addressing Marion. "We are protectors, not servants. Our oath is not one of indentured servitude, and we bend neither our skills nor decisions to the will of the Durupinen. Our role is just as important to the continuation of the Gateways as your own. This young man is doing his duty. You will not fault him for it."

Marion turned in exasperation to Finvarra, who was not looking at her, but rather tracing a finger thoughtfully around her mouth.

Finvarra's penetrating gaze blazed between Finn and me like a searchlight. "If you remain here, as you say, in fulfillment of your oath, then I must conclude that you believe Jessica to be in danger if she is left here in the company of this Council without you. Am I correct in this assumption?"

Finn did not speak at first, but caught my eye. I gave my head the tiniest shake I could manage, and he blinked. It was too much to hope that Finvarra hadn't caught the exchange, but I could hope that she wouldn't be able to interpret it.

"High Priestess, look at her. She seemed to be in no danger last night when we parted company, and yet here she is, gravely injured," began Finn. "I don't yet know how this came to pass, and I'm not sure that she does either. Until we do, I must assume that Jessica could be in danger anywhere. At her request, I will stay with her until I understand the nature of this situation, and how she can be best protected. I would be remiss in my duties if I did not do so."

Carrick nodded sharply, looking at Finn as a proud father would look at his own son. Finvarra seemed to be weighing Finn's words very carefully on some internal scale before answering.

After a long moment, Finvarra gave her reply. "Very well. There is some wisdom to what you say. Although I can see that you would have remained regardless, you may do so now with my open invitation."

Finn clicked his heels together and bowed formally. "Thank you, High Priestess."

Marion seemed to melt back into her seat, although not without a last venomous look at Finn. Carrick stepped back and resumed his position just behind Finvarra.

"Let us continue, then," Finvarra said. "Jessica, we are here, as you know, because of the most extraordinary drawing with which you've covered the entire entrance hall. It is my understanding that you have produced Psychic Drawings before."

"Yes," I answered.

"How long have you been able to do this?"

"Since last year."

"And since coming to Fairhaven, you have been exploring this gift with Fiona, is that right?"

"Yes."

Finvarra seemed to be waiting for me to elaborate, but when I didn't oblige, she turned to the Council benches. "Fiona? Can you give us some details from your sessions about the nature of these drawings?"

"Yes, High Priestess," said Fiona, rising to her feet. She was clutching my leather portfolio from our lessons under her arm, along with a bundle of scrolls. My heart sank. I must have left the portfolio in her office the day of Pierce's Crossing; I'd been far too distraught since then to notice it was missing.

Fiona's eyes darted to me, and their expression, although brief, seemed to be asking my forgiveness. She walked carefully down the steps to a table that had been placed at the base of the benches. She set the scrolls to one side, then lay my portfolio open on the polished wooden surface.

"Jessica came to us with an extensive collection of her own art and an untrained but considerable natural talent for drawing."

Despite the gravity of the situation, I couldn't help but feel a faint hint of pride at the compliment, which was the first Fiona had ever paid me. I watched as she rifled through the stack of papers in the portfolio and slid one out.

"This," she said, holding a drawing up for everyone to see, "is the first Psychic Drawing Jessica ever produced. It was pulled merely from a physical object with an attached spirit, although the spirit was not present at the time."

I had to crane my neck to see it. It was the drawing of Lydia

Tenningsbrook, which I had unwittingly produced in my very first class with Pierce. The corners of my eyes began to burn, but I blinked the tears away impatiently. I didn't have time to fall apart over Pierce now; I needed a clear head.

"During her time with me," continued Fiona, "we have explored her ability, which from the start has been surprisingly sharp and accurate. She has connected with many spirits here at Fairhaven Hall, both in class and outside of it. The detail she's been able to provide through her drawings has been the most rich and specific I have seen in a very long time. However, the information she has sensed and drawn has always been relative to the past or the present. I have never witnessed anything of a prophetic nature."

My drawings floated among the Council, passed from member to member and examined over and over again. I wanted to leap from my seat and snatch my works out of their hands: It was a violation, they had no right to touch them. The drawings weren't theirs—they weren't even really mine. They belonged to the spirits who had trusted me enough to depict them, to pour their hearts and lives into me and out onto the pages. And right there on the floor of the Council Room, for the first time since I'd discovered who I was, I felt a surge of protectiveness, almost a possessiveness, for the spirits who had forced their way so unceremoniously into my life.

"It was determined through our mentoring sessions," said Fiona, "that Jessica is a Muse—not a Prophetess. We have proceeded accordingly with her training. But the drawings upstairs are, quite obviously, a different story."

Heads all around the room nodded gravely, and many turned to look at me. I was not imagining the fear and hostility in many of their faces, but I couldn't spare a single emotion for any of them. My entire being had frozen on the word *Prophetess*.

Prophetess. The Prophecy.

They knew. They had to know.

Finn looked down at me inquisitively, sensing my tension. Whatever it was he saw on my face put him on high alert. He placed a hand firmly on the back of my chair, so that I could feel the pressure of it against my shoulder blade.

Fiona cleared away my portfolio and unrolled several of the scrolls very carefully. She laid them out on the table deliberately, as if each scroll required a specific placement to form a whole. Then she stepped away from the table and averted her eyes as though the resulting image made her feel ill.

"As you requested, I've brought all the records that exist of prophetic art throughout our history. We have come to learn over time that they all relate to a single prophecy, like pieces of a puzzle that have revealed themselves over the centuries. When put together in this configuration, they create a single, continuous image."

All of the Council members rose instantly to their feet, craning their necks to view the scrolls. A few of them filtered down the aisle to get a closer look.

Finvarra called out over their hushed conversations. "Mr. Carey, perhaps you could bring Jessica forward. I think that she needs to see this."

Finn stepped behind me and wheeled me forward. It took an unnaturally long time to reach the table, as though the room were an optical illusion where the table never seemed to get any closer. Finally, Finn turned the chair around the side of the table and the image lay before me, pieced together from a dozen tattered and ancient pieces of parchment.

What I felt was not shock, but rather a heavy weight of confirmation that dropped like a stone into my gut.

Before me lay the very same image I had drawn onto the walls of the entrance hall. Horror bled from scroll to scroll, a continuous scene of utter chaos and despair. And there, at the heart of it all, was a tiny, dark-haired figure in silhouette, arms raised and standing in the center of an open Gateway.

Finvarra's voice was quiet, but nevertheless carried clearly over the stunned silence that had fallen. "This image depicts the Prophecy. It was revealed to us over many centuries, beginning nearly a millennium ago. It tells of the fall of the Durupinen and the rise of the Necromancers. Marion, please bring the *Book of Téigh Anonn*."

Marion hoisted the enormous volume off of her bench and lay it open on Finvarra's lap. Finvarra turned to the tome's very back pages, which appeared to be blank. She held her right hand suspended over the open pages and began to chant silently, her lips moving unnaturally fast. When she opened her eyes again, words had seeped up out of the pages.

Then Finvarra read the words that would change everything.

When Keeper and Protector shall unite
And forth from this forbidden union shall be spawned,
Two as one from single womb, and Keepers both,
Then shall the greatest of battles commence.
For One shall be Caller with powers unmatched
To reverse the Gates, and call forth the Hordes
To bend to her will and that of our foes.
And One will have to make The Choice
'Twixt blood and vocation, 'twixt kindred and kin,
For she will have the power of sacrifice to end all,
And leave the world until the end of days
To the Darkness or the Light.

20

AS IT IS WRITTEN

"**J**ESSICA?"

I came back from the far side of the new landscape that Finvarra's words had painted.

"Yes?"

"Have you heard the Prophecy before?"

"No."

"You told Celeste that you do not remember making the drawing in the entrance hall."

"Right."

"Can you give us any understanding of how you came to produce that drawing?"

A great wall rose up before me. There was no way around it, no way over it. The moment had come to tell the Council everything, and face the consequences—whatever they may be.

"It was Mary."

Finvarra stared at me. "Who is Mary?"

"She is one of the spirits here. You know her as the Silent Child."

Muttering began to ripple around the room in unsettled waves. I waited for them to die away.

"She has been trying very hard to communicate with me since the very first day I came here."

Still Finvarra stared, bewildered. "I've never known the Silent Child to approach or attempt to speak to anyone."

Again a ripple went through the Council, caused, this time, by shaking heads.

"She couldn't speak," I replied. "She couldn't communicate with anyone at all. She's been Caged for centuries."

"Caged?" Finvarra whispered.

"Yes," I said, with a sick, hot anger rising inside me for the pain that Mary had been through. "Do you honestly expect me to believe that not one of you ever realized it? Never once stopped to wonder what kept her here, terrified to approach any of you?"

Silence greeted my words. Here and there, a guilty squirm.

"All of your preaching about our duty to the spirits, about our sacred calling. What bullshit!" I shouted as impulse shot me up out of my wheelchair.

Finn placed a restraining hand on my shoulder, but the wave of nausea and dizziness landed me back in the seat before I'd even gained my footing. I shoved his hand away.

"You expect us to give up our lives, everything we've ever known, to become one of you. Everything that's ever been important to us—our relationships, our education, our plans for the future—we're just supposed to hand it all over with a big fucking smile on our faces. And if we doubt for even a second, if we dare to question, we're treated like outcasts!

"This path destroyed my mother's life. It destroyed my sister's life. It nearly destroyed mine. But Hannah and I, we came. We came here and we trusted you. We gave up everything because we really believed you meant what you said—that it's all for the spirits, for those that cannot help themselves. Maybe that's still true for a few of you, but for most of you—" and I shot a poisonous look at Marion and a few other unnaturally beautiful faces, all frozen in shock at my outburst, "it's all about what you can take for yourselves. You claim to want to help these spirits, but all you do is suck them dry. You could've known everything you wanted to know about the Prophecy ages ago, but why would you pay any attention to a ghost like Mary? You don't bother with them if you can't see what's in it for you. But she risked everything to help me. She endured terrible agony every time she tried to speak to me, just to warn me about what was coming. It's too bad no one was there to warn her."

"That's enough!" Finvarra ordered, rising to her feet. Her expression reflected a nearly undecipherable collision of emotions. She was obviously furious with me—her tone alone subdued me into a seething silence—but she seemed unable to decide how to proceed. I noted with satisfaction that I had unnerved her, and felt a huge pride as I realized she wasn't contradicting me. In fact, when she next spoke, she didn't even fully meet my eye.

"What did Mary tell you? How did she speak to you if she had been Caged?"

"We... I Uncaged her," I said, changing tack mid-sentence. No reason to drag the whole crew down with me.

Siobhán piped up for the first time. "That is an incredibly complex and dangerous Casting! How did you learn such a thing? We certainly don't teach it, and I don't think anyone here has ever performed one."

"The library. It was all in there, if you knew where to look," I said.

"What did Mary tell you?" Finvarra repeated.

"She didn't want to talk to me at first, until she could be sure that we were alone. But last night, I followed her down to the dungeons and she told me the truth about her death. She was murdered by the Durupinen because of the Prophecy." I pointed a shaking finger at the *Book of Téigh Anonn*, where the conjured words had once again hidden themselves in the pages.

Shock wiped every face blank except for Finvarra's, which crumpled instead into a mournful expression. She brought one hand over her eyes and held it there for some time. When she lowered it again, her eyes were eerily bright.

"The Prophecy speaks, as I'm sure you've realized, of an illicit relationship between a Durupinen and a Caomhnóir. This relationship would result in twin girls, who would both be blessed with the gift. These two girls would hold the fate of the Durupinen in their hands, with potentially cataclysmic consequences. There were some," she said quietly, "ages ago, who felt sure that the devastations laid forth in the Prophecy were imminent. They chose to destroy all possible risks for fear of its fulfillment. Can I assume that Mary was the child of a Durupinen and a Caomhnóir?"

"Yes," I said.

Finvarra nodded. "The Prophecy was the very reason that relationships between Durupinen and Caomhnóir were forbidden. But those who first heard the Prophecy allowed their fear to overwhelm their logic. There followed what can only be described as a witch hunt for the children born from these unions. It was a very shameful time in our history. I assure you that we are not proud of it."

"She wouldn't Cross over," I said. "She wanted others to know what had happened to her, to warn them of the dangers. When the Durupinen couldn't get rid of her, they silenced her with a Caging instead."

"When I first arrived here as an Apprentice, the Silent Child had long since hidden herself in the shadows," Finvarra said. "I must admit that I never gave her a second thought. She fled from us at the first sign of attention, and she was one of very, very many spirits that haunted these grounds. In the many years since, I've never known her to attempt communication with anyone. But she sought you out, Jessica."

"Yes."

"Why."

It was not a question. Finvarra already knew; she had realized the truth, as I had—she was merely waiting for me to state it aloud.

"She knew I was in danger because I am like her. She was afraid for me, so she kept fighting against the Caging to warn me."

"Because somehow she knew what even you did not," Finvarra said. "She knew that you were a child of a forbidden relationship."

"An abomination. That's what she called me," I whispered.

"Unfortunately, that's what such children were called, in the early days."

"I don't know how she knew it," I said. "But she recognized me right away. She attacked me within hours of my arrival here, and she's been coming to me in dreams and drawings for months."

"And she feared, as you do now, that you and your sister are the ones spoken of in the Prophecy."

I swallowed back the impulse to be sick. "Yes."

The silence that followed was one of the longest of my life. I felt nauseous again, and the pain from my burns began seeping back into my limbs.

I pushed the pain aside, and instead focused on the Council members. Several of them were sitting motionless, their eyes accusing me of being the very abomination Mary's murderers had thought her to be. Others looked merely bewildered, as though they hadn't yet caught up with the implications of what all this meant. Siobhán hung her head and shook it back and forth slowly like a mournful pendulum.

"We have no proof," Finvarra said at last, "of your parentage. Even with all our resources, we were never able to discover, in all of our searches for your mother, any information regarding your father's identity. She wiped it quite clean. You are sure you have no information about him?"

"Nothing," I said. "She would never speak a word about him."

I'd always thought my mother's silence was because the memory of my father was, for whatever reason, too painful. Now I realized that she was doing everything she could to protect me... to protect us.

"Very well then," Finvarra said. "We must take Mary's actions quite seriously. Marion, please draft a letter summoning a meeting of the Caomhnóir Brotherhood. We will need all members here immediately. A formal inquiry must be made before—"

Braxton appeared in the doorway. "Excuse the interruption, High Priestess. I've found the other Ballard girl." His huge paw of a hand was clamped tightly around Hannah's upper arm. "These two girls," he pointed over his shoulder at Mackie and Savvy, who were hovering nervously just behind him, "were trying to help her leave the grounds."

"Thank you, Braxton," said Finvarra. "What about Lucida?"

Braxton shook his head ruefully. "I could not locate her, High Priestess."

Finvarra rolled her eyes. "Why am I not surprised? When is Lucida ever where I need her to be? Very well, please keep looking."

Braxton clicked his heels together and marched from the room.

"Mackenzie, Savannah, please sit down. I shall speak with you in a few moments," Finvarra said. Mackie, trembling from head to foot, sat immediately. Savvy made a brave attempt at her usual swagger, but also sat without protest.

"Hannah please come here and join your sister," Finvarra said.

Hannah shuffled forward, looking smaller than ever in the vast cavern of the hall. As she reached my side, Milo shivered into view beside her.

"Are you okay?" she whispered, reaching out to touch me but unsure of where she could safely place a hand.

"I'll live," I said, winking at her. She didn't smile.

"Are you sure?" Milo asked. "No offense, really, but you look like hell."

"I feel like hell, so that seems appropriate," I replied. "But really, I'm alright. I've got some bad burns on my arms and hands, but—"

"Does the ghost need to be present for this?" Marion asked.

Milo's eyes snapped up to meet Marion's with the ferocity of a mother tiger in her den. "The ghost has a name, Miss Thang, and would appreciate it if you'd use it. Also, the ghost is a Spirit Guide, Bound to protect these girls, so you bet your sweet ass he needs to be present for this."

Marion's face twisted into a sour knot, but she raised no further objection.

"That's enough," Finvarra said sternly. "Hannah, why were you trying to leave Fairhaven?"

Hannah swallowed hard; the voice that escaped her was barely more than a whisper. "Jess told Mackie I should get out of here. She didn't tell me why, but I trust my sister," she answered, as she shrunk nervously behind her messenger bag as if it were a shield.

"And did you see the entrance hall? Are you aware that your sister created that image?"

Hannah nodded, her eyes filling slowly with tears. "It... it looks terrible."

"It *is* terrible," Finvarra said. "It is a depiction of the Prophecy, made many hundreds of years ago. Perhaps its importance will make more sense to you if you hear it for yourself."

Finvarra repeated the Incantation, bringing the pages to life once more. We listened to the Prophecy again. When it was over, Hannah was so pale that she could have been a ghost herself.

"A Caller?" she asked.

"Yes," Finvarra said, closing the book once more.

"And you think the Caller in this Prophecy is me? That I have the power to..." she looked down at her own palms, as though she suddenly found them to be deadly weapons rather than just tiny, scarred hands.

"We must proceed under that assumption. Which brings me back to my orders. Marion, please draw up a letter to—"

"With all due respect, High Priestess, I must protest," Marion said, rising from her seat. "I contend that we have no time for the drafting of letters or the calling of meetings. We need to act, and act swiftly."

"Please clarify yourself, Marion," said Finvarra. Carrick stirred nervously beside her.

"I move that we separate these girls and confer them immediately to the dungeons, where they will be placed under Castings of containment until we can decide what further actions should be taken to protect ourselves from them."

An outburst from the entire Council met her words. Savvy was immediately on her feet, shouting. Celeste and Fiona were likewise protesting. But it was apparent that the general tenor of the noise was that of assent; most of these women, as they stared down at us in alarm and mistrust, were agreeing with Marion.

"That is preposterous and I will not allow it!" Finvarra's voice boomed over the racket, which quieted to a buzz. "This is not the dark ages, Marion, and these girls have done nothing wrong."

"It is not what they have done, but what they are capable of doing that we must prevent!" Marion said, standing her ground.

"There is no proof!" said Celeste. "No evidence at all that what you are saying is true!"

Marion turned on her. "What do you call that monstrous display marring the entrance hall? What do you call the behavior of the Silent Child? If these things are not evidence, I don't know what would please you."

"You can't lock them up! You have no right!" Celeste cried. She had crossed the room and now stood between us, with one hand on Hannah's arm and the other on my shoulder. "And what would you tell their aunt? Karen would never allow it!"

"We have every right!" Marion replied with a dismissive wave of her hand. "We have not only the right, but the responsibility as members of this Council to protect the Durupinen from the utter destruction these girls will surely cause."

Voices from the Council members rose in a swell of frantic agreement. Celeste rejoined the group as she continued to defend us. Marion's fear-mongering was whipping them into a frenzy.

I looked up at Finn. He was standing poker-straight, with his fists clenched and his eyes darting furiously around the room for the first sign of attack. I knew that despite our rocky relationship he would fight with his last breath to protect us, if it came to that.

"Stop this at once!" Finvarra shouted, slamming her hands down upon the arms of her throne with a resounding crack. "I will not allow our fear to turn us into monsters! There is no reason at all why we should—"

"This is not a question of ethics!" Marion cut across her. The disrespect inherent in the gesture elicited gasps from several of the Council members, and Carrick actually planted himself defensively between the two women, as though the interruption were a physical threat to Finvarra. "This is about safety. It's about protecting our way of life! You saw the horror defiling the walls of our sacred hall. Will you really stand by and allow those images to become our reality?"

The murmur of the Council grew louder, angrier, as Marion's words further sparked fear. Under cover of the noise, I leaned in toward Finn.

"Should we be nervous right now?" I hissed.

Finn did not take his eyes from the heated debate in front of us, but he nodded his head. "I think so. If she rallies enough of them to her side, we may be in trouble."

"What can we do about it?" I asked.

"I'm thinking," he said. His eyes were still darting around the room, but now they were assessing the closed doors and the high windows; there was no good escape route.

"What I will not do," Finvarra declared, "is stand by and allow two of our own to become scapegoats. Marion, I must ask you to step down."

"No, Finvarra. I must ask *you* to step down," Marion said, her voice ringing with cold satisfaction. She pulled a scroll of paper sealed with gold wax from the pocket of her jacket.

It was as though someone had stopped time. No one moved. No one spoke. Finvarra's face was a mask of shock, as was Carrick's beside her.

"I have here," Marion continued, "an order of no confidence, signed by a majority of the Council members. We have long expressed concerns about your refusal to act decisively. We begged you not to bring these girls back into our fold after their mother's disgrace. We told you this Caller could be dangerous. We evoked the Prophecy. You did nothing. Now the survival of our order hangs in the balance. We will not let you destroy all that we stand for. This order gives us the right, here in this assembly, to vote for your expulsion from the office of High Priestess."

Marion suddenly stomped her designer boot three times against the stone floor of the Council Room; at this signal, in marched all of the Senior Durupinen in residence at Fairhaven Hall, with the exception of Lucida, who was still nowhere to be seen.

As these women seated themselves on the benches at the far side of the room, Marion's voice rose bombastically. "As is procedure, this vote must be witnessed by at least a dozen Durupinen beyond the Council."

Finvarra did not speak, but merely stared in disbelief at the monster that Marion had become, then looked woefully at the Durupinen who had entered the room. Finvarra must have been both furious and hurt, but she held her emotions in check; clearly, she would meet this challenge to her authority with dignity.

I felt like a spectator, an outsider looking in on a situation that I surely could not be a part of. The detachment was the only way to fend off my panic and think rationally. We were the "issue" they were talking about, as if my sister and I were a poorly-enforced pest control regulation. How could Marion look us both in the eyes, as she was brazenly now doing, and talk about us in this manner? How could she demand our imprisonment... and who knew what else? How had she managed to get so many of the Durupinen to bend to her will? Even knowing what I knew of her, it seemed too cruel, too cold. And yet she plowed on.

"This should come as no surprise, Finvarra. Your decisions have been debated and called into question for months now."

"I little expected," Finvarra said through clenched teeth, "for commonplace disagreement to disintegrate into an insurrection as underhanded as this. How long have you been working to collect these signatures? I think this rather smacks of mutiny."

Marion opened her mouth to answer, but I did not hear her reply. At that moment, Carrick vanished from Finvarra's side and instantly began speaking quietly in my ear—although he did not materialize as he spoke. I jumped violently at the sound of his voice, but no one other than Finn and Hannah noticed. From the widening of her eyes, I could tell that Hannah could hear him, too.

"You must find a way to get out of here. If the vote comes out against Finvarra, there will be nothing she can do to protect you."

"But how?" I asked. "The entrance is guarded! And look—" Caomhnóir were now flooding the room; they entered not in their usual regimented lines, but burst in like a SWAT team.

"Hannah, you will need to use your abilities. You need to harness the power of the spirits to create enough of a distraction to cover your escape."

"I can't," Hannah said in a tiny whimper. "I'm not allowed to. Lucida has been teaching me to keep the Calling under control."

"It's time to break the rules, Hannah," said Carrick. Were I not engrossed by the imminent danger, the irony of a Caomhnóir—dead or otherwise—telling us to break the rules for our own protection might have registered more fully. "This has turned into a witch hunt, and Marion will not rest until she sees you imprisoned... or worse."

"But I can't control it," she hissed. "When I try to control the spirits like that, I don't know what will happen. Remember when I hurt you?"

"And I am perfectly fine. It is a risk you will have to take to save yourselves." Carrick's voice was firm yet gentle, but also very urgent.

Marion's voice rang throughout the hall, drawing our attention back to her.

"I ask now for the support of the Council on this matter. I ask you to raise your hand if you believe, as I do, that new leadership is needed to deal with this grave matter of Durupinen safety. We cannot risk the future of our order. We cannot sit silently by as this clan lays waste to all we hold dear. This woman," Marion pointed an accusatory finger at Finvarra, "would have us bide our time, drawing closer and closer to the inevitable doom now smeared in terrible detail on the walls of our great castle. We cannot let this be. We will not let this be. Let us vote. All in favor of expulsion of the High Priestess?"

Nine hands rose into the air. Then after a tense, tremulous moment, a tenth rose to meet them; Siobhán kept her eyes on the floor as she betrayed us. The only two who refused to seal our fate were Celeste and Fiona, who kept their arms defiantly at their sides, although their decision would do nothing to help us. The motion had carried.

Several voices shouted in protest from all around the room. Celeste was speaking now, trying to make an argument, but her words were lost in the uproar. The Caomhnóir were spreading further into the room, making quieting motions to the crowd as they moved. Finvarra was still standing in numb disbelief.

Silently, unnoticed by anyone but me, Hannah closed her eyes and began to mutter under her breath. I felt the subtle change at once; the current of energy that accompanied her Callings began zinging over my skin like the snaps of electricity in the air before a storm.

A really big storm.

Marion tossed her head triumphantly. She held up her hands for silence, but the crowd did not quiet itself right away. She called over the commotion. "The Council has spoken. Witnesses were present. Finvarra, you have been removed from the office of High Priestess. You will step down at once and relinquish your amulet."

Finvarra's did not move at first. Her hands were clenched in white-knuckled fists at her sides. Then, in one swift motion, she wrenched the large golden amulet from her neck and threw it down upon her throne, where it thudded with echoing finality. Carrick had reappeared beside her; he placed a spectral hand upon her shoulder.

Many Durupinen around the room began to applaud and shout, their faces and voices full of fierce satisfaction. They were the faces of those who had respected Finvarra—revered her—mere hours ago. This was perhaps the most frightening thing, the suddenness with which the tide had turned; it had swallowed her whole and washed her away within minutes.

Under the cover of the commotion, degree by degree, the temperature in the Council Room began to drop. One or two of the Caomhnóir shifted uncomfortably. In the crowd, several faces had torn their gazes from the scene up front and were looking warily around the room. Hannah's hair began to blow gently around her face, as though it were floating in water.

Finn glanced at me, his eyebrows raised quizzically. As quietly as I could, I told him, "She's Calling the spirits. She's going to use them to get us out of here. Get ready."

Finn nodded slightly, but never relaxed his stance. His darting eyes now began landing on Hannah every few seconds, in tense anticipation of the moment to act.

"As first officer of the Council, I will fulfill the duties of the High Priestess until a proper election can be held, as is procedure and tradition," Marion declared, making no effort to restrain the exultation in her voice. She reached for the amulet and held it up before her eyes; it hung there between her fingertips for a moment, with the light of the many candles glinting off of it as the reflections played across Marion's jubilant face. Then she dropped the necklace over her head and nestled the amulet carefully against her breast.

Again, a burst of applause followed, punctuated by scattered cries of protest that were quickly swallowed up. No one could spare a glance, it seemed, for the girls they were all supposedly so terrified of. While they ignored us, Hannah's trance was deepening, and I could tell her connection was reaching farther than it ever had before and gathering the masses of the dead to come to our aid.

"Seamus," Marion called to one of the senior Caomhnóir. "You are to escort Finvarra to her chambers and make sure she stays there. Under no circumstances is she to leave. Is that clear?"

Seamus looked stunned at first, but hitched his look of stony indifference back onto his face with commendable speed. He stepped forward, motioning for Finvarra to follow him. Carrick floated between them, ready for a fight.

"Carrick," Marion said sharply, "if you cause any trouble here, you will be expelled."

For a moment, it seemed like Carrick very much planned to risk expulsion, but Finvarra looked at him and shook her head; she realized she had no choice. Carrick drifted back to his customary place by her shoulder, with bitterness etched into every line of his face.

With her head held high, Finvarra descended from the platform and stood beside Seamus. "Enjoy the amulet while you can, Marion. I assure you, you will not be wearing it for long."

"I'm afraid you have no say in how long I wear it, Finvarra," Marion countered. "That will be for the rest of the Durupinen to decide. I doubt very much they will put their support behind a leader who would allow this," and here she gestured to the scrolls still spread on the table, "to become our reality. But they just might be interested in a leader who took decisive action to ensure our safety. What do you think?"

Finvarra didn't answer, but brushed away Seamus' guiding hand roughly. "I do not require your assistance, I assure you," she spat at him.

They had only made it halfway across the chamber when Finvarra halted. "What is that?" she asked to no one in particular.

"We are not interested in your delays, Finvarra," Marion said.

"No, everyone stop. Can't you feel that?" asked Finvarra. There was an edge of fear in her voice.

"What are you babbling about?" Marion cried. "I don't feel—"

"No, she's right!" Siobhán said, rising from her seat. "I feel it, too. Something is happening with the spirits!"

Marion looked from Siobhán to Finvarra impatiently, and then, quite suddenly, Marion detected the energy too. All around the room, Durupinen and Caomhnóir began shivering and shuddering as the dropping temperature and rising spirit energy penetrated their senses at last.

"It's Hannah! Look at Hannah!" one of the Council members cried.

Hannah was so deeply engrossed that she didn't realize we had been discovered. Her hair was whipping around her face now, and her mouth was moving alarmingly fast. The air around her was crackling and popping with building energy. Beside her, Milo's expression had gone blank, as though he were hypnotized.

"What's she doing?" shouted a voice.

"Someone stop her!"

"Hannah! Stop this at once!" Marion shouted.

Abruptly, Hannah opened her eyes. Her hair floated harmlessly down onto her shoulders, and her face became utterly calm. "Yes, High Priestess."

Marion's shoulders were heaving. Her eyes darted around the room. "What were you doing just now? What have you done?"

"I've just been setting up a contingency plan," said Hannah.

"What do you mean? Explain yourself."

"We—that is to say, Jess, Finn, and I—are going to leave now. We don't want anyone following us, please," she said with a politeness that clearly shocked Marion.

"And how exactly do you propose to do that? Powerful Wards protect this place, and the Caomhnóir have no intention of letting you leave this room—unless it is under their guard on the way to the dungeons. You understand why I must act so, in light of the Prophecy."

"We are going to leave here peacefully," said Hannah, "or every spirit within a hundred miles is going to descend upon this hall and attack on my command." Her words echoed through the cold silence, dancing on her tiny, frosty puffs of breath.

Marion gave her an appraising look. "I have been carefully monitoring your progress with your Calling. I have spoken to Lucida regularly, and based on our conversations, I don't believe you have the ability to Call that many spirits, let alone to force them to do your bidding."

"Really, Marion?" I asked, hoping my voice sounded more confident than I felt. "You believe her capable of unleashing the spirit hordes to destroy us all, as told in the Prophecy, but you don't think she can do this?"

Marion shifted her weight as the smug expression on her face faltered slightly. "What she can do now and what she may grow to do are two very different things."

"Yes, they are," I said. "You cannot condemn us for something we may or may not eventually have the power to do. Finvarra understands that. I'm sure others in this room understand that, too, even if they are too scared to oppose you."

Marion looked around at the crowd of Durupinen women. Many were staring at us in unmitigated terror. Others looked unsure what to believe. Their doubt only stiffened Marion's resolve. She squared her shoulders and fixed on us once more with her imperious gaze.

"I will do my duty to the Durupinen and the future of our order. I will not allow you to bring about our destruction. Caomhnóir, do your duty to protect us all. Seize them."

In a voice I hadn't heard her use since the day we escaped from New Beginnings, Hannah declared firmly, "Remember, you had a choice."

I glanced at Hannah's face; it was alight with a power and ferocity so strange that—although I knew my twin stood beside me—I didn't know who she was in this moment.

Immediately, Hannah flung her arms wide and threw back her head. Like a tidal wave of the dead, spirits flooded through the walls and ceiling, cresting in a great arc before descending on the screaming crowd. Windows smashed and the stained glass showered down on us like jewels. Finn threw himself on top of me, shielding me from the blast. My burns screamed with pain.

The cold sucked the air from our lungs and pierced our skin. The spirit army dived into the panicking crowd, and one by one each of the Durupinen collapsed in pain, writhing and screaming as the ghosts attacked. Benches and chairs and tables exploded into the air. The great golden chandelier crashed to the ground, and—within moments—the Council Room's heavy purple wall hangings were aflame.

Finn tugged me to my feet, where I swayed dangerously. "We need to go. Now!" he cried. "You've got to try to run, Jess."

I turned to Hannah, who was still lost in her Calling. Her eyes were shining, transformed by her power.

"Hannah! Can you hear me? We have to run! We have to go!" I grabbed her arm with my bandaged hand and swung her around to face me. "Hannah! Hannah look at me! *Stop!* You have to stop!"

She stared at me for a moment without seeing me, but then the manic sort of glow behind her eyes extinguished itself. Her face fell into lines of terror. She looked around the room as though seeing it for the first time. "What did I do?" she asked.

"You saved us, but it's all going to be for nothing if we don't run! Let's go!"

We tore from the room, dodging the flying scrolls and furniture and ducking beneath the choking clouds of smoke. As we approached the massive doors, I saw Mackie flailing and shrieking on the floor, with the spirit of a woman tearing at her.

"Expel it, Finn!" I cried.

He muttered his Casting and thrust his hands at the spirit, which detached at once and vanished. He lifted Mackie to her feet.

"Are you alright?" he asked, shaking her shoulders.

Mackie, still sobbing, nodded weakly.

"Where's Savvy?" I asked her.

"I d-don't know! Lucida snuck in about ten minutes ago and they left together. Jess, I'm sorry. I'm so sorry, we tried to get Hannah off the grounds, but—"

Her apology was lost as a blast of frigid air caused the massive doors before us burst open. We sprinted through them, with Finn practically dragging me as I fought to stay on my feet. We into the entrance hall.

"Find Brenna and get out of here! That fire is spreading," he ordered. Mackie stumbled away.

The hall was full of the other Apprentices, clad in their pajamas and bathrobes, all of whom had clearly been waiting for the outcome of the Council meeting.

"There's a fire in the Grand Council Room!" Finn shouted. "Everyone find the other half of your Gateway and get outside! *Now...* by order of the Caomhnóir!"

The Apprentices scattered and began frantically calling for their sisters and cousins. We ran across the room and out into the night.

"We'll have to try to get one of the cars," Finn panted, as we skirted the wall of the castle towards the garages. "It's the only chance we'll have of getting out of here without being caught."

"Wait!" Hannah cried, stopping abruptly. "I have to call them off!"

"What do you—"

"The spirits! I have to release them!" Hannah said, and closed her eyes.

She probably took no more than five seconds, but to us it seemed an eternity. Finally, Hannah opened her eyes and nodded, and we took off again across the grass. As the garage loomed up in front of us, we heard the screeching of tires. A black SUV, high beams flaring, whipped around the corner and pulled up beside us. Finn pulled at us to cut back across the lawn, but a familiar voice called out.

"Oi! Get in the damn car!"

Savvy was waving frantically from the back seat. We ran for the car and Hannah jumped in, but I skidded to a halt, my bandaged hand coming to rest on the door handle.

"Why are you here?" I asked.

Lucida grinned at me from behind the wheel. "I'm saving your arses, if I'm not very much mistaken."

"Jess, what are you waiting for?" Hannah gasped. "Get in!"

Still I did not move. "Why should we trust you? You're one of them!"

"I trust her!" Hannah said. "She's my mentor!"

"We were supposed to be able to trust everyone in that room!" I cried, pointing back to Fairhaven, which was already engulfed in billowing black smoke. "And most of them voted to have us imprisoned and maybe even killed!"

"You've got two options love," said Lucida impatiently. "Either get in this bloody car and take your chances with me, or stay here and take your chances with them."

I followed her gaze over my shoulder. At least twenty Caomhnóir were sprinting toward us from the castle doors.

We had no choice. I jumped into the car; Finn followed behind me and slammed the door shut as Lucida hit the gas and sped off along the winding drive.

I turned to Savvy. "What are you doing here?"

"Lucida took me out of that meeting—not a single one of 'em noticed us. She said you were in danger—well, I'd already figured that much out—and that she needed my help getting a car... just in case. I've... uh... assisted Lucida in the past."

"What do you mean?"

"Your mate there is the fastest hot-wirer this side of the pond," Lucida said. "I overheard her talking about it to her cousin, and I've engaged her services a few times when I needed transport. The Caomhnóir are so over-protective of their vehicles. Speaking of which, none of them will be able to follow us. We disabled the rest of the cars in the garage."

"I still don't understand why you're helping us," I said, glaring at Lucida's reflection in the rearview mirror. "Don't you care about the Prophecy... and how Hannah and I are going to destroy us all?"

"I think prophecies only come true if you choose to fulfill them," said Lucida. "I faced a good bit of suspicion and ridicule when they first discovered I was a Caller. They put me under house arrest in my room at Fairhaven for weeks before they decided I wasn't a threat. Wasn't about to let that happen to my girl," she said with a grin toward Hannah, who smiled back.

I opened my mouth to say, perhaps childishly, that Hannah was not "her girl," when Milo materialized between us. He looked shaken, even for a ghost.

"I can't believe we got out of that!" he said. Then, seeing Fairhaven's flames behind us, he turned to Hannah. "Are you a pyro now? What's going on with that fire?"

"It was an accident," Hannah said, dropping her face into her hands. "I didn't mean for there to be a fire, but some of the spirits knocked over the candles and—"

"Don't you apologize for using your abilities to save your own life!" Lucida said. "They forced you to drastic measures, love. It's their own damn fault."

"Do you think everyone is okay?" Hannah asked, her voice merely a muffled squeak from behind her hands.

"Yes," I lied. "We told them all to get out. I'm sure they listened."

"We can't wait around to find out, anyhow," Lucida said.

§

We reached the main road. As the adrenaline of the escape wore off, all of the fatigue and pain from my earlier ordeal came creeping back into my body. My vision clouded and I found it difficult to keep my eyes open.

"You should try to rest," Finn said, his voice much gentler than I'd ever heard it.

"Where are we going to go?" I asked. "What the hell are we going to do now?"

"I don't know."

"And the Necromancers. Neil. How are we going to… oh my God, I haven't even told you about—"

"You can tell me later. It will be okay."

"How?"

Finn couldn't answer that. No one could. So he just said again, "You should try to rest."

I wanted to protest, but I'd lost the energy. I turned my head on the headrest as Fairhaven fell out of view.

Just before I drifted away, I realized that the Silent Child's messages to me were a prophecy of her own: For as the flames leapt and danced high into the star-strewn darkness, Mary's tiny lonely figure rose, silhouetted by the flickering light of the inferno behind her, as Fairhaven Hall burned.

Acknowledgments

Here's the bit where I do a completely inadequate job of thanking all of the many people who have helped bring this book to life. But here I go, nonetheless.

Most of my thanks must go to my husband, Joseph Holmes, who not only designed the interior of this book, but has become my one-man marketing team. It is entirely thanks to him that anyone anywhere, apart from my family and friends, has picked up this series, and I will never be able to thank him enough for his unwavering support and unflagging enthusiasm for this story and all of its occupants.

Many thanks to James Egan at Bookfly Design LLC for his beautiful and thoughtful cover design. Much gratitude must also go to Norm Gautreau and Susan Reynolds, our friends, mentors, and supporters on this exciting journey. Thanks for your advice and for the many delightful hours we shared talking about writing, publishing, editing, and everything else under the sun. Looking forward to raising a glass (and maybe a Pimm's and soda) to celebrate.

To my dear friends who are always supportive and eager to hear the next chapter of the story: thank you for picking up on all of my tiny references and for harassing me to finish the next book already. I'm so lucky to have you all in my corner.

To my daughter Lily, thank you for all of the many tantrums you threw while mommy was trying to work on her manuscript. You are such a helpful little bugger, and also the light of my life. I'm enjoying my time with you, repeatedly reading One Fish, Two Fish, Red Fish, Blue Fish, and looking forward to the many other books we will share together.

Finally, to my readers, I honestly cannot thank you enough for taking a chance on this series, and for your enthusiastic and overwhelming response. I am humbled every single day to interact with you, and I hope that reading this second installment in The Gateway Trilogy gives you as much enjoyment as writing it has given to me.

About the Author

E.E. Holmes is a writer, teacher, and actor living in central Massachusetts with her husband, two children, and a small, but surprisingly loud, dog. When not writing, she enjoys performing, watching unhealthy amounts of British television, and reading with her children. To learn more about E.E. Holmes and *The World of the Gateway*, please visit www.eeholmes.com

CPSIA information can be obtained
at www.ICGtesting.com
Printed in the USA
LVHW091351100222
710767LV00004B/99